D1287091

How to Seduce a Ghost

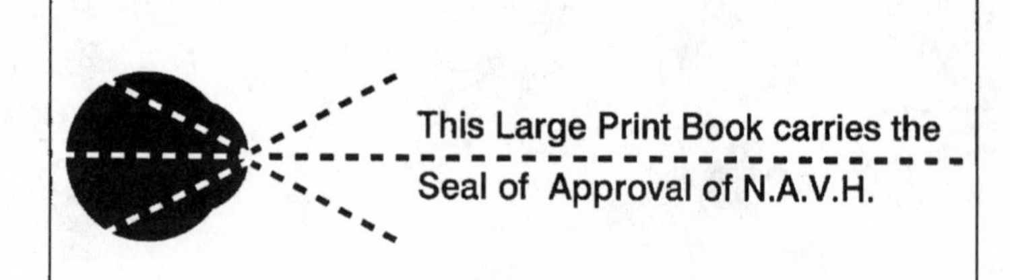
This Large Print Book carries the
Seal of Approval of N.A.V.H.

How to Seduce a Ghost

Hope McIntyre

This book is a work of fiction. Names, characters, places, and incidents are the product of the author's imagination or are used fictitiously. Any resemblance to actual events, locales, or persons, living or dead, is coincidental.

Published in 2006 by arrangement with Warner Books, Inc.

Wheeler Large Print Hardcover.

The text of this Large Print edition is unabridged.
Other aspects of the book may vary from the original edition.

Set in 16 pt. Plantin by Elena Picard.

Printed in the United States on permanent paper.

Library of Congress Cataloging-in-Publication Data

McIntyre, Hope, 1946–
How to seduce a ghost / by Hope McIntyre.
p. cm.
ISBN 1-59722-199-6 (lg. print : hc : alk. paper)
1. Notting Hill (London, England) — Fiction. 2. Arson — Investigation — Fiction. 3. Women ghostwriters — Fiction. 4. Large type books. I. Title.
PS3571.P33H69 2006
813′.6—dc22 2005034423

For my friend, ghostwriter extraordinaire
Cheryl Merser.
And for Clare and Joy.

National Association for Visually Handicapped
serving the partially seeing

As the Founder/CEO of NAVH, the only national health agency solely devoted to those who, although not totally blind, have an eye disease which could lead to serious visual impairment, I am pleased to recognize Thorndike Press* as one of the leading publishers in the large print field.

Founded in 1954 in San Francisco to prepare large print textbooks for partially seeing children, NAVH became the pioneer and standard setting agency in the preparation of large type.

Today, those publishers who meet our standards carry the prestigious "Seal of Approval" indicating high quality large print. We are delighted that Thorndike Press is one of the publishers whose titles meet these standards. We are also pleased to recognize the significant contribution Thorndike Press is making in this important and growing field.

Lorraine H. Marchi, L.H.D.
Founder/CEO
NAVH

* Thorndike Press encompasses the following imprints: Thorndike, Wheeler, Walker and Large Print Press.

Acknowledgments

During the time this book was written I underwent major surgery and built a house, and I could not have completed *How to Seduce a Ghost* without the help of many friends. While I waited for construction to be completed, my life was peripatetic to say the least and I would like to thank the following people who gave me shelter from the storm and a place to write.

London
Louise Allen Jones
Hilary Arnold
Deborah Rogers and Michael Berkeley
Annie and Francis Shaw
Jacqui Graham and David Pelham
Clare Alexander and Guillermo Gil

Devon
Kate Bartholomew
Lindsay Bell

Oxfordshire
John Lloyd and Sarah Wallace

West Cork, Ireland
David and Patsy Puttnam

New York City
Annabel Davis Goff
Sonny Mehta

Rhinebeck, NY
Ann Patty
Joy Harris
Katherine Russell Rich

Portland, Oregon
Shawn and Mary Levy
Whitney Otto

Amagansett, NY
Joe Dolce and Jonathan Burnham
Richard and Betina LaPlante
Judith Kuneth
Annemarie McCoy
Susan and Murray Smith
Michael Nader

I also owe an enormous debt of gratitude to yet more people who helped me with the book: Kristen Weber, Ernie Hamm, Judy

Piatkus, Alexia Paul, Hope Harris, Miranda Davies and last, but most definitely not least, Dermot Keating, Detective Superintendent, New Scotland Yard.

Chapter 1

When Astrid McKenzie went up in flames at the end of my road I was fast asleep in my bed, dreaming about my mother.

Had they ever met, I think Astrid and my mother would have got along rather well. They are two of a kind, which is to say they are everything I am not. I didn't really know Astrid except to nod to in the street but the word in the market — on which I rely for virtually all my gossip — is that she was a live wire. My mother is a naturally gregarious person, who leaps about the place like a mountain goat most of the time. Frankly, I'm amazed they haven't signed her up to model for one of those over-fifty-five fitness programs that offer to rejuvenate your mind and body, or a fashion spread in *Saga* magazine. She has that lithe, eager-beaver look about her and I imagine talk of a party will still get her ears flapping when she's ninety.

I, on the other hand, am what they call a

loner. Or, and here's a word that really makes me cringe, a homebody. I like to live vicariously. I realized pretty early on that my aim in life was not to sit night after night in the Met Bar getting smashed and going home with the first hot guy to buy me a cosmopolitan. Nevertheless I wanted to hear about the people who did, just as when I refused invitations to glamorous parties and sat home, happily watching the box, I looked forward to the calls the next morning from all and sundry with a detailed account of everything I missed.

I never got the point of going out all the time. I never had the stamina for a start, but I also always preferred being one-on-one with someone and you could have a cozy dinner à deux at home just as easily as going to a crowded restaurant. The problem is, while I don't think there's anything wrong with spending a lot of time on one's own, I have to admit that my antisocial lifestyle is not the norm. I mean, I don't know anyone else like me, and it worries me sometimes. Everyone's always saying things like *You should get out more, You're only young once, It's not healthy sitting at home on your own all the time.* I think it makes them uncomfortable having a friend who's not like them but I notice it doesn't stop them making me a captive audience for all their problems. They seem to like the idea that, more often than not, I'll be home alone and ready to listen. Of course I turn on the answering machine and screen my calls for days on end and that really turns me into a hermit. It's been particularly bad lately and if I don't get a grip on myself soon, I am in danger of becoming seriously unglued. Sooner or later my life is going to require a major shake-up or else I'll join forces with Astrid and spontaneously combust. I'm talking about all areas — work, living arrangements, and most important, my love life for, despite my reclusive nature, I do have a long-standing boyfriend. But, I find myself wondering far too often lately: For how much longer?

I feel terrible that while Astrid crackled away I was totally oblivious to her suffering. My mother maintains you always dream in opposites so I suppose it makes sense that in my dream she was running toward me with her arms outstretched, ready to embrace me. This simply does not happen in real life, which is probably why I was so deeply ensconced in the dream, enjoying something I never normally experienced, that I never heard the crackling of the flames only a little way down the road.

Astrid was a children's television presenter. I was always mildly intrigued that she was one of my neighbors because she was a minicelebrity and celebrities are my stock in trade. I'm a ghostwriter. I'm the "as told to" or the "written with" in small type you see underneath the celebrity's name on the cover of their autobiography. Every time I hear the name of someone in the news I automatically start asking questions, filing away a mental profile, just in case. Although Astrid was hardly likely to need a ghostwriter now.

But Astrid, it seemed, was not responsible for the blazing inferno that killed her. I first learned about the fire when I watched the local news on breakfast TV. It had started just after midnight. I must have slept through all the sirens. Seeing the street where I lived on television was unnerving. I pulled a pair of jeans on and rushed outside to look at the charred remains of Astrid's little mews house. The crowds and the press had already accumulated in the street outside and I noted that one or two of the women wearing particularly high heels were having a problem with the cobblestones in the mews. This was exactly the kind of inappropriate detail I would take into account rather than facing up to the unpleasant fact that there was a dead body lying in the house. She'd gone to the trouble of painting the outside pale pink and she must have started very recently because only yesterday the postman had come away cursing the pink paws he received when he tried to put her mail through the letterbox. What a shame, since it was now almost totally blackened by soot, I thought irrelevantly. Anything to ward off the images that would begin to terrify me at any moment.

"It's all right, love, they already took her away." Chris, a merchant I knew from Portobello Market touched my elbow. "You look terrible. Did you know her?"

I shook my head. "No, I never met her."

"Well, you won't now. I heard she was dead when they carried her out. That's her bedroom up there" — he pointed to a window toward the back of the house overlooking the mews — "that's where they found her."

And then it began to hit me. I had a sudden flash of Astrid waking up to a wall of fire around her bed. I wondered what went through your mind when faced with something like that? Did you automatically leap out of bed and try to wade through it?

Would you stop to think about anything at all in the face of such danger? What would it be like to know that in a few seconds you would be subjected to heat that would cause your flesh to fry, your blood to boil, and your bones to snap, crackle, pop into powder. These were the kind of thoughts that would now begin to haunt me. Sometimes I lie awake, working myself up into a state of panic imagining the worst kind of violent death I could encounter. Plane crashes have always been favorites. Boating accidents and drowning feature high on the list. It doesn't matter that I made the swim team at school and passed the life-saving exam. Somehow I will be caught in the perfect storm with drowning the only option. Elevator cables snapping, tornadoes hurling the car I am in through the air, sharks lurking beneath the surface in a bay where they have never been seen before, waiting to bite my leg off. I've entertained all these eventualities and many more.

And then of course there's murder. They're all out there waiting for me but murder is the worst. One night, while I'm fast asleep, someone is going to creep into my bedroom and smother me with a pillow. It doesn't help that I live in Notting

Hill, an area of west London that has more than its fair share of crime. The carnival that takes place over the August Bank Holiday weekend is known for its race- and drug-related violence and there has been a stabbing at the end of my road two years running. I hear talk in the market of people opening their front doors in the morning to find blood on their doorsteps. It doesn't seem to matter that mine is a designated "ritzy neighborhood" to which tourists flock on a Saturday afternoon. What they never mention in the guide books is that living side-by-side with the celebrity residents gathering their organic groceries and frequenting the amazing number of fancy bars and coffee shops that have sprung up all over the place, are junkies, prostitutes, and dealers armed to the teeth. The only clue is the crumbling facade of the stucco-fronted crack house whose walls abut a millionaire's mansion.

I know the kids who grew up across the street from me and with whom I used to play hopscotch on Saturday mornings are now busy heating up their cocaine in a solution of baking soda until the water evaporates and they have their base cocaine. Many a night I can hear the whirring of police helicopters hovering overhead and I know that someone's getting stabbed somewhere. I force myself to ignore them and the danger their presence signifies. I huddle away in my house and pretend I'm safe. I know I'm behaving like an irresponsible ostrich, but once I allow even a snippet of the outside world to penetrate, my imagination starts to run riot.

So Astrid's death at such close quarters had really shaken me and I couldn't stop thinking about her. Nor, it seemed, would I be allowed to banish her from my mind even if I wanted to. Clearly, the fire was all anyone in my neighborhood was going to talk about for quite a while.

"You know," said Chris, looking at his watch, "it's eight forty-five. She'd have been on round about now for her morning slot. Johnny, two stalls down, told me his wife always parked their youngest in front of her when the older kids left for school. It upset him seeing his brothers and sisters leaving him, but Astrid took his mind off it. She was a lovely person. Did you watch her at all?"

"Never. Was she married? Did she have kids of her own?" I realized I didn't know much about Astrid beyond seeing her in the street and the pictures in the *Sun* the market merchants sometimes showed me of her leaving nightclubs on the arm of footballers or B-list pop idols.

"No, she had a bit of a problem in that department."

"She couldn't have children?"

"Don't know about that. I meant the married bit. She wasn't."

"Why was it a problem?"

"She went in for the wrong sort of bloke. You could tell she . . . No." He stopped. "Shouldn't go into that. Don't want to speak ill of the dead. Listen, gotta run. I'm supposed to be picking up a couple of sacks of potatoes from the lockup. Carrots are lovely this week and I've got some of them sweet potatoes I know you like. Stop by later."

I went home to tip Tommy out of bed and get him off to work. Tommy Kennedy is the "love life" I've begun to wonder about that I mentioned earlier, my boyfriend if you can call a man in his early forties a *boy*friend. He'd stayed the night, not something I encourage on a regular basis but I'd had too much to drink and when that happens my resistance is low. I knew I'd regret it later.

Tommy got in under the wire about eight years ago and while we're still seeing each other, the precarious state of our relationship is something I keep pushing under the carpet along with the rest of my worries. The problem is he's ready to get married and have kids and I'm not. I've got the biological clock — I'm nearly forty — but he's the one keeping time. He'd settle for just moving in with me but I don't want that either. I'm quite happy on my own. I take my ghostwriting very seriously. The last thing I need is an overweight radio engineer cluttering up my life, demanding meals on the table, and turning up the television to full volume whenever Chelsea score a goal. I need peace and quiet to order. Or, to put it another way, I'm just terrified what would happen if we spent too much time together. Tommy has the patience of a saint but I don't know how he'd react when faced with constant exposure to my neurotic phobias. I keep telling myself I love Tommy and that I don't want to lose him but I'm not 100 percent sure I still believe what I'm saying. I pretend to myself that we're doing fine as we are and the more people urge me to think about settling down, the more I resist it. The thing is, I *am* settled down. Marrying Tommy would only unsettle me.

Tommy works for the BBC in the bowels of Broadcasting House and he has the complexion to prove it. He's gray. If I had the time I'd spend a week spying on him to check if he ever sees daylight. He works underground in a studio all day and I know he doesn't go out to lunch because if he ever does stay the night here, I have to make him sandwiches to take to work the next morning. Cheese and pickle on white. I keep a jar of Branston specially. That's about the extent of my culinary activities as far as poor Tommy's concerned. I have to make at least four sandwiches. They didn't call him Thomas the Tank Engine for nothing when he was at school although I confess I find his solid bulk reassuring when the helicopters are hovering and the police sirens are roaring up Ladbroke Grove.

We met when I went along to the recording of a late-night chat show with one of my subjects, as I call them. I think it was the medium. I seem to remember she did a lot of radio. Spooky phone-ins with people calling to see if their loved ones would get in touch over the airwaves from the other side.

Tommy wandered in and out of the studio with earphones hanging round his neck and did a lot of very pretentious fiddling with knobs. Then he asked me if I'd like to go for a Kit Kat and a cup of BBC tea.

The basement of Broadcasting House is not the most romantic venue for a first date. He led me down a long underground corridor to a vending machine, asked me if I had any change before we progressed to an empty canteen. We sat under the kind of harsh fluorescent lighting that probably gives you bags under your eyes and wrinkles if you are under twenty, let alone approaching forty. But it didn't seem to bother him.

He didn't say much but I found his presence oddly reassuring. I always have. The only thing I remember about that first encounter was that he asked:

"Why are you so nervy? Why do you look so worried? Why do you keep lining up the salt and the pepper and the ashtray?"

"I don't know. I probably have an obsessive-compulsive disorder or whatever it's called. I have to touch things a certain number of times, I won't walk through a door until I've touched the jamb four times. I can't go to sleep if I don't have a certain pillow."

"Weird," said Tommy. "I suppose you wash your hands fifteen times a day."

"You're not taking me seriously."

"I'm taking you perfectly seriously," he told me, smiling. "I just think you're talking a lot of rubbish, that's all. I suspect you might be a bit neurotic, a bit of a worrier rather than this obsessive thing. Still, something seems to be bothering you, you're all jumpy."

"It's the radio show," I confessed. "Listening to her just now, it reminded me of all those people she got in touch with who died such violent deaths. I hated doing the book, writing up all the gory details and the way they were still in pain when she caught up with their spirits."

" 'Caught up with their spirits'! You believe all that crap?" Tommy was incredulous but when I started to tell him about how freaked out I could get at the thought of someone coming to a grisly end, his face softened. He listened in a way nobody else ever had and he didn't laugh at me the way most people did when I tried to explain how the mere mention of physical danger could start my imagination working overtime.

"You funny old thing," he said affectionately when I'd finished. "What a waste of energy."

"It's not that I think I'll die tomorrow," I said, "just that when I do it'll be horrible and agonizing."

"It's all in the mind," he said. "You do know that, don't you? You're no more likely to encounter the kind of violent end you keep thinking about than you are to slip away quietly in your sleep. So stop worrying. It's a waste of time. Just deal with problems when they turn up, that's what I do. I don't see the point of fretting about something unless you can actually do something about it. Like right now. I'm not going to hover in the background while they record the show. They'll holler if they need me."

At that point they hollered and he disappeared, but first he scribbled down my phone number.

When he called I don't know what made me say yes to a pizza and a movie just as I don't really know why we're still together after all this time. I had a bunch of snotty friends at the time, cynical up-and-comers. People with whom I had nothing in common other than that we were fellow journalists, destined to go in opposite directions. I don't know how I drifted into such a disagreeable crowd but I was too young and callow to be able to extricate myself from their midst. Unwittingly, Tommy managed to do this for me. They took one look at him and dubbed him the Radio Nerd assuming he'd be out of my life so fast they needn't bother getting to know him. As it turned out they were wrong. I found myself spending more and more time with Tommy and losing touch with them. He began to grow on me until it got to the point where he was a more or less permanent fixture in my life. Radio Nerd he might be, but he turned out to be an expert lover. Must be something to do with twiddling all those knobs. Yet it was more than that. He was so completely my opposite that his very presence was beneficial and I began to relax for the first time in my life. And the one time we did split up for about four months — when he realized I was serious about not letting him move in with me — I discovered to my horror that I missed him dreadfully. It was as if someone had removed my television or my toaster or some other reliable and intermittently rewarding object in my life.

Tommy was emerging from the bathroom stark naked and dripping wet from the shower when I walked in.

"Tommy, you're making the floor all wet . . ." I began but he waved me away. He had the phone clamped to his ear.

"Christ, Genevieve, was it right here in

this road? Are you sure? Is she dead? I never heard a thing. Good God, I'd better tell Lee, she's just walked in. Yeah, I'll tell her. I'll get her to call you if she can't make it." He hung up and returned to the bathroom to grab his towel. He looked a lot better from behind, I noted. His bum was still in quite good shape and he'd always had sensational shoulders. His biggest problem was his budding paunch that was starting to hang over the top of his jeans in a mildly off-putting manner. He reemerged rubbing himself vigorously with the towel and shaking his head so I was showered with beads of water.

"Lee, listen. You'll never believe what's happened right here in our street while we were fast asleep. Just up the road, incredible! That kids' television woman lives here, did you know? Well, let me tell you —"

"Tommy."

"No, let me finish. You never let me finish. This is really something. She's dead. Her house burned down last night. Let's go down and see if it's on TV yet."

I explained to him I had already seen it on TV and been down the road to look at the aftermath of the fire. He looked predictably crestfallen.

"You might have woken me up. Why did

you let me miss all the fun?"

"I'd hardly call it fun. Somebody died, Tommy."

"Yeah, yeah, you're right. It's awful." He looked sheepish.

"So what did Genevieve want so early in the morning?" Genevieve is my agent.

"Well, she wanted to be the first to call you about the fire and she has a job for you. She was very mysterious. Wouldn't say who it was who needed a ghost, she wants to surprise you. Can you go to her office at three this afternoon? She's out and about till then so only call her back and leave a message if you can't make it. Otherwise just show up. So, did your mother get off okay?"

I caught the note of resentment in his voice. My mother had just been over from France where she lives. She was with me for five days and I banished Tommy from the house for the duration. It had nothing to do with them not getting on — the few times they met, they appeared to have rather liked each other. What I couldn't stand was the thought of having the two of them in the house at the same time, getting in my way while I was trying to work.

It's a bit exhausting having a whirlwind for a mother. Tommy's mother, Noreen, whom I adore, couldn't be more different. She's got a mind of her own and plenty of opinions to go with it but she'll sit and listen to you for hours if she senses you've got a problem. My mother races through life going a mile a minute and expects everyone else to keep up. To be honest I gave up years ago. She's always been like this. She used to have a pretty impressive career in advertising — I remember being taken to her office when I was a child and watching her boss a lot of people around — but she gave it all up when Dad retired and off they went to France, and that too was impressive. Dad was a lifelong Francophile and it had always been his dream to cross the Channel for his retirement. Instead of fighting it, my mother supported the idea from the start but it must have been a huge sacrifice for her to leave her busy London social life and bury herself in the French countryside. She can't even count on me to live it for her and I think she takes her frustration with her current state out on me. I know my hermitlike existence is a huge disappointment to her and whenever I see her now, I revert to being a seven-year-old and stand there letting her berate me for not living the life she had lined up for me.

It always made me sad the way she failed to get the point of me but I accepted it. I appreciated her need for an active social life and all the conventional trappings that went with it. I wanted her to have all the things that made her happy but at the same time I knew it was a waste of time expecting her to reciprocate. That's what upset me. She loved her daughter, Lee, some abstract person I barely recognized, but I never felt she loved *me.* How could she? She'd never taken the trouble to find out what made me tick.

As usual her visit caught me on the hop. She never gives me any warning, just turns up, lets herself in, and proceeds to give me hell the entire time she's here. Of course she's entirely justified. My parents and I have a deal. When they retired to France a few years ago, they said I could live in the house on condition that I took care of its upkeep. I said, *Wow! Thanks, yes please, no problem.* Living rent free in a four-story Georgian house in the middle of Notting Hill Gate is probably the best deal anyone's likely to get even if it's no longer a particularly fashionable part of London — but I'm this close to blowing it. I've let the house fall to wrack and ruin and pretty soon there is going to be the most almighty showdown. Every time I pick up the phone to call the plumber, the carpenter, or the window cleaner I start thinking about the noise and the disruption to my precious solitude and I hang up. Men on ladders are my particular aversion. They always leave them propped against the window so someone can hop up them, climb in, and murder me while I'm asleep. Or while I'm awake, come to think of it.

I know I'm unbelievably spoiled to have such a big house all to myself. I tell myself that over and over again and at least once a week I get into bed and *swear* just before I fall asleep that I'm going to get everything taken care of first thing in the morning.

Never happens.

I'm still not quite clear of the real purpose of my mother's visit, if indeed she had anything else in mind other than terrorizing me. She charged about the house brandishing a list and flapping it in my face.

"The pressure in the shower on the top floor, it's nonexistent, Lee. They must be able to do *something.* What did they say?"

I kept quiet, always the best thing to do. Most of her questions were rhetorical anyway.

"The gutters are full of leaves, you absolutely must get them cleared. The window-sills are falling apart inside and out, I mean they are literally *crumbling.* And I thought we agreed you'd get the floors in the living room sanded."

We agreed no such thing. I wasn't going to put up with the noise and the smell of that awful sanding machine in a million years.

"And there's no bath plug in the guest bathroom. There never is. I bought six last time I was over. What do you do, throw them out the window when you get out of the tub?"

I was rather intrigued. Losing six bath plugs was something of an achievement. I opened my mouth to say Tommy was the only person to use the guest bathroom and then shut it again. I didn't want her demanding to see Tommy.

"At least you got the dishwasher repaired." I kept quiet there too. There'd never been anything wrong with the dishwasher so there was no way I could have had it repaired. "But the water in the sink doesn't run away. It must be blocked. What have you done with the plunger?"

I looked at her. I don't think I'd recognize a plunger if you whacked me over the head with it.

But of course all these things were nothing compared with the big problem: The Damp. I had riffled through the Yellow Pages a few times looking for ads that included the words "damp course" and that was as far as it went. But I had the drop on her here. I had taken the precaution of locking the door to the basement and hiding the key. If you opened the door the smell of the damp festering below smacked you full in the face. But I was on safe ground for the simple reason that I couldn't for the life of me remember where I had put the key. No one was going to have access to the basement unless they bashed the door down.

When it became clear that the only item remaining on her list was the damp, I took the drastic step of diverting her attention by inquiring what she and my father were planning to do for Christmas.

"You and Tommy are coming to stay with us in France. New Year's too if you want."

This wasn't quite what I'd asked. Nor was it what I wanted to do for Christmas. And there was something else. I'd had my father on the phone a couple of weeks ago and I had distinctly heard him say he would be in London for Christmas and was looking forward to seeing me then.

"Dad said —" I began.

"I don't care what your father said. I want you to come to France."

"But —"

"Lee, please, *PLEASE,* just this once. Come to France, bring Tommy, let's make it a nice family Christmas."

I could have sworn there was a slight catch in her voice, as if she were about to break down, but this was so unlike my mother that I dismissed it. But she was suddenly looking so forlorn for some reason that I said "I'll speak to Tommy," knowing I would do no such thing.

She perked up immediately. "We'll have such fun. Now while I'm here I'm going to call people to come and deal with all these repairs."

"I'll do it." I held out my hand for the list. If I didn't take charge there would be nonstop banging throughout the house for the next seven days.

"Well, I know how it interferes with your work," she said, handing it over. I was amazed. She was never usually so considerate about my writing. "So making the calls is the least I can do, but if you're sure?" She looked doubtful. "Anyway, I've been thinking, Lee, maybe I should get a lodger in the guest bedroom and leave him or her in charge of the upkeep of the house — for a lower rent, of course. Then you wouldn't have to worry about it all."

This was one conversation I did not want to get into. I was leaning over the counter and I had my back to her. I picked up a pen and pretended to be writing something, acting like I hadn't heard her. Then I took her list and Scotch-taped it to the front of the fridge.

"There," I said, "now I can't possibly miss it. So let me take you out for dinner, Mum. How long did you say you were staying?"

When she finally left, her list had increased right down to the bottom of the page. She'd added to it every day in her tiny handwriting that looked as if a bird had dipped its claw in ink and scratched away at the paper. It reminded me of the indecipherable scrawl on a doctor's prescription. That was as good an excuse as any. *Sorry, Mum. Couldn't take care of anything. Couldn't read your writing.*

"So how was she?" Tommy had finished drying himself and was on his hands and knees searching for his socks under the bed. "By the way the pressure in your shower's a disaster. You ought to do something about it."

"Tommy," I said, fishing one of his socks

out from halfway down the bed, “you want it fixed, *you* do something about it.”

I stomped out of the bedroom and up to my office where I tried to ignore the sound of the Dixie Chicks coming from the radio in the kitchen five minutes later. Why Tommy always had to have everything going full blast was beyond me. And of course when I heard the front door slam behind me as he rushed out, late for work as usual, I had to stomp all the way down to the kitchen to turn the radio off, something it would never occur to him to do.

By the time I left for my meeting with Genevieve later that day, the *Evening Standard*, which appeared at noon, had the story.

ASTRID MCKENZIE DIES IN BLAZE
Suspicious Fire at
TV Presenter’s Notting Hill House

Suspicious fire. I read the whole story. They were very careful, it was all supposition, bets were hedged all over the place, no concrete statements that could get them into trouble, but the message was pretty clear. Check in with them later. They might have an arson story to print.

I stopped by Chris’s stall in the market. I

pay him a visit three or four times a week to pick up my fruit and veg. He's part of my marketing routine. I shop at the same places until they close down and I am forced to go elsewhere. I've lived in the Blenheim Crescent house for as long as I can remember and my mother sometimes used to send me along the road to pick up a last minute lettuce or some parsnips or something. In those days you wouldn't think twice about sending a little girl out on her own on an errand. The stall had been in Chris's family going back two generations and there'd be a welcome from his mother once I arrived. I'm such a creature of habit that I continued going to the same stall even after she retired. Besides, it wasn't as if I didn't know Chris. He was about five years younger than me, and as he was growing up, he'd be there behind the stall on Saturdays, helping his mum. I remember him as a cocky little boy. There didn't appear to be a father anywhere in the picture and I never learned the reason why although it didn't seem to bother Chris. He could shout louder than anyone else in the market even when he was a young lad.

"Seen this?" I flapped the *Standard* in his face.

"Doesn't surprise me. I didn't want to

mention it earlier but what the hell? Word on the market is she fancied a bit of rough. Got herself beaten up pretty bad once or twice. Someone probably had it in for her."

"You mean . . . ?" I didn't like the sound of this.

"Sure as eggs is eggs. I'll bet you two pounds of Golden Delicious she was murdered."

Chapter 2

I'd left it too late to take a bus — my transport of choice — to Genevieve's so I was forced to travel by underground. Needless to say, I have a horror of descending to the underground. If I know that a lift shaft is particularly deep — Russell Square springs to mind, unless they've renovated it since I was last there — I always take the stairs but then I get a panic attack halfway down and can't go any farther. There's no lift at Notting Hill Gate but by the time I'd stepped off the escalator to board the Central Line, I was quaking. What I'd have done in the Blitz, I can't imagine.

To make matters worse, by now I had worked myself up into a real state about Astrid. Had someone really set fire to her on purpose? Were they working their way along Blenheim Crescent? Would it be my turn tonight? It was just so dreadful to think that she had died in agony, probably screaming out for help and no one had heard her.

My cell phone rang and I jumped a mile.

"Hello," I whispered. I don't really know why I even have a cell phone given I hardly go out the house. And I hate the way everyone glares at you when you have a conversation in a public place.

"So what else did you find out?" It sounded as if Tommy was eating the cheese and pickle sandwiches I'd made for him. He had a habit of stuffing them whole into his mouth and chewing while he was talking.

"About what?"

"Her. Astrid thingy. How she got fried alive."

"Oh, don't be so *disgusting!*" I yelled and of course all the other passengers looked up and glared at me.

"Sorry. Don't get upset. Please don't get upset." Tommy's voice softened. He's good at apologizing, I'll give him that.

"I'm not upset" — total lie — "it just freaks me out what happened to her, Tommy, and we didn't hear a thing."

"I expect I was snoring too loud."

"I expect you were." I managed a laugh. "See you tonight?"

"You mean that?" He couldn't believe his luck. We rarely saw each other two nights running these days but I knew I didn't want to be alone in the house.

"Give me a call when you finish work," I told him, blew him a kiss, and switched off the phone before he could get back to Astrid. I forced myself to put her out of my mind. I'd make myself ill if I carried on fretting.

I wondered who it could be that had got Genevieve so excited. I ghost for women mostly and for some reason they always seem to be in the arts or entertainment world. I've never done a politician or a captain of industry. But I draw the line at sleazy madams or silly supermodels. I have my standards. Actually, scrub all of the above. I do whatever Genevieve can get for me to keep the wolf from the door and she's wise enough to team me up with people with whom she thinks I might have some affinity. Of course her dream is for me to land someone like a royal butler. Now and again she hints that I might want to find myself a job like this. I wonder if she knows what a recluse I am? Maybe she imagines I go to dinner parties every night where the hostesses employ the fallout from Kensington Palace. She probably dreams about me handing them my coat and saying *Come and tell me your story when you've served the coffee, don't leave out a thing, and, trust me, we'll have a book in six weeks.*

I like what I do. Writing someone's autobiography with them means you are going to write something nice about them. I used to be a profile writer for magazines, and I wasn't comfortable with the way I had to get people to hang themselves. I'd go into their homes and smile and charm them and worm out of them all their little secrets and hang-ups and then expose them in print because that's what my editor said made a good story. But I always felt bad, even if I hadn't much liked the person I'd been sent to interview. I am well aware that I am more judgmental than most people but I try to keep my thoughts to myself. I never got much of a kick out of putting people down in public.

When the first commission to ghost a full-length autobiography came along, it was something of a relief to make them sound as exciting and salable as possible. I had the time to turn in some presentable writing and I was paid a good deal more money. The truth is I never had any particular ambition to write the Great West London Novel and I'm under no illusion that what I produce is art. I suppose some people — my mother, for instance —

would say I'm happy to hide behind my subjects and maybe they're right. But why not? I like being a ghostwriter, it presents its own unique challenge — to capture the voice of someone else and tell their story in as entertaining a way as possible. More often than not I think I do them justice and that for me is fulfilling.

So who would it be this time?

I adore my agent even though we have nothing in common beyond our professional relationship. Genevieve's very good for me. She will not tolerate my black moods and insecurities. She is very brisk and businesslike. Click here and she'll get you a deal, sell your translation rights all around the world via a host of subagents, negotiate a serial sale, analyze your royalty statements. And all with immaculate makeup and pale pink tailored suits with a lilac patterned scarf artfully tucked into the opening just above the top button. Manicured nails, a short no-nonsense haircut softened by highlights and lowlights, short legs and thick ankles excused by tiny feet in high-heeled Manolo Blahniks. Genevieve is always so well groomed, I cannot imagine what she looks like all rumpled first thing in the morning. I always feel a complete wreck beside her, not that she ever says anything.

But underneath it all she is enormous. There is no getting away from it. The impeccable grooming is a kind of sugary camouflage to mask her excessive circumference. I do not understand why she is so large. She never appears to eat very much and her tiny feet and hands indicate her natural size to be considerably smaller. Maybe she binges in secret. Whatever she does, it doesn't matter. I could not imagine Genevieve being any other way. There is a cuddly quality to her that is extremely attractive. I sometimes think she ought to be the star of a TV show that reassures people that it can be okay to be fat. She is so totally comfortable with her bulk, she almost makes me want to gain thirty pounds. Because above her ruff of double chins, Genevieve has one of the prettiest, daintiest faces I know. Her features are small and perfect. Navy blue eyes, a cute little turned up nose, and a rosebud mouth. And I would kill for her baby-soft skin.

Genevieve's attitude toward me is perfect as far as I am concerned. I allow her total confidence in me as a professional writer to encompass everything else about me even though her inquiries about my private life never extend beyond the perfunctory. I would never dream of unburdening myself to Genevieve about my personal problems just as I know next to nothing about her own life beyond the agency. I suppose I could interpret this distance as lack of concern but I choose to view it as a desire to avoid being intrusive for which I am grateful. Genevieve leaves me alone, which is what I would like everyone to do, yet at the same time she is mumsy. There is no other word for it. Within the confines of our professional relationship, she fusses over me with affection, clucking away about my career like a mother hen.

"So did you know her?" Genevieve asked as soon as I walked through the door.

"Did I know who?"

"Astrid McKenzie."

"Saw her in the street, said hello. Never really met her to talk to."

"Well, I saw her last night," said Genevieve triumphantly. "Sit down, dear."

I sat, gingerly, because her chairs for visitors are rather spindly. God knows what would happen if she ever subjected them to her own alarming weight.

Genevieve's office is like a large cupboard. It is meticulously tidy, which always makes me feel rather uncomfortable. As far as I can see she has absolutely everything on disk. There is never a scrap of paper on her desk, no manuscripts lying around. For quite a while I thought there was no fax machine and no filing cabinets. Then I accidentally opened a door while searching for the loo one day and found a walk-in closet that housed both these things. They were crammed in, along with a small sink, a fridge, an electric kettle, a wine rack full of champagne, an ice bucket, a few glasses and mugs and a large bottle of Gucci Rush, a fragrance I particularly dislike.

Her office is a tiny room up some stairs in a very fancy part of Covent Garden just behind Long Acre. She doesn't have a conference room. For a meeting comprising more than two people, she always contrives to convene at the publisher's office or in a restaurant. I have a terrible feeling that if anybody does get inside the door she pretends her office is the reception area. I suppose she isn't really a literary agent like any other. She handles ghosts and people don't normally publish their autobiography more than once so maybe only her clients, her ghosts, are allowed into her office. Everyone else she meets elsewhere. It's a tiny operation but she runs it with maximum efficiency and because it's so small, she's always available.

"So put me out of my agony, Genny. Who have you got lined up for me?"

"Selma Walker."

Selma Walker?

She'd got me all the way over here to talk about a soap star? But even as I heard the name I experienced an involuntary prickle of excitement.

Selma Walker meant money. Serious money. She was hugely popular. An American actress who had been imported into *Fraternity*, one of our long-running soaps, as Sally, the brash American bride of one of the family of brothers on whom the series was based, brought back from a business trip he'd made to New York. For anyone who is prepared to admit they are old enough to remember *Dallas*, it's as if the Ewings have been picked up and put down in the north of England. The appearance of Sally and her ritzy New York style had really set the cat among the pigeons, the pigeons in this case being her more down-to-earth sisters-in-law, none of whom could stand her. Television audiences, however, loved her and the ratings soared. Not since Joan Collins appeared in *Dynasty* had a bitch antiheroine so completely captured the viewers' imagination.

"So how did you meet her?" I asked Genevieve.

"I was at the Ivy last night with one of the cast members of *Fraternity* and I got him to catch her eye and go over." I resisted the temptation to quiz Genevieve on what she was doing out with an actor. Occasionally I longed to break the rules and engage her in a bit of girly gossip but our mutual respect for each other's privacy was paramount.

"You mean you set this up?"

Genevieve shook her head. "No, I didn't actually. That's the weird thing. She was at that far corner where they can push the tables together and seat about ten people. She was right in the corner, no way I could get to her, and she wasn't even the person I wanted to talk to. There was a record producer at her table I've been after for some time. He's put the word out he wants to do his autobiography. Business stuff. Not your kind of thing." She smiled to show she didn't mean to be patronizing. "Anyway, I thought if we could get invited over for a drink after dinner, I could make a move. Well, we were and I wound up seated next to the record producer and I suppose I must have been pitching him quite heavily because suddenly Selma

Walker who is now very close to me says, *What is it that you do exactly?* She'd been eavesdropping. Well, after that the record producer was toast. She virtually rearranged the table so I could be right beside her and she started quizzing me. It turned out *she* wants to tell her story and is looking for a writer. But before I could tell her about you she up and left, went home to get some sleep because she had an early call. As she's leaving she says *Call me, okay? Jerry has my number.* Jerry's the record producer."

"Who's toast," I reminded her.

"Not necessarily." Genevieve winked and I laughed. I loved the way she kept all her options open. "But no sooner had she left than this guy called Buzz someone slips into the seat beside me. Very good looking but quiet. Introduced himself, said he'd seen me chatting to Selma and told me he was her manager. When he heard what we'd been talking about, he told me to call him first thing this morning so that's what I did and we set up a meeting for you to meet him next Wednesday at five. He has an office in her house and, you're not going to believe this, but did you know she lives right around the corner from you?"

"Sounds like it was meant to happen," I said. "So what's her story? Is it a good one?" I realized I didn't know anything about Selma Walker beyond the fact that she was American and starring in one of our most popular soaps.

"Oh, bound to be, dear."

"You mean you didn't ask?"

"Well, it's not exactly the sort of thing you get to grips with first, is it?" Genevieve amazes me sometimes. She wants me to write someone's story with them but she doesn't even know if it's a good one.

"So what did you and Buck —"

"Buzz, dear."

"So what did you and Buzz discuss?"

"Oh, the marketing. How much publicity the book would get, author tours, foreign sales, the fact that she's an American would secure a big sale over there."

"Not necessarily," I pointed out. "Has *Fraternity* been sold in the U.S.? What was she doing before she came over here?"

"And I know I could get a huge serial sale."

"Only if there's some juicy gossip."

"Which you'll find out, won't you, dear?"

This was beginning to sound rather familiar. I'd been here before when I'd written profiles. Go for the dirt. That's what sells.

"Only if she wants to divulge it." Once again I was the voice of reason. "It's her autobiography, don't forget. She'll have control over what goes into it."

"Oh well, you'll have no trouble dealing with that," said Genevieve with confidence.

She disappeared into the cupboard to make me a cup of coffee.

"You'd better give me the address," I said wearily when she reappeared. Not much time to do my homework. "What did you tell the manager about me? Are you sending over my work in advance? When do I get to meet her?"

"I already did. And I guess he'll set up a time for the two of you to get together. Now, that's enough of that. Give me all the details about Astrid McKenzie. Did you see the body? Was it horrible? I'd never seen her in the flesh before. She has this milky white skin. The thought of it turning black and disintegrating into soot is —"

"Genevieve, *PLEASE!*" What was the matter with everyone? First Tommy and now Genevieve, thirsting for the gruesome details. How would they feel if they had to go home to the scene of the fire knowing that someone might be out there lurking, ready to strike again?

I described my brief visit up the road that morning and told her what the guy in the market had said.

"But where did you see her last night?" I asked her.

"At the Ivy. It was when I was talking to Buzz. She was coming down the stairs from the ladies' on her way out of the restaurant and she looked straight at us. And she freaked."

"What do you mean, she freaked?"

"Just what I said. It was really spooky. She saw Buzz and she freaked. Her face changed, she looked terrified, and she started almost to run. She couldn't get out of that restaurant quick enough. He didn't notice her, he had his face turned toward me, and it was as if she wanted to get away before he saw her."

"What time was it?"

"About ten thirty."

"She must have gone home and . . ."

"Oh my God," Genevieve squeaked at the thought. "I might have been the last person to see her alive."

"Except for her murderer," I said without thinking.

Chapter 3

Tommy and I are not on speaks.

It's actually quite serious. All went well for a couple of days after the fire. He stayed with me for two nights running, snoring gently beside me like a catarrh-ridden tabby cat, while I clung to him, wide-awake, and sniffing the air for the first sign of burning. Then I asked him to do something really quite simple for me and he failed me and I went for him in the vicious ugly way that only I know how. It's how I sometimes behave when I am disappointed — usually by life in general but in this instance because I had actually believed Tommy and I were beginning to remedy the rather bad patch we seemed to have been going through. Now he had ruined it by screwing up the one small thing I had asked him to do. And so had I by letting it get to me and losing control.

Our standoff has been going on for a week. Our record is nine days so I'm getting a tiny bit nervous. If there was ever a time when I needed Tommy to stay the night it was now. When the constant nocturnal fire alert became more than I could bear I would have to get up and pad about the house until I was satisfied nothing was burning and there was no one outside brandishing a blazing torch.

On the whole, Tommy's quick to say sorry when I berate him but then there are times when he insists it isn't his fault and he won't climb down. I suppose if you live with someone this sort of thing gets cleared up in a day or two but it's a little tricky if you're each waiting at opposite ends of London for the other one to say sorry.

This time Tommy had failed to record a gardening documentary on BB2 I particularly wanted to see but would miss because I had to show up at the book launch for one of my subjects. It's funny how some of them want you to disappear off the face of the earth once you've turned in the last chapter and others insist on making you their best friend. All I needed, when I got home and found he'd forgotten, was for him to say "Oh, sorry. How stupid of me. Let me take you to Paris for the weekend to make up for it." And I would have been fine about it. He didn't even need to mention Paris. I am very easily disarmed. But that was too hard for him. Oh no, he'd been lounging around on my sofa with a Chinese takeaway, waiting for me to return and when I went ballistic, his response was:

Why'd you want to watch it anyway? It's not as if you even like gardening.

It's a waste of time explaining to Tommy about having dreams for a cottage in the depths of the countryside with acres of peace and quiet all around me. His vision of the future never goes much beyond me marrying him and having loads of little Kennedys. Try as I might, I just could not get him to admit he'd done anything wrong. He didn't think I needed to watch the bloody documentary so therefore it didn't matter that he'd forgotten to record it for me.

Even though I am stubborn, somehow I am always the one who reaches out first and calls a truce. But this time I was seriously pissed off with him. It wasn't a question of having missed the documentary; I'd got beyond that long ago. It was the fact that he hadn't cared enough about me to record it. That rankled. And I would have let him stew for at least another four days if I hadn't left my tape recorder in the back of a cab. I always took a tape recorder with me when I worked, even for the first introductory meeting, and once I'd met her manager, I could be set up for the first interview with Selma Walker any day now. The more I thought about it the more I felt I bloody well wasn't going to go out and buy a new one just because Tommy had forgotten to record my documentary for me.

There is a connection here. I didn't need to go out and buy a new one because I knew Tommy's flat would be stiff with tape recorders and all I had to do was go around there and take one. But I wasn't speaking to him and I didn't have a key. I'd had to give mine to his cousin from Newcastle when he'd last come to stay and I'd never had it back. I knew Tommy kept a spare hidden somewhere but I didn't know where.

If I wanted to find out I'd have to make contact.

His answering machine picked up the night I called. This was outrageous. Where was he? He had no right to be out enjoying himself without me. I left a terse message stating what I wanted to know, would he please get back to me. I couldn't resist adding a triumphant closing sentence about how I'd landed a lucrative new job writing Selma Walker's autobiography. Bit of a fabrication given I hadn't even met her yet.

He called and left a message on my machine while I was at the dentist. Had he known that I had an appointment that morning? Had he called then deliberately so as to avoid speaking to me?

"Key's taped to the back of the fourth dustbin from the right." His voice resounded in my kitchen as if he was standing right beside me. *Key taped to fourth dustbin from right,* I scribbled on a bit of paper. Asking for trouble, I would have thought. "Take the Aiwa," he continued. "It's in the chest in the hall and I know I put in fresh batteries the other day. Built-in microphone. Selma Walker's a bit of all right. She's a Chelsea supporter. Keep me posted. Cheers."

Why Tommy lived in Bow was beyond me. It's not as if it's convenient for Broadcasting House. Or, more important in Tommy's view, Stamford Bridge in Fulham. Chelsea Football Ground. I doubt that he's registered that it has become fashionable to live in the East End. Notting Hill, the area I live in, used to be a cool address and was even catapulted into the international limelight by a film of the same name starring Hugh Grant and Julia Roberts. The film's mammoth success meant the property prices went through the proverbial roof in Notting Hill. Now anyone with any sense is selling up and buying houses in Shoreditch or Hoxton or even a loft in Exmouth Market.

If I ever feel myself weakening and thinking of agreeing to live with Tommy, all I have to do is make a trip to his flat to be reminded why this would be such a foolish move. Talk about Men Behaving Badly. And it's not as if there's two of them to make such a mess. There's only Tommy. Though I know he says yes to anybody who asks him for a bed. The only problem is he hasn't got a spare bed so his guests have to sleep on the floor in a sleeping bag. Anyone would think he was still a teenager. Walking into the place you always have to start by kicking a path through the mounds of clothes on the floor. Everywhere I could see evidence of Tommy's habit of becoming obsessed with something and then abandoning it halfway through. A book entitled *How to Write Screenplays that Sell* lay open facedown on an armchair, its pages filled with dust, a testament to his ambition to change careers about six months ago. Discarded manuals littered about the place revealed a variety of other ambitions that had fallen by the wayside. A model airplane minus the wings had pride of place on his dining room table, the glue open and congealing beside it. A jigsaw with the outer edges completed and the rest of the pieces lying scattered across a desk. Crosswords with only half the clues filled in. CDs out of their cases. This was how he spent his time away from me. I confess I felt a little guilty. Tommy is someone who likes company. He's popular down in the bowels of Broadcasting House, he has his mates at the BBC. But away from work they probably assume he's spending time with me. They probably don't realize that there are long periods when I banish him from my life while I work on a book. All around me I could see proof of his attempts to occupy his spare time, time he would much rather spend with me.

I went into the kitchen to make myself a cup of tea but one look at the mound of washing up left in the sink, the jars of jam, Branston, and Marmite standing around with their lids off, the upturned packet of cornflakes, changed my mind.

I went back to the hall to retrieve the Aiwa tape recorder before I forgot why I'd come. Suddenly I felt depressed by the sight of Tommy's lonely bachelor existence. This was not the home of someone who was happy living on his own. But would he be happier if I gave him the boot and set him free to find a suitably chirpy and gregarious girlfriend?

Suddenly I couldn't wait to get out of there fast enough but first I needed to pee. I was washing my hands in the bathroom and staring at myself in the mirror of the medicine cabinet, not that I could see much, it was so filthy. I looked tired. I really did need a rest. The last thing I needed was to plunge into another exhausting ghosting job when I would have to give someone else my full attention for as long as it took and receive virtually nothing in return. In fairness, sometimes the person's life fascinated me and sometimes I really liked them. But much of the time it was a case of leave your own ego at home and be prepared to boost someone else's for the duration.

I've been told I look Italian. Or Latin, at any rate. My natural expression is rather a mournful one and my nose is long and fine. But my mouth is very wide and they say I have a great smile.

My cheekbones are high and my bone structure gives my face what people call a Madonna look and they're not talking about the singer. But the best thing about my face is my eyes. I know they're beautiful. Huge and almond shaped, dark, sometimes almost grapelike in their color in a certain light. Soulful.

I was admiring my eyes and on the verge of cheering myself up when on instinct I reached out and opened the door of the medicine cabinet, as you do. I don't know what I was looking for. I didn't need anything.

Tommy is a terrible hypochondriac so I wasn't surprised to see endless packets of Panadol Xtra, cough syrup, Olbas Pastilles, and a whole shelf of weird-looking homeopathic remedies. Another craze begun and dropped. I was about to close the door when I saw something that definitely didn't belong there.

A bottle of mist pot cit. Potassium citrate.

I knew what that was for. I'd had recourse to it myself when I'd been suffering the agonies of cystitis.

Men didn't get cystitis, did they? I scanned the medicine cabinet for any other sign of a female presence. Nothing. I tiptoed gingerly through the debris of discarded clothes in his bedroom looking for something pink and frilly. Again nothing. So what was Tommy doing with a bottle of mist pot cit in his medicine cabinet?

I was still pondering the answer to that question when I arrived back home to find a policeman standing on next-door's doorstep, talking to my neighbor, Mrs. O'Malley. When he saw me going into my house, he abandoned Mrs. O'Malley and rushed over, yelling "Just a minute. Miss. Please."

I waited at the top of the steps while he puffed his way up to me.

"You're Vanessa Bartholomew?"

"No, I'm not," I told him, "that's my mother. She and my father live in France now. I'm Nathalie Bartholomew. Their daughter," I added when he consulted his notebook.

"Did you know Astrid McKenzie?" he asked me.

"Of course. Everyone did."

"Were you friends?"

"Oh, no, I never really talked to her."

He looked understandably confused. "You just said . . ."

"I meant I knew who she was. On the TV. With the kids. Was it arson?"

He didn't answer that. "Where were you on the night of the fire?"

"I was right here in this house, upstairs, fast asleep in my bed. Was her death suspicious?"

He didn't answer that either.

"Were you . . ." Whatever he'd been about to say, he decided to rephrase it. "Was there anyone else in the house?"

"Yes, my boyfriend, Tommy Kennedy. He was in bed with me. So you think it might have been murder?"

The way he hesitated — only for a fraction of a second but it was enough — told me I'd scored a bull's-eye.

"I never said . . ."

"What do you think happened? How did she die?"

"Smoke inhalation." And before I could tackle him further, he said, "We're going to need to contact Mr. Kennedy. Did you or he hear anything, see anything?"

"No, not a thing. In fact I'm amazed I slept through it all. As for Tommy, you'll have to ask him." I scribbled down Tommy's number and gave it to him.

"Did you notice anyone going in and out of her house in the days prior to the fire? Anyone hanging around outside in the last week or so?"

I shook my head. "So how did the fire start? Did someone set it deliberately? Have you got any suspects lined up?"

"I'm sure you'll hear the outcome of our investigations in due course."

"Murder investigations?" I couldn't resist it.

"Good afternoon, Miss Bartholomew." He knew he wasn't going to get anywhere with me and he'd had enough. Once inside the house, I peeped through the blinds in the bay window of my kitchen to see him return to Mrs. O'Malley. Good luck to him. She was a sour old puss and her son Kevin picked his nose whenever he saw me.

I found a message from Tommy's mother on my answering machine. I made myself a cup of coffee and settled down for a nice chat on the phone. I knew why she'd called. She always did when she sensed there was some kind of friction between us — beyond the ongoing problem of me not wanting to settle down with him. She was with Tommy on that one, the sooner we got married the better, as far as she was concerned.

"You're the best thing that's ever happened to him," she told me not long after Tommy and I began seeing each other.

"That's nice to hear, Noreen, but I don't really understand why," I said.

"That's because you don't know what he was like before he met you. He's a changed lad ever since you came into his life. He never had a woman who lasted more than a month. I was like some unpaid therapist, the amount of time I spent mopping up their tears. He treated them appallingly, chased them, seduced them, and then lost interest. Lord knows what he was searching for but it looks like he found it when he met you."

I found it hard to reconcile this image of Tommy the Wild One with the hopeless character who acted like he was ready for a pipe-and-slippers-by-the-fire existence. But Noreen Kennedy was no fool. We respected one another and the knowledge that she thought Tommy and I were right for each other had always made an impression on me.

But I was wrong about why she was calling me.

"I heard what happened," she said as soon as she came on the line, "that fire down the road. Sounds dreadful! Do they think it was set deliberately?"

"Looks that way. Tommy and I slept through the whole thing."

"I doubt you'd have heard anything above Tommy's snoring. But I expect you're glad to have him with you. Not nice to think of someone out there burning down houses."

I didn't say anything. Noreen knew how to press my buttons. She was probably well aware Tommy had spent the last week at his flat.

"Give him a call, love," she went on, confirming my suspicions. "It's just his stupid male pride that's stopping him picking up the phone. He wants to. I know he does. In fact, you know what I'm going to do? I'm going to call him myself, tell him to get in touch with you."

I grinned at the phone. "Thanks, Noreen. I'm pretty scared being all alone in the house."

"I thought you liked being on your own."

"Well, that's right, I do. Normally I don't need anyone at all but it's like you said — there's probably an arsonist at large and who knows where he's going to strike next."

"Strike next. That's a good one. You know what you need, Lee? I was just thinking about this the other day."

"What's that?"

"You need a lodger to keep you company in that great big house. There must be somewhere you could put a person where they wouldn't disturb you when you were working, and then you'd know you weren't alone."

Right now that sounded like a very good idea, and I was grateful to Noreen for not suggesting that Tommy move in permanently, which is what I know she wanted.

"Would you like me to come over and be with you tonight, love?"

"No, Noreen, please, I'm fine." What a sweetheart she was. Just the thought of her being prepared to navigate the buses all the way from Islington in the rain was heartwarming but I couldn't ask it of her.

"Well call someone and get them over. You never talk about your girlfriends, Lee. There must be someone who could be with you tonight."

We chatted on for another twenty minutes or so and as we did I began to feel one of those tension headaches creeping up the back of my neck. I knew exactly when it started: the minute she said *You never talk about your girlfriends.*

She was right. I never talked about my girlfriends because that would remind me of Cath, the one friend I wanted to see more than anyone — and couldn't.

I have to admit I've been a bit stupid when it comes to girlfriends. Just because I live alone and like it doesn't mean I don't need people to turn to every now and then. Lord knows now is one of those times, but I made the mistake of putting all my girly eggs in one basket and for years I relied on one person as my sole confidante. Cathleen Clark grew up down the road from me in Notting Hill. Her parents ran a little café up near Westbourne Park Road and they lived above it in a pokey little flat. It was a far cry from the four-story house that was — and still is — my home on Blenheim Crescent but that didn't seem to bother us. We were best friends from the age of twelve until we fell out in a totally unexpected and distressing way several years ago. Just thinking about it increased the pain in my head considerably.

Cath had headaches. In fact they were more than that, they were migraines. She had to take to her bed and I would go over and prepare ice packs to lay on her forehead. She used to protest that I made too much fuss but I made her try everything. I persuaded her to give up one food after another that was supposed to be high in tyramine or tyrosine or whatever it's called.

Cheese, chicken liver, chocolate, citrus fruits, and red wine went out the window but nothing helped. Sometimes I just sat by her bed and held her hand. I tried to work out what it was that caused the migraines. Unlike me, she was always so capable. She never seemed to worry about anything, she just took care of it. But there must have been inner demons tormenting her that I didn't know about. The fact that she never exhibited any sign of stress while she fretted away under the surface, wasn't that the sort of thing that caused migraines? Not showing who you really were.

I admired Cath. She was a teacher at a local elementary school. At least she did something worthwhile instead of ghosting silly celebrities' autobiographies. I liked the fact that we came from totally different backgrounds. My parents elected to send me to a state school rather than indulge in the private education they could easily afford and Cath and I were in the same class.

I remember the first time Cath came to our house, the one I live in now, because it was the first time I realized my mother had a ghastly pseudoliberal streak in her that would embarrass me from that day on. My mother worked very hard to cultivate my less privileged friends in a way that did not seem genuine. She spent a long time quizzing Cath about her parents' café and saying she must go there some time, and then she asked her if she knew "Lee's little black friend" that I'd brought home for tea the day before. Cath stared at her in amazement but my mother appeared to have no clue as to how patronizing it sounded. There was a kind of desperation for her to be accepted by these kids and their parents that enabled her to disregard their obvious discomfort in her presence. Eventually I decided she was too much of a liability and I stopped taking friends home altogether.

Except Cath. Somehow, after that first awkward encounter, Cath seemed to know how to handle her. She also understood me, and how uncomfortable my mother made me feel. Better still, she tried to help me understand myself.

"You haven't the first clue about yourself, Lee, that's your trouble. You let people get the wrong idea about you. You're so private and you have to be careful there. People mistake it for hostility if you don't tell them anything about yourself."

She was always telling me what was wrong with me, and trying to help me see what I could do about it. I never presumed to give her advice although I often wondered about her migraines and whether they might be caused by some defect she refused to admit. But I didn't call her on it. Maybe I should have because the day was fast approaching when I would wonder if I really knew Cath at all.

If she pointed out my flaws, she also spent a considerable amount of time telling me good things about myself as if she sensed that my confidence needed boosting. "You're a good listener," she told me once. "I really feel I can talk to you. I know where I am with you and that means a lot to me. You're so reliable and all it does is get you hurt and disillusioned."

"What on earth do you mean?" There were times when I didn't recognize myself as the person she was describing.

"You just need to learn to take yourself more seriously," was one of her favorites. "Of course, you're pretty hopeless about people. You're so unbelievably impressionable. Look at all those worthless creeps you run around with. They're exploiting you, can't you see it?" She was referring to the crowd I hung out with just before meeting Tommy, the ones who never got the point of him, or her for that matter.

Needless to say she approved of Tommy and he of her. But it was because of Tommy that I lost touch with her.

It happened after he proposed to me. He'd stayed the night and I came downstairs the next morning to find he'd rearranged the magnetic alphabet on my fridge door to read:

WILL YOU MARRY ME?

I pushed all the letters to one side, knocking some of them onto the floor in the process and left the words:

NO THANKS. NOT RIGHT NOW.

I didn't mean to hurt him. That was the last thing I would ever want to do. I thought he was just having a laugh but it turned out he was deadly serious and I felt terrible. I would never have left him such a flippant magnetic reply if I'd thought he meant it.

He brought it up that night at dinner and I stopped eating when I realized what he was saying.

"We've known each other for five years. I was thinking the other day that I cannot imagine my life without you. I cannot even remember what it was like before I met you. You're a neurotic, difficult, unpredictable person, Lee, but you're always interesting."

We were out of wine. My glass was empty. I picked up his and finished it off while I searched for the right words to tell him yet again that I just wasn't ready. I hated it when he brought up the subject of marriage. I loved him. I wanted to make him happy. I just didn't think marrying him would do that.

He went on before I could say anything. "I just can't bear to think of you struggling through life without me. You'd worry yourself sick if I wasn't there to sort everything out for you."

This was so sweet I think I might even have given in and said yes if Cath hadn't rung the doorbell and marched into the kitchen. What nobody seemed to realize was that every now and then I felt such a wave of affection for him that I came very close to asking him to move in. Often it was the very fact that people felt they had to point out what an idiot I was that made me withdraw once more into my shell.

"You're being a silly stubborn mule," was Cath's opening gambit and it dawned on me that he had invited her round to fight his corner.

"Hello, Cath, and very nice to see you too. Didn't know you were coming over tonight. I hope you've brought a bottle.

We're right out of wine by the looks of things."

"Tommy asked me to come round and talk some sense into you."

"About what?" I looked at Tommy.

"You know what," he mumbled into his chest.

"We care about you, Lee." Cath sounded uncharacteristically pompous. She stood up and moved to perch on the end of the kitchen table right in front of me. What was she trying to do? Hold me prisoner? "That's why we're here."

"I'm touched," I said.

"Don't be like that!" she said. "I'm totally serious. You can't go on like this."

"Like what?"

"Living this kind of half life. Half with Tommy, half without him. It's not fair."

"Not fair on whom?"

"I meant not fair on Tommy but in fact you're not being fair to yourself either. You've got to take your relationship to the next level."

"You make it sound like some kind of management hierarchy. And I don't see where I take it is any concern of yours, Cath. Butt out and stay out." I knew I'd taken the first step into the minefield but I felt really provoked. Leave me alone and you'll never have any trouble with me. Try to interfere, try to make me change my life and you'd better run for cover. Cath had to know she was breaking the rules.

"I will not! Or rather I would if I thought you'd ever do anything off your own bat but you never do. You're the least proactive person I've ever met. You just sit there like a lump until something happens to bring about a change in your life."

I didn't say a word mostly because I knew she was absolutely right. But where was the Cath who told me how great and reliable I was? who understood that I needed my privacy?

"Lee." She sat down next to me and turned the chair round to face me. She took both my hands in her lap and leaned in till her face was very close to mine. "Lee, someone like you who spends so much time on their own, who never goes anywhere where they might run into someone interesting, has about as much chance of meeting a husband as a polar bear in the Arctic. So if you let Tommy go . . ."

I glanced at Tommy. He didn't seem to be going anywhere.

"I like that," I told her, laughing, hoping to diffuse her earnestness. "You're absolutely right. I *am* a polar bear. They're the ones who live apart, right? The female and the male, they don't live together, they only come together to mate. That's exactly what I've been trying to tell Tommy. If and when I ever want to have a baby, that'll be the time to shack up together. Meanwhile, you're just going to have to accept that I'm a little unconventional, Cath. I'm not like you. I'm not like most people. I know that. As you keep telling me, I'm my own worst enemy. But hasn't it ever occurred to you how lonely that makes me feel?"

"There you are," she pounced. "We don't want you to be lonely."

"I'm not!" I screamed at her. "Inside here, on my own I'm not at all lonely. It's only when I listen to you describing how you see me that I feel lonely. You're describing a freak and I'm not a freak, I'm not!"

"You're not a very happy bunny, are you?"

This was the last straw. She was smothering me with understanding. Just once I wished she would scream something back at me so we could have a stand-up row and clear the air. She was always so mature and well behaved and she never lost control like I did. I had faults and I admitted them but Cath somehow always seemed so perfect. And she was so patient with me. However much I ranted and raved she always told me how much she loved me.

"It's not going to work, Tommy" — she looked at him — "the more we try to persuade her, the more she's going to dig her heels in and say she doesn't want to get married."

"Stop talking about me as if I'm not here." My voice was still far too loud.

I was beginning to feel cornered, as if they were ganging up on me. I began to panic, just a little. I didn't want to lose Tommy but at the same time I would not be controlled in this way.

I think we all knew that this was no longer about whether I married Tommy or not. Somehow it had become an ugly battle of wills between Cath and me. All kinds of resentments were festering inside me. It appeared some kind of sea change was occurring in our friendship whereby our roles were shifting. Up to now Cath had always been the adult whose advice I, the wayward child, had always sought. But now I was feeling rebellious.

"Oh, now you're just being silly. You sound like you're still in kindergarten." She actually had the nerve to smile and try to pat me on the head.

"Fuck off!" I leapt up, totally furious now. "Leave me the fuck alone, Cath. I've had enough of you always telling me what to do. I need you to give me a bit of space to work things out for myself. It's not my fault I'm not as perfect as you. Why do you always have to make me feel so inadequate?"

She gave me one of her knowing looks that said *You do that all by yourself.* But I wouldn't let it go.

"I mean, what is it with you, Cath? Why is it so important to you that I marry Tommy? You keep on telling me to get married but I notice you're not getting very far in that direction yourself. Why haven't we seen *you* walking down the aisle with anyone yet?"

It was just something I threw out but Cath's reaction was instantaneous. I seemed to have hit a nerve somewhere inside her. She flushed, opened her mouth but didn't say anything.

"Come on!" I taunted her. "What's the big deal? Why do you have to stick your nose in? You must have a reason and don't say it's because Tommy asked for your help because you know as well as I do that you could have told him it wasn't appropriate for you to be involved."

"It wasn't appropriate," she repeated, an altogether quieter Cath. In fact she looked shellshocked.

"What's the matter?" I asked.

"Nothing," she said, "you're right. You're absolutely right, Lee. I won't interfere again. I'm leaving now. I'll let you two sort yourselves out."

To my astonishment, she came and placed her palms either side of my face and gave me a quick kiss and I saw there were tears in her eyes.

"I want you to marry Tommy. Don't ask me why but I do."

"I *am* asking you."

"Forget it," she said. Now she sounded quite fierce, not at all like calm, rational Cath. I hadn't realized she was capable of such passion. I backed away but I wasn't going to give up now.

"I won't forget it. You can't just barge in here and interfere like this and then say *forget it.* I want an explanation."

"Okay!" Suddenly Cath totally lost it. "Okay! Don't marry him if you don't want to but I just want you to know I think you're crazy beyond belief. Utterly crazy and stupid with it. He's a beautiful man. He's sweet and funny and sexy and I just don't understand how you can't love him like I —"

She stopped then and ran out the door. It was just as well. Maybe she could pretend we hadn't heard and retain a little bit of dignity.

But we had heard and we stood there like dummies until I forced myself to break the silence.

"Did you know?"

He nodded. "I had an idea. She made it pretty clear a couple of times. I don't think she meant to come on to me or anything. She probably didn't realize how she came across. Nothing ever happened, Lee. I always backed right off."

I believed him. What I couldn't understand was why hadn't I spotted it too. "Why didn't you say anything?"

"Give me a break, Lee. What *could* I say? Oh, by the way, have you noticed your best friend's in love with me? Besides, I wasn't sure if maybe the drink didn't have something to do with it."

"The drink?"

"She hasn't talked to you about that? She calls me up sometimes at the Beeb when she's really loaded and wants to talk."

"You mean she has a problem? With alcohol?"

"I can't believe you haven't noticed. You spend a lot more time with her than I do."

"She barely drinks at all, just a glass of wine occasionally and if it's white she'll always mix it with Perrier and make a spritzer."

"I think she tries to hide it from you. She thinks you'd disapprove, she told me."

"Me disapprove of her? That'd make a change. How long has she — you know?"

"I'm not sure. All I know is that recently she's started to worry that it's getting out of hand. She keeps waking up with these dreadful hangovers and very little memory of how she acquired them."

"Well not with me, that's for sure." I thought about the migraines. Were they in fact hangovers? No wonder my suggested treatments hadn't worked.

"Is she seeing someone? I mean, does she go to — ?"

"Is she in a program? I don't think so but the fact that she's acknowledged she's got a problem means she might take the next step and enroll in one."

I was silent for quite a while. I didn't say anything to Tommy but I felt I'd been left out of the equation in some major way. Maybe I was being even more self-absorbed than normal but I just couldn't understand why Cath hadn't talked to *me* about her alcohol problem, if indeed she had one. Coming on top of her revelation about her feelings for Tommy, it was a little too much to handle. I knew I should feel concerned for her but I just wished that I hadn't learned about it this way.

Tommy seemed to be reading my mind. "You know, she would have told you about it sooner or later," he said gently.

"I didn't know she called you up at work."

"I wished to God she hadn't. I was pretty freaked out by her calls. I was on the point of asking you to speak to her about them. I don't suppose you're going to believe this but it was at the back of my mind when I asked her over here tonight. She assumed I wanted her to back me up about the whole marriage thing but really I hoped I'd get a chance to persuade her to talk to you about the booze."

"So what are we going to do now? I suppose I'd better call her tomorrow."

"I suppose you better had," said Tommy sadly, almost as if he anticipated what was going to happen.

Because that was the last time I saw Cath. I called and called but she screened her calls forever and when I left messages, she never got back to me.

After about six months I gave up trying to reach her and tried to come to terms with the fact that I no longer had her as a friend. Once I ran into her at the home of a mutual acquaintance and she was civil and smiled and kissed me hello but there was no follow-up. Tommy kept telling me she'd get in touch one day but it hasn't happened yet.

So when Noreen said I never talked about my girlfriends, it hurt. I wanted to pick up the phone and call Cath and tell her about Astrid McKenzie and how scared I was, and how my mother's repairs list was longer than ever, and how Tommy and I hadn't spoken for a week. But I couldn't — not least because I knew she'd moved and I had no idea where she was living these days.

I wondered if Noreen would succeed in persuading Tommy to call me. And I wondered again about the mist pot cit in his medicine cabinet. But what was I thinking? This was the faithful Tommy we were talking about, not some tabloid lothario. How could I even imagine Tommy playing away, as he would undoubtedly put it?

At least we'd always had that. The knowledge that we were faithful to one another. Despite the fact that I don't seem to be able to commit to a mutual living arrangement with Tommy, there's no way I would ever cheat on him.

Chapter 4

I don't usually go to the homes. Normally I am summoned to the agent's office or a restaurant whenever a meeting is required, otherwise I work via telephonic contact. Going to the home was a real treat, taking me back to my profile-writing days when I had to get as much as I could from the person's living room to inform me of their personality. Being nosy by nature, I was thrilled to be allowed a peek into Selma Walker's house and I wondered how Genevieve had wangled it.

Selma had obviously resisted the temptation to sell up and move from Notting Hill, although at a rough guess her house would command an asking price of four million, minimum. She might live only two minutes' walk from me but her house and mine were not in the same ballpark. While her house exuded wealth and was obviously the object of constant upgrading and renovation, mine — or rather my parents' — conveyed a message of woeful neglect and there were no prizes for guessing who was to blame for that.

I counted eighteen stone steps up to the front door. I stood between a couple of silly little bay trees planted in terra-cotta pots and rang the bell.

The man who answered the door had just bitten a chunk off the piece of toast he was holding in his hand. When he saw me he munched furiously in order to be able to speak.

"Sorry. Thought you were going to be a messenger delivering something. I'm convinced they lurk outside the door till I've just made myself some tea and toast or stepped into the bath before they ring the bell. Happens every time. Lee Bartholomew?"

"Yes," I said. "My agent Genevieve LaBache said you'd be expecting me. I'm here to talk about writing a book for Selma Walker."

"Ah, Genevieve. The famous Genevieve." He grinned. "Vision of loveliness in pale pink and lilac. She called this morning to remind me. Come in." He held the door wide in an exaggerated gesture. "I'm Buzz Kempinski."

"You're Selma Walker's manager?" I

stepped into a beautiful spacious hall with a floor of York stone. I glimpsed my reflection in an antique mirror above a marble-topped console that reached almost to the ceiling. I was surprised to see I was looking good but then I remembered old glass is invariably kind.

"I suppose you could say that," he said over his shoulder. What was that supposed to mean? "My office is on the top floor but why don't you come into the kitchen and join me in a cup of tea. Or would you like a drink?"

"What I could really do with is a cup of coffee," I said. "Instant would be fine."

"In a kitchen like this?" he waved toward a Gaggia espresso-cappuccino maker, a caffetiere, and an electric coffee machine lined up on a far counter. "Have one of each, otherwise the others will feel left out."

I laughed.

"Is Selma Walker going to join us later?"

"Selma's not here. She's in Manchester all week, didn't you know? They tape the show in the studio up there. But it doesn't matter if she's not around. I'm the one you need to see. So what is there about Selma's story that you think would make a good book?"

Damn. Because I had been so unnerved

by the fire — not to mention the latest fracas with Tommy — I hadn't taken the time to prepare for my meeting. I'd broken one of my golden rules and shown up without having first sought out background information on Selma Walker from the Press Association or the Internet so I would know what I was talking about. I believed in doing homework. It was professional. Now I'd have to wing it.

"Well," I began, "she's a woman who's successful in her own right playing a similar sort of woman. She has control over her own destiny. She's . . ."

Mercifully he interrupted me before I could utter any more embarrassing clichés. But the force of his comeback surprised me.

"That's all a load of crap. She doesn't have control of her own destiny. The network does. Tell me something, have you ever actually watched *Fraternity*?"

I shook my head. There was no point in lying. It was obvious I wasn't suitable for the job. I'd finish my coffee and leave. Get on with the renovations to the house and amaze my mother.

"So you know absolutely nothing about Selma?"

"Well, I *have* heard of her . . ."

"I love it. Don't say another word. Congratulations, Lee Bartholomew, you've got the job. Now relax and tell me all about yourself. You'd better tell me about the ghosting jobs you've done recently. That way I can convince Madame you're the best there is. Shall we have a drink now? To celebrate?"

I looked at him in astonishment. "You're hiring me? Just like that? Why?"

"Because if you know nothing about her, you'll be objective. You'll tell the real story. I hope you know what you're in for."

"That sounds ominous."

"Wine? Vodka? Lager?"

"A vodka and tonic would be great, thanks. How long have you been her manager?"

"Long enough."

"So you were with her in America?"

"Wasn't everybody?"

"Why are you being so evasive?"

"Am I?"

I was beginning to get annoyed by his attitude. I couldn't quite place him. His accent was English and he had that languid upper-class grace, long legs, slim build, fine brown hair flopping over his eyes.

"Why are you called Buzz?" I asked suddenly.

"My energy. I buzz about a lot."

"Do you sting like a bee?" I couldn't resist asking.

"I try not to. Actually, I think it's something to do with my childhood. Isn't there a rhyme that goes 'Isn't it funny how a bear likes honey, Buzz buzz buzz, I wonder why he does?' I like honey. Or maybe I had my hair chopped off in a buzz cut and somebody came up with the nickname. Who knows? I've had the name so long, I honestly can't remember."

"What's your real name?"

"Can't remember that either. Or my age, so don't ask."

Of course, now he'd brought that up I was dying to know. I guessed we were about the same age. I was about to ask how old Selma was when he butted in.

"So, you don't watch much television?"

"Just because I don't watch *Fraternity* doesn't necessarily mean I don't watch television. There are other programs, you know."

"Bit of a culture vulture, are you?"

I wasn't sure about his tone. I couldn't quite work out if he was sneering at me or not.

"Sorry. Don't look like that. I'm not having a go, honest." He grinned. "I'm just curious as to why anyone would be a ghostwriter. Don't you want to write your own story, not someone else's?"

"Not much to tell. It would bore the pants off the reader. I'd have to jazz it up and make it fiction."

"Not up to that?"

There was no getting away from it. He was taunting me. Throwing down some kind of gauntlet and waiting for me to pick it up. The annoying thing was that I found I wanted to impress him and it had nothing to do with whether he would think I was suitable for the job or not. I wanted him to think I was smart.

"I don't know," I said evenly. "I haven't tried. Ghostwriting is more difficult than you might think. There *is* a craft involved, you know."

"Well, writing's a craft, sure," he said, "but I would have thought it would be more a case of dealing with your subject's ego without them being aware that you're the one calling the shots."

I was amazed. He'd got it in one. My friends never understood the kinds of problems I faced being a ghostwriter. They assumed it was all one big party hanging out with a celebrity and then going away and writing their life story, whereas there's a whole lot more to it than that. You have to establish a relationship but there's always a very delicate balance to that relationship. You have to both subsume your own ego *and* exert it because ultimately you're the one who is the writer, the one who has to deliver the book, the one who has to shape the work. And somehow you have to make your subject subsume his or her ego without them ever knowing it and this is hard because inevitably you're dealing with very strong personalities.

And this is what Buzz seemed to understand.

"I guess it's a bit like seducing a woman," he said.

Now he had my attention.

"How so?"

"Well, a man sees a woman at a party, hears about her from his friends, and then they introduce her to him. Or he sees her picture in a magazine, bumps into her somewhere, whatever. He meets her. He wants her. She becomes his prey. Once he's met her he has to chat her up, flatter her, pander to her ego, give her his undiluted attention until she's putty in his hands. Once he has control, he goes to work until he's got what he wants out of her. That sounds rather like the way you'd treat someone whose book you were writing."

"Then once the job's completed he moves on to the next woman?"

"I never said that."

He didn't have to.

"I mean, look at it this way" — now he was really warming to his theme — "even if you're writing someone's autobiography you're the one asking the questions to get the story out of them, you choose which anecdotes to include, which emotions to highlight. You have control. Do you like jazz?"

He had a disarming way of changing the subject just as I was about to open my mouth.

"I don't know much about it. I think so."

How pathetic that sounded. Tommy was a country music nut. He liked sentimental songs about women treating men bad thus enabling them to console themselves with too much alcohol. Sometimes the lyrics made me laugh out loud. Only the other day he'd been listening to a song in which the singer proclaimed "I like my women a little on the trashy side, they wear their clothes too tight and I know their hair is dyed." I wasn't quite sure whether this was what had made me laugh or the sight of Tommy singing along and leaping round the kitchen, shaking two artichokes as pretend maracas.

"Listen to this," said Buzz. "Bought it yesterday, been playing it all night. Houston Person. Amazing tenor sax."

The sound was rich and full and dreamy. And undeniably romantic. It was like an animal wailing across a valley to its mate. Urgent and desperate. Then repeated softly, pleading, irresistible.

"Ron Carter on bass," Buzz told me and suddenly I felt rather flattered. He assumed I knew who Ron Carter was. I hadn't a clue.

When it finished he asked me if I wanted to hear Johnny Lytle do "St. Louis Blues." I said yes. At least I'd recognize the tune.

"Who's on bass?" I asked, trying to sound as if I knew what I was talking about.

"Peter Martin Weiss. David Braham on organ."

"Yup." Casual. Like I knew all along.

Then something rather disturbing happened.

He had his back to me. He had reached down and taken a bottle of wine out of the fridge. He turned and held it up with a corkscrew in his other hand. *Want a glass?*

I nodded. He seemed to have forgotten I'd asked for a vodka and tonic. I didn't dare say anything. I realized I was thinking something I hadn't thought for nearly eight years.

I was thinking that I knew with absolute certainty that I would go to bed with this man.

Now let me get one thing straight. I don't believe in infidelity. I'm a one-man girl. I know I'm old-fashioned in this respect but the thought of it really does make me uncomfortable — no, more than that, it makes me sad. I maintain that when someone cheats on his or her partner, they are not fundamentally happy in that relationship. Add to this the fact that I have had very few boyfriends, only two of any significance before Tommy. I'm attracted to very few men and if I'm seriously involved with someone, my eye just does not stray. But on the rare occasion when I am drawn to a man for his looks, then I'm in trouble.

I always used to know ahead of time. I'd meet someone and I'd know and I was always right. Even if it turned out to be just a one-night stand and I felt like a slut afterward. It was a chemistry thing, nothing to do with how I felt about the guy. I just knew if something was going to happen and it always did.

Amazingly enough, this was the first time I'd *known* since I met Tommy. After all, I'd had that same weird certainty all those years ago when I'd sat down to drink a cup of BBC tea with him. Given that he was pasty-faced, exhausted, and exuding virtually zero sex appeal, it was something of a miracle that I latched on to him at all. But I'd picked up on something and I'd been right. In bed, even on the rare occasions we still got it together, Tommy and I were dynamite. Of course, since I'd been with him, I'd met countless men whom I'd recognized as good looking and attractive but I'd never come across one where I'd *known.*

I *knew* about Buzz. This guy was a cinch and there'd be nothing I could do about it.

He held out his arms.

"Wanna dance?"

His sweatshirt had been washed in some sweet-smelling fabric conditioner. It was all I could do not to bury my nose in his chest as he rocked me back and forth in front of the Miele Novotronic washing machine, the one I'd looked at last week in John Lewis and reluctantly decided I couldn't afford.

He wasn't taking a blind bit of notice of me. He seemed to be completely lost in the music even to the point of ignoring the phone when it rang suddenly, its shrill sound competing vainly with Johnny Lytle et al.

The machine picked up and a rather vulnerable American voice played into the room as the track came to an end.

"Buzz? Are you there? Pick up, will you? Can you get a car to meet me at the airport? I'll be on the seven o'clock from Manchester. Town car will be fine." A woman. Sounding very tired.

"I can never get her to understand we don't call them town cars over here. Oh well, back to work."

"That was Selma Walker?"

"The one and only."

"So when am I going to be able to meet her?"

He looked at me, puzzled. "You want to meet Selma?"

"Well, when we start working on the book, I'm going to be spending a lot of time with her. My subjects usually want to check me out first even if it's only a formality."

"Oh, Selma won't have time to do the interviews herself. Her filming schedule's crazy. I just told you she's away all week and at the weekends she'll just want to relax."

"But how am I going to get her story?"

"Through me, of course." He smiled. "Why do you think I arranged for you to come here today?"

"*You're* going to give me her story?" I was flabbergasted.

"Sure. I can tell you everything you need to know about her."

It was totally irregular. It wasn't how I normally worked and whatever happened there would come a time when I would have to sit down with Selma herself.

But something told me now was not the time to push it.

"So what's your number?" he asked me. "I'll give you a call, set up another meeting."

I found my handbag and gave him one of my cards.

"Oh, you're local?" he said.

"Right around the corner."

"In that case I'll walk you home."

He touched my arm briefly, shepherding me out the door and I felt as if I'd been wired for electricity. To cover my confusion I made a reference to Astrid McKenzie's fire, expecting him to pick up the thread and tell me about her. After all, hadn't Genevieve said she'd seen Astrid look at him in the Ivy as if she knew him?

He didn't answer me, just kept walking along Elgin Crescent.

"The word is she was murdered," I said, pepping up my stride to keep up with him.

"I wouldn't know," he said.

"What was she like? She lived almost next door to me but I never met her."

"How would I know?"

"But I thought —"

"Well you thought wrong," he cut in abruptly.

I didn't dare ask him if that meant he didn't know her or that I'd got it wrong about her being murdered.

"Listen," he said, half turning toward me, "there's something I ought to tell you about Selma."

"You want to warn me about her, don't you?" I asked him as we turned the corner into Ladbroke Grove. It was getting cold. Winter was setting in and the afternoons now imposed a five o'clock curfew on anyone who didn't want to be out after dark. "It often happens. I'm used to it. I'm always being told such and such a person's a nightmare, I won't get anything out of them, or they'll call me day and night, do I know what I've let myself in for. Didn't you say something like that yourself earlier on?"

"Did I? No, what you ought to know is that she didn't know you were coming round today. I thought I'd see you first, find out if you were suitable."

"And am I?"

"Totally," he said and then added almost under his breath, "at least as far as I'm concerned."

We were standing outside my house. I'd stopped, ready to go in. I was annoyed that he hadn't been entirely straight with me and I knew I ought to tell him so, thank him for walking me home, then let myself in my front door and close it firmly behind me.

Instead I allowed him to kiss me for several minutes in full view of my extremely nosy neighbor, Mrs. O'Malley. And I was still standing there in a daze for quite some time long after he'd pulled away and disappeared around the corner to sort out Selma Walker's ride home from the airport.

Chapter 5

I called Genevieve and reported the gist of my meeting with Buzz.

"We're sort of back to square one," I told her. "He never even told Selma he was going to meet with me. He says I don't need to see her at all and that he can tell me everything I need to know."

"That's ridiculous." Genevieve sounded annoyed. She does not like to be thwarted in any way. "Leave it with me. I'll sort it out, don't you worry."

Of course I didn't say a word to Genevieve about what had happened between Buzz and me on my doorstep. Truth to tell, I was so confused I wouldn't have known what to say anyway. I was still trying to work out in my own mind why I had allowed him to kiss me and I was reluctantly coming to a rather worrying conclusion. One thing I know I need in a relationship is attention (read: affection). I didn't get much from my parents when I was growing up and I have a kind of simplistic psychological theory that tells me I seek in my lovers what I didn't get as a child.

Up until fairly recently I had been smothered in attention from Tommy, but lately I had sensed his withdrawal no matter how much he told me he loved me. I fully acknowledge that it is partly — if not mainly — my fault because I prevaricate so much about the question of our living together and this only adds to my confusion. Why am I like this? Why don't I welcome him with open arms? What is stopping me from embracing the intimacy that other people seem to accept wholeheartedly?

Only the other day Tommy shouted at me, "It's like I can't tell you enough times, Lee. You *never* seem to believe me." And when he said that I felt so lonely because it was true. I didn't truly, really, absolutely believe it when he said he loved me. I didn't truly, really, absolutely *feel* it and there were times when I wondered if I ever would. And yet I knew it was because I'd created a barrier around me. I knew that slowly but surely I'd been pushing him away and having done that I'd laid myself open to being seduced by someone else in my eternal quest for affection.

If I told Genevieve I wanted out of the job she'd want to know the reason why and I didn't feel like giving her the answer. I needed the work, I told myself firmly. Whatever happened with Buzz would happen. Or not. If Tommy and I made up soon then my kiss with Buzz would just be a momentary lapse. I'd deal with it. Tell Buzz I'd had too much to drink and finesse my way out of any further advances.

I went on-line to check out Selma's Web site, something I should have done before I went for the meeting, and found it to be strangely lacking in information. All I learned was that she was American and that she'd worked in the odd daytime soap opera over there that wouldn't mean much to people in England — *As the World Turns*, *All My Children*, *Days of Our Lives.* It was her role in *Fraternity* that had made her famous in the UK but beyond that she didn't seem to have done any interviews about her personal life and that was odd. It looked like she was going to turn out to be one of those people you think you know but actually you know nothing.

That intrigued me. She was a big name. But it was beginning to look as if anything I put in her autobiography would be news.

I could be on to something here. When Genevieve called back to say she'd tried to reach Selma in Manchester without success, I urged her to keep trying.

"See what you can do, Genny. Please. You've got the address. Write a letter. Give her my credits. Do a real number on me. You never know, she might make the effort to find the time."

"Will do," said Genevieve. "Now, I've got a bit of news for you." She lowered her voice as if she imagined there were people listening in on our conversation. "I've found out a thing or two since we last spoke. Astrid McKenzie wasn't the saint she appeared to be. She liked being beaten up."

"Oh yes?" This bore out what Chris had hinted at.

"My friend Toby worked with her on children's TV couple of years ago. He said she kept her life pretty much to herself but he was screwing a makeup artist on the show and she said Astrid McKenzie came into work sometimes with some pretty nasty bruises that took a fair amount of covering up."

"That could mean someone was hitting her, Genevieve. It doesn't mean she *liked* it."

"Whatever. It means she had a bit of nastiness going on in her private life. Think about it. It never made the press, did it?"

She was right.

"So you'll let me know when you've made contact with Selma Walker and set up a time for me to meet her?"

"Sure thing. Sit by the phone like a good girl."

I had no intention of doing any such thing. In fact I willed myself to forget all about Selma Walker and everyone concerned with her.

And while I was at it, I'd try to stop thinking about Astrid McKenzie.

Except that she haunted me. Her face stared up at me from every newspaper vendor's stand. They'd chosen a particularly ethereal photo of her where her fine blond hair seemed to be lit from behind and floated around her like a halo. To my horror, she began to exert a strange morbid power over me from beyond the grave, or the morgue or wherever they'd taken her toasted corpse. A power that prompted me to actually buy the papers that carried her picture and leave them lying around my bedroom like some kind of shrine. It was a mistake. The press had portrayed her as being too good to be true to the extent that you were turned right off. The inside photo spreads included soft-focus pictures of her in meadows surrounded by children holding flowers and she looked as if she were modeling for a fabric conditioner commercial. Quotes attributed to her always had her extolling the virtues of other people, and saying how lucky she was to be working with such a wonderful crew on children's television, how she adored children and hoped to start a family of her own one day. I finally stopped buying the papers when I came across a picture of her that was so pious it made me want to vomit. It showed her standing outside a church, holding the hand of a little girl who was gazing up at her adoringly. "Astrid and Baby Jesus are my two favorite people in the whole wide world" read the caption.

And yet if Genevieve was to be believed, when the cameras weren't on her, this apparent blessing to society went looking for trouble. Each time I went past what was left of her little mews house, I shuddered at what must have gone on within its walls and even when I had locked myself inside my own home, I still didn't feel safe. I needed the comforting bulk of Tommy beside me. This standoff was lasting an unusually long time. I resisted the temptation to call Noreen for an update. Of course I could always pick up the phone and call him but each time I thought of that, I remembered Buzz. What had I been thinking of? It was so unlike me. I never acted on impulse like that. Okay, so he had kissed me but I hadn't exactly fought him off.

I had enjoyed kissing Buzz. It was as simple as that. And if I called Tommy I'd have to deal with it. Well, I'd deal with it if and when he called me.

But he didn't and neither did Buzz and I always had to come back to Noreen's suggestion that I get a lodger.

I actually had the idea of renting out the summerhouse in the middle of the night. I'd barely been asleep ten minutes when I was awakened by the sound of dustbin lids clattering to the ground outside. I lay rigid for about twenty seconds and then forced myself to get up and pad barefoot into the bathroom where I could open a tiny window and peep down into the alley.

There was someone down there. I couldn't make out who it was but the light from the street lamps in Blenheim Crescent threw a shadow onto the wall of the alley. The shadow was moving back and forth and I could hear footsteps below me.

I ran back to my bedroom and dialed 999.

"There's a man trying to break into my house and he's going to set fire to it." This was completely unfounded but the woman on the other end of the line merely took down my name and address and said someone would be with me right away. "Just stay on the line till they get there," she added.

When the doorbell rang about five minutes later, I left the phone off the hook and ran downstairs to open it. A man in a brown leather jacket charged past me and up the stairs, flashing some ID at me as he went. I padded up after him in my nightie.

"Where'd you see him?" he yelled over his shoulder. "Come and show me." He was standing at my bedroom window looking out over the mews at the end of the garden.

"I didn't *see* him. I heard him downstairs in the alley. I saw his shadow."

"You didn't see anyone over there" — he pointed to the back of a tall house rising up above the mews — "someone climbing up that scaffolding?"

Just then a voice shouted up the stairs.

"It's okay, guv. We got the bloke in the alley. It's only old Alfred, drunk as a skunk, peeing all over the walls but nothing worse than that."

The man in the leather jacket slammed his hand down on the windowsill in a fury and I squeaked in shock.

He turned to me. "Sorry, luv. I'm after a rapist. Woman one street away was assaulted last night. Thought he might be paying you a visit tonight. The uniforms downstairs'll take your drunk away."

Arson, rape, a drunk and disorderly, all in a night's work to them but I was left to stand at my bedroom window and wonder how much longer it would be before I wound up like Astrid McKenzie or the woman who'd been attacked the night before.

And that's when it came to me that the summerhouse would be the perfect place for a lodger. I was staring at it from my bedroom window, standing there bathed in moonlight looking really rather inviting.

It was a pretty little building, built against the back of a mews house at the end of the garden. This house formed the back wall. Two additional stone walls jutting out formed the sides of the summerhouse and the front was made up of a wood frame and glass doors. It was a proper little house, quite a big area, not at all the garden shed some people dubbed their summerhouse. If anything that was erring on the side of understatement. When I was a child, I always wanted to turn it into the most wonderful playhouse and invite my friends for sleepovers but my mother never got the point of that idea. My parents had long ago had it wired for electricity. All it needed was heat. I could imagine how snug it would be in there if it could be heated. *Imagine.* That was the key word. Somehow the summerhouse began to fire my imagination so that was why I knew, as I got back into bed and lay wide awake for the next hour, that it would take precedence over the work that needed doing to maintain the house itself.

The next day I was fidgety. I realized I had inadvertently psyched myself up to start work on another book and now it didn't look as if anything was going to happen. For about twenty seconds, I pretended I was going to get on with sorting out the repair work on the house. I made a list of what needed doing. The damp appeared to be rising up out of the basement and into the laundry room. I say "laundry room"; in fact it was just an alcove off the kitchen where I kept the washer and dryer. I had a ludicrous habit of embellishing parts of the house to make them sound grander. Tommy said it made me sound like a real estate agent.

So. Apart from the damp, what was next on the list? The toilet on the first floor was leaking. The windowsills were all rotting. Something needed to be done about the gutters. The first four items on a list that eventually numbered eighteen jobs, and that was just my list. I had yet to unearth my mother's and remind myself what was on it.

But making the list was as far as I got because as I was writing it, I remembered my idea about the summerhouse. It was perfect. I'd find a nice friendly soul, someone reliable and quiet, and they'd be far enough away so as not to disturb my routine but I was bound to feel less nervous knowing there was someone within shouting distance of my bedroom window.

I went mad. I invested in a couple of kerosene heaters and installed them. I dragged a large multicolored shaggy rug across the lawn, shook it free of leaves and laid it on the summerhouse floor. The sun was shining and the sunlight picked out the rug's swirling patterns through the glass doors, making it seem like a golden tapestry. There was a small queen-size bed in the second guest bedroom on the first floor and I called a couple of men in the market Chris recommended and had it moved into the summerhouse, pushed it against a wall and covered it with cushions. It would serve as a bed/sofa since there wouldn't be room for an armchair. I went to Ikea and bought shelving, a clothes rail and a bedside locker. Finally, I went round my parents' house appropriating the other necessities. A small chest of drawers. A mirror in an oval wooden frame. A reading lamp and a standard lamp. A couple of chairs. A small chest on which to stand a television. Then the television itself, swiped from the kitchen, one of four in the house. A tiny fridge that had been sitting unused for years. I switched it on. It still worked. On the shelf beside the fridge I placed an electric kettle, a toaster, a tiny Baby Belling electric cooker, the kind you can boil a pan of soup on, some mugs, plates, glasses, cutlery.

Within a week it had all come together. My final contribution came from Portobello Market. An eighteenth century china washing bowl and pitcher. I put it on a table in the corner with a pile of bright blue towels beside it. A bit cold but maybe some hot water could be added from the electric kettle.

There were forty-five replies to my ad in the *Standard* and indeed most of them were from women. Women who seemed totally bewildered as to why they were being marched to the end of my garden. Women who took one look at the little nest I had created and stared at me as if I was mad.

"The ad said 'enchanting garden pied-à-terre'," one woman told me accusingly.

"Well, there you are," I replied.

"But where's the bathroom? The kitchen? The loo?"

"There," I said, pointing across the garden to the wrought iron steps leading up to my back door. "There's a bathroom just to the right. And your kitchen's right here." I gestured to the Baby Belling, the electric kettle.

"If you're offering a shed at the end of your garden, I think you ought to say so," I was told.

But before I could word a new ad, Angel arrived on my doorstep.

The doorbell rang and there stood a short buxom creature with peroxide hair. Her face was very pretty. I took in that much before she announced.

"Hi. I'm Angelina O'Leary but you can call me Angel."

"I'm Nathalie Bartholomew but you can call me Lee," I said automatically.

"Can I? That's great. So how much is it then? It never said."

"How much is what?"

"The room? How much is it? Can I come in? It's nippy out here."

I was stupefied. I had never envisaged having a five foot two mini-Marilyn as tenant and nighttime backup. I toyed with the idea of telling her the room had gone but then I thought, *What the hell?* She wouldn't want it anyway if she was anything like the other viewers.

She wasn't and she loved it.

"Ooh, it'd be like living in a summer'ouse."

That was one way of putting it.

"You like it then."

"Oh yeah. It's all so cozy. Makes you want to curl up and hug yerself."

That was exactly the way I saw it.

"Don't you want to see where the bathroom is? And the toilet? The kitchen?"

"Oh, there's more?" She seemed astonished. "I mean, you put that jug and bowl there and them towels. And what with an electric kettle and that, you could boil water and you'd be laughing." She looked around. "But I see what you mean about the toilet."

"And wouldn't you want to have a bath or take a shower now and again?"

"Oh, I could run round to me mum's for that. But I do need to go to the toilet, don't I?"

I led her back across the garden and showed her the bathroom. She said "Ooh lovely," about four times but when she saw the kitchen, her mouth dropped open.

"It's like what you see in films. You don't ever think you're going to be in one of these fancy kitchens yerself, do you?" She seemed to be appealing to me as if I were standing in my own kitchen for the first time. My mother had fancied herself as a bit of a cook and her ambition had manifested itself by the transformation of our comfortable family room with the cooker, fridge, and sink at one end into a minimalist designer kitchen with bare counters and everything hidden away, even the fridge. You pressed a cupboard at thigh level and out popped the dishwasher. You hit another with your knee and there was the garbage disposal. Sometimes if you accidentally leaned against something without thinking, you got the fright of your life by exposing revolving shelves of saucepans that clattered into your shins.

But if Angel liked it, she could have it. I wouldn't show her the pantry where I made my suppers of an evening. "Pantry?" said Tommy predictably when I referred to it as such in his presence. "Oh, please. It's a larder with a cooker in it."

"Bit of a cook, are you, Angel?"

"Me? Never. Takeaway girl, me. So how much was you thinking of for the room?"

"You say your mother lives in the area?"

"Yeah. Portobello Court Estate. Council flat. Five minutes from here."

"You live there now?"

She nodded. "Bloody nightmare it is. Five of us in a two-bedroom flat. I'm the eldest. I've got three little brothers and they're all in the one room. Me and me mum share the other room. The other bed. Me dad was Spanish but he run off when I was five." She said it as if his nationality and his departure were connected. "Mum went back to her old name. I don't even think they were married. My brothers are all O'Learys. I mean, we've all got fathers somewhere but we're not bothered who they are or whether they're the same guy. I know mine was Spanish because Mum always said he chose the name Angelina and he used to call me his little Angel. Well, till he run off. There's always been Spanish people up Golborne Road way. I went to a Spanish restaurant up there once, kept looking at all the waiters thinking maybe one of them was my dad. Anyway, time I moved out. Mum saw your ad. She was looking for a cleaning job. You wasn't looking for a cleaner by any chance, was you?"

"Not at the moment, thank you. Now, would you like a cup of tea?"

"I'll make it. Where's your teapot? How do you open these doors?" She was running round the kitchen trying to find handles.

"Like this." I showed her, reached in, and retrieved a teapot.

"Shall I get the kettle from outside?"

"No, it's all right." I smiled. "I've got another one. So you don't want to live with your mum. How old are you? If you don't mind me asking?"

"Nineteen," she said, with enough defiance to make me think she was probably younger. "And I've got a good job so you don't have to worry about the rent."

How do you know? I wondered. *I haven't said what it is yet.* The truth was I hadn't really worked out what it would be.

The other people who had come round had been so instantly dismissive, it had never come up.

"Milk and sugar?" I asked, stalling. "Where do you work?"

"Tesco," she said proudly. "In Portobello. On the checkout. One day I'll make duty manager."

Her face did look familiar. Or was I just imagining it? I went to Sainsbury's for my big shops and popped round to Tesco for the odd top-up during the week but I generally ran in and out so fast, I barely noticed the checkout girls.

"So how much is it? I could manage a hundred a week. Will it be as much as that?"

A hundred pounds a week in one of the most fashionable areas of London? She'd be lucky to get a room for less than three hundred. But then it looked like I'd be lucky to find someone who didn't mind running across the garden at two a.m. in their nightie if they wanted a pee.

"Tell you what," I said wondering if I'd regret it for the rest of my life, "why don't we say you give me eighty pounds a week and you give your mum the other twenty for her to give the place a good clean every now and then."

She looked at me for a second. She knew what I meant. If she kept the place clean herself, then she could pocket the extra twenty. But if she wanted to help her mum out, well then it was up to her.

I wasn't renting the summerhouse out because I needed the money. I was doing it so I wouldn't be totally alone at night while there was an arsonist running round the area. Plus it helped me procrastinate about the chores in the house yet again, which was par for the course, and it gave me a certain amount of satisfaction. It was something I'd feel good about doing and how often did that happen these days?

"There's no phone." I said, suddenly remembering the one thing I'd forgotten.

"No worries." She fished a mobile out of a little purple crochet bag. "My boyfriend give it to me for Christmas."

"You've got a boyfriend?"

"Did have. We broke up."

The doorbell rang and she jumped down off the stool, spilling her tea.

"Shall I get that?"

"Will it be for you?"

"Oh, no, I was just trying to help."

I felt bad. She was a nice girl. No side to her. She genuinely wanted to help.

"It's all right. You sit tight."

It was Tommy, back at the worst possible time.

"Mum said you wanted to see me," he said casually, giving me a peck on the cheek. He made it sound as if he'd just been in the next room instead of totally out of my life for the last ten days. He rarely turned up unannounced because he knew it infuriated me. I could see him preparing himself for what he called "one of your telling-offs." He perked up considerably at the sight of Angel.

"Pleased to meet you. We've just made a cup of tea," she told him before I could get a word in. "What's your favorite color?"

What an odd question, I thought, but Tommy didn't seem in the least put out.

"Beige," he said, "red second. What's yours?"

"Blue. And golden. Because of my name. Angel."

"Blimey. What's your last name? Gabriel? I'm Tommy." He held out his hand.

I had never seen Tommy hold out his hand before and what was all this rubbish about favorite colors?

"So what's your porno name?"

Weird question but God help me, Tommy had an answer.

"Fluffy Marriot."

"Kitten?"

"Rabbit. Yours?"

"Frisky O'Leary. Hamster."

"Suits you."

Angel giggled. It was like they were talking a foreign language. I felt totally excluded.

"Will one of you please explain what is going on?"

"Which bit didn't you understand?"

"Well, for a start why did she need to know your favorite color?"

"It's just a thing you ask someone when you first meet them, a way of getting to know them," said Angel.

I had never asked anyone what their favorite color was.

"And the porno name? Getting to know them better?"

"Oh, it's just a game you play." Everyone but me obviously. "You take the name of the first pet you ever had and you add your mother's maiden name and that's your porno name. You know, on the Internet. So what would yours be, Lee?"

I thought for a moment. "Moby Dick Pilkington-Scott. Goldfish."

"Don't think you'd get very far with that," said Tommy.

"Angel's moving into the summerhouse," I said to change the subject.

The joy on her face made my day. I'd obviously enabled some kind of dream to come true. "We'd better discuss dates," I said, Lady Bountiful personified. "It'd have to be next week at the earliest, I'm afraid. Here's my number. Give me a ring and we'll sort something out."

She took the hint and stood up. "Well, better be getting along."

"Do you live far from here?" Tommy asked.

"Five minutes. Portobello Court Estate. Just past the mews. I'm going to walk back past her house and take a good look. Ever so sad, wasn't it? She was the last person anyone would want to kill. She was such a sweetheart. Everyone loved her. She was successful. She was happy."

I noticed we didn't even have to say Astrid McKenzie's name anymore.

"How do you know she was happy?"

"I read it in the *Sun*," said Angel cheerfully. "I'll let you know if I see anything juicy."

"Would you like me to walk you home?" said Tommy. "It's dark outside."

"It's all right," she said, smiling. I understood why he asked. She was such a dainty little creature if you looked beyond the breasts. "I'll run all the way except when I stop at hers."

She left, kissing us both rather embarrassingly on both cheeks before she went.

"So, Tommy, this is an unexpected pleasure. Shall I put the kettle on again?"

"It was a slow day so I came round to see if you wanted me to help clear out your office. You said the other day you'd been meaning to do it for a while and I thought you could use a hand. I got off early. Just a thought."

This was often the way we approached our reunions after a row. We didn't address the reason we hadn't seen each other in a while, just found an excuse to get us back together and carry on as if nothing had happened. Tommy would invariably redeem himself by offering to help at exactly the right time. His actual assistance was a bit perfunctory and he wasn't much use if I was really worried about something. He had a small selection of soothing stock responses like "Take your time" and "Don't worry about it" while I rattled on about what had upset me and then I'd glance at him and see he wasn't even looking at me.

But I let him help clear my desk and lug a lot of rubbish downstairs to the bins.

As he was preparing to take the last load he looked out of the window of the room I use as an office.

"You'll be able to see her coming and going," he commented. "You'll be a right concierge, I'll bet."

"Who?" I asked, as if I didn't know.

"Angel," he sighed. "Bit of all right, that Angel."

I was relieved to see him again but nevertheless once we'd finished clearing out my office, I pretended I was going out, just to get him to leave. It was the first time I'd seen him since I'd kissed Buzz and it felt weird. When we parted at the corner of Portobello Road, I gave him an unusually passionate farewell kiss fueled no doubt by my feeling of extreme guilt.

"Boy!" he shouted at me as he started off down Portobello. "That was something. Won't wash for a week!"

I hadn't told him Angel worked at Tesco. I didn't want him offering to do the shopping and then going around and ogling her over the bar codes. But I did make a trip to Tesco myself a few days later. I believed her. I trusted her. But I just wanted to check out for myself that at least her Tesco story was true.

I saw her sitting there on aisle 4 as I

went in and she saw me so I had to go around and pretend to do a shop. I grabbed a cart and began to fill it at random, not really concentrating on what I was doing. As a result I found I had selected items I didn't even like. Celery. I hate celery. It would sit in the fridge and go bad. Bananas. They'd go brown but maybe I could make banana bread. Pasta sauce in a jar. Horseradish. *Horseradish!* A carton of vichyssoise. Some sweaty packed ham. A carton of Bio yogurt. I left my cart by the cheese and wandered off down the aisles to search for something I really might need. When I returned, loaded with paper towels (you can never have enough), Kleenex, fabric conditioner, heavy bulky items, the cart wasn't where I'd left it.

I'd lost my cart. It had come to this.

"Shall I take those from you? You look like you're going to drop them any second."

I glanced over my shoulder. Straight into Buzz's eyes. They were, I registered to my surprise, dead eyes — flat, staring — but somehow their sleepy expression made them sexy. He was standing very close behind me. He maintained constant eye contact as he took each of the items out of my arms. Then he turned around.

"Follow me. I've got your cart over here."

"You hijacked my cart?" I accused him. "That's a violation of some kind. Has to be."

"Not the kind I have in mind."

When we got to the checkout I made sure I went to Angel's and she chattered away while she rang up my purchases.

"I'll call you soon. Honest. I've just been so busy. I really really have. Oh, d'you use Pantene shampoo? I do too. Dead creamy. We'll be able to share."

Out of the corner of my eye I could see Buzz standing at another cash register, his gaze fixated on Angel's large breasts.

Of course I'd bought so much stuff I couldn't carry it all home by myself and he had to help me. Why hadn't he bought anything himself? Had he been stalking me? Lying in wait outside my house and following me to Tesco?

You wish, said a voice I tried not to hear.

"What did she mean, 'we'll be able to share'?" he asked. "I couldn't help overhearing."

"I'm renting out my summerhouse to her."

"For sunbathing?"

"It's a long story."

"I've got time."

I suppose it was as good an excuse as any for him to get his foot through my door. Or at least through my front door. Twenty minutes later he'd made it through my bedroom door. They call it *carnal* knowledge and I know why. There's absolutely nothing spiritual or cerebral about it. Tommy never even crossed my mind for the simple reason that my mind wasn't functioning — only my body.

Buzz unbuttoned my shirt and ran his hands around my back to unhook my bra while I tried not to shake. I hadn't had new sex with someone in eight years and I was nervous and shy at exposing my body.

I was tense and he sensed this and he was gentle with me. As our kisses became more urgent my brain slowly began to register how desperately attracted I was to this man. His skin was light brown and the hairs on it silky. He was long limbed and he moved with extraordinary grace above me. I could feel his passion but he had it under control. He whispered to me every now and then, words I couldn't make out but I understood nevertheless. Was I okay? Was I ready? Now? Yes? I heard myself moan, felt myself smothered by his embrace.

I've heard it said that you should always

listen carefully to what men say when they've just had sex because their defenses are down and they tell you the truth. Buzz was holding me close and muttering away into the hair on the top of my head but although I heard Selma's name a couple of times, my left ear was pressed to his chest and I couldn't really make out what he was saying.

People always seemed to be going on nowadays about whether they had feelings for someone. I didn't know what to make of what I had just experienced with Buzz. The only feeling I had at that second was that after such good sex, I was so hungry I wanted to go straight down to the kitchen and make myself a peanut butter sandwich.

And if he wanted to lie in my bed muttering something about Selma Walker, the only feeling I had about that was that it was just as well I hadn't heard anything more on that score because by now I had almost certainly burned my boats. To the best of my knowledge ghostwriters were not in the habit of securing jobs on the casting couch.

Chapter 6

Guilt about Buzz made me do the unthinkable. Chelsea were playing at home and I invited Tommy round to watch. Wednesday night. Live on TV. 7:45 kickoff.

Tommy was understandably confused. I had long since established that there were two definite no-go areas in my house: live football on the box and country music. Recently I had begun to relax the country music rule a little because actually I quite liked it. The old stuff. Tammy Wynette. Waylon Jennings. Willie Nelson. Hank Williams. Dolly Parton. The late lamented Johnny Cash. And Don Gibson's "Sea of Heartbreak" was one of my all-time favorites. It was these new people I couldn't be doing with. Garth Brooks. Faith Hill. George Straight. Shania Twain. And Tommy's new discovery, the Dixie Chicks, although ever since one of them had declared herself ashamed that George W. Bush was from Texas — presumably because she was too — I'd begun to view them in a different light.

But I definitely didn't like any kind of football.

I think the thing that really bugs me about Tommy and Chelsea is that it always seems to make him revert to the little boy he used to be in the playground. He even admitted it once.

"When I was at school, in the playground they asked me who did I support so I went home and asked my dad and he said Chelsea. It was the sixties and loads of celebrities supported them so I just went along with it."

Now he has the same boring routine for every match. He always goes with the same four guys whom he's been going with since he was seventeen, eighteen — I think they were at school with him. They always sit in the West Stand. They always meet outside the betting shop opposite Stamford Bridge at a quarter to three every other Saturday when Chelsea plays at home. One of them will have already bought the programs. After the game they always go to the same Italian café for baked beans on toast. Only Tommy could order baked beans in an Italian restaurant. Then they always move on to the same pub from which I usually receive a drunken phone call with some excuse as to why he can't make dinner.

The enormity of what I'd done with Buzz hit me full force when Tommy called to remind me he wouldn't be seeing me on Wednesday because Chelsea were playing an evening game at Stamford Bridge. It wasn't just that I had slept with Buzz and betrayed Tommy that made me berate myself. It was the fact that I knew with absolute certainty that I planned to go on betraying him. If Buzz made contact with me I knew without a doubt that I would see him however shocked I would be at my own behavior. I could not remember when I had been so motivated to do anything. I'd had an unsolicited shot of adrenaline in the form of Buzz Kempinski and I could already tell it was going to be addictive.

But did this mean the end for Tommy and me? I had betrayed Tommy but did this mean that I no longer wanted him, that I wanted to move on? I had slept with another man and if I did so again, that man would have to become the only one in my life.

In the meantime I was doing my utmost to accommodate Tommy in an effort to assuage my guilt and hating myself at every second. When he had said he was going around to his mates to watch the match on the box I heard myself say:

"Why don't you come round and watch it here?"

There was a silence. He was probably wondering what kind of penance I'd extract in return for this extraordinary offer.

"What's the deal?" he asked suspiciously.

"There's no deal," I replied. "I could make us some supper."

"But I'd want beans on toast." Now he was beginning to sound incredulous.

"How hard can that be?" I said reasonably. "Although I might make myself some pasta and salad if that's okay with you?"

Of course what really threw him was when he arrived I suggested we go upstairs and watch the match on the TV in my bedroom.

"In bed? You sick or something? It's only six thirty."

Yes, I'm sick with an insane lust for another man and I want you to seduce me with the same intensity he did so I never want to see him again, so I know I've made a terrible mistake and will never again succumb to temptation. I want you to have carnal knowledge of me, Tommy, in a way that will reignite our relationship because I know that's what it will take to stop me being seduced again.

"I'm fine," I said. "You've got time for a shower before kickoff. Up you go."

Tommy kept things like clean boxers, T-shirts, shaving stuff at my house. Actual space in my wardrobe was banned because he was so messy. I knew he'd take over my bedroom if I gave him half a chance, but I'd given him a couple of drawers and he appeared to have sneaked in a pair of pajamas when I wasn't looking. He was sitting up in bed in them when I brought up his baked beans.

Pajamas! How big a turnoff was that?

"Where's the ale?" he wanted to know.

"We're not having beer in the bedroom. I don't want to go to sleep in a pub."

He started looking grumpy so I compromised by offering to open a bottle of champagne. Tommy perked up. He doesn't actually like champagne very much but like most people he equates it with some kind of celebration, so maybe he thought opening a bottle would bring Chelsea luck.

So there we were, halfway through the first half, sitting up in bed clutching champagne flutes with Tommy bouncing up and down beside me and spilling his fizzy all over my Egyptian cotton.

I didn't say a word. I sat bolt upright because every time I lay down I saw Buzz's face hovering above mine and my body turned to jelly. Instead I tried to concentrate on the game. I had long since given up thinking I might have the kind of sex with Tommy that would enable me to dismiss Buzz from my mind, mainly because Tommy was yelling "crazy!" whenever a Chelsea player moved a muscle. It was his new word. "Crazy!" It had replaced "cool!" in what he imagined was his hip vocabulary. "Cool" had replaced "wicked" and so on. I wondered what Buzz said. A buzz word, naturally. I giggled at my own stupid joke and Tommy hugged me thinking I was joining in the spirit of things.

Dear Tommy. I might loathe football but it touched me to see him enjoying himself so much. He was happy sharing this with me. He had no idea what was running through my head and I had no idea how to broach it with him.

I was wondering what sport Buzz liked, if any, when Tommy yelled "CRAZY!" with such force that I looked at the screen. Chelsea had scored just before halftime. The phone rang on Tommy's side of the bed.

Would it be Buzz? Who hadn't called me since the day he'd been lying exactly where Tommy was now.

"I'll get it. That'll be Shagger about the score. I told him I'd be here."

Shagger Watkins. One of the trusty group who accompanied Tommy to Stamford Bridge. I assumed Shagger's parents had given him another name at birth but if they had I'd never heard it.

"Hey, Shagger? What about it, mate?"

There was a short silence after which Tommy began apologizing profusely.

"Genevieve, I'm really sorry. No. No. Don't be like that. I thought it was going to be someone else. Yeah, hold on. She's right here. I'll pass you over. It's Genevieve for you," he said unnecessarily. "She's a bit pissed I called her Shagger."

"And you're surprised? Genevieve?"

"It's a go," she informed me triumphantly.

"What is?" I asked stupidly, wondering if she'd kept it a dark secret from me all these years that she too was a Chelsea supporter.

"Selma Walker. She wants you to do it."

"Buzz called you?" I held my breath.

"No, she called herself. From Manchester where she's filming in the studio. She wanted to know why I hadn't called her! She was furious when I told her you'd actually already met with Buzz. Anyway, she's flying back tonight and she most certainly does want to meet with you herself. She's talking about a breakfast meeting tomorrow morning since you live around the corner from her."

I'd never had a breakfast meeting in my life.

"What time?" I asked nervously.

"Oh, ten-ish. Actually we agreed ten and I just said I'd call her back if you couldn't make it. But you can, can't you?"

"Yes," I said feeling weak. Would Buzz be there?

"Lee, there's something else." Genevieve sounded nervous which was highly unusual for her. "Now she's decided to do a book she's in a hurry. I don't understand why but when I explained to her about how you'd have to do a proposal for us to sell before you started the book, she nearly threw a fit. She wants you to start straight into the book, to write it on spec."

"But how are you going to sell it?"

"I guess we're going to have to wait until you've done a chunk of it, then I'll sell it on that."

"And you'll go along with that?"

"I don't see what choice we have unless you drop out altogether. Of course if her story's crap you can pull out in twenty seconds. You'll have to assess it as early as you can."

I didn't know what to say. It all sounded a bit irregular.

"Well, I'd better let you go and get your beauty sleep," said Genevieve. "Don't let Tommy keep you up too late. Call me when you've seen her."

Chelsea won 3–1 and Tommy appeared to have downed most of the champagne. His euphoria manifested itself in some rather drunken groping of my breasts before he fell asleep. Champagne gives most people a lift but then I've long since given up hoping that Tommy will behave like most people.

Except in many ways he does. I was the oddball. Tommy wanted a normal life. He liked us doing things as a couple. He was always on at me to go to Sainsbury's and Tesco with him on Saturdays to get the weekend shopping. He'd be in his element if we were pushing a pram in front of us and he had a toddler perched high on his shoulders, a miniature Chelsea supporter. He yearned to go to places like Homebase except he didn't have his own home to shop for. I'd tried to indulge him in his fantasies by letting him do as much do-it-yourself around my house as I could find but he was so hopeless at it, it wasn't worth the effort.

I fell asleep after an hour of lying awake feeling unbelievably sad. I was deceiving Tommy, not only sexually but because I hadn't told him why I had invited him around this evening. I had expected him to behave in the same wildly uncharacteristic manner I had suddenly adopted for no reason whatsoever and that was totally unfair of me. And yet I had a strangely fatalistic attitude toward my infidelity with Buzz. I knew that what I was really doing was putting my own feelings for Tommy to the ultimate test. I had fully anticipated that when I spent time with Tommy again, when I climbed into bed with him, I'd be instantly cured of Buzz's hold over me.

But that hadn't happened. If anything I felt an even stronger pull toward Buzz and a split-second moment of unease filtered through my mind. Was I spending my last night with Tommy?

The next morning I awoke in a state of exhaustion. I made Tommy some sandwiches in a daze. God knows what I put in them. After I'd packed him off to work, before walking over to Selma Walker's, I went around the corner to one of the plethora of newly installed coffee shops that had sprung up all over Notting Hill. I needed a shot of espresso and a rush of sugar in the form of a couple of chocolate croissants. It occurred to me as I was munching that I was consuming the breakfast I was supposed to be having with Selma. On my way through the market, where the merchants were bundled up in an assortment of woolly hats, scarves, and mittens against the December cold, I bought a *Daily Mail* and read the story entitled "My Friend Astrid." A woman who had once shared a flat with her in her more impoverished days had come forward to announce that Astrid McKenzie was nothing like the portrait that had been painted of her in the press since her death. She described Astrid as a hard-drinking, good-time girl who used foul language and was frequently involved with disreputable characters. I didn't recognize the names of any of the men mentioned. They were probably well-known hoodlums for all I knew. But one thing was clear: The tide had turned. The press had gone to town building up a picture of Astrid the Saint but now they were ready to shoot her down.

The low-key early-morning rhythm of the market was something I treasured about living in Notting Hill. I loved to wander along as the merchants set up their stalls. Apart from the odd truck delivering produce, the street was devoid of vehicles. Sleepy pedestrians on their way to work roamed all over the street. I stopped to buy an apple at Chris's stall.

"See you've been reading about her," he said, tapping Astrid's picture in the paper over my shoulder. "See that geyser over there" — he pointed to a burly creature arranging a display of cauliflower across the road — "she had a bit of a thing with him."

"She did?"

"Oh yes! It was all a bit brazen. She started buying veg from him, never went near anyone else, then one day he starts bragging about how he's had her in her little mews house. And not just the once by the sound of it. He's a nasty piece of work, beats his wife black and blue. The police know him of old, the number of times they've been called round to the house, but there's not much they can do when it comes to domestic violence. His wife calls them in a panic and then she denies everything when they get there."

"Did she know about Astrid?"

"Who knows? Thing was, Astrid herself

turned up to buy her parsnips with a couple of bruises a few days later. Weren't that long ago."

"What does that have to do with her house being burned down?"

He shrugged. "Search me. By the way" — he was giving me a rather suggestive look — "who was that bloke I saw coming out your house round lunchtime the other day? Tall geezer, bit on the thin side, dark hair. Good looking, like me." He grinned. "I've seen him somewhere but I can't place where."

I smiled back wondering whether or not he was joking because poor Chris is not good looking. He's probably one of the ugliest blokes on the planet. Short, squat, bald head, stubby nose like a bulldog, but there is one thing: He has the longest eyelashes I've ever seen on a man.

"I can't think who it could have been. Why do you ask?"

"No reason except one place I know I've seen him is round Astrid McKenzie's house. Saw him there the day she died, as it happens."

"Have you told the police?"

"What, about seeing him at Astrid's or at yours?"

"Hey Chris, over here," someone yelled

to him before he could answer my question and he patted my arm.

"Gotta run."

"Me too," I said, looking at my watch in horror. I was late for my meeting. I scuttled along Elgin Crescent worrying about what Chris might have told the police and then as I was crossing Ladbroke Grove I calmed down. Why would the police ever want to question me about who came in or out of my house?

Selma Walker had an agenda. I think I realized that as soon as she opened the door to me. It was the way she ushered me inside as fast as she could. We had a great deal to do and there was no time to waste. This was the message her body language sent me and who was I to argue?

My first meeting with a subject is always a little awkward. You smile a lot and act as if you're going to be buddies for life but behind the charm and the professions of goodwill, you're usually working like crazy to size the person up. And they you.

Selma Walker was pretty blatant about it. She kept turning around and giving me penetrating looks from top to toe as she led me down a long stone passage to the back of the house. The smell of freshly ground coffee wafted after us, competing with the overpowering fragrance of Selma's scent, something French and expensive I couldn't recall the name of. Was Buzz in the kitchen seducing one of the coffee-makers? There was no immediate sign of him and for this I was grateful. I looked terrible. I'd slept badly and my attempts to camouflage my tired-looking skin hadn't worked. And the two chocolate croissants had managed to push my stomach out to the max in record time.

Selma wasn't at all what I expected. For a start her appearance was a shock. I'd seen her black-and-white image in the media often enough and I'd caught an episode of *Fraternity* the day before so I'd be prepared for her in color but the flesh and blood woman bore no resemblance to her character in the soap. She had no makeup on and I reckoned she was at least ten years older than I had imagined. I'd assumed she would be early forties, a bit older than I was. This woman was in her fifties. And she wore a wig in *Fraternity.* In the TV series her character was a little fireball with flaming red hair. The woman who stood before me had a mane of black hair. It fell halfway down her back in what I imagined must be a pathetic attempt to hang on to a girlish appearance. She was tiny and fragile looking with pale blue eyes and very white skin. She wore jeans, the chic designer kind, pressed and crisp, and a powder blue cashmere sweater with a boatneck.

But it was her manner that intrigued me more than anything. There was something about the eyes that I noticed immediately. There was apprehension in them, fear even. She didn't come across as a glamorous figure. She didn't exude confidence, quite the opposite. In fact I had the distinct impression that in spite of the beady looks she kept giving me, she was nervous, almost shy.

She took me into a room that ran the width of the house and benefited from the morning sun through three floor-to-ceiling sash windows. You could step out of them onto a wrought iron balcony with steps leading down to the garden below.

Giant sofas upholstered in white calico were dotted around the room. In fact, apart from an old French linen cupboard, which people seemed more inclined to have in their living room nowadays than in their bedroom, and a few well-tended plants that actually looked more like trees, the sofas were the only major furniture.

There was the odd, strategically placed steel and glass coffee table on which to place drinks and a tapestry-covered ottoman stood in front of the fireplace, but otherwise that was it.

Selma flopped on one of the sofas and gestured for me to do the same. I had the presence of mind to see that if I sat opposite her on the other side of the fireplace I'd be miles away from her. So I positioned myself in the corner of the sofa she was lying on and tried not to look at the crinkled soles of her tiny little feet, bare now that she'd kicked off her embroidered slippers. She huddled away from me into the corner. Her tiny frame, dwarfed by the epic proportions of the furniture, put me in mind of a toy lapdog curling up on a cushion for a nap.

Before we could speak the door opened and a woman came in bearing a tray that she set down on the ottoman.

"This is my precious Bianca," said Selma. "She takes care of me better than anybody I have ever known."

It was rather a dramatic statement. Clearly Bianca was someone I needed on my side.

"Hello." I smiled. Bianca didn't. In fact she regarded me with a great deal of suspicion. She was medium height, and had an attractive Latin face. Middle-aged, probably around fifty, her figure concealed by a starched white housedress. On her feet she wore white tennis shoes.

"Is coffee," she informed me. "You want the milk and the sugar?"

"Just milk, please."

She handed me a cup, still without smiling.

"Miss Selma, I pass the Hoover in the next room. Is okay?"

"Sure," said Selma and made to get up and reach for her coffee.

"Miss Selma, don't move. You must take care."

Suddenly I saw it. As Selma reached out to take her cup of coffee, her sweater pulled up to reveal her bare back and the tail end of a livid bruise to the left of the base of her spine.

She saw my reaction.

"Stupid!" she exclaimed. "I slipped in the kitchen the other day, fell against one of the counters. Hurt like hell. It was over a week ago but I can't seem to get rid of this bruise. Nothing broken but Bianca is a bit overprotective. I'm fine. So let's get started. You come highly recommended, by the way. I know a couple of people you've ghosted so I called them and they said you were a star. Is there anything you want to ask before we begin?"

Was there anything I wanted to ask? Surely there was *everything* I wanted to ask. I had nothing to do but ask her questions. I started with the one I always asked first.

"Why do you want to write your autobiography?"

"Why do you want to write my autobiography?" she countered.

Now she had me.

"Selma, I have a confession to make. I know next to nothing about you other than that you've come over here because you're in *Fraternity.* But I also have to confess that I don't recall ever seeing any in-depth interviews with you and I do go through the papers quite thoroughly as part of my job."

I held my head high as I said this and looked her in the eye. I wished she'd let up with the penetrating gaze. She'd done her homework on me, hadn't she? She seemed to think I'd passed her test. What was it that she still wanted to know that warranted this X-ray vision boring into me?

"Well, you can save yourself the trouble," she said, tipping her head forward and jerking it back suddenly to get her mane of hair out of her face. "There's not much. Oh, you'll find plenty of dumb pieces about me going to a party or a premiere or a football match but you won't find out anything about my life. I have a degree in privacy. I hate publicity."

"So why would you want to tell your life story?" I didn't get it.

"You'll find out," she said mysteriously. "But let's talk about practicalities. Our biggest problem is going to be my filming schedule. I'm up in Manchester four days a week so I was wondering if I could talk into a tape recorder on the plane there and back from London and in my dressing room when I'm waiting around at the studio? Then I'll bring the tape back down, hand it over to you and you'll have four days to transcribe what I've said. We'll meet while I'm in London and go through what you've done so far and I'll hand you a new tape. How's that sound?"

Like I was being steamrollered into writing the book like an automaton with no creative input of my own, no chance to fashion the material into the kind of book I would be proud of. I wasn't happy. At the first meeting I was always the one who was in control of the proceedings. However famous or talented the person was, they instinctively handed over the reins to the ghost because they knew they were in the presence of someone who could do something they couldn't. If they could write, they wouldn't need a ghost.

Plus I just didn't get it. What Selma was suggesting was totally at odds with what Buzz had told me about her not having time for me. She seemed to be bending over backward to accommodate me. But I decided to keep quiet about this. The less attention I drew to Buzz the better.

"It's not how I usually work," I ventured. "I'd prefer to conduct the interviews with you face-to-face rather than have you talk into a tape recorder on your own. That way I can steer your story in the direction I want to take in the book. I live in the neighborhood. I could come round whenever you wanted."

"No!" Her little palms flew up in protest. "We won't be doing the interviews here. You can come round to pick up more tapes but no face-to-face interviews on a regular basis."

"But why?" I was thrown. "Where will we be working? I'd like to sit down with you for a couple of hours every four or five days for the first few weeks and then go away and write a first draft of your early life. Come back and talk some more about the next stage and so on."

That way she would get to know me, trust me, I could draw her out, persuade her to really open up bit by bit. Her guard would drop by the fourth or fifth week, if she was anything like the other people I'd worked with, and the real Selma Walker would emerge.

But she wasn't like anyone else I'd ever worked with, I sensed that much already.

"Why do you want to know about my early life?" She was wary and she didn't try to hide it. "Maybe I should have made it clear earlier. I want to start with the present. That's where the action is. Believe me, I may have kept my private life private but now I'm coming clean and boy do I have a story to tell."

My ears pricked up. *She had a story to tell!* I could be on to something. Maybe I had better shut up and let her do it her way, see what she had to offer me and then ask for more if I needed it later on. I knew it sometimes paid to be flexible. I just wished she'd stop staring at me as if she was trying to figure out if I was someone she could trust. It was almost as if she had something in this house she wanted to hide.

"There's one other thing I have to ask you," she said suddenly. "Are you discreet? Can you keep a secret? I have to know that you can keep a secret."

"I think so," I said, bemused. Selma Walker was full of surprises. Cautious, suspicious, and now maybe a little paranoid to boot.

"I want you to promise me that you'll keep my story to yourself. Only when it's ready to go to a publisher can you speak about it to anyone."

"I can't even tell Genevieve, my agent?" Although even as I said her name I knew I wouldn't tell Genevieve anyway. Genevieve couldn't keep a secret for twenty seconds. I think she'd gossip to the speaking clock if she couldn't get anyone else on the phone. The only person she never dished the dirt on was herself.

"No one," said Selma. "Not your mother, not your sister, your girlfriends, your boyfriend, no one. And that includes people who work for me. Do you have a boyfriend by the way?"

I nodded, surprised at her interest. "He works for the BBC."

She pounced. "Well, there's the first no-no. You can't tell him. No talking to the media."

I didn't exactly think Tommy the pale-faced Radio Nerd slaving away in the bowels of Broadcasting House could accurately be described as the media but she wasn't to know that. And in any case, the way things were going, how much longer would I be talking to Tommy?

"He's just an engineer. And anyway we don't live together and I don't see him that often anyway."

She looked at me questioningly.

"I'm just not ready for marriage and living together and commitment. Or babies," I burbled. "I need more time." Why was I blurting out my life story all of a sudden? I was supposed to be extracting information from her, not the other way around. Although this was a tack that sometimes worked with recalcitrant subjects. I chattered away about myself until they relaxed and joined in. Before they knew it, they were often divulging all kinds of repressed information.

"How long have you been seeing him?" she asked.

"Eight years."

"You definitely need more time." She laughed for the first time and I was enchanted. Her face changed completely, opening up and relaxing. She was really extraordinarily pretty in a doll-like way. "But tell me," she said, "and I hope you don't mind my asking, why don't you want to live with him? Are you afraid of him?"

"Of *Tommy?*" I was incredulous but then how could she possibly know that Tommy was the least threatening person in the whole world? "Tommy is the last person I'd be afraid of, he's much too sweet."

"For you, maybe," she said dryly. "But you shouldn't take him too much for granted."

"I don't take him for granted," I began, and then stopped because of course that was exactly what I did. "Okay, I do. He's kind and reliable, I can't fault him really. It's just it seems to have got to the stage where I am just as happy when I'm on my own as when I'm with him. In the beginning I seem to remember we never ran out of things to say or do and it was fun. Then somewhere along the line he seemed to sort of lose it."

"And you didn't?"

I sat up. I hadn't been challenged like this in quite a while, not since Cath really, and I missed it.

"I don't think you could say I lost it," I defended myself. "I happen to enjoy my own company but I am constantly being made aware that it is highly unconventional to spend so much time on my own. I think it's more a question of not needing to be with Tommy as much as he needs to be with me and —"

I came to an abrupt halt. I longed to open up to her and tell her about the unbearable situation in which I now found myself. That I had managed to bring my relationship with Tommy to a crucial turning point and he had no idea. That the way I was behaving was flying in the face of everything I believed in and I couldn't understand why.

She smiled. "You're slightly dodging the issue but I see what you're getting at. At the moment you two lead somewhat separate lives and the arrangement suits you. But he wants to do what he thinks is right by you and this is making you jumpy. It's not the end of the world. You know, it could be a lot worse. He could —" She stopped suddenly.

"He could what?"

"What I mean is there are an awful lot of women who would give their right arm for a man like your Tommy. Oh, I understand why you find him irritating but the most telling thing is that you haven't left him.

There has to be *something* about him that keeps you hanging in there? Do you know what that is?"

I thought very carefully for a few seconds and then, knowing she wouldn't let me get away with anything but the absolute truth, I told her something I'd never admitted to anyone, not even Cath.

"I'm scared. I may live alone and make a lot of fuss about how much I love it but I like having someone in my life. I look around me and I see women on their own everywhere. Lonely divorcées, or women who have put their careers before their families and their man has gone off with a more accommodating model. I see them and I think if I kiss Tommy good-bye that will be me. I'm not getting any younger, it'll be pretty hard for me to find another man so I suppose I have to confess it's a question of better the devil you know."

"Except he's not a devil, he's an angel, and that's why you've grown just a little bored with him." She stood up, stretched, and then walked around the coffee table to face me. I looked down so she wouldn't see my face redden because of course she had unwittingly knocked the proverbial nail right on the head.

"But let me tell you something," she

went on. "It's possible that as time goes by you will no longer crave the kind of high-voltage relationship you think you want. You'll slow down. You can't imagine it but you will. It's not as if you've found someone else to take his place." The look on my face must have given me away. "Uh-oh. There *is* someone else?"

"He's the most exciting man I've ever met." I was aware that this was really over the top even as I said it. "I don't know what I'm going to do."

"Get rid of him," she said sharply. "Excitement doesn't necessarily bring happiness. Quite the opposite in my experience."

What is your experience? I wanted to ask, dejected by the cold shower she had poured on my revelation.

"I didn't mean to tell you what to do," she said, looking rather ashamed. "I'm sorry. When we get to know each other better I think you'll understand why I feel like I do. In the meantime I can see that you feel trapped. You've allowed yourself to become frozen inside the relationship like a fish that's been netted. Every now and then you thrash about a bit but you don't get anywhere. You think you want excitement and adventure, you don't want to settle for being a domestic goddess. Believe me, I understand. But be careful what you wish for. He may seem boring to you but men like Tommy could change the lives of a lot of women in this world."

Fine, let them have him, I thought uncharitably. Maybe I'd see the wisdom of Selma's words when I'd advanced as far into middle-age stagnation as she had. Now of course I felt rather embarrassed that I had given away so much about myself.

"Selma, this is meant to be you telling me about your life rather than the other way around. So when can we start?"

She sighed. "I don't want to do face-to-face interviews until I'm a little more settled with you. Nothing personal. You want to know the truth? I'm embarrassed and ashamed by what I have to tell you and I'd prefer to do it privately. And I don't want anyone in this house to overhear me. You'll get your material, Lee, you'll just have to agree to work a little differently with me. Or maybe I should look for someone else?"

But I was already far too intrigued and I guessed she knew that.

"Whatever you want is fine with me," I said quickly. It was clear she already knew how the story was going to be told. She was going to tell it. All I was going to be was the conduit through which she told it. Wasn't that what most people probably thought my role was anyway? A siphon. But I liked to think I was more than that. I turned to her. "You have an office here, don't you?"

"On the top floor, although in fact it's Buzz's. He takes care of everything up there."

Aha! Was he up there now? Had he been in the house all along?

The front door slammed. Selma's reaction was instantaneous. She jumped up and her face went dead white.

"Talk of the devil," she said.

My hands began to shake slightly. And when he came into the room they began to shake a lot.

He was even more gorgeous than I remembered. I managed to get to my feet and stood there wobbling a little. I didn't know what to do. Would he come over and kiss me hello? Would he make any reference to our last meeting?

He did neither. He just stared at me.

"Hi, honey," said Selma. It was little more than a whisper. She turned to me. "You've met my husband, haven't you, Lee?"

Chapter 7

Buzz followed me home.

I walked back from Selma's telling myself firmly that that was it, he was married and there was no way that my thing with him would be going any further. Thank God I had found out in time, before I was in too deep to be able to resist him.

I was letting myself in through my front door when he came running round the corner and up the steps behind me.

"You forgot this," he said, pushing me inside and placing Tommy's Aiwa tape recorder on my hall table before scooping me up in his arms and slipping his hand up the slinky jersey knit skirt I had selected to impress his wife. He caressed my buttocks before moving his fingers around to execute a strange little flicking movement over my clitoris that nearly made me come on the spot.

I was stupefied. I more or less collapsed in his arms and together we slumped to the floor and made love there and then in my hallway, crushing the mail that had come through the letterbox while I was out.

Afterward he reached beneath us, fished out my bills, and read them to me.

"You owe AmEx seven hundred quid. Visa only four hundred. Poor Visa. Graham and Green are having a sale. Twenty percent off everything down in the basement until Christmas. Better hurry over there with your Visa. Let's see, what's this? Corney and Barrow. Wine merchants. Only you didn't order any wine during the month of November. Just two thousand bottles of Smirnoff. And the gas man came. You were out. He says he was a hunk. You missed him. What a shame."

I didn't respond. I couldn't bring myself to look at him. I got to my feet, silently berating the body I no longer felt was my own for refusing to listen to what was going through my mind.

I went into the kitchen and began to make myself a cup of coffee and tried to collect what wits I had left, if indeed I'd ever had any in the first place. What in the world had I been thinking?

"Okay, so why didn't you tell me you were married to Selma?" I said as soon as he joined me in the kitchen. The question

I should have asked him before he got me down on the floor.

"Why didn't I tell you I was married to *Selma?*" he repeated. "That's an odd way of putting it. I kept waiting for you to mention my wife."

"How was I supposed to know you were married?"

"The usual way." He held up his hand with the wedding ring on his finger.

Damn! Damn! *Damn!* I'd never even noticed. How could I have been so stupid?

"I thought you weren't saying anything deliberately, that you were trying to be cool about it," he said. "Actually I did bring it up, in your bed, that first time, but I had a feeling you weren't listening properly. You interrupted me, said you were going downstairs to make a sandwich so I took that to mean you thought sex with a married man was no big deal. I should have persisted."

"Yes," I shouted at him, appalled at what I had done, "you should have. You're married. You had no right flirting with me like you did."

I was making like it was his fault but I'd flirted just as much.

"You appear out of the blue on my doorstep and completely knock me out. What am I supposed to do? Turn you away? It's called sexual attraction. Chemistry."

Now he was making like it was *my* fault.

"It's just I had no idea *she* was married," I pointed out in a pathetic attempt to get myself off the hook, "and I don't think my agent did either. Does anyone know?"

"Of course people know. The entire cast of *Fraternity* knows. Why would we keep it a secret? Just because it was never in the newspapers, you assume no one knows? It was just a small registry office wedding but there were two witnesses. But we chose not to broadcast it to the world just yet. Selma's in no hurry to tell the press."

"Why do you think that is?" I was intrigued.

"Who can say?" Buzz shrugged. "I think she's a bit nervous about the public's reaction to her marrying a boy toy. Doesn't bother me but she's quite sensitive about it. There's twenty years between us. Might not look too good. But the other thing is, she hasn't introduced me to any of her friends in New York yet. They know about the marriage but I don't think she's told them how old I am. I think she's scared they'll be unhappy about the age gap. To tell you the truth, I think she may have even lied about it."

"When does she plan on telling them?"

"She's going over there at Christmas. Alone. I don't know why she's so sensitive about it but I'm not going to argue. Any way she wants to play it. I keep trying to tell her they probably all know anyway. That sort of gossip travels fast."

"Well, it's going to come out in the book," I said, referring to her marriage. "She was quite open about it to me or didn't you notice."

Actually, it wasn't so much that she was open about her marriage, it was the way she was all over him that I couldn't get out of my mind. From the minute he'd walked into the kitchen she'd metamorphosed into a lovesick Stepford Wife. After she'd introduced us, she'd flitted about the kitchen making him coffee, arranging cookies on a plate, while I traipsed after her trying to say good-bye so I could extricate myself from the ghastly situation I had found myself in. But I couldn't get her attention; as soon as he appeared it was all focused on Buzz. She chattered to him incessantly. *Honey, I'm making coffee. You want it in here or shall I bring it up to the office? How was the meeting? I made a reservation at Orsino's. I'm taking you there for lunch.* No calling for Bianca, she was taking care of him herself. Every now and then she crossed the kitchen to touch him. She clasped his upper arm. She patted his cheek. It was as if she'd done something wrong and was trying to make it up to him. I was freaking out about whether she'd pick up on any spark of electricity there might be between Buzz and me. But at the same time I couldn't help observing that even though *she* was the star, *she* was his boss, *she* had the money and the big house, it was *he* who clearly had the power in the relationship.

"Sure," he said, "she introduced me as her husband. Why wouldn't she?"

"Well, she didn't mention you before you arrived on the scene," I pointed out. "Not once. And she seemed sort of proprietorial."

"Oh, I know what that was all about. You're an attractive younger woman. She was stating her territorial rights over me."

"You make it sound like you're her possession."

"Got it in one. She owns me." He laughed.

"You don't mind?"

"What's to mind? I have a good life with her."

Do you still fancy her? was what I was dying to know but didn't have the nerve to ask.

"Where did you meet her?"

"I met her the very first time she came over to talk about the series. I was a young agent representing one of the cast of *Fraternity.* She was pretty forward. She introduced herself to me, asked me to lunch, asked me to represent her, asked me . . ."

"Asked you to fuck her?" Why was I being so coarse? The truth was I was spellbound by his revelations in an awful, gruesome way. I wanted to hear all the lurid details even though I knew I would probably be sickened by them.

"More or less." He grinned. "If the Diva wants something, she goes after it, wants control of it. I was sort of swept along in her wake. Although I admit I was impressed by the notion of being involved with a name actress."

At least he was up front about being a starfucker.

"Did she ask you to marry her? Get down on one knee?"

I was joking but he didn't smile.

"Not quite. Probably because we were in a restaurant. Valentine's Day. But she did get me a ring." He flashed the signet ring on his pinky at me. "She came over all teary and sentimental. What could I do?"

Run like hell!

"Listen, I care about her," he said, looking steadily at me as if he could see what I was thinking. "I really do. Or at least I did. She may not be in the first flush of youth but her career as a soap opera actress is on the up-and-up and I'm right there to mastermind it. We're a good partnership. And it's a great house, don't you think?"

There was something cold and clinical about the way he was describing the woman who had been his bride for so short a time. I could detach myself and listen to him talk and know that he sounded like a potential monster. Yet at the same time I could revel in his words because they validated my passion for him. I felt desperately sorry for Selma. I had wondered what she meant when she said she was ashamed and embarrassed by what she had to tell me. Could she have been referring to her marriage? And if so, would she come clean and admit she knew the husband she adored saw her as little more than a business partner?

"You said she's not exactly in the first flush of youth. How old is she?"

"Fifty-five but you never heard it from me."

So he was thirty-five. Younger than I was.

I had turned away from him when he had been talking about Selma. Now he came up behind me and put his arms around me, his hands coming up under my sweater before I could stop him, stroking my breasts.

"You're so soft," he whispered. "She's getting older, you know. Things change for women in their fifties. She's getting so dry, like she's been baked, left too long in the oven. She's not my little cupcake anymore." He sounded genuinely wistful.

I hated myself. I could feel my body responding to him even though my mind was in shock at how cruel he was being about her despite the fact that he had obviously cared about her once. It wasn't so much sexual attraction as sexual addiction to him. And it wasn't as if I even knew that much about him. I tried to think back to the time before Tommy when I had gone out on dates. Hadn't there been that period of getting to know a person before you let them tear your clothes off? Hadn't I known all about a guy's family, how many brothers and sisters he had, all that first-date stuff, before I let him kiss me? I'd let Buzz get as far as actual penetration knowing more about his wife than I did about him.

And as for what he said about Selma — God knows, it would happen to me too when my time came.

We went upstairs. We undressed. We got into my bed and we had sex twice.

And I learned something. That it is very easy to sit in judgment of other people — as I had done several times in the past — on the subject of sexual infidelity when you were not one of the lovers involved. But I had already slept with Buzz *before* I knew he was married and knowing I was experiencing severe doubts about Tommy. It doesn't matter what other people say, it doesn't matter what *you* say, unless you're a block of wood your body takes over. What I had just done was morally reprehensible and no doubt I would pay for it but there was nothing — absolutely nothing given that I was a flesh and blood human being and not a saint — I could have done to stop it.

Then, as we were lying there, warm and relaxed, he murmured, "So what did you two talk about? What did she tell you?"

He was making an effort to sound casual

but I felt his body tense beside me.

"Oh, she just wanted to meet me, I think, and you know you were wrong about her not having time to work with me. She really wants to do it and she's going to do all the interviews by tape and give them to me to transcribe."

I expected him to say how great that was but all he said was, "Well, believe it when it happens."

"It almost sounds like you don't want her to do this book," I challenged him. And regretted it twenty seconds later. He probably didn't like the idea of the two of us working together after what had occurred between him and me. And he was right to be concerned. I was going to have to think pretty carefully about whether I could handle doing Selma's book given what had happened.

But it turned out that wasn't the reason.

"I don't think she should do it, if you really want to know." He rolled over and looked straight at me. His eyes were inches from mine. "I can't see how it can sell any copies. There's no story. She's just a soap opera actress. A picture book, maybe. Some kind of souvenir for the fans but I don't see how you're going to get much mileage out of Selma's life story. I've already told her what I think and I'll be honest with you. I'm going to try and talk her out of it."

I rolled away from him slightly. I felt rather deflated by his lack of enthusiasm. Suddenly something struck me.

"Where does Selma think you are right now?"

"Returning your tape recorder to you."

He'd been here nearly two hours. I threw back the bedclothes.

"Calm down. I often go out for hours on end. She's not my keeper. But she did say she'd booked a table at Orsino's for lunch so I'd better be heading back."

He dressed in front of the window with his back to me.

"If you don't mind me asking," he asked over his shoulder, "why do you have all that furniture scattered around your garden?"

I was out of bed in a second. He was right. Looking down, I could see that the summerhouse doors were wide open and its contents littered all over the lawn.

"I have a lodger, remember?" I explained and reminded him about seeing Angel at Tesco.

"I'll call you," he said as he reached the door and looked back.

I opened my mouth to ask *When?* and stopped myself just in time. I listened for the sound of the front door slamming behind him but I didn't hear it. And then, as I hopped from one foot to the other pulling on my jeans, I saw him appear below me in the garden. As he walked toward the summerhouse, Angel emerged, the shape of her voluptuous little body still visible underneath a pair of overalls. Her blond curls were fettered by a ribbon tied in a huge bow on top of her head, which made her look like Minnie Mouse. She was brandishing a paintbrush.

I watched in horror as Buzz held out his hand and she took it, smiling up at him. Did she recognize him as the man who had been with me in Tesco? I didn't think she'd even noticed him but how could I be sure? Was he introducing himself to her? Telling her he was a friend of mine? Was he totally insane? She'd already met Tommy and she was highly likely to see him again. She could easily tell him about Buzz. But then as quickly as I had begun to panic, I relaxed. I had a perfectly legitimate reason to know Buzz. I was going to be working with his wife and he was her manager. He had come around to deliver the tape recorder I had left behind. I couldn't quite come up with why he'd chosen to go for a wander in my back garden but no doubt I'd get there.

Suddenly Angel burst out laughing. She seemed to be literally shaking with mirth. And she couldn't take her eyes off Buzz. I wondered if she realized she was standing very close to him. They chatted for a few minutes and then he leaned over to give her a quick avuncular peck on the cheek. He didn't see me watching as he came back up the garden but Angel did and she pointed to the summerhouse, miming that I should come down and see what she'd done.

I hadn't been the only one spying on Buzz and Angel. When I entered the summerhouse I found a gangling youth having a bit of trouble with a paint roller over in the corner where the bed had been. He had stringy hair, sported pimples on his face, and a protruding Adam's apple but when he turned to face me, I got the point of him. He had the bluest eyes I had ever seen, except they never looked in my direction. They were fixated on Angel's tits.

"What do you think? It's called Warm Lilac. Fred chose it. Fred's my new boyfriend."

"Hi, Fred," I said with as much enthusiasm as I could muster. "Angel, don't you think you should have consulted me before you . . .”

“What? You mean about the color? You don’t like Warm Lilac?”

To be honest, if anyone had said *I’m thinking of painting your summerhouse Warm Lilac, what do you think?* the very sound of it would have made me throw up. But in fact I was pleasantly surprised. It really was warm and a very pretty shade and I had no doubt it would enhance the atmosphere of the little room. I felt she should have asked me before going ahead and painting my property, but what the hell. I should give her some leeway. Didn’t want to get a reputation as the Wicked Witch Landlady too soon.

I smiled. “It’s beautiful. Well done, both of you. One thing I am worried about though is what will happen to all this furniture if it rains before the paint dries?”

“Oh, Fred will give me a hand getting it indoors. And if not he’s got a big tarp to cover it all. My mum knows Fred’s mum down the bingo. That’s how we met.”

“Good for you.”

I made my excuses and left before I became too embroiled in Angel’s long-running soap opera. Fred hadn’t said a single word and the only reason I knew he actually had a tongue in his head was because I had seen it literally hanging out at the sight of Angel's cleavage.

Angel mentioning her mother had made me remember my own and the e-mail she had just sent me reminding me that I had said I would go and spend Christmas in France with them. I had said no such thing but I knew better than to expect my mother to accept that. At least she wasn't asking about the damp. The real problem was that she had also sent an e-mail to Tommy at the BBC so there was no chance I could get away with not telling him and pretending he couldn't make it. She'd get him out there whatever it took. She was already asking what he liked to eat so she could impress him with her culinary skills.

Maybe it would be a good thing to get away, with or without Tommy. Buzz was bound to be tied up with Selma. I had a horror of turning into one of those clichés, the girl with the married lover. I'd read all those silly women's magazine articles about how Christmas was the worst time because he always had to be with his family.

Although I'm not sure you could describe Selma Walker as family.

Besides, once he was no longer in the

house I found I was able to think a little more rationally about Buzz. I wanted him, of that there was no doubt. But I couldn't help noticing that I didn't feel that overwhelming sense of joy you experience when you begin a new affair. I wasn't going around with an idiotic smile on my face the whole time. On the contrary I was edgy and miserable. He was married. Moreover he was married to *Selma Walker.* I could give up the job — but then, why should I?

The more I thought about it the more I began to understand that the right thing to do — the *only* thing to do — was to give him up.

And when he called, I'd tell him.

Except he didn't call.

I didn't sit by the phone. I was much too mature for that kind of behavior. I just paced around and around it, staring at it, willing it to ring.

Anyone who did ring got extremely short shrift because I wanted to get them off the line as soon as possible. The only person I engaged in conversation for longer than two minutes was Genevieve who called with the most amazing news. She was on the point of actually doing a deal for Selma's autobiography. She said she'd sounded out a few publishers and the response had been overwhelmingly positive. It was as I had suspected. People were intrigued because, while she was a national celebrity, not much was known about her private life.

I pointed out to Genevieve that strictly speaking she wasn't Selma's agent and maybe she ought to meet with Selma and Buzz before she tied up a deal. When Genevieve asked how things were progressing, I fought back the urge to say *Once in the hall, twice in my bed,* and restricted it to:

"Genevieve, why didn't you tell me Selma Walker was married to her manager? I almost made a complete fool of myself."

What did I mean, almost?

"You're not serious?" Genevieve sounded amazed. "How come I didn't know?"

"You're asking me? You're supposed to know these things and tell me. You're out there. I'm just the writer who stays in the background and never goes out and relies on you for all the news from the front."

"Oh, spare me. Listen, I have to get off the phone and tell as many people as I can find."

I could imagine cell phones whirring all over London. What had I done? Would

Buzz be furious with me? But then he'd said himself it wasn't exactly a secret. Well, it certainly wouldn't be now Genevieve had got hold of it.

I was surprised she hadn't mentioned Astrid McKenzie. Rumors in the market were rife. The market merchant Chris had pointed out to me, the one he said had had an affair with Astrid and beaten her up, had been taken in for questioning. The word around the fruit and veg was that his wife had been telling anyone who would listen that he'd been out the night of Astrid's fire and he hadn't come home till the small hours. She wasn't the most reliable of witnesses given that every time she'd called the police when he raised a fist to her, she'd denied it when they turned up. It seemed now she'd really picked her moment to nail him.

And before I even had a moment to draw breath, I had Tommy on the phone in a state of uncontrollable excitement. When were we going? *As late as possible. With luck then there wouldn't be any flights left.* What should he get my mother for Christmas? *He couldn't go wrong with a boxed set of sleeping pills.*

I was being ridiculous as usual. It was the same old story. I looked forward to seeing my parents and at the same time I dreaded it. My mother would be on my case from the minute I stepped off the train. How far had I got with the house renovations? All I ever wanted to do was sleep, read, eat, go for long walks, and generally have a rest but my mother always used my visits as an excuse to be madly social. But somehow I treasured my time with them. I had this idealistic notion that we were a happy family unit and when I was with them I was safe.

But with Tommy in tow, I wouldn't have them to myself at all.

I thought of something. I needed to tell Selma I was going away. As I dialed her number my hand shook in anticipation of Buzz picking up.

"Oh, hi, Lee. I've been meaning to call you. I was really so happy to meet you the other day." It was Selma and she sounded as if she genuinely meant what she said. I felt worse than ever. "Did you realize Christmas was so close or am I the only one with my head in the clouds? It's right around the corner, just like you. Are you busy right now? Come on over and have a Christmas drink and we'll figure out what to do. I haven't told you my new plans. And isn't it fabulous about the book offer?

Your agent Genevieve just called me."

"There's been an offer?"

"Six figures. I'm so thrilled. I can't wait to tell Buzz. He never wanted me to do a book, you know?"

"Really?"

"Yes, he never thought anyone would be interested in my story. Well, how wrong was he! Come on over and we'll celebrate."

Bianca the housekeeper opened the door. I smiled. Once again she didn't.

"Miss Selma is in the kitchen. She make the mince pies." Bianca was clearly unimpressed with such industry. She didn't take my coat. She didn't even hold the door open for me. Why did I get the distinct impression Bianca didn't like me? I was being paranoid. She'd barely met me.

"Is Buzz here?" Very daring of me.

"*Mr.* Buzz no here." Oh, *excuse* me. *Mr.* Buzz. "He upstairs."

What was that supposed to mean?

She didn't bother to show me to the kitchen. I had a shock when I entered. Selma was sitting on a stool, stirring something vigorously in a mixing bowl with a wooden spoon. A bottle of champagne, half empty, stood on the counter beside her. The smell of mince pies baking in the oven made me peckish.

"So you like to cook?" The mixture looked interesting, not least because of the strong smell of brandy emanating from it.

"Christmas cake for Buzz. I'm leaving him on his own for Christmas. Least I can do is bake him a cake. Have a glass of champagne."

His remark about her being left too long in the oven like a baked cake popped into my mind.

"You're leaving him on his own for Christmas," I repeated stupidly. "Where are you going?"

"I'm going to New York to see my family. It's been too long since I had a family Christmas."

"But can't Buzz go with you?"

"I'll let you into a secret. It probably sounds crazy but I'd kinda like to break it to them gently that I've married a man twenty years younger than I am. I know, I know" — she raised her hands in protest when she saw my look of disbelief — "I should have told them way back when but I was chicken. I'm old-fashioned about these things. I'm worried about what people will say. So I'm going on my own. It'll only be a quick trip. It's not as if it's our first Christmas together and I won't be gone long. So what I was going to suggest to you, Lee, is that we all take a break for the Christmas holidays and you and I get down to work in January. I rather like that, starting my autobiography right at the start of a New Year. What do you say?"

Sorry I've slept with your husband, I'm never going to do it again.

Instead, I said, "Well, now it looks like we've got a book deal, we'd better think about producing the actual book. The sooner we start the better."

"What book deal?"

Buzz had come in so quietly I hadn't heard him. I didn't dare turn around to face him.

"I've had an offer on my book," Selma told him, rather defiantly, I thought. "A good one. And apparently there are plenty of other publishers interested too."

"And you know this how?" Buzz had come to stand beside her now and his face was grim. In the midst of trying to remain calm in his presence, I couldn't help wondering why he didn't seem a little more pleased at the news. Maybe he just hated to be proved wrong. He was standing very close to Selma now and I suddenly noticed she was trembling.

"Lee's agent told me," she said.

"Lee's agent should have told *me*," snapped Buzz.

"Well, I expect she will. So what are you doing for the holidays?" she asked me, rather obviously trying to change the subject.

"I'm going to France. My parents live there."

"Very nice," said Buzz casually. "What part of France?"

"The Lot-et-Garonne. The southwest. My parents retired there a few years ago. It's a beautiful old barn, woods, church on a hill, idyllic country setting."

"Sounds dreamy, lucky you," said Selma. "So will you be taking — excuse me, I can't remember his name — the boyfriend you told me about, the one you've had for eight years." She winked at me and I could have killed her.

"Tommy," I muttered.

"Tommy. So is Tommy going too?"

I nodded.

"Well, it's nice the two of you will be together. When I get back we'll have to have you and Tommy over for dinner, won't we, Buzz?"

"Absolutely," said Buzz. He put his arm around Selma's shoulders and I saw her flinch. And when she did so, he held her even more tightly as if to stop her moving altogether.

"I can't wait to meet Tommy," said Buzz. "Tommy and Lee. Sounds good to me."

Chapter 8

I left for France not knowing if the man in the market had been charged with Astrid's murder. Nobody had seen him around the market, and his wife, who had been minding his stall, had disappeared. They might have gone away for Christmas or he might be hanging up his stocking in the clink. Nobody seemed to know. I couldn't quite work out why I was still so uneasy about Astrid's fire. After all it had nothing to do with me. All I knew was that I wouldn't relax until they had a suspect in custody.

Tommy and I had to fly to Paris because I'd left it too late to get two seats on the Eurostar. At Charles de Gaulle we jumped in a taxi to the Gare d'Austerlitz and then took a fast train down through the center of France to Cahors. On the plane, Tommy was so excited he could barely contain himself. I am someone who likes to read on long train journeys, or stare out the window at the countryside racing by and lose myself in uplifting fantasies about a possible future life living in an idyllic spot in the middle of nowhere. I never look people in the eye as they approach the empty seat next to me and I never initiate a conversation. Though, of course, on a plane to Paris just before Christmas, an empty seat was out of the question.

Tommy is the opposite. On the plane flying over the Channel, he chattered to other passengers across the aisle and in the seats behind us, telling them all about our plans for Christmas and how my parents lived in France, and then he asked them what they were doing. All in all there were a lot of heads popping over the back of the seat and people crouching down in the aisles and the poor Air France flight attendant had her hands full trying to restore order. The thing about Tommy is that he can be very engaging and people instinctively trust him and want to tell him everything. I wasn't really terribly interested in the fact that the woman sitting diagonally across the aisle from us had had a terrible problem with her teenage daughter who had refused to accompany her mother to Paris, preferring instead to remain with her boyfriend in London. If anything, judging by the mother, I thought the daughter probably had a point. And by the time Tommy had her going into details about her messy divorce and how the trouble with the daughter had begun at the same time, I noticed other passengers were beginning to look a little irritated too.

Mercifully, after about an hour, Tommy fell asleep on the train and I was able to read. There had been a slight problem at a bar at the Gare d'Austerlitz when it had dawned on him that he might have difficulty ordering half a pint of Guinness in France. He'd settled for a bottle of Beaujolais and downed it so quickly, it was rather surprising he didn't nod off before we boarded the train. I watched him sleeping for a few minutes. He was very proud of the new sweaters he had brought along for the trip to France, one of which he had insisted on wearing for the journey, even though I had pointed out to him that it would be filthy and travel-worn by the time he arrived. To my surprise, I approved of his choice. Tommy never made much of an effort with his clothes unless he was going to see his mother and it had never occurred to me that he would extend a similar courtesy to mine. This was a beautiful sweater. Charcoal gray with a crew neck. But what surprised me the most was that it was made of the softest cashmere. This wasn't Tommy's style at all. He was usually in and out of Marks and Spencer in approximately seven minutes, grabbing an exact replica of whatever had fallen to bits on him that morning. Once I had witnessed him stripping down to his vest and putting on a new sweater right there in the store before paying for it and handing his old one to the person behind the cash register to throw away. She was too surprised to protest. I wondered where he'd bought this new one. I was tempted to look at the label but that might wake him up, so I resisted.

Inevitably my thoughts turned to Buzz. I remembered the look he'd given me when Selma had asked after Tommy, and I felt sick. I'd half hoped he'd turn up on my doorstep demanding an explanation but the days went by and there was no sign of him. Christmas was drawing closer by the minute and in desperation, I telephoned the house. If Selma answered I could always find some excuse for calling her, but the machine told me they were out. *They.* This was something new. When I'd called before the machine had just said *Leave a message and I'll get back to you.* No mention of any name but it was her voice. Now the message had been changed. It was Buzz's voice. We're *not home right now . . .* We. Us. A couple. Was I being paranoid or was this new message directed at me? Had he changed it deliberately to make some kind of point?

I reached him eventually and the conversation was awkward to the extent that I never even came close to saying what I had intended — that I thought it best that we ceased to have any kind of physical relationship.

"So who is this Tommy?" he asked when we'd barely said hello.

"Tommy's just Tommy."

"Your boyfriend."

"You never told me you had a wife."

"We've been through that. At least you knew of Selma's existence and that she had some connection to me. You never even mentioned Tommy."

I didn't say anything. This wasn't exactly going as I had planned.

"You haven't told him about . . . ?"

"Of course not."

"You make a habit of cheating on him?"

"It's the first time it's happened."

"How long have you been together?"

"Eight years."

"Eight years and I'm the first?" I could hear his disbelief. I was miserable in my ambivalence. I cared about Tommy and I knew this was the moment when I should tell Buzz I didn't want to see him anymore but I remained bewilderingly silent.

"So, isn't it great that there's so much interest in Selma's story?" I babbled.

He didn't say anything and I could hear the rustling of paper on the other end of the line. I jumped when he suddenly snapped: "Give me your agent's number. I seem to have misplaced it."

"Why do you want —"

"Just give it to me." He sounded so hostile, all I could do was read out Genevieve's number.

It was horrible. We left everything unresolved. He wished me a happy Christmas in a curt, dismissive tone. I asked if I could call him from France. Maybe by then I would have summoned up the courage to explain what I wanted.

"When do you get back?" he asked, evading my request.

"New Year's Eve."

"Well, have a great time."

I had to make do with that.

When I called Genevieve, ostensibly to wish her a happy Christmas, she started talking about Buzz before I had time to say hello.

"The man was yelling at me, Lee. I mean he was literally *yelling* at me. I had to hold the receiver well away from my ear. Why is he so unhappy with the fact that we're this close to a deal? You would have thought he'd be a happy man. But no, he more or less told me the book wouldn't be happening. Made it sound as if it was a pointless exercise. What is wrong with the man?"

"He can't do anything to stop it, can he?"

"I get the feeling that's why he's so mad. The money's good, the publisher is the perfect home for the book, and Selma's more than willing to cooperate. There's not a damn thing he can come up with that makes it look like a bad idea. Yet he's being extremely unpleasant. We'll just have to hope she'll have a killer story to tell to make it all worthwhile. And you'll see to that, won't you, dear?"

I could have done without the word "killer" and the mounting pressure on me to come up with the goods was beginning to unnerve me.

Tommy's head was resting on my shoulder. I looked down at his sleeping face and, as always, liked what I saw. He has a pleasant face. Wide. Open. The thing about Tommy is that he looks safe. People trust him.

And the thing about Buzz, I reflected, was that he looked dangerous and that was why I was attracted to him. His face had a streak of cruelty, something about the mouth.

I could tell the minute we stepped down from the train at Cahors that my mother was in a state of high excitement about our visit. She was pacing up and down the platform, rubbing her palms together in front of her, a habit she'd adopted ever since she gave up smoking five years ago. She was whippet thin. How could she have lost even more weight since I'd last seen her? She has a small head perched on a long neck and her face is all bones — cheekbones, prominent nose, pointed chin — and huge eyes. I've always thought she had the eyes of a wicked child. They have a constant look of amusement, as if she's just done something terribly naughty and you won't scold her, will you? Because if you do, she'll giggle and swear she didn't do it. I noticed her hair was expertly cut, very short and close to the head exposing the angular bones of her face. But I was troubled that despite the fact she had turned up the collar of her jacket in rakish fashion, it did not detract from the roundness of her shoulders and the by now quite prominent hump at the top of her spine.

My mother was lithe and she prided herself on her energy level. But in the way that you can observe a person with added incisiveness when you have been separated from them for a while, I noted a change in her. She stooped a little, she no longer held her head quite so high, she was, I realized with a sudden pang, growing old.

What I hadn't realized was that in a way Tommy and my mother were two of a kind. Overenthusiastic people who threw themselves into projects without really taking the time to think them through. The way she'd thrown herself into my father's plan to go and live in France was a case in point. Just as my father had been about to retire they'd taken a holiday in the Dordogne and moved on to explore the Lot whereupon my mother had suddenly decided, while driving along the river through one of the beautiful gorges, that this was where they would live. To give her her due, she had masterminded the move single-handed, even going so far as to take French lessons at night school in order to be able to deal with the intricacies of buying a house there. Unfortunately her accent was so atrocious that no one could understand a word she said. The upshot of this was that instead of taking their time to look for the perfect retirement home, my parents had vastly overpaid for what was little more than a cowshed in 1989 and then spent a small fortune — and several years — converting it into a habitable two-bedroom barn. It stood just outside a village, perched on top of a hill in the middle of a field. Granted, the view was spectacular, but it was a far cry from the comforts I enjoyed in the house they had left behind in London.

"And how are you, Tommy?" asked my mother as soon as she had packed us into her little Deux Chevaux, "I can't tell you how delighted we are that Lee was able to bring you." Her voice was high and squeaky and somehow too girlish for her age. She always chirped like a bird rather than spoke.

"Listen," said Tommy, "I'm the one who's excited. I've never been to France before."

"No!" My mother was suitably amazed. "Not a single pop across the Channel?"

"Not a one. Don't know why. Been to

Spain on a plane but never France."

"Spain on a plane. You're a poet, though you didn't know it." My mother giggled.

I almost groaned out loud. How long were they going to keep up this inane patter?

"How's Dad?"

"Don't worry about your father. He's in heaven," was my mother's rather peculiar answer. "Tommy, tell me all your news. Are you still at the BBC? What are we going to do with you while you're here? Do you bicycle? There are some marvelous views."

"Mum, it's the middle of winter," I pointed out.

"Well, we can't just sit indoors doing jigsaws and playing cards," she said. "It's Tommy's first visit to France."

"How do you play poker in French?" asked Tommy and my mother giggled happily and said, "Oh, it's going to be such fun having you here."

I didn't need to worry about them, I realized. I sat in the back of the car — my mother had insisted Tommy sit in front beside her so he wouldn't miss anything — and listened to them chattering away. They thrived on the kind of banal small talk that I always found such a struggle. Tommy was just carrying on the conversation he had begun with the passengers on the plane. He liked to chat, didn't really matter to whom, and my mother was the same. I could probably get through the entire Christmas break never having to open my mouth again.

There was no sign of my father when we arrived at the house.

"Damn him." My mother stopped in the middle of the yard in front of a pile of wood. "I told him to call the farm and get them to send a boy to split the logs. What are we supposed to put on the fire?"

"Don't worry about another thing." Tommy began rolling up his sleeves. "I can take care of that."

"Give me your nice new sweater first." I took his bags from him. "I'll take these upstairs."

"What an angel you've got there," said my mother as we went indoors.

He was an angel fit for absolutely nothing when he staggered upstairs an hour later. He was so hopelessly unfit that splitting one log — let alone twenty — left him gasping for breath.

"I'll run you a bath," I told him, "then you'd better have a nap before dinner otherwise you'll never go the distance."

"This is a bit short," he complained when he lay down on the *lit bateau* — a sort of mini-Napoleonic bed shaped like a boat that my mother had insisted on putting in the guest bedroom.

"It's French," I pointed out to him, "and from now on you're going to love everything that's French. Like these coarse linen sheets that will scratch our sensitive skin and the long stiff bolster that's so hard it'll probably give us a headache. What do you think of my mother by the way?"

I lay down beside him and looked around the guest bedroom, thinking that it must seem a little strange to him. There was no plaster or paint on the old stone walls because my mother had thought it amusing to preserve the original cowshed image. Medieval-looking tapestries were hung all over the place made from untreated wool obtained from the local shepherds. They had a rather unusual smell and as far as I was concerned it wasn't wise to go too close to them.

"She's a darling," he said, yawning. "Why do you ask?"

"Do you think she's happy living out here?"

"Haven't a clue," said Tommy helpfully. "What do you think?"

"I think she's lonely. Look how excited she was to see us. I think maybe she got it wrong and she doesn't like to admit it."

"Got what wrong?"

"That retiring to France would be a great idea. As you've probably already noticed, the house is a disaster. Some people are blessed with vision and can look at a broken-down cowshed and see the idyllic rustic home that can be made out of it. My mother isn't one of them. She just sees the picture in a coffee table book of someone else's dream and imagines hers can be conjured up just like that. She's always trying to be something she's not. She's not meant to be buried in the countryside like this. I'd be better off living here than she would."

Tommy opened his eyes and looked at me in alarm.

"It's all right, I'm not moving," I reassured him. "It's just it makes me sad to see how things don't work out for my mother, that even after all these years she isn't getting what she wants."

"Maybe she doesn't know what she wants. That's probably what the trouble is."

I glanced at Tommy. Sometimes he can hit the nail bang on the head when he's not even trying.

"But you can't say that about me. It must be hell for her having a daughter like me. I don't think I really satisfy her on any level. She used to want me to be a high-flyer like her. Now that she's resigned herself to the fact that I'm *just a writer,* her words, she'd still prefer a daughter she could go shopping with, someone who'd give her grandchildren, someone she could compare recipes with. I imagine she wishes I were a best-selling novelist with her picture in the paper rather than the ghost behind the scenes."

"Yeah, I see what you mean. The last thing she needs is a reclusive writer who never lets her boyfriend anywhere near her. No chance of a coffee morning deciding what the bridesmaids are going to wear. No knitting needles clicking for the grandchild. What a miserable old age she's going to have."

"You're a beast." I kicked him. "Anyway, we seem pretty close right now." It was true. Somehow our arms had become entwined and we'd fallen into our familiar embrace. It felt good. Not exciting like it did with Buzz but comfortable and relaxed. I felt a rush of affection for Tommy.

"Come here." He pulled me to him and we rubbed noses. It was something we did.

Tommy had started it after what had become known between us as my Polar Bear Speech to Cath. She was gone and I missed her but my stupid pride would not allow me to show my misery to Tommy. Until one day he very firmly took me in his arms and announced, "If you're going to be a silly polar bear for the rest of your life, you'll need an Eskimo kiss from time to time to make you feel at home." Whereupon he nudged my nose with his in such a gentle, tender movement that I opened my mouth without thinking and the ice melted.

I was so stupid to have worried about this visit. Tommy knew exactly how to make my mother happy. I was the one who was going to have to work overtime to show her that her efforts were appreciated. And I would. My mother and I were not on the same page, a favorite expression of Tommy's in view of the fact that I was a writer. Indeed, this was the kind of infantile sense of humor he shared with my mother. There were times when I felt we weren't even in the same book given the extent to which we failed to get the point of each other.

Tommy fell asleep in the middle of kissing me. Looking down at his rather wide head resting uncomfortably on the bolster, I was reminded of a Labrador retriever. Somehow Tommy had taken on the role of pet in my life. He was faithful and trusting, he was occasionally allowed to sleep on my bed, and he looked forward to his meals. He didn't like being parted from me and he loved me unconditionally. And I loved him. But I had relegated him to a kennel on the edge of my consciousness, infrequently petting him and paying attention to him as one would a dog.

But unlike dogs, you couldn't take Tommy for a walk unless the path led straight to a pub, so I took the opportunity to slip out of the house without him. I remembered my own special route to the village, taking a path down the hill that led past a place where a natural spring gushed out of the rock into a pool. One half of it formed a drinking trough for cattle and in the other the local washerwomen still came to rinse their laundry and scrub it on the large stone slabs, shooing away any cows that came too close. Although in late December I didn't expect to see any.

There was a reason I was making for the village. I had a handful of Euros in my pocket and Buzz's number scrawled on a piece of paper.

He wasn't in. The phone rang and rang until I realized with a shock that the answering machine wasn't on. There was no way I could communicate with him.

Tommy had awakened and joined my mother in the kitchen when I returned. She was showing him how to make an *omelette aux truffes* for supper and a dressing for the salad using the local walnut oil. I was tempted to point out to her that he would have much preferred egg and chips or beans on toast but I refrained. But I did produce a jar of Branston I'd brought with me for my father who liked a plowman's lunch as much as the next man and Tommy's face brightened.

My father came home around seven and I noticed my mother didn't greet him or ask him where he'd been. As with my mother, I noticed a distinct change in my father but if anything he looked younger than when I'd last seen him. He had always been an attractive man who took care of himself but now he seemed especially vibrant. Unlike my mother he still held himself reasonably erect and at six foot three he was even taller than Tommy. He was a vain man who took excessive care of his appearance, but whereas my mother tended to overdress, my father always got it absolutely right. His well-worn corduroy trousers and Shetland polo neck looked like they afforded him the good quality comfort he'd expected when he bought them. His once black hair had turned completely white, his face was creased with wrinkles and folds in skin that had been roughened in all weathers but his eyes were the same eyes I had looked into as a child.

I looked into them now as he reached for me, enveloping me in one of his bear hugs.

"Nathalie, my favorite daughter," he said. He never called me Lee and the "favorite daughter" line was an old joke between us. I was his only child.

He turned to Tommy. "Fancy a drink? Bottle of Guinness do you? I keep a few for special occasions. You need a reward for splitting all that wood."

As I watched him put Tommy at his ease I thought what I always thought about my father: That he was this charming stranger. He had the gift of switching all the attention onto you and making you feel wonderful but at the end of the day you realized you had no idea what he was thinking. But when a man behaved like that with his own daughter, could it still be described as a gift? In his own manipulative way, my father was as much a loner as I was.

Supper was unexpectedly enjoyable, for the first half at any rate, before the conversation took a rather difficult turn. My father, usually the more silent of the two, always the listener, was surprisingly loquacious.

"Where do you live in London?" he asked Tommy suddenly after they'd exhausted everything there was to say about the Chelsea Football Club. I hadn't known my father was a Chelsea supporter. In fact I strongly suspected he might have become one at the beginning of supper just for the purposes of finding a common topic of conversation with Tommy.

"East End," said Tommy. "Bow. Vanessa, this really is yummy." He was enjoying a second helping of the *gateau de marrons* my mother had whipped up since our arrival. "Can you teach Lee how to make this?"

"I can teach you, Tommy. How hard is roasting chestnuts? I'll show you how to make the caramel tomorrow and of course you mustn't forget the brandy."

"Like I'd ever forget about the brandy," said Tommy. "Isn't she amazing, Lee?"

"Utterly," I agreed. She really was. Her

cooking lessons were one of the few worth-while things she had taken up and not abandoned. But what I most admired was the way she never made a big deal of it. Anyone could do this, was her attitude.

"Good part of the world, Bow? Bit of an up-and-coming area?" My father was still looking at Tommy. "What do houses go for around there these days?"

Pointless thing to ask Tommy who had never had a clue about property. He'd never owned a house. He rented his flat.

"So how are the renovations to our house coming along?" asked my mother as I had known, inevitably, she would.

"Fine," I said.

"What renovations?" asked Tommy before I could give his shins a good kick under the table. "Oh, you mean the summerhouse."

"The summerhouse?" echoed my mother.

"Yes, it's great. She's gone and got a renter in there. Put in a heater and everything. It's dead cozy."

My parents stared at me.

"Is this true?"

I nodded.

"Well, you'd better get him or her out immediately." My mother's tone was quite sharp. I looked at my father, expecting him to reassure me it was fine.

"What kind of lease arrangement do you have with this person?"

"Well, nothing really. It's all on a friendly basis. There's no lease as such."

"No lease!" My mother was shocked. "But suppose you have to get them out. They probably have squatter's rights by now."

"I don't want to get her out."

"You may not want to but what about us? It's our house in case you'd forgotten."

"Any French people in the neighborhood?" inquired my father. An odd question; I couldn't see the connection.

"In Notting Hill? I expect they're a few," I replied. "I don't come across them much if there are. They probably prefer to be down by South Kensington, near the Lycee."

"Your father's got a bee in his bonnet about all these French tax exiles."

"What French tax exiles?"

"Oh, there are loads of them. Didn't you know? Sixty-five thousand Britons in France and two hundred and fifty thousand frogs in the UK. The French are desperate for properties in England."

"Don't call them frogs," said my mother.

"I'll call them what I like," protested my

father. “It’s a term of endearment for them. No one could accuse me of being anti-French.”

“Lord knows, that’s true,” said my mother, rather sourly I thought.

“I haven’t told you about our murder,” I said, knowing that would ensure their full attention. “That children’s television presenter, Astrid McKenzie, died at the end of our road.”

“You know, I think I read something about that,” said my mother. “I had no idea she lived in Blenheim Crescent and I didn’t realize she was murdered.”

“She lived in the mews and it’s a pretty sure bet she was murdered. They’re holding a man who works in the market.”

“Not anymore,” Tommy interrupted me. “While you were out for your walk I called the BBC. I always feel sorry for the poor sods who have to work over Christmas, wanted to wish them season’s greetings and all that. They’ve let that bloke go. Even though his wife said he wasn’t at home, no one actually saw him at Astrid’s either.”

“How do they know about this in your office?” I asked.

“We’ve been following it all pretty closely,” Tommy said, surprising me. “After all, I was there when it happened and, in any case, just about everyone I work with has worked with Astrid at one time or another. They reckon it was only a matter of time before she got more than she bargained for. Liked the rough stuff more than was good for her."

"But it was arson," I pointed out. "Someone killed her by setting fire to her house while she was in it."

"Well, she had a fair amount of bruises on her from what I heard," he said.

"How will the fact that there's been a murder in the area affect house prices?" asked my father suddenly and for an instant I was thrown by his question.

And my mother replied, "Not now, Ed," which was even more bewildering. "Let's have coffee next door by the fire," she went on. "Lee, come and help me."

I followed her into the kitchen. She had smiled and chattered away through supper but I had the weird feeling that she was preoccupied, that something was bothering her.

"Mum, what's wrong?"

She had her back to me but I saw her tense. "Nothing, nothing at all," she said in a way that told me something definitely was but before I could press her, Tommy joined us.

"Your father's gone upstairs to make some calls. No coffee for him."

"That's what's wrong if you really want to know," I heard my mother mutter, speaking so softly she might have been talking to herself. And then she turned around and handed Tommy the tray of coffee cups and they retreated safely to their designated roles of charming hostess and obliging guest.

On Christmas morning my mother served us bowls of steaming hot chocolate and brioches for breakfast and then marched us into the freezing cold conservatory where, for some reason best known to herself, she had elected to place the Christmas tree.

When Tommy presented my parents each with a large square box wrapped in red paper covered in a rather lewd little Santa pattern, I held my breath.

But I need not have worried. Tommy's present was a huge success, far more popular, in fact, than my cookbook for my mother and CDs for my father. Tommy had given them clogs. Bright red shining clogs so they could go clomping round the house making an unholy din on the stone floors.

"Lee told me the house had stone floors

and that can get pretty cold," he explained. "And the thing about clogs is that you can wear as many socks as you want and your feet still keep warm, they're so high off the ground."

He was right. Now that I thought about it all the villagers wore them. It was an intelligent and thoughtful present and I could see my parents were pleased.

"*Civet de marcassin* for Christmas lunch," announced my mother cheerfully. I opened my mouth, poised to explain to Tommy that we would be having wild boar rather than the traditional turkey but he was already beaming with delight and saying "Great. Crazy. Can't wait. And do let me help you in the kitchen again."

"I'm going out for a couple of hours," said my father.

On Christmas Day? I waited for my mother to explode but she didn't.

"Don't forget I've asked the de la Falaises, you know, from the château, to come for a drink. Around six," she reminded him.

As it was, he only made it back by five, missing lunch altogether. Curiously, my mother made no mention of the fact that he hadn't reappeared so I took my cue from her and didn't remark on it.

My parents seemed to have progressed to first-name basis with the de la Falaises, which was a relief because I hadn't a clue how you introduced a French count. Now it was Henri and Coco all over the place. Henri spoke excellent English but Coco, clearly not the first *comtesse* and probably younger than Henri's children, didn't speak a word. Uh-oh, this was going to be rather stiff. My mother's French was incomprehensible. As far as I knew, Tommy hadn't a prayer. Ironically, I realized I couldn't speak for my father but I knew that my own French hadn't progressed much beyond GCSE standard. Still, the sound of popping champagne corks could always be relied upon to loosen tongues.

It was only after I'd been chatting happily to Henri — in English — for about fifteen minutes that I became aware that someone else had arrived. Another Frenchman. He was behind me somewhere talking to Coco. I turned my head slightly but couldn't see anyone.

My mother appeared at Henri's side with a bowl of cashews.

"You never told us," she said to me.

Never told them what?

Then Tommy appeared and grabbed a handful of nuts.

"Vous n'avez pas d'accent. Du tout! Incroyable!" Henri said to Tommy.

I was about to translate when I realized what he'd said.

"*Merci. On m'a déjà dit. Aucune idée pourquoi? J'ai — comme on dit en Anglais* — a good ear."

Tommy spoke French. Not only did he speak French but he spoke it with an incredible French accent. He was fluent.

"But I thought you'd never been to France?" I spluttered.

"I haven't."

"So how . . . ?"

"Radio program a few months ago. Teaching French. I was the engineer but the broadcaster, a teacher, she taught me a few things and she said I was a natural. She gave me lessons. Trouble was I only ever talked to her. I never knew until just now if it would work with any other French people. Talking to Coco here was a bit of an experiment, but it worked okay, didn't it, Coco?"

"Comment?" she looked very confused.

"J'ai dit qu'on a bien parlé ensemble — en Français."

"Très bien." She giggled and suddenly I thought it was high time Tommy stopped talking to her.

Still, later that night, thrown together in the cramped confines of the *lit bateau,* I had to admit that the fact that he could speak French did make him seem a little more sexy. That and the quantities of my father's champagne we had consumed.

"Tomcat?" My pet name for him that I hadn't used in months.

"Mmm?" He was almost asleep.

"I can't tell you how impressed I am by your French. It's made my Christmas."

"Thanks."

"So what were you and Countess Coco yattering on about while my back was turned then?"

"She was asking me all about your house."

"*My* house? In London."

"Well, your parents' house."

"Don't remind me. What on earth for?"

"They're thinking of buying it. Her and the Count. Tax exiles."

"Tommy, are you crazy? Are you sure you understood correctly? Your French . . ."

"I understood perfectly. I was as surprised as you are. I made her repeat it several times."

"Oh, Lord, I'd better tell Mum and Dad."

"I think you'll find," said Tommy, burrowing his head in my hair, "that they already know."

Chapter 9

Tommy was right.

I cornered my mother in the kitchen the following morning while he was still in bed nursing his champagne hangover.

"How on earth did you find that out?" she asked, stunned.

"*La Comtesse* told Tommy last night. Is it true? Why do they want to buy our house?"

"They want to move to London like all those French exiles your father was going on about."

"What on earth would make them think it was for sale?"

"Simple," she said, turning to face me, "we told them."

Now it was my turn to be stunned.

"Oh, it's okay. Nothing's going to happen for a while. They haven't even seen it yet. They'll probably be over in the next month or so. That's why I want you to keep me up to speed about the renovations. I want the place to be in mint condition when they see it. And I want that lodger in the summerhouse out."

So they were going to sell the house. I knew it had been too good to be true, living rent free in the middle of one of the most fashionable parts of central London. What would I do now? Hope Selma Walker made me a ton of money so I could grow up and finally buy a home of my own?

My mother seemed to be reading my thoughts. "I have to confess that's one of the reasons we asked Tommy to come with you. We wanted to get to know him a bit better, because you'll probably move in with him now, won't you? I mean, it's been, what? Eight years?"

"Mum, you've got it all wrong. I'm not going to live with Tommy. I'm not even sure you can really call us a couple."

Now why had I gone and said that? I waited for her to ask me why but she just looked at me sadly and said, "Oh, not you as well?"

"What do you mean?"

"I had an ulterior motive for getting you down here for Christmas. I needed to tell you something. Your father's got a mistress. He's had her for a while. One of those wretched *Parisienne* divorcées who seem to take it into their heads to run away down here and bury themselves in the countryside. Lord knows where he met her but he wants to marry her. He wants me to give him a divorce and he needs to sell the London house to pay me off. The de la Falaises came along at just the right moment."

"Oh Mum." I felt a wave of sympathy for her. Well into her sixties and being forced to start a new life on her own. I moved toward her to put my arms around her.

She almost let me do it. I had my hand on the back of her head and was starting to stroke her hair, expecting to feel a tremor of emotion in her body, when she jerked her head back.

"I'm fine," she said, moving away from me.

Same old story. Every time I tried to show her any affection, she brushed me off. When I was a little girl, the excuse had always been that I would mess up her appearance. Now she didn't even bother with an excuse. It wasn't as if she sent out signals, *Keep your distance; I'm not one of those touchy feely people.* She worked hard on her warm and hospitable image. God knows, Tommy had fallen for it. But it was a front. She had a problem with any kind of intimacy. I had a sudden, fleeting insight into my parents' sex life. Had she flinched every time my father had reached for her? No wonder he had looked elsewhere.

Feeling guilty that I should even see my mother in such a light, I shut down that train of thought as quickly as it had crept up on me.

"You can't be fine," I insisted. "It's an awful thing to happen to you. No one would blame you for feeling terrible. It's understandable."

"I do not feel terrible. I am totally in control."

That was the problem. If only she'd snap now and then and freak out like the rest of us.

"So why can't you sell this house and keep the one in London?" Answering a practical question might help her to open up.

"Because we'd get about four times as much for the house in London, that's why," said my mother and I saw her point. "Of course, if we don't make a quick sale to the de la Falaises, then I'll probably have to come back and live in the house with you till we do sell it. I'll have nowhere else to go."

"But you live here, Mum. You live in

France. Why can't you stay in this house now you've done it up?"

"Because your father wants to live here with Josiane and I want to get as far away as possible. I tell you, Lee, it'll be a relief to get away. This place is the pits. I'm quite looking forward to starting a new life, if you really want to know."

"That's right, Mum. That's a good positive attitude. What's she like, this Josiane?"

"She's another Coco de la Falaise. Younger than springtime and hard as nails." I heard the bitterness in her voice but said nothing. "But it's not that bad," she went on. "As I said, I really am quite looking forward to a new life. It wasn't a one-sided thing, you know, this breakdown between me and your father. As soon as I got him down here and he had nothing to do, I realized what a mistake I'd made. I had no one else to talk to and you may not see it, Lee, but your father is pretty boring. I don't know how I put up with him for so many years. He has no conversation. He gets you to do all the talking and you think he's unbelievably charming and because of that he fools you into thinking he's also fascinating. I remember when I first met him. He was the most handsome creature I'd ever seen. That's the danger with good-looking men. You never think to look any farther till it's too late. Ed was a great listener because he had to be. He had nothing to say for himself. Sorry, darling." She turned to me and for one glorious second I thought she was actually going to embrace me.

But she didn't move.

"I shouldn't go on about him like this. He's your father after all. But I should warn you, I intend to get as much money out of him as possible. In fact, if they sold Josiane's house down the road for a good price then perhaps he could buy me out of the Notting Hill house. We own it together."

I didn't tell Tommy until we were in bed that night. I imagined my mother in the next room, telling my father that I knew. And then I realized that even though my parents were on the point of getting a divorce, they still shared the same bed. Or were they forced to because Tommy and I were in the guest bedroom? Had they been sleeping apart for months? Would my father move his stuff back into this room as soon as my mother had put us on the train? I found it extraordinary that my father and I were in the same boat, both of us putting on a show of normalcy, he with my mother and me with Tommy. At least my mother knew about Josiane.

"Who'd have thought your dad would go off with someone?" Tommy remarked. "It's the quiet ones you want to watch."

"It explains a lot," I said. "I could tell when we arrived that something was troubling her. Yet *he* was strangely elated and I couldn't figure out why."

"He's a good-looking man," Tommy observed. "He takes care of himself."

"Oh, he always has. That's what he does best," I said, aware that I was sounding a little bitter. "He's pretty vain in many ways, pretty selfish too."

"Lee, I have to say something." For once Tommy appeared to be wide awake. "You don't sound as if you like your father very much." He looked at me anxiously as if he was worried he might have said something he shouldn't.

To my surprise I answered immediately, "You may be right although I look at Dad and think what's not to like? I don't dislike him. I'm happy to see him. I've never had much of a conversation with him. I confess I don't think about him much when I'm away from him."

"You sound like you're talking about a near stranger."

"Well, that's probably because I am. You might say the same about Mum. My parents have never seemed like parents to me. They're like an older couple I know. I visit them from time to time and they've been kind enough to loan me their house to live in."

"That's shocking," Tommy muttered, clearly appalled.

"Is it? I've never really talked about it before. When I was a child we were like three adults living together. Except I couldn't be left on my own. But half the time they acted as if I didn't exist."

"I never realized you were so unhappy as a kid." Tommy bundled me into a rather clumsy embrace. "There's so much I don't know about you."

"I don't think I was unhappy, really. I just learned to be completely self-sufficient. I learned not to depend on my parents for anything. I was perfectly happy in my room with my books. And I had plenty of friends. To be honest, I always felt that my mother made very little distinction between me and my friends. She behaved exactly the same to all of us. Very entertaining, loads of delicious food, but in terms of genuine feeling and emotion, we could have been refugees from another planet for all she cared."

"So how's she going to take it now her husband's dumped her?"

"You mean will she finally see that what she needs is a shoulder to cry on? I think she's probably known that for quite a while but whether she'll actually admit it is another matter. Oh God, why does this have to happen at this stage of their life?"

It was starting to hit me as I had known it would. I had been trained by my parents not to show emotion in their presence so I had maintained a calm front during the talk with my mother and throughout the rest of the day. But now I was beginning to crumble. My parents were splitting up. Up to now I had been able to fool myself that we were some kind of family unit. I had a vision of my parents being picked up by a huge anonymous hand and thrown into the air in two different directions. I saw my mother landing in my arms and my father in the arms of a glamorous stranger who turned on her heels and carried him away. I was having childlike fantasies about my parents' future instead of facing up to the reality. Josiane was probably a perfectly nice woman who would treat me exactly as my mother had for thirty-something years.

"You see, Tommy," I said, "you see . . ."

"See what? You're getting yourself all worked up."

"You see why I don't want to get married? My parents have been married for nearly forty years. What's the point of marriage if it can just be dissipated by an affair after all that time?"

"You think it'd be any better if they'd been married for eighteen months and then split up?" asked Tommy reasonably. "They were probably very happy for at least twenty of those years and that may well be more than your father will have with Josiane. Besides, that's not why you don't want to get married."

"It's not?" I sniffled and pulled a bit of squashed Kleenex out from under the bolster. "What's stopping me then?"

"You're just plain scared. You look upon marriage as a kind of trap, I know you do. You worry away thinking your whole life will change if you share it with someone else and you won't be able to do any of the things that are important to you."

"And that's bullshit?"

"Total bullshit. I know who you are. I know you're a neurotic, territorial polar bear who needs her space and I'd give it to you."

"I like the space you give me now. Why

do you have to live with me?"

"Because I love you and I want to know absolutely everything about you. I want to know what you do when you're alone, I want to see all your little quirks, I want to hear what you say when you talk to yourself. I want to know you inside out and then I'll give you all the space you desire."

"See," I grumbled although I was secretly touched by his declaration, "you'd drive me nuts for the beginning of our marriage, crowding me, smothering me, and then by the sounds of things, you'd get bored with me and dump me."

"I wouldn't. I promise."

"I bet that's what all the husbands say. Women who believe them are the ones who get married."

"And cynical, jaded creatures like you know better."

Hearing that unleashed my tears. Tommy knew what he was doing. He knew me inside out. That was what I could never make him understand. He didn't have to move in with me to get to know me any better. He knew all about my insecurities yet still he was prepared to wait till my resistance broke down and that was what made it so hard to give him up. Would I ever find anyone else who knew me the way Tommy knew me?

Having him here with me now when I had to deal with the shock of my parents' divorce meant a lot to me. The thing about Tommy was that I knew I could always rely on him. Sometimes this faithful canine quality was irritating and sometimes it reminded me why I needed him.

My father looked very sad when it came time to say good-bye.

"I'll get in touch when we come to London," he whispered in my ear. I assumed by the *we* he meant himself and Josiane. "I was going to come over before and tell you about Josiane but your mother insisted I stay so we could have a family Christmas together and the truth is I'm glad we did. Don't worry. Everything will work itself out."

I wanted to ask umpteen questions like *How long has it been going on?* and *Are you happy?* but maybe they would have to wait until he came to London. If he ever did.

Tommy and I arrived back in London at about eight o'clock in the evening on New Year's Eve. I felt considerably closer to him than I had when we left London. I knew that I was deliberately pushing all thoughts of Buzz to the back of my mind because the way things had gone over Christmas had left me feeling very confused about him. I knew that continuing to see him would only complicate my life even further. The shock of what had happened to my parents had left me feeling more guilty about Tommy than ever.

But the minute we hit London it was as if the bond that had reunited us in France was severed. We had each been invited to several parties individually, which once again highlighted the fact that we just didn't have that many friends in common, if any. We took the Heathrow Express to Paddington and on the ride in from the airport, a heated argument erupted between us because I refused to be dragged to Shagger Watkins's home in God knows where to see the New Year in with a lot of drunken Chelsea supporters. I had invitations from some of the old crowd who referred to him as the Radio Nerd. I hadn't wanted to subject him to their patronizing attitude so I hadn't included him in the acceptance and this had upset him. By the time we arrived at Paddington Station he had collapsed in a major sulk, sitting slightly turned away from me. When I leapt up to grab the bags, shouting to someone to hold the doors open, he stayed put.

"Tommy!" I yelled. "Help me. I can't carry all these bags by myself."

"You don't need to take mine." He glared at me. "I'm not coming with you. I'm going to Shagger's without you."

Oh, Tommy, I thought, as I struggled with my bags toward the taxi stand beside platform one, *why does something like this always happen between us?*

It was about six o'clock at night when the cab turned off Ladbroke Grove into my street. The sky was strangely light, I noticed. There was still a kind of lingering pink glow or was I imagining it?

"How's the weather been?" I shouted to the cabbie. "Was it sunny today?"

"Nah, sweetheart, rained all day."

"But it's so bright outside."

"Yeah, you're right," he agreed. "But it's not like that all over. Just over there" — he jerked his head in the direction of the house — "someone's havin' a bonfire in the garden. 'Allo. Looks like it's got a bit out of hand."

He turned the corner into Blenheim Crescent and the cab came to an abrupt halt. Three fire engines were parked in the road outside my house with their lights flashing. Their hoses were snaking down the alley to the side of the house and a crowd had gathered to watch.

I leapt out of the cab and up the steps to the front door. I had no idea what I planned to do once inside the house but I imagine I must have wanted to save whatever I could from the fire. I found myself racing up the stairs, taking them two at a time and hauling myself up by the banister until I reached the top floor where I had my office. I went straight to the cupboard where I kept my laptop and grabbed it together with the little wooden box in which I kept my disks.

As I stood up I looked out the window and saw that the garden below me was illuminated. Suddenly I realized that there had been no sign of fire in the house when I rushed upstairs in such a reckless fashion. It was the summerhouse that was ablaze. I stood mesmerized, watching the flames leaping into the air like the ones from the bonfire the O'Malleys had built next door on November fifth. The firemen looked as if they were beginning to get it under control but it didn't matter now, the damage was done. The place that had made Angel's face light up with joy would soon be a mass of blackened wooden stumps and ash-covered rubble.

"Angel!"

I dropped the laptop and hurtled out of the room straight into the arms of a burly giant of a man who had just reached the top of the stairs.

"Hold on, miss." He had reached out to restrain me and I began to beat him off in panic. I didn't have a prayer. He lifted me up, literally, and set me down in my office.

"I'm Detective Sergeant Richard Cross," he told me. "You're not meant to be here. We've got to get you out of the house."

"Of course I'm meant to be here. I'm Nathalie Bartholomew. I live here. It's my house. I need to get my things."

"No you do not," he insisted. "You need to leave everything here and come with me. Now."

"But the house isn't on fire. It's the summerhouse. Look."

"I know that, miss." I could tell he was trying very hard to be patient with me. "But we have to get you out of the house before you destroy any evidence."

"Evidence? You make it sound like a crime's been committed."

He didn't say anything, just took my arm and propelled me toward the stairs. He was being gentle, he wasn't hurting me in any way but he was exerting just enough pressure to make me realize I didn't have much choice. I was leaving the house whether I wanted to or not.

As I went downstairs, through the windows on the landing I could see the police were beginning to section off the back of the house with yellow tape.

"But what about Angel?" I turned around on the stairs to face him above me. "Was she in the summerhouse? Did she get out in time?"

I sensed him pause behind me for a second. "She?" Then he made a swiveling motion with his finger, instructing me to turn around and carry on down the stairs.

"Yes. Angel. My tenant. She lives in the summerhouse. I mean she did."

"No," he said.

"You mean no, she wasn't in the summerhouse or no, she didn't get out in time?" I was frantic to know.

But he didn't answer, just kept propelling me down the stairs. As I came into the hall I saw two police officers go into the kitchen carrying equipment of some kind. Outside the pavement had been cordoned off with more yellow tape and the crowds had been moved back up toward Portobello Road.

"This way, miss." Sergeant Cross marched me across the street to a police car.

"Hey, that's her. She owes me a fiver." I saw the cab driver I had abandoned on arrival.

"Where are my bags?" I yelled at him. "What have you done with my bags."

"Who's this?" A tall man standing beside the cab driver asked Sergeant Cross. His lean frame beside the sergeant's huge bulk put me in mind of Laurel and Hardy. "Hey! Where are you going?" He suddenly darted across the road and waylaid the men with the yellow tape coming out of the alley. "I want that potting shed over in the corner sealed off as well as the summerhouse and the garden. And then you'll have to do the ambulance. But most important, I want you to seal off this alleyway and any access routes you can find although if these firefighters keep on trampling over all the evidence, we might as well not bother. So." He came back across the road, still yelling. His voice was surprisingly powerful for such a slender-looking man. "You live here?" He glared at me.

"She got in the house before I could stop her, sir. Says it's her house."

"How far'd she get?"

"Right up to the top, sir."

"Fanbloodytastic!" The man scowled.

"Get her taken down to the station. Get her clothes off her first. I'm going in the ambulance."

"Is he dead, sir?"

The man threw up his hands in exasperation. "No, Richie, he's not dead. That's why we're taking him to hospital."

I saw the ambulance then, parked in front of the alley. The back doors were being closed. There was someone inside. *He's* not dead. It wasn't Angel.

"Where's Angel?" I shouted at Sergeant Cross. "You never told me you'd found her."

"Oh great, Richie. You've been chatting away to her, have you? Why don't you go on the six o'clock news, tell the whole bloody world while you're at it?"

"Sorry, sir. We'll need you to give us your clothes."

"No," I said firmly. "I want to know what's going on. I want to know how the fire started and who you've got in that ambulance."

The tall man's face softened for an instant. "Look," he said wearily. "*We'd* like to know who we've got in the ambulance and the sooner we can get him to hospital, the sooner we'll find out. I'm Detective Inspector Max Austin and this is Detective

Sergeant Cross. You're going to be taken down the police station where we'd like you to answer some questions. Thank you very much."

"But why?" I shouted but he'd already crossed the road to the waiting ambulance. As I got into the police car I heard the wailing siren start up and saw the red light flashing through the rear window.

Sergeant Cross didn't accompany me to the station and the driver just smiled reassuringly at me in the rearview mirror whenever I asked him a question. On arrival I was shown into a waiting area. I was fingerprinted and I let them take a DNA sample and then I was joined by two detective constables and their first request had me staring at them in total astonishment.

"We'll need your clothes, so if you'd just like to go in there and remove them for us, you can put this on instead." They handed me what appeared to be a white paper dress as substitute clothing.

At that point I gave up hoping I would find out what was going on. They were being perfectly nice. There was no sense of threat or menace but I couldn't help feeling as if I were about to be tortured. I put on the paper dress and I handed them my own clothes to take away.

And then I gave them my name again and answered their questions as best I could. *Whose house was it? Who lived there? Where were those people now? Where had I been for the last twenty-four hours?* On and on it went and they never indicated whether or not they were happy with what I told them. I didn't complain. I was dog tired and past caring.

I read through my statement and signed it and just as I was about to fall asleep, there was a commotion at the entrance to the station and the tall man who had introduced himself as Detective Inspector Max Austin walked in. The detective constables who had been interviewing me got up and went over to talk to him in his office. I saw him look in my direction several times.

"Can I go home now?" I asked when he finally came into the interview room and I felt an ominous shiver go through me when he shook his head.

He took a seat opposite me and said something quickly into the tape recorder between us. "Now," he said, leaning forward, "as you know there was a fire in the summerhouse in the garden of what you say is your house."

"It's actually my parents' house. They live in France."

"They live in France," he repeated slowly. "You've given us their contact details?" I nodded. "Okay. Why we have you here is because the body of a man was recovered from the fire and that man has subsequently died. Now I'd be grateful if you'd answer some questions for me. You've told my detective constable you were on your way back from France at the time of the fire —"

He didn't spell it out; he didn't have to. I knew as soon as he said that the man had died that he was treating the death as a murder inquiry.

Chapter 10

I was suddenly ravenously hungry. I hadn't eaten the night before. In fact I hadn't eaten since I'd left France.

"I'm starving," I told DI Austin and resisted the urge to tell him he could do with a bit of fattening up himself. He looked positively undernourished. I'd never met a murder detective before but he looked more like a university professor to me, not that I knew many of those. The thing about Max Austin was that he didn't look slick like they do on TV. He was still wearing his raincoat and he had one of those long college scarves wound around his neck. He was kind of droopy. I think it had something to do with his height. He was like a beanpole, all arms and legs and a face looking down from about a foot above me. "And I'd like to call my boyfriend," I added.

But what a face! He was the same physical type as Buzz, liquid brown eyes, floppy dark hair, fine features, sensational bones. But while Buzz was an eagle, fierce and impatient, this guy looked like a soft, approachable rabbit.

"Your boyfriend?" He looked up sharply. "Who's your boyfriend?"

"Bu—" Looking at him had started me thinking about Buzz and when on earth I was going to see him again and how much I'd like him to come here and rescue me.

"Tommy Kennedy. We've just come back from France together."

"Oh yes." He seemed to know about Tommy already. "What were you going to say just now?"

"I was going to say 'But when can I go home?' " It was a white lie. I did want to know when I could go home.

"When my men have finished in the house."

"But what are they doing? How long will it take?"

He ignored the first question. "Could be up to three days."

"You're joking?" He shook his head. "You mean I can't go home for three days? What am I supposed to do?"

"I said *up* to three days. It'll probably be much sooner than that but we can't let you back into the house because you might disturb the evidence. Maybe Mr. Kennedy can help? Now can we go over your statement, please. You left your parents' house in France when?"

He took me back over every step of my journey from France, what time had the plane arrived? How long had we had to wait for a train to Paddington? Had there been a queue for a taxi? What time had the taxi arrived at the house? Could I give him my parents' address and telephone number?

"Why don't you ask the taxi driver? He'll confirm what time he picked me up at Paddington. He'll tell you he brought me straight to the house."

"I have," he said.

"Well, why don't you check with Air France? They'll confirm I was on the flight and what time it arrived and everything." But I knew as I made the suggestion what his answer would be.

"I will," he said with a hint of a smile. He looked as if he hadn't slept for days. I wondered if he had a wife or a girlfriend and what they thought about him being gone half the night, chasing murderers. And then I was reminded that there might have been a murder at the bottom of my garden and I started shaking. He noticed and began to look worried so I sat up straight, stamped my feet on the ground to still them and told him:

"Well, your Sergeant Cross can take over from there. He can tell you what time he found me at the top of the house. The fire was well under way by then, wasn't it? And they'd found the body — who is it? Tell me, who it is, who did they find? Who died in my summerhouse?"

"A Mr. Frederick Fox." He leaned back and studied me, waiting for my reaction. The name meant nothing to me and the expression on my face relayed that to him.

"You didn't know him?"

I shook my head impatiently. *No!*

"Miss O'Leary says you did."

"Miss O'Leary? Oh my God, Angel! Where is Angel? Is she okay?"

"So you know Miss O'Leary?"

"Of course I know her. Angel O'Leary. She's my tenant. She lives in the summerhouse or rather she did before —"

He didn't say anything, just looked at me, waiting for me to go on. I stared back at him and then the penny suddenly dropped. I felt a fierce jolt of pain in my head from the sudden tensing of the muscles in the back of my neck. Frederick Fox. Angel. It was Fred. Dear sweet Fred of the pimples and the bobbing Adam's apple. Fred was dead. Dead Fred. The rhyming words reverberated around my brain, colliding with each other each time I tried to speak. Finally, I nodded stupidly.

"I knew him. He was Angel's boyfriend."

"Was he?"

"Yes," I said, "you can ask her about him."

"We have. She said he used to be her boyfriend but they broke up before Christmas."

"You've spoken to Angel already? Where is she? She never told me she'd finished with Fred."

Again he didn't answer my question.

"So what was he doing at the summerhouse if he wasn't her boyfriend anymore? You have to tell me, is Angel okay?"

He relented for a second. "Miss O'Leary's fine. She's here. We found a key on the body. It didn't melt in the fire. She told us who had a key to the summerhouse far as she knew. Frederick Fox was the only person to have one besides her. And yourself." He added softly, "It was a male body —"

And Angel and I were females.

"Well, you'll find mine in the kitchen, hanging up on a rack just inside the door."

"I'm sure we will," he said. "Now you've given us a list of all the people who have been to the house recently. Mr. Kennedy, eh, Tommy. Miss O'Leary. Your parents and you've given us a list of the people who service the house — the plumber, electrician. So who else? What about your friends? People coming to the house for a meeting, that sort of thing?"

"I can't be expected to remember every single person who ever came to my house. I've given you the main people. I'm not a very gregarious animal, inspector. I'm a writer. I spend a lot of time on my own. But you can check my diary if you must. It's in my office at the top of the house. No, it's not, it'll be in my bag, the one I left with the taxi driver."

"We've got that. Miss O'Leary mentioned a woman who looks after your garden. Said she turns up and starts planting things in the flowerbeds without warning. Does she go in the house at all?"

"Felicity Wood. She's a friend of my mother's, runs a garden club somewhere near here. My mother doesn't trust me to take care of the garden properly so she has Felicity pop over now and then and sort things out. No, she doesn't come in the house, at least not unless we invite her in for a drink and that hasn't happened for at least a year." Of course there was one person I hadn't mentioned but from the sound of things, Angel hadn't said anything about him either. If she had surely Max Austin would have nudged me. *Miss O'Leary mentioned a Buzz someone.* Why had Angel kept quiet about him?

Of course I would tell him about Buzz eventually. I had to. But I wasn't going to say anything until I had spoken to him first. I couldn't put him in such a compromising position without giving him some kind of warning.

"What time was Miss O'Leary expecting you back last night?"

"I have no idea if she was expecting me back at all. I don't inform her of my comings and goings. We live separate lives."

"She said she was at a New Year's Eve party and spent the night with a friend."

"Well then I expect she was."

"And you were on good terms with Miss O'Leary? No friction between you of any kind?"

"None whatsoever that I'm aware of."

"What about her and Frederick Fox? Do you know why they broke up before Christmas?"

"No, I don't. Now you've got to tell me,

why are you questioning me like this? I feel like a suspect but a suspect for what? What happened to Fred? Do you think someone started that fire deliberately?"

"I can't discuss any of that with you at the moment." He sounded quite apologetic for a change. "I understand it must be frustrating for you and we'll let you know as soon as we can."

"But why can't I get back into my house?"

He hesitated for a second as if trying to decide how much to tell me.

"*If* the fire was started deliberately — and I'm only saying if at the moment — then whoever started it might have had access to the garden through the house. We need to forensicate your house."

"But how did they get into the house? There was no sign of forced entry. They would have needed a key."

"Yes," he said, looking straight at me. "Who has a key to your house? Besides yourself, of course."

I was getting fed up with this. It always seemed to come back to me. And every time I supplied him with a bit of information it seemed to provoke more and more questions. Why did I have the distinct impression he was trying to trip me up?

Another hour went by before he finally stood up and left the room followed by Sergeant Cross who had been sitting behind me for the whole interview. I was impressed at how such a large man could make himself so unobtrusive. He hadn't said a word the whole time Max Austin had been talking.

"Hey, what about me?" I called after them. "Can I go home now?"

Sergeant Cross popped his head back around the door.

"Not just yet, I'm afraid. Few more things to clear up. I'll be coming back with PCW Mary Mehta. Family Liaison Officer."

"What's that?" I wasn't a family.

"She'll be the person you'll be in touch with on a regular basis. Family Liaison Officers keep in close contact with the victims."

"You see me as a victim?" I was astonished.

"Leave it out, Richie." I heard Max Austin's voice. "Don't make her feel even worse than she has to."

Richie Cross came back with a tiny creature with flickering doe eyes, a small straight nose, and dainty chin. She had one of those red dots in the middle of her forehead. I always wanted to lick my finger and wipe them away. I wondered if she'd been born here like my school friend Ayeesha whose grandparents had insisted she have Hindi lessons so she could converse with the husband they'd found for her in Delhi.

"Miss Bartholomew? What a nasty thing to happen. Sorry we have to keep you here like this. I hear you've been very cooperative. You must be exhausted. We'll get you some refreshments. How about an early breakfast?"

"They say I can't go home. I need to call my boyfriend, see if I can go there."

"Oh, it's okay. He's been in touch. We've got your mobile and he phoned that. He's expecting you. Richie, breakfast, now, tea, eggs, bacon, the works. Get a move on. What are you? Paralyzed?"

Poor Sergeant Cross. Between Little Miss Dynamite here and Max Austin, I didn't imagine he got much peace.

She was good, Mary Mehta, I'll give her that. She neatly evaded all my questions but she bombarded me with queries of her own, all of them sneaked in under the guise of chatty girl talk. How long had I known Tommy? Was it a nice place to live, Blenheim Crescent? Bit pricey, no? Oh, it was my parents' house, was it? What did I do for a living? Oh really and whose book was I ghosting at the moment? Not *that* Selma Walker? The one in *Fraternity*? Not that she ever got much chance to watch it. How long had I lived in Blenheim Crescent? Did I know my neighbors? How long had I known Angel? Was she a good tenant? Did she have many boyfriends? Was Fred the jealous type? Did I think he'd come round to cause mischief? Well, they do sometimes, if they've been dumped, don't they? With each question she proffered an opinion of her own so it looked as if she was just making conversation. Very clever — but she didn't fool me for a second.

And then Max Austin suddenly came in and muttered something to her.

"I'd be grateful if you'd telephone PC Mehta every day, especially if you remember something you think might be of use to me. She'll know where to get hold of me. We've got a car to take you to Mr. Kennedy's. We'll let you know when you can get back into your house in a day or two. Thank you for your help."

That was it. No promises to get in touch and keep me posted as to how the investigation was progressing. *I've finished with you so now you can go off and play with*

PC Mehta like a good little girl.

"Come on, give us a smile. You're in the clear. He spoke to your parents, you've been alibi'd out. You can go now." She took my arm and helped me get to my feet. I was so tired, I could barely stand.

"But why did he need to get me here in the first place? He's a murder detective, right? What was he doing at a fire?"

"Well, I suppose I can tell you" — she looked at me doubtfully — "there was another fire in your area —"

"Astrid McKenzie!" I pounced.

Mary Mehta nodded. "That fire was started deliberately. They're treating it as a murder investigation so when there's another fire so close to her house, they think it's too much of a coincidence. It might turn into a murder investigation. We'll know as soon as we get the fire report but until it's ruled otherwise, your house, your garden, your summerhouse, your potting shed, your alley — they're all crime scenes and Inspector Austin is in charge."

"So why do you think Astrid was murdered? What's the connection with Fred?"

"Can't give you an answer there, I'm afraid. Now, do you want to leave us or shall we have the pleasure of your company for a bit longer?"

I followed Mary Mehta through the hubbub of the station and as we were going out the door to Ladbroke Grove I bumped straight into the last person I'd expected to see there.

Cath was coming in and she was in a hurry, running so fast, she slammed right into me.

"I'm *really* sorry," she began, barely pausing to look at me and then she saw who it was. It took me a second to realize she was going to keep on moving, that she didn't plan to stop and say hello. I grabbed her by the arm and wouldn't let go.

"Cath, it's me, Lee. Cath, how *are* you? You know, I called and called and you never called back but it doesn't matter. I always thought we'd run into each other. I'm amazed it's taken this long. What are you doing here?"

She looked at me and hesitated for a second. I was still holding her arm and I tried to draw her in and give her a big hug but she wriggled away and said sharply, "I'm sorry. I can't stop. There's someone I have to see in here. Some other time, okay? 'Bye."

Her dismissal of me was so abrupt I felt tears coming because when I'd seen her on the steps my first thought had been that she'd somehow heard what had happened to me, and had come to offer her support. She had looked beautiful, glowing almost. Pale white skin, long red hair falling down her back, wild and unkempt and the same old Oxfam raincoat with the belt tied around her waist in a knot instead of buckled. It would have been a perfect re-union — there was no one I would have been happier to see. But clearly I was the last person she was expecting to see.

Mary Mehta had seen it all.

"She seemed like she was in a hurry," she remarked. "I expect she'll have more time tonight if you give her a call."

"I don't have her number," I said and this was the truth. I'd tried to call her about six months ago only to find she was no longer living at the same address. "Do you know what she's doing here?"

"Couldn't tell you. I've seen her around a couple of times. Red hair like that, you can't miss it. Never really noticed who she's come to see. Come on now, love. We've got to get you across London."

Angel was waiting for me in the back of the police car. She looked hideous. Her eyes were swollen and red from crying and her makeup had run, revealing badly pock-marked skin I'd never noticed before. She clung to me as soon as I got in the car and I looked down on a dark patch where her roots were growing out. She had black hair and blemished skin. What else was I going to discover about her that I hadn't already known?

"It was my fault," she kept saying. "It was all my fault."

I told her no it wasn't and she mustn't think like that and she should get some rest.

"Where are you going to go?" I asked her. "I mean right now. Of course once I'm allowed back into the house, you can have a room there till you find somewhere else to live."

"Can I really?" She looked so pathetically grateful, I felt embarrassed. It was the least I could do. "I'm going back to my mum's. I wanted to go to Scott's but she's freaked out and says she wants me near her."

"Scott's?"

"Yeah, well he's who came after Fred. You know?" She looked decidedly awkward.

We delivered her into her mother's arms and I promised to call her as soon as I knew we would be allowed back in the house. Then, on the long drive across London to Tommy's, I sank down into the backseat of the police car and began to take stock.

Had someone started the fire deliberately? And if so had they just wanted to burn down the summerhouse or had they known there would be someone in it? Because if it was the latter then the chances were that it was Angel they were after. Fred's visit had to have been unexpected. No one could have counted on him being there. But why would anyone want to set fire to Angel?

Tommy was sitting in a heap in front of the TV when I let myself in. He'd left his key in the door. The driver of the police car shook his head in wonder at such stupidity.

"Happy New Year," said Tommy. "We're a fine pair, we are. Is the summerhouse totally destroyed?"

"Totally," I said. "Why are we a fine pair? What's your problem? Did you get legless at Shagger's and now you can't understand why there are little green monsters throwing darts inside your head?" I was annoyed with him for not making more of an effort to console me.

"I didn't go to Shagger's," he said, not looking at me.

"Why ever not?"

"Mum's been taken to hospital. That's why I called you on your mobile. I nearly had a fit when the police answered and said they had you at the station. She's at the Royal Marsden on the Fulham Road. I'm due there in about an hour. Maybe you could pop along later in the day?"

"What's the matter with her?"

"She has cancer of the pancreas. They found a tumor. It wasn't near the intestines or the bile ducts so they were able to operate successfully. Last night."

He looked shellshocked. "She must have known," he said almost to himself. "She never told me."

"So what do they do now? Will she be okay?"

"I don't know what they're going to do. Look, I was just about to get dressed and go over to see her. Make yourself at home. Have a kip or something. You're probably exhausted."

"Call me when you've seen her. I need to know Noreen's going to be okay. I need to know you're okay. Tommy, will you call later? Or just come straight back?"

I don't think he really heard me. He just said, "Talk to you later," and walked out the door.

After about an hour — which was as

much as I could stand of the chaos of Tommy's flat — I followed him. I didn't really know where I was going except that I felt the need to get back to West London. I felt totally cut off in the East End. I had established that the next visiting hours at the Royal Marsden weren't until two o'clock in the afternoon so I had an hour to kill.

I found myself getting off the tube at Notting Hill and walking up Portobello Road. I planned to wander along Ladbroke Grove and stand at the corner of Blenheim Crescent, look down it, see how they were getting on. I had toyed with the idea of banging on my neighbor Mrs. O'Malley's door and asking if I could go upstairs to her flat on the top floor so I could watch whatever was going on in my garden from there. But Mrs. O'Malley was a nosy old gossip and she wouldn't stop interrogating me as to what was happening. She'd be worse than Max Austin and she'd probably call him up and tell him I'd been there. Something told me that would get me into trouble.

So it was probably just as well that I never got as far as the O'Malleys'. As I was going round the corner into Blenheim Crescent, I bumped straight into the top of someone's head. At least that was all I could see until she stepped away from me.

"Happy New Year, Bianca," I said as cheerfully as I could, smiling down at her. I hadn't registered until now quite how short she was.

She looked up at me blankly. She was wearing a red duffel coat. Her face was framed by black curls inside the hood of the duffel, and with her pointed nose and eyes like black beads she reminded me of a malevolent Mrs. Tiggywinkle, the hedgehog in one of my childhood Beatrix Potter books, wiggling her snout suspiciously at me.

"I'm working with Selma Walker," I reminded her. "You saw me at her house. So why are you here, Bianca, on New Year's Day?"

"Miss Selma ask I clean house for Mr. Buzz. She make mess."

"Selma? Selma's back?"

"No. Tomorrow. Next week. Soon. Young lady make mess. I clean before Miss Selma come home."

What young lady? "How's Mr. Buzz?"

"He fine. Why you ask?"

Why indeed? I wouldn't say another word about him. Didn't want Bianca on my case any more than was necessary.

"So anyway, Bianca, I'll be seeing —"

But she'd gone, beetling away to Elgin Crescent to pounce on an unsuspecting Buzz. It was lucky I'd run into her because what I'd really come here for was to go and see Buzz and warn him that I'd have to tell Max Austin that he'd been to my house, that he'd been in my bedroom, in my bed.

And that he could never expect to be there again.

But now, with Bianca glowering about the place, I couldn't go near him.

"They've put me with the wrinklies," Tommy's mother hissed at me when I finally arrived at the hospital and bent to kiss her hello.

"They do that on purpose, Noreen," I told her. "They know a young thing like you'll cheer them up."

Looking around, I could see that at seventy-four, Noreen Kennedy was by no means the most youthful patient in the ward but it wouldn't hurt to let her think she was.

"There's an empty bed over there." She pointed across the ward. "Poor old thing died in the night. They all came running and pulled the curtains around the bed. Lot of whispering, then it went quiet. They wheeled her away on a gurney and never brought her back. Shame!"

"I've brought you freesias." I thrust them at her. "Where will I find a vase?"

"Oh lovely. Why don't you pinch that vase from her in the next bed? Her flowers have been dead for two days and from the look of her, she'll join them soon most likely. Just change the water in the sink in the lav. You know, it's a crime if they leave that bed empty for long what with all the overcrowding in the NHS hospitals. I half expected to be given a bed in a corridor. Did you read that story about the hospital where the patients were put in a laundry room? The government give us all this talk about tax hikes to increase funding for the NHS but the trouble is, they'll get their sums wrong like they always do and they still won't have enough at the end of the day. I remember when Nye Bevan reckoned a hundred and seventy-six million pounds was going to be enough for a couple of years in 1949. Turned out we needed four hundred and thirty-seven million pounds for just one year. Fat chance they'll find the right amount today. I tell you, Lee, I —"

I listened with half an ear. Noreen could talk the hind leg off a donkey and it didn't look like a little thing like cancer would stop her. She had voted Labour her entire life but she made no secret of the fact that she had no faith in Tony Blair. "His eyes are too close together," she'd complained when I'd asked her what was wrong with him. "You can tell a lot about a person from their eyes."

"Noreen," I said firmly, "you're very sick and I have to tell you, I'm pretty angry with you for keeping us in the dark about your cancer."

"I thought about it," she admitted. She slumped against the pillows for a second, fiddling anxiously with her bed jacket. I hated to see her looking so frail. She was a tiny woman with a shock of curly white hair cropped short. Her features were small and even and she must have been incredibly pretty as a young woman. Her once porcelain skin was now dry and flaky with age and marked with a mass of fine lines around the mouth, but her dark blue eyes, that Tommy had inherited, were as lively as ever. She was looking at me intently. "It's funny, Lee. You were one of the first people I wanted to tell but then I thought to myself, what right do I have to burden her with my troubles? It's not as if she and Tommy are even engaged."

"Don't start, Noreen," I warned her.

She leaned forward and lowered her voice.

"I didn't come in here yesterday like I told Tommy. I've been in over Christmas. I didn't tell him because I knew he'd cancel his trip to France and I know how much he was looking forward to it. He had the time of his life by the sound of it."

"While you had to spend Christmas in hospital and we never knew." I felt so awful for her I burst into audible sobbing.

"You're not much good at this hospital visiting, are you?" Noreen said gently. "What's up, love? You had a gloomy look on your face when you arrived even before I'd told you my news. Tell me, what's bothering you? Is it your parents' breaking up? Tommy told me all about it. I'm so sorry."

"There's that and then I came home and it all started to go from bad to worse."

She listened to my story about the fire, patting my hand every now and then and reaching out her arms toward me when I told her about Fred.

"At least I've had most of my life," she said. "I'm seventy-four. My, my, I'm lying here wondering if I'm close to dying but you seem to be having a worse time of it being alive. Go on, give us a smile. That was meant to be a joke."

"I just wish I could go home. One of the reasons I couldn't live with your precious son, Noreen, is that he turns rooms into pigsties within seconds. Why won't they let me into my house? What do they mean, *forensicate* it?"

"They'll be after DNA," said Noreen cheerfully. "They'll be wanting to know everything there is to know about anyone who's been in that house."

"But they're acting like I'm a suspect."

"Well, you are in their eyes. They can't discount anyone till they can prove that they weren't there, that they have an alibi. I mean, you could have caught an earlier plane back from France, rushed home and set fire to the summerhouse then gone back to Paddington and hailed a cab."

I looked at her in total amazement. "But Tommy would have told them I didn't do any such thing."

"Yes, but he's not a reliable witness. He loves you. He'd cover up for you, pretend you traveled back from France with him. And who's to say you didn't hire someone to carry out the murder for you? Your detective will have to take all that into consideration. I expect you're wondering how an old lady like me knows all this stuff.

Tommy's father's best friend Pete was a detective like your Max Austin. He once told me that at the beginning of each case he suspected absolutely everyone until he had very good reason not to."

"He's not *my* Max Austin," I said rather crossly.

"Pete once took me through every stage of a case he was working on. He probably shouldn't have, I don't think they're meant to talk about their work but they do. I think he was sweet on me, to tell you the truth, and it was a sure way of getting my attention. Max Austin is going to be looking to find out absolutely everything about anyone who was in your house or your garden or anywhere near it at the time of the crime. They'll all be interviewed, you'll see. There'll be hundreds of witnesses who'll come forward with all sorts of stories."

"Do you suppose he's working on the Astrid McKenzie case too?"

"Oh no, he'll only have one case at a time but I expect he'll have got all the details from HOMES —"

"What?"

"Home Office Murder Enquiry System," said Noreen. By now she was quite puffed up and excited at being able to expound her knowledge. "He'll have got on the computer and cross-referenced all the details. Of course, it might all be different now. Everything's changing so much these days —"

I made an apologetic *must be going* signal, kissed her on the top of the head, and made my getaway. Once Noreen got started on the state of Tony Blair's police force, there'd be no stopping her. *I'll be back soon,* I mouthed, running down the ward, feeling rather guilty that I'd revved her up so much when she was supposed to be resting after her surgery.

Without the aid of a police car racing through the traffic it took me hours to get back to Tommy's and he wasn't even there to greet me with a comforting bowl of soup. Feeling disgustingly sorry for myself, I staggered upstairs in search of some painkillers for my aching head. The mist pot cit for cystitis was no longer in the medicine cabinet. Maybe I had imagined it. I crawled into bed at eight o'clock and began to cry for Noreen and, surprisingly, since I'd barely known him, for poor Fred. For some reason I felt an unmitigated sadness at the thought of his death.

I knew it had to happen sooner or later but I was so tired, I really did think I would drift easily into a long and rewarding sleep. I had closed my eyes and I was just about to nod off when all the trauma of the last twenty-four hours began to rise to the surface in my consciousness. I wasn't fully awake but on the other hand I knew I wouldn't fall asleep until I had dragged myself through every grisly detail of the fire. I wasn't there so there was no way of knowing if it was accurate or not, but somehow my imagination took hold and began to conjure up what might have happened.

I saw Fred turning out of Blenheim Crescent into the alleyway where he paused to fumble in his pockets for cigarettes. I watched him stick a fag in his mouth, bow his head and strike a match to light it, shielding it from the wind in hands cupped inside his anorak. Then he chucked the match away into a bush.

I paused in my fantasy. Did the fire start then and engulf him? No, he wasn't in the summerhouse yet and that was where they found his body.

The curtains were drawn when he reached the summerhouse. He knocked on the door and when there was no answer, he let himself in with his key. He lay down on the futon to wait for her. He was tired, hungover maybe. He fell asleep.

Then came the bit I wasn't sure about. Either he'd lit another cigarette and left it burning or someone opened the door and threw in a burning torch of some kind.

Fred woke up and leapt to his feet to be confronted by a wall of fire as high as his knees and climbing. In panic he made a fatal mistake. He opened the door and tried to jump over the flames. Air rushed into the room inciting the fire and in an instant his jeans were alight. He grabbed a blanket off the bed, wrapped it around his legs, and subdued the flames but now he was trapped. To go forward and escape he would have to literally wade through fire. And behind him was the brick wall that formed the rear of the summerhouse. The blanket wrapped around his legs caught fire. The rug beneath his feet was blazing. He couldn't see outside through the smoke. He couldn't breathe. He couldn't call for help.

He couldn't survive.

It was the worst nightmare I'd ever had and I wasn't even asleep.

Chapter 11

They let me go back home after two days. Just as well. I couldn't settle down in Tommy's house. I spent the first day huddled under the bedclothes after my visit to Noreen. I think I was experiencing some kind of delayed aftershock. On the morning of the day after they'd sent me to Tommy's, I had to go back and answer more questions, which as far as I could make out were identical to those I'd answered before. *Who had access to the house? Who had keys? Had I been expecting anyone to go there? Who would have been likely to go into which room? Was there anyone who was likely to be there at the time the fire started?* I found myself getting a little paranoid. What if there was someone to whom I'd given a key and I'd forgotten?

If they'd actually come right out and asked me if I'd entertained any gentlemen callers other than Tommy in my bedroom, I'd have told them of course. But they didn't. I'd tried to call Buzz to tell him what had happened. I needed to tell him I was going to have to come clean about him being in my bedroom, so he'd be prepared when the police questioned him but each time I had got the answering machine and the message *We're not home right now.* If I left a message, Selma would hear it.

Tommy had accompanied me because of course they wanted to talk to him too. I'd told him about running into Cath and asked him what he made of her unwillingness to talk to me.

"It's sad," he said after a moment when I sensed he was as shaken as I had been. "You two should get back together. I feel bad about the whole thing."

"*You* feel bad."

"Well, it's because of how she says she felt about me —" He didn't seem to know what to say next.

"Have you seen her at all?" Maybe he'd run into her and hadn't wanted to tell me.

"Why would I do that?" he said and that was it. I hated it when Tommy answered my questions with one of his own.

"So what did they ask you?" I demanded to know on the journey back to his house.

"What did they ask *you?*"

"I asked first."

"Oh, usual stuff," he said maddeningly.

"What usual stuff? Do the police haul you in for questioning a lot, Tommy?"

"No, of course not," he admitted. "I meant they just asked what you'd expect. Did I know Fred? How long had I known you? How much time did I spend there? Did I know Angel? What did I think of her? What did I know about the relationship between you and Angel? Did you get along well? When exactly had we come back from France? Why wasn't I with you when you arrived home? Where did I go once we split up?"

Of course I wanted to know what answers he'd given them but he closed his mouth very tightly for several seconds in an irritating way he has and finally said: "Give me a break, Lee. What do you think I told them? You can work it out for yourself. I'm not going through it all again. You're worse than they are." And I knew I wouldn't get any more out of him. He can behave like a stubborn elephant when he feels like it.

But then he added, "Thanks for going to see Mum," in such a forlorn voice that I forgave him instantly.

"What do you think is going to happen with her?" I asked him.

"We'll just have to wait and see," he said. "She's a tiny little bird but she's surprisingly strong. She might well pull through but whatever happens, it's going to take a lot out of her. She really ought not to go on living on her own. She won't like it. She's as independent as you are in many ways. I'll have to think what to do."

"You know I'm here if there's anything I can do to help," I said and meant it. I was genuinely fond of Noreen and funnily enough it hadn't dawned on me that we had our love of independence in common until Tommy had mentioned it.

When we got back to Tommy's, I spent the rest of the day clearing up his mess. Clearing up, not cleaning. I am hopeless at cleaning and my way of clearing up was to move things from one part of the room to another. But it kept me busy and when Tommy came home he seemed to appreciate my efforts. We were on our best behavior with each other, trying to be supportive of our respective dramas, but I knew I wouldn't be able to take much more of him asking me *You all right? You're sure?* every five minutes.

They sent a police car to pick me up and I realized that was one thing I could get used to very easily: being driven about the place and never having to do battle with London Underground. As soon as I was back in the house I rushed to open all the windows. The lingering stench of the fire was still in the air and somehow it had permeated throughout the house. Then I slammed shut all the ones at the back that gave onto the garden because having them open only made it worse. The summerhouse was a good hundred feet away from the main house but it was still going to take me quite a while to get used to living with the smell of burned toast. I went around to Graham and Green and bought up their entire stock of scented candles and as I began lighting them all around the house, it occurred to me that at the rate I was going, I'd probably start another fire.

To begin with it seemed I had found the house more or less as I had left it, no mess except a film of silvery ash where they'd dusted for fingerprints. But then I noticed they'd taken the tape out of the answering machine and I began to panic. I am completely hopeless at erasing messages once I've listened to them. I am always convinced I will have written a number down wrong and will need to play the message again. But the most worrying thing was that I had no idea who had called me while I had been away.

Had Buzz called? Had he said his name?

But then I calmed down and reminded myself, not for the first time, that there was a perfectly legitimate reason for him to call. I was ghosting Selma's book and he was her manager. Presumably he wouldn't be so dumb as to leave a message saying something like *Did you find the briefs I left on your bed?*

The first thing I did was to call PC Mary Mehta and give her the third degree.

"So what's happened? Did they find anything in my house? Was it arson? Who killed Fred?" I was literally pummeling her with questions down the line but I couldn't stop. "When am I going to get my answering machine tape back? Who called me?"

"Not pumping me for information by any chance?" PC Mehta laughed. "It's a waste of time. We'll be letting you know as soon as we've got something to tell you. Trust me on that one."

I hated it when people said that. It immediately made me *dis*trust them.

"But can't you even tell me who called?"

"There were a few hang-ups, I'm afraid." *Buzz?* "And someone called Genevieve wanted you to ring her when you got back."

"That's my agent," I said quickly. "I'm a writer."

"Yes, we know that," she said. "You'll keep in touch, won't you?"

Of course I'd keep in touch. It was clearly the only way I was going to find out what was going on.

While I had been talking to her, I had registered the sound of a cab stopping outside, someone running up the front steps and the letterbox slamming shut as something was pushed through it. I went into the hall to retrieve whatever it was.

It was a tiny Jiffy bag about eight by six inches. Inside was a tape and a note from Selma.

> I've been trying to deliver this ever since I came back but your house has been closed off as a crime scene! Today is the first day I've been able to get near your front door. What's going on? Hope you had a good Christmas. Selma.

I propped the tape up against the marmalade on the kitchen table and called Genevieve who said *What about lunch?*

And that just this once she was prepared to cross town and come over my way. She said she wanted fish so I walked down Westbourne Grove to meet her at Livebait.

"You look terrible, dear. Completely washed out. What's the matter? I've already ordered by the way. The seafood platter, you can share it if you want."

I filled her in on what had been going on in my life in the relatively short period of time since I had last spoken to her. She emitted little squeaks of distress, the soft rolls of fat below her chin seeming to ripple in shock at each new detail.

"This is dreadful, Lee. Dreadful. Dreadful." She repeated the word several times. I sensed that she was totally taken aback. Of course she'd never had to deal with anything troubling in my personal life. We'd always kept it professional. Maybe I shouldn't have dumped my problems on her.

She popped a prawn into her mouth without bothering to peel it first and I heard a crunch. She licked her fingers daintily. "I'm sorry, Lee. I just don't know what to say."

"Don't worry about it," I said a lot more cheerfully than I felt. "So anyway, why did you call me? You said you wanted to talk."

Genevieve looked relieved. "I wanted to discuss what kind of book you're going to write. Selma's got a following here but she's an American and this is her first British TV show and we don't yet know how juicy the material will be. The offer's still on the table, of course, but now they're demanding to know the contents. Whatever her story throws up, at the moment, if we look at her audience, we're talking pretty downmarket. A juicy bit of gossip would be good but keep it at street level. We don't want her going all high and mighty, 'I'm a serious actress,' on us, do we now? I watched the Christmas omnibus episode and Selma Walker's character now has a stalker. Well, that's the sort of thing we want in the book."

"I'll see what I can do," I said dryly. "I'll phone rent-a-stalker. By the way, she's given me the first tape so when I've listened to it I'll have a better idea of what's going to go into the book."

"I found out something else about Buzz, by the way. Besides the fact that he's her husband as well as her manager."

"Really?" Act cool, I told myself, don't be too eager to hear what she has to say.

"Guess whose boyfriend he was a while back?"

"Genevieve, I have no idea. Tell me." I didn't like the sound of this.

"Go on. Guess."

I held my palms up in a gesture of defeat. "Don't know. Give in."

"Astrid McKenzie."

"You're kidding!"

"Not at all. Don't you remember, I told you I saw her at the Ivy the night she died and she acted so strange around him."

"I don't remember you saying they talked."

"They didn't. In fact he acted like he didn't register her at all. And she ran away the minute she saw him. I heard it ended pretty badly between them."

I flashed back to the first time I'd met him. Why had he acted as if he didn't know Astrid?

"So how did you find out about them? How long ago was it?"

"Several years, I think. It's not a secret. Once one person told me I discovered loads of people knew. It just wasn't that interesting until someone made the connection after the fire. It'll be in the papers pretty soon, I bet. Now tell me, dear, are you going to be all right after *your* fire? You were insured, weren't you?"

Was I? Or rather were my parents? Of

course they had insurance but did it stretch as far as the summerhouse? I was so ignorant about stuff like that. And what about poor Angel? Would her belongings be covered? Probably not.

Genevieve didn't say anything about Fred. There was a very simple reason for this. I hadn't told her a body had been found. I don't quite know why but I didn't want her to know about this until she absolutely had to. There'd been a tiny piece buried in the *Standard* about a Frederick Fox dying in a fire in Notting Hill but if Genevieve had read it, she would have assumed it was an accident. And because I wasn't a celebrity like Astrid McKenzie there was no mention of it being anywhere near my house. So Genevieve didn't know that a murder might be involved and probably just as well judging by the way she'd reacted to the news about the fire. Let her make do with speculating about the Astrid McKenzie scenario for the time being.

I walked home after lunch feeling weirdly fatalistic. Of course I could demand to be taken off the Selma Walker project but I knew I wasn't going to do that. At least not yet. I knew that I ought to walk away from it because my entanglement with Buzz spelled nothing but trouble. I was feeling edgy because I still hadn't reached him. Ironically, working for his wife looked like my only way of staying in touch with him.

I made up my mind what I was going to do. I would go home and listen to her tape. If it turned out to be boring predictable stuff, then I would call Genevieve and ask her to extricate me from the assignment. But if the material was intriguing or provocative in any way, then I would hang in there, write a best-selling book, and remain in contact with Buzz.

I made myself a cup of tea and pressed PLAY.

Selma's throaty voice resounded around the kitchen, telling me that all I was getting was an introduction and that she'd have more for me in a day or two. But when she started to speak, I was so completely mesmerized, I stood there with my eyes bulging in amazement until she'd finished. It was all rather flowery and melodramatic in style. It didn't really sound as if she was speaking to me, more like she was addressing what she assumed would be her readership. It was as if she'd actually tried to begin writing the book herself, as if she was reading text she'd prepared in advance.

"I am going to tell you a secret," *she began.* "I am going to tell you something I have been wanting to share with someone for nearly three years. I kept quiet because I was afraid and I was embarrassed. But most of all I didn't think anyone would believe me.

"Recently I have begun to plan my escape from a world of terror. This book is a way of precipitating that escape, of forcing out into the open that which has been hidden.

"You know me as Sally McEwan in *Fraternity* but of course I have a life behind the scenes as all actors do. It is a horrific life and one you will probably not be able to equate with my high profile and the fact that I am a successful woman from a wealthy middle-class background. But it is for that very reason that I have decided I must tell my story, so that people will understand mine is a problem that affects all levels of society.

"Although this is a personal story of fear and tyranny, it begins in paradise. I was born in New York on November 9, 1946, the only child of a prominent surgeon and his wife. My mother did not work. We lived in a ten-room apartment on Park Avenue. We had servants to cater to our every need. We summered in the Hamptons and in Maine and every February we went to the Bahamas.

"When I decided at the age of seventeen that I wanted to become an actress, two phone calls from my father were enough to secure a place for me in a series of elite acting classes. I had dreamed of a glittering career on the Broadway stage but not even my father's money could buy the kind of talent that required, so when I landed a role in *As the World Turns*, my career as a soap opera actress was launched.

"But this book will not be the story of my career. Nor will it deal with my life before I came to England. All you need to know about that time is that for fifteen years I was the mistress of a married man. I was never under any illusion that he would leave his wife. He was a devout and guilt-ridden Catholic and it was never a consideration. But even if he had taken the plunge and abandoned the marriage, I don't think I would have been able to live with his remorse. Still, like many 'other women' passionately in love, I indulged in fantasies from time to time whereby his wife dropped dead and he was free to be with me.

"My dream came true — but not in the way that I imagined. I was destined to play a role in a real life soap opera. When his wife was diagnosed with leukemia and subsequently died a painful, lingering death, he did not turn to me but married her live-in nurse with whom he had been betraying me — and his wife — for several months. In the months that followed I believed I had to be at the lowest ebb in my entire life and I believed that if I could just get myself through it, nothing would ever be as bad again.

"I was wrong.

"To get away from New York and all it reminded me of, I accepted a role in *Fraternity* and fled to London to start a new life.

"Within a year I had met the man who would become my husband. I fell deeply in love for the second time in my life and believed I had found someone who would love and protect me.

"Once again I was wrong.

"Even before we were man and wife, my so-called lover and protector had begun to batter me, to appear out of nowhere, and hurl me against the wall so that my body would be black and blue for weeks at a time.

"And, like so many women who, I hope, will read this book and find comfort in recognition, I stayed with him. I could not leave. Now, finally, I am preparing my getaway and I hope that my message in this book will encourage them to do the same before they too are battered within an inch of their life."

I stood there in silence, too stunned to reach down and press STOP. Either Selma Walker was a complete nutcase with a bizarre imagination or I had had sex with a man who was capable of extreme violence. What chilled me more than anything was that I never for one second doubted the truth of what Selma said about Buzz. I had been infatuated with him but I think I always sensed he was some kind of monster.

I was scared, so scared that without thinking twice about it I took the unprecedented step of dialing Tommy's direct line at the BBC and inviting him to move in with me.

Five minutes later I called him back and added:

"Don't go getting any ideas, Tommy. It's just for a little while — until they find out who's been setting fire to houses in this area."

"Just let me pick up my hose and my helmet and I'll be right over," said Tommy and the relief that flooded through me gave me quite a shock.

Chapter 12

Of course Tommy being Tommy, he didn't get it together to come over right away. Even though he had spent the last four years begging to be allowed to move in with me, now he came up with every kind of excuse to procrastinate. He needed to arrange for his mail to be forwarded, he'd have to stop the milk being delivered, and it would take him a day or two to sort out what to bring with him. He even tried to turn it around and suggest that I move back in with him but I knew I'd rather face my fear of being alone in my own house than spend another minute trying to exist amongst Tommy's chaos.

So I was left to fret. I had to train myself not to go near the back of the house because then I would look out the window and see the devastation left by the fire. I called my mother in France but there was never any reply and that was weird. I left a message and in return I had an e-mail that indicated she knew all about the fire. I realized Max Austin must have filled her in when he contacted her to establish my alibi and I found it strange that she hadn't called me in hysterics. But instead her instructions were brisk and straightforward. Here was the number of the insurance people and would I also get Felicity Wood around to see about repairing the damage to the garden.

There was nothing about Fred so maybe she didn't know there'd been anybody in the summerhouse and I was surprised by how much this upset me. I wanted everyone to mourn Fred. I could not get over what had happened to him. I kept seeing him standing there outside the summerhouse ogling Angel with such adoration it seemed all the more appalling that she appeared to have given him the boot before he died. I kept going back to the nightmare I had had while staying at Tommy's house. I wasn't in the habit of reliving the dreams I had when asleep let alone something like this where I had been conscious, but it had been particularly vivid. I felt absolutely certain that Fred had gone to see Angel to try and persuade her to take him back and it had turned out to be a fatal mission.

The more I thought about it, the more I

convinced myself that this was what had happened and that I should tell someone about it. One of the reasons I was allowing my imagination to run riot like this was because no one was giving me any concrete facts. I needed to share my dream with Inspector Austin and the sooner the better.

Mary Mehta was having none of it.

"Let me get this straight. You want to tell Inspector Austin what you've been dreaming about." She laughed to show she didn't mean to put me down but she wasn't about to let me talk to him.

"I'll tell him you called," was as far as she would go. "Everything else all right? Settling back into the house, are you? We didn't leave too much of a mess, did we?"

Well, that's that, I thought after we'd hung up. I've blown my chances of them keeping me in the loop. Might as well get on with my life and try to put it all behind me.

But Mary Mehta called back within the hour.

"Inspector Austin would like to see you."

"You told him about my dream?"

"I didn't, actually. I thought I'd leave that to you. It must be telepathy. Right after you called he came and said he needed to see you. Will half an hour be okay?"

I was still wearing the T-shirt I'd slept in and my sweatpants were old and faded. *What do you wear for a meeting with a detective?* I wondered as I showered. The Ladbroke Grove police station was just down the road. The sun was shining. It'd be a nice ten-minute walk. I put on a pair of jeans, a gray polo neck sweater that came down below my hips and a cashmere pea jacket I had splurged on in the January sales the year before. By the time I reached the police station my cheeks were glowing from the cold air and I felt invigorated, ready for anything, even running into Cath again — and this time I wouldn't let her go.

"What are you doing *here?*" Mary Mehta squeaked when I asked for her. "They've just left to go to your house. Oh, never mind. I'll call Richie on his mobile and get them back here. Take a seat over there for a few minutes, will you?"

I don't know why I'd automatically assumed I had to go to them rather than the other way around. She hadn't asked me to but then she hadn't said they'd be coming to me either.

I was all revved up by my walk and I couldn't sit still. I got up and wandered over to look at some photographs displayed in cheap frames on someone's desk.

I can never resist being nosy like this. I have a bizarre passion for looking at total strangers and trying to figure out who they might be and what they might be like. Except one of the people in the photo was not a stranger to me. I picked up the frame and stared at Cath's face smiling back at me, freckles all over her nose and cheeks, and her long red hair swung over one shoulder.

Whoever sat at this desk knew Cathleen Clark and rather well by the looks of things. This was clearly the person she had come to see that day I had seen her. I tried to remember if Cath had a brother or a sister who was in the police force and all I could come up with was her younger brother Billy who had gone to live in New York. I looked around. There was a young WPC across the room looking at me suspiciously so I put down the frame and returned to my seat.

Max Austin came in looking like thunder. He nodded at me and jerked his hand in a *follow me* motion and I almost had to run after him as he disappeared into his office. Glancing over my shoulder I saw Sergeant Cross pause at the desk where I'd found the photo of Cath.

"Have a seat," said Max Austin. He took off his jacket and hung it over the back of his chair. "Very good of you to come and see us here."

I didn't say anything. I wasn't sure if he was being sarcastic. He had lowered his lanky frame into the swivel chair, reclined a little and stretched his long legs out under the desk. You could have said he looked relaxed if he hadn't rested his elbows on the armrests and begun tapping his fingertips together so hard they made a noise. The sound made me nervous in the way that I always winced when peopled cracked their knuckles. I thought about asking him to stop, even wondered if he was doing it on purpose. My eyes kept straying to a large pile of dirty laundry spilling out of a plastic bag behind his chair. I noticed the shirt he had on was clean but decidedly crumpled. A page torn from a notebook was pinned to the corkboard behind his head. I screwed up my eyes to read the list scrawled in pencil. *Brillo pads. Milk. Parsley. Stamps. Kitchen roll. Marmalade.* The parsley intrigued me. It was like those lists we were given at school. Which is the odd one out? Parsley implied that he might actually be cooking something.

"Very nice office," I said, parroting the small-talk tone of *Very good of you to come and see us here.*

"It's not my office. Mary's here and Richie has a desk here but my office is over at Paddington Green." He sat up sharply and leaned forward over the desk. "You're a ghostwriter, Mary Mehta tells me."

The switch was so abrupt, I was thrown. I nodded.

"And you're about to start work on Selma Walker's autobiography?"

I nodded again. "I hope so. I haven't actually begun the book yet."

"But you've met her, yes? And so you know her manager, a Mr. Robert Kempinski?"

"*Robert* Kempinski?"

"Maybe you call him Buzz?"

"That's how I was introduced to him." I knew I sounded defensive.

"And you met him at her house?"

"Yes."

"He never came to your house?"

Oh Christ!

"Well, I think he walked back with me one day. She lives just around the corner, you know?"

"Would that be . . ." He consulted a sheet of paper on his desk and came up with the date of my first interview with Buzz. I nodded.

"But he didn't go into your house?"

I shook my head. Well, he hadn't. Not that day.

"That's what your neighbor Mrs. O'Malley said. That he just left you on your doorstep."

I was going to kill that nosy cow. She must have been peeping through her curtains again. How much had she seen? How had she known who it was?

"So he's never been in your house?" Max Austin continued.

I thought quickly. "Well, he might have come in at some point. I am working with him —"

"Which rooms in the house *might* he have come into?" Max Austin's tone was sneering.

"I don't know, I —"

"You don't know? Maybe I can help you out here. We found his prints in the hall, in your kitchen, on the banister going up the stairs, and in your bedroom. Mr. Kempinski was in your bedroom."

I knew the color rising up my face must give me away. "If I tell you about it, does it have to go any further?" I said, not looking at him.

"Does it have to go any further?" Why did he have to keep repeating everything I

said? "Miss Bartholomew, this is a murder investigation. That young lad was burned to death and it's almost certainly related to the death of Astrid McKenzie. If what you tell me has a bearing on the case and I take it home and put it under my pillow and sleep on it, that's not going to be of much use to anyone. Is it?"

I didn't answer.

"IS IT?" he roared at me.

"It was a one-night stand," I said. "Everybody has them."

"WELL, WHY DIDN'T YOU TELL ME WHEN I ASKED YOU WHO HAD BEEN IN THE HOUSE?"

I glanced through the glass partition to see if the rest of the station were listening in.

"It's called," he said, speaking very slowly now, as if to an idiot, "obstruction. Do you have any idea what I could charge you with? Did you think we weren't going to find out that you had been entertaining Buzz Kempinski?"

I stayed silent. It seemed the best thing to do under the circumstances.

"We know Mr. Kempinski of old," Max continued. "We've got his prints. Had him in years ago when he beat up Astrid McKenzie. She was his girlfriend a while back. She called us in once but in the end she said she didn't want to press charges — they rarely do — and we had to let him go. So when he popped up in connection with your fire, being the manager of the person you're working with, we ran a check, just to be sure and *bingo!* They're his prints in your bedroom *and* on the can of kerosene. We got him in and of course he's saying he's never been to your house but now you're saying he has."

"What can of kerosene?" Half a second ago I'd been worrying whether he was about to throw me in jail for obstruction but that was before he'd mentioned Buzz and kerosene in the same breath.

"The can you keep in the potting shed by the summerhouse. The one that was used to start the fire. We sent the spaniels in and they sniffed it out immediately. I got a whiff of it when I arrived at the crime scene even after the fire brigade had drenched the place. Why do you keep kerosene, Miss Bartholomew?"

"I don't," I stated, mystified. "Why would I want to do that?"

"Because, as I said, we found a can of it in your potting shed."

"Well, I didn't put it there. Maybe my father was doing something with kerosene when he was last over from France."

"And that would be when?"

"About a year ago. He came over Christmas before last."

"This can was purchased pretty recently. It came from a shop in Westbourne Park Road that's only been open a month."

"Well, I didn't buy it. You said you found fingerprints on it."

"Oh, we certainly did. We found Mr. Kempinski's prints on the can of kerosene and on the door latch. We also found another set of prints on the latch, small enough to be a child's."

"Kevin O'Malley," I said with a certain amount of satisfaction.

"Yes, we've talked to him," said Max Austin. "We think he was the last person to talk to the deceased. Told us he liked Frederick Fox because he took the trouble to kick a football around the garden with him."

"*My* garden?"

"That's what he implied."

"I've never seen him in my garden. His mother and I don't really get on. But he could have been hanging out with Fred while I was in France. So Kevin saw Fred on New Year's Eve?"

"Mrs. O'Malley saw Miss O'Leary leave

at five, which was the time she told us she left. Then about a half hour later Frederick Fox turned up looking for her. Young Kevin was outside and asked Fred if he wanted a game but Fred said he didn't have time. Apparently he was a bit under the influence, according to Kevin, and he kept shouting that Miss O'Leary was his girlfriend and he had to see her."

"YES!" I punched the air as if I'd just won match point at Wimbledon.

Max Austin looked at me.

"This all ties in with my dream," I explained.

"Your dream," he repeated. But he didn't sound skeptical. "Tell me about your dream."

"I'm not like that, really," I protested. "I don't go in for all that dream analysis stuff. And it wasn't really a dream. I was on the point of falling asleep when I had this instant replay in my mind of what might have happened. It was a kind of vision but it felt like a dream."

I was aware that I was waffling away like an idiot.

"Just tell me about it," he said quietly.

When I got to the bit about Fred lighting another cigarette and leaving it burning, he stopped me.

"You know he smoked?"

"Well, no, I just assumed —"

"Because we asked Miss O'Leary and she said he didn't as far as she knew. And there were no butts anywhere."

"Well, maybe someone threw in something that started a fire?"

"That's what you saw in your — your 'vision.' " Now he was beginning to sound a bit skeptical.

"I just ran that through as a possibility," I confessed.

"Go on," he said.

I stumbled through the rest of my description of Fred's demise as he became engulfed in the fire, my voice becoming strained as I relived the moment once again.

"But it was dark. You couldn't actually see this," Max Austin asked.

"I never saw any of it. It's all in my mind. I wasn't there." I stared at him. What was he suggesting?

"It's quite possible Frederick Fox died just the way you've described. The firemen determined that the fire was started deliberately."

"With a can of kerosene." I didn't want to think about the fact that Buzz's prints were on that can and what that implied.

"You found Kevin's prints on the can too?" I asked hopefully.

"No. Not Kevin's, although we found footprints right outside that were a match with his sneakers."

"Well, if he was playing football —"

"And we found another kid's footprints but Kevin insists he only played with Fred and that he wasn't in your garden on New Year's Eve."

"And you believe him? So who's the other kid?"

"That's what we're trying to find out because those footprints were also found outside Astrid McKenzie's house the night of her fire."

Now he had my attention.

"But I thought you were questioning a man for that?"

He looked at me rather coldly. "Yes," he said slowly, "of course we've talked to those people we've tracked down whose prints were found *inside* her house but I'm talking about the prints that were found outside, all over the letterbox for example. Someone pushed a rag soaked in kerosene through it and then tossed a lighted match after it. That's how the fire started at Astrid's and whoever fiddled around trying to get the rag through the letterbox was dumb enough not to be wearing gloves. We're talking about an amateur."

"A child? She was a children's TV presenter after all."

He looked at me so askance that I just knew he hadn't put that together until I mentioned it. I felt rather pleased with myself.

"We don't *know* it was a child," he said shortly, "but we're not ruling it out. We've got a witness who was looking out of one of the windows of the house next door to yours. He says he saw a kid running down your garden at about the time Fred died. He couldn't give us a description because the kid was wearing a parka with the hood up. He couldn't even be certain if it was a boy or a girl because it was so dark, just this little shadow going down the lawn. Kevin says he wasn't in your garden but we think maybe he's lying. He knows he wasn't supposed to be there. Apparently his mother has forbidden him to play in your garden. We're getting a list of his friends and we'll be talking to them."

"So there were kids in my garden?" I said.

"Oh, that's just the half of it. Your garden's pretty well enclosed. The only access really is via the alleyway that runs down the side of the house so we've been asking for witnesses who saw anyone going into that alleyway around five o'clock on New Year's Eve."

"And?"

"Besides the witness looking out the window who saw the child in the anorak, there's a woman across the road who says no, they were wearing an anorak but they were too big to be a child. She noticed the little — or big — anorak because they were in such a hurry. And she says it was later, closer to six. Then there's a man who was putting leaflets through all the letterboxes in the area that afternoon and he's come forward to say he saw a woman coming *out* of the alleyway 'after five o'clock' — that's as close as he can make it — so we have to find her. Then we've got one of the market merchants who says he knows you —"

"Chris?"

Max Austin looked at his notes. "Christopher Petaki, yes. He was making last-minute New Year's Eve deliveries from his stall. Does he deliver to you, Miss Bartholomew?"

"No, he doesn't." When Chris had taken over from his mother, he'd started a new service of running along the road to restaurants and certain favored customers to deliver produce directly to their door, but I'd always thought part of the fun of shopping in the market was actually going there.

"Anyway, he saw a man go into the alleyway at six o'clock. He says he stopped to look at him because he knew it was your house and you were away."

"Buzz?"

"He fits the description. Tall, dark but Mr. Petaki says he was wearing a brown leather jacket and Mr. Kempinski says he'd never wear a leather jacket, not his style."

"So you've got a man, a woman, and a child. Do you have prints for all these people?"

He nodded. "We've got a ton of prints because of all the firemen tramping about all over the place. We're still eliminating them."

"What about Angel?" I said. "Did she say she'd seen anyone unusual in the garden?"

"She said the only people she'd ever seen were the deceased and her new boyfriend — Scott."

I thought about telling him that Angel knew Buzz had been to my house but before I could say anything, he said:

"I need to ask you about your relationship with Mr. Kennedy." He'd done it again. Jumped from one subject to another without warning and caught me off guard. "You don't live together."

"Well, we're about to start — he's moving in with me." *Until you sort all this out and I feel safe again,* I wanted to add but didn't. "So the person you're looking for," I said slowly, "is someone who would have had a motive for setting fire to both Astrid McKenzie and Fred?"

"Not Fred," he said.

"You think it was someone different who torched Fred?"

"No. I just don't think it was Fred they were after."

I let that sink in.

"Angel? Someone wanted to set fire to Angel?"

"Well, she was the person who was supposed to be there. And it was dark so if we assume that your vision was pretty close to what actually happened then whoever torched the summerhouse would not have been able to see it was Fred and not Miss O'Leary in there. A blurred shape through the curtains maybe but that was it."

The thought that Fred had died because someone had mistaken him for Angel was almost too much to bear. I didn't say anything for quite a while and I must have looked pretty grim because Max Austin suddenly stood up and told me to go home.

"You're letting me off the hook, even though I didn't tell you about Buzz?" I was amazed.

"If you think there is anything — whatever it is, however small — that you think I should know, you are to pick up the phone and call either me or Mary Mehta and tell us. If I find you are withholding evidence again, then I will charge you. Do you understand?"

He looked straight at me and I felt quite scared for a moment or two. I nodded frantically. "I'll come running," I promised.

"Anyway," he muttered, his face softening, "you've been a great help and I'm sorry you have to be drawn into it like this."

I was touched by the sudden gentleness in his voice. His temperament really did seem to be highly mercurial. I had the distinct impression that I only ever had half his attention and that the other half of his mind was busy working out something else while he was talking to me. I held out my hand but he had already turned away so I slipped out of the room before he thought of something else to ask me.

Sergeant Cross was sitting at the desk where I had seen Cath's picture.

"Why have you got a picture of Cathleen Clark on your desk?" I asked him.

"She's my girlfriend." He looked startled by my recognizing her.

"Since when?" I asked.

"Since about eight months. You know her, do you?"

"I haven't seen her in a while. I've lost touch with her. She used to live at number twenty-four All Saints Road. On the second floor."

"Not anymore. She lives with me now. We got a flat together Shepherd's Bush way. Bit of a bargain, it's got a roof terrace, not that I spend much time there." He gave me a rueful grin. It was cases like my summerhouse fire that kept him away from it.

"We grew up together," I explained. "We went to school together, we were — like — best friends and then we sort of lost touch. I'd really like to see her again. Maybe you could give me her —"

His phone rang. He held up his hand to me, mouthed *Don't go away,* and then his face broke into a big smile.

"How did you know to call right this minute?" *It's her,* he mouthed at me again. "Listen, you'll never guess who I've got standing right in front of me, says she hasn't seen you in a while. Nathalie Bartholomew. Here, I'll put you on so you can talk to her. Hello? Hello, Cath? Are you there? What? Oh, okay. I'll tell her. Yes, tonight. I should be back on time. We'll talk then. Fine. Bye." He looked at me. "She says she'll call you. I'll give her your number tonight."

"She's got my number," I mumbled. Then someone called his name from across the room and he excused himself. I could tell he was embarrassed and I wondered what Cath had said about me in the brief moment she'd had him on the phone. As he walked away I surreptitiously picked up his phone and dialed 1471. Cath hadn't blocked her number and I wrote it down and pocketed it.

On impulse I went back and popped my head round Max Austin's door to say good-bye. He had his back to me and was sorting through his laundry. He was talking to someone while he did so.

"What do these wretched signs mean, Sadie? How am I supposed to know if I can put them in the machine or not?"

I stepped into the room and looked around the door. There was absolutely nobody else there.

I knocked on the door. "Can I help?"

He jumped and turned around. "Oh. Hi. Just trying to figure out which of this stuff gets dry cleaned. I never understand what these little pictures mean. I always seem to arrive at the launderette when the woman who runs it is on a break so I have to do it myself."

I think it was the fact that he was so helpless that prompted me to study the washing instructions on each individual label. "This means wash separately. This means don't put it in the dryer. This means don't let the water get too hot, no more than thirty."

I couldn't believe it. He wrote it all down and stuck a yellow Post-it on each item of clothing. "I'll never remember otherwise," he said. "Thanks."

"I just came by to say good-bye."

"Well, yes. Good-bye."

I was almost out the door when he yelled after me, "And if you keep anything else back from me, I'll have you locked up!"

I imagine everyone in the entire police station heard. Mary Mehta touched my arm.

“Don’t mind him,” she said.

“Who’s Sadie?” I asked her.

“Sadie?” She frowned. “She’s his wife. *Was* his wife,” she corrected herself. “She’s been dead five years. Why?”

“Oh nothing,” I said, “nothing at all.”

Chapter 13

I knew I should call Selma now that I'd listened to the tape. She must be sick with anticipation wondering what I had made of it. But the astounding revelations had made me more than a little nervous about calling her house. What would I say if Buzz picked up the phone?

But before I had time to do anything, Angel moved in. She just appeared on my doorstep and I made good on my offer to give her a room. It was the least I could do. I used it as an excuse to rearrange the house a little and only when I had finished did I stop to wonder if I should have consulted my mother beforehand.

From the outside our house looked vast. If I hadn't known I would have guessed it had at least six or seven bedrooms. In fact, it only had four and one of these I had converted into my office. Within a week of my parents disappearing to France, I appropriated the master bedroom on the second floor with its accompanying luxurious bathroom. My mother had installed a Jacuzzi bath and a power shower and Tommy's biggest gripe was that I wouldn't let him use this bathroom when he stayed the night. I relegated him to the one at the top of the house but now I supposed I'd have to share mine with him otherwise he'd start walking in on Angel soaking in a bubble bath. On my way up to the top of the house to inspect this bathroom, the one where my mother complained the shower didn't work, I stopped at the little box room on the half landing. I had intended to put Angel in my old bedroom on the top floor but it suddenly struck me that this little room would be perfect for her. I spent the rest of the day emptying the room, carrying the boxes downstairs to the basement where they should have been in the first place. I had found the key to the basement at the bottom of a tin of Vienna roast that I'd just finished. I must have just tossed the contents of a new packet into the empty tin without noticing the key.

Unfortunately the strong aroma of the coffee lingering on the key could not mask the vile reek of the damp that hit me full in the face when I opened the door to the basement. I carried the boxes down breathing out through my mouth, placed them gingerly on the floor, and switched on the light. Near the floor the walls looked positively bruised, great patches of blue mold splattered all over them. Higher up the moisture-sodden paper billowed out from the walls. It was much worse than when I'd last been down here. Here and there the damp had risen all the way up and the ceiling was buckling and sagging. It looked as if any minute now the kitchen floor could cave in.

I rushed upstairs and called the first damp fixer I could find in the Yellow Pages. They said they'd be around first thing in the morning to take a look. I felt so pleased with myself I wanted to call my mother so she could give me a pat on the back. And then I thought, *Hold on, you call and tell her you're getting the damp fixed, she's going to ask how come I didn't know about this damp and why has it taken you so long to do something about it?*

I might grumble about Tommy procrastinating but I managed to fritter away an entire afternoon preparing Angel's room. Besides buying flowers and arranging them just so and laundering a pretty blue bedspread, I emptied a closet for her clothes, found a fleecy bedside mat, made sure her reading lamp worked, and cleared some shelves for her books. When I finally surveyed the room, it looked extremely cozy. I turned up the heat on the radiator so it would be really toasty when she arrived and went upstairs to scrub the tub for her. I was still up there at midnight, rearranging the furniture in the spare bedroom that had been my office and wondering whether it might make a nice TV room. I barely registered the rotting windowsills, the leaking radiator, and the crumbling cornice. Give me a break, I'd called someone about the damp, hadn't I? When I finally fell into bed, I wrote *CALL CATH* on a Post-it and stuck it to my alarm clock.

In any event, all my thoughtful effort on Angel's behalf proved to be a waste of time. She didn't need any of the things I'd prepared for her. She brought a pathetic amount of clothes with her. Virtually everything she owned had been destroyed so she didn't need much closet space. She didn't read in bed and when I mentioned bookshelves she looked bewildered and it began to dawn on me that maybe she didn't read at all. And when I asked her if she needed a desk — that really made her laugh. *What do I need a desk for? I don't* do homework no more.

Then there was the food problem. I went overboard to begin with, preparing freshly squeezed orange juice followed by coffee and croissants every morning. Angel ignored them and made herself a pot of tea, heaping sugar into every cup she poured. And in the evening she brought home fish and chips and sat at the kitchen table, eating them out of the newspaper. The smell permeated the entire house and when I tried to remonstrate with her about her unhealthy diet, she just laughed in my face and said, "You want some, don't you? You're just jealous. Nothing beats fish 'n chips." So I shut up because of course she was absolutely right.

But I made a point of being there in the evening to share a meal with her, even if we both ate totally different food. Angel was putting a brave face on things but I could see she was jittery. For the first couple of evenings we skirted around the fire and Fred until finally, on her third night there, she suddenly burst into tears in the middle of squeezing an upturned ketchup bottle over her cod and chips. Her sobbing coincided with the ketchup finally emerging from the bottle in a disgusting noisy splurge that sent drops of bloodlike goo flying onto her triple-D cups straining against her pristine white T-shirt.

"It used to drive Fred mad when he couldn't get it out. He could never understand why they couldn't make ketchup that poured easily."

I tried to picture the docile, pimpled Fred getting mad with the ketchup and failed. I didn't say anything, sensing this might be the moment when she would release her pent-up misery.

"I mean who would want to kill him? Fred was such a gentle boy. Tell you the truth, Lee, that was one of the reasons we broke up. He was sweet but he just wasn't that exciting. I dumped him and when I told him it was over, do you know what? He cried. And now he's dead because of me."

"It's not your fault, Angel. You have to understand that. You can't blame yourself. You really can't. You didn't ask him to come round and see you on New Year's Eve, did you?"

"No," she said, "no, I didn't. But it didn't surprise me. He was always turning up. He couldn't accept it was over between us."

"I expect it was hard for him. Was he jealous of the new boyfriend?"

"New boyfriend?" She gave me an odd look.

"Scott. You told me about him in the car, remember?"

"Oh, yeah, I suppose he was upset about Scott. You know what the police thought? They reckoned it was someone after me, not Fred. They kept asking me if there was anyone I'd had a falling out with. If I had any enemies. Lee, do you think someone wanted to kill me and they got Fred instead? Do you think they'll try again? Do you think they'll break in here? Like tonight?"

It was terrible to hear those words coming out of her mouth as she sat there at my kitchen table with blood all over her chest. I knew it was ketchup but it looked as convincing as it does in the movies.

"Well, we'll be safe as houses." I tried to sound reassuring. "Tommy's coming tonight. He'll protect us."

But I had no idea if I was speaking the truth. Tommy might be a great big reassuring presence but his abilities as a bodyguard had never been put to the test.

He walked through the door half an hour later, mysteriously bearing his wok before him.

"Your Christmas present, remember?"

he said proudly. I'd given it to him the year before thinking stir-fry would be a way of getting him to eat vegetables. He was worse than Angel in the junk food department.

"This is only temporary," I hissed at him, true to form, "while this whole investigation is going on. You do understand that, don't you?"

Yet I had to confess I was extremely glad to have him there.

But as if having Angel and Tommy in the house wasn't enough, the next day I came home from a routine visit to the dentist and found my mother sitting at the kitchen table with the two of them. When I saw her all I could think of was that the damp people had never showed up and I had forgotten to call Cath. The two things that had been of paramount importance to me a couple of days ago had gone clean out of my mind. Trust my mother to make me feel guilty before she'd even opened her mouth.

Despite the by now familiar smell of fish and chips, they were tucking into plates of grilled vegetables. All of them. Angel waved a charred parsnip at me by way of greeting.

"Your mum's turned me on to this whole

new way of eating," she informed me. "You're going to love it, Lee."

"Oh, it was terrible," said my mother, talking with her mouth full. "I walked in and she was eating fish and chips. *Fish and chips!* And that was all she was going to eat. No roughage. No greens. Just a load of fat and grease and salt. And there were all these lovely fresh vegetables just sitting here. Carrots, sprouts, parsnips. I showed her what to do. Peel them, put them all in a baking dish, sprinkle them with a smidgen of oil and sea salt, add some chopped up parsley, and pop them in the oven with a baked potato. And of course she thinks they're delicious. So much better for her. Darling, I'm sorry I didn't give you any warning but here I am. We were questioned by the police, you know? Via Interpol or something. Had to tell them what time you left. It felt like you were a suspect."

I thought of all the rich food my mother had served us in France and wondered how that compared with fish and chips in the healthy diet department. Tommy, I noticed, wasn't eating anything.

"Sit down and join us," said my mother. "We were just talking about your murder."

"*My* murder," I repeated flatly. "Why

does it have to be *my* murder? He was Angel's boyfriend."

"Was he really?" My mother turned to Angel in dismay. "You never said. I am so sorry. Oh my God, that really is terrible."

She was genuinely shaken.

"He was an old boyfriend," said Angel. As if that made it any better. "Before Christmas."

I noticed Mum didn't get into that one.

"Well, there's something fishy going on," said my mother. "Two fires on the same road within six weeks. We must get an iron gate put up across the alleyway. We've got to cut off any access to the garden at the back of the house. We should have done it years ago. This area just isn't safe anymore."

"Was it ever?" I said gloomily. Any minute now she was going to want to see how I'd got on with the repair work on the house.

"There's nothing we can do," said Tommy quietly, squeezing the back of my neck as if he knew exactly how edgy I was feeling, which he probably did since he was working on easing the tension in my muscles. "If there's anything to discover the police will find it. That's their job, not ours." He gave my skin a little pinch and I yelped.

"The roast vegetables were just an appetizer," said my mother as if she sensed the subject needed changing. "So what's for dinner, Lee?"

Tommy felt my panic. *You never told me you were coming. There's nothing in the house.* "It's okay," he said. "I'm going to cook you all a meal in my wok. You will be amazed. Lee's going to chop everything up for me, right, Lee?" Another sharp pinch.

He was backing me up in the only way he knew how. We were all in a nightmare situation. My mother's marriage had broken up. Angel had lost all her belongings and was a potential murder victim. Tommy's mother had pancreatic cancer.

"Right," I said, hesitating a little, "but there's nothing in the fridge. Where did those vegetables come from, by the way?"

"That bloke in the market brought them round from his stall," said Angel. "Said he wanted to do something to help as you was having a bad time."

"Chris?" I said, smiling. "How kind of him. What an incredibly sweet guy he is." Angel made a face. "You don't think so, Angel?"

She shrugged. "Well, he may be underneath but he's not much to look at, is he? He was ever such a pest recently, kept hanging about at his stall waiting for me when I come out Tesco in me dinner hour. Hope he's not going to keep showing up here and all."

"I'll see him off if he's a nuisance," said Tommy. "Now, we've got to get to work. We're going to make my special dish. It's called the Caught on the Hop stir-fry. I do it all the time. Just get everything out of the fridge, chop it up and throw it in."

He cleared a space on the kitchen table and we all went into action, arms reaching into the refrigerator. Soon we had accumulated a nice little pile of ingredients. My mother acted as editor, removing no-go items like a wedge of brie and a slice of chocolate cake. Finally we were left with four carrots, two onions, a stick of celery, three zucchinis, the remains of a cold roast chicken, a bunch of rather tired parsley, some boiled rice, a couple of slices of ham, and several miserable-looking mushrooms.

"Okay, get to work." Tommy handed Angel the chicken. "Pull all the white meat off that. Vanessa, open some wine and then maybe you could lay the table. Lee, over here with me." He handed me a paring knife and a chopping board and began to amass the onions, the carrots, the celery, and the zucchinis in front of me.

We didn't exactly work fast because we kept stopping to sip our wine and check on what everyone else was doing. My mother injected an air of ceremony into the proceedings by bringing out the best silver, the candelabra, and the linen napkins we kept for special occasions. She placed not one but two wineglasses beside each place and added a water glass. She made a show of presenting first a white wine and then a red to Tommy for his inspection. I had never seen her like this and it was fun. Her final masterstroke was to remove all the silver except for the serving spoons and replace it with chopsticks, laying them lightly across the bone china plates.

Angel happened to be wearing black. She took a white dishcloth and adjusted it about her person so that it resembled a waitress's apron. She ran around asking each of us, "May I take your order now?"

It was all totally mad but I loved it. God knows we needed a bit of levity and how long had it been since I had heard giggling in my kitchen? I imagined we'd all feel guilty later on about having some fun so soon after Fred's death, but as long as Angel's spirits were being lifted, I was all for carrying on.

Tommy had just tossed in a little oil to

heat up in the wok when the doorbell rang.

"Be right back," I said, padding barefoot into the hall. Lord knows why but I had felt the need to take my shoes off to chop up vegetables.

Buzz stood before me when I opened the door. I had trouble breathing because he appeared even more handsome than I remembered. He had grown a little designer stubble and it made him look rough and sexy and —

Matching sets of prints in my bedroom and on the can of kerosene in the shed. Why didn't Max Austin have him locked up?

I slammed the door in his face.

The bell rang again and Tommy stuck his head out into the hall.

"What's going on?"

I offered no explanation and smiled reassuringly at him till he retreated into the kitchen.

I opened the front door again. "Go away!" I hissed at Buzz. I raised the paring knife without thinking.

"Why?" he said. "I heard about your fire. I just wanted to see if you were okay." He licked the two index fingers of his right hand and brought them to my lips. I nearly screamed out loud.

"Go *away!*" I said again. "What are you doing here? I have people . . ." I gestured behind me with the paring knife.

"What's-his-name?" He looked amused. "The boyfriend? Put that thing down, will you?"

"As a matter of fact, yes." Why didn't he leave? Out of the corner of my eye I noticed a small FedEx package propped up against the doorstep. I stooped down to pick it up and saw it was from Selma. I thrust it behind my back before he could see the label and made as if to shut the door.

He looked at me quizzically. "Okay, okay. I get it. But you asked what was I doing here? Aren't I allowed to want to see you? I haven't spoken to you since before Christmas."

I shrugged. "But it's —"

"Dangerous? I know. Look, don't I even get a kiss?"

"Lee. It's almost ready," Tommy yelled from the kitchen. I shut the door on Buzz. Let him make of that whatever he wanted.

"Who was that?" asked my mother as we began eating.

My heart was hammering away and my hands were shaking. On top of everything else, chopsticks were not exactly my instrument of choice for conveying my food to my mouth. I was doing okay until Angel said, "It was Buzz," and everything slithered back onto my plate.

Angel had seen him.

"You know Buzz?" I decided feigning ignorance was the best way to play it.

"Yeah, 'course. He come into the garden that day I was painting the summerhouse with Fred." She frowned a little as she said his name. "He introduced himself, said he was working with you because you were writing her book. I was ever so excited."

"Who on earth is Buzz?" said my mother.

"He's the manager of the actress whose book I'm about to start ghosting. He's —"

"He's wicked," Angel interrupted. "He's got floppy hair, dark, and he's tall and a bit skinny to tell you the truth, but it doesn't stop him being sexy. He's got these dreamy dark eyes. They're like them black pools you see at the bottom of very high mountains. You know, they're so deep the water probably keeps going down forever and his eyes are the same. When he looks at you for more than a minute you feel like you might drown in them."

I'd never imagined Angel could be so poetic. And I knew exactly what she meant.

Buzz's eyes had just immersed me almost to the point of panic.

"Where have you seen these mountains with their bottomless pools, Angel?" I asked her.

"Me mum's got this calendar. It's been hanging up on the back of the kitchen door since about 1997. I won't let her take it down because I love the pictures. I've never seen real mountains. I keep meaning to pop back home and get it to put in my room here."

"So who's the actress?" said my mother.

"Selma Walker." Too late I remembered Selma didn't want me telling anyone I was ghosting her book.

"Oh, I forgot to tell you, she called," said Angel. "Said she'd sent you another tape by FedEx."

"You spoke to her?"

"No, I never answer your phone. We agreed I'd use my mobile. I heard her voice on the answering machine." On the new tape I'd had to buy since the police still had my old one.

And she'd probably listened to anyone else who called. Just as well Buzz hadn't.

"Who is Selma Walker? I've never heard of her," asked my mother.

"You've never watched *Fraternity*?" I

could hear the astonishment in Angel's voice.

"What's *Fraternity*?"

"Britain's number-one soap opera, Mum."

"Oh, a soap opera actress." I could hear the disdain in her voice. *Not a story worth bothering with.*

"It's an art just like any other form of acting," I said, suddenly feeling the need to defend poor Selma. She'd set out to conquer Broadway but she'd wound up on the soaps. Well, she was a success and she should be proud of herself.

"I take it you watch *Fraternity*?" My mother looked at Angel. "What's your real name, by the way? I can't call you Angel."

"Don't blame you," said Angel, now sounding remarkably cheerful, "especially as I'm a little devil. It's Angelina. Yes, I watch it but I don't like her at all."

"Why ever not?" I was intrigued.

"She's such a cow. The way she bosses her husband around and all her sisters-in-law."

"But that's Sally McEwan, the character she plays. It's not Selma Walker," I protested.

"Whatever." Angel didn't look convinced. "But I don't know what she's doing married to someone as cool as Buzz. She's old enough to be his mother."

"Tommy, put that down," I said. He was brandishing the percolator far too vigorously for my liking and if he dropped it we'd have to spend hours making drip-drip individual coffee through a plastic filter. "Do we all want coffee?" I didn't sound encouraging because I didn't want everyone to sit up late discussing Selma Walker.

"I'm ready to go upstairs," said my mother. "I've come all the way from France and I haven't even unpacked."

"I'll come and make up the bed for you, Mum." As good an excuse as any to leave the room.

Of course I wound up watching as she made the bed up herself. She always relegated me to the sidelines when anything needed doing, and I always let her, partly out of sheer apathy and my natural tendency to procrastinate and let someone else take care of business if they were willing. And partly because I knew that however much she might exhort me to bestir myself, she got a kick out of taking charge of a situation herself. Besides she appeared to be making no fuss about the fact that she wasn't in her old bedroom and would be sharing a bathroom with Angel. Normally I vacated the master bedroom for her but this time I'd had no warning. Maybe she was just too tired and I'd be given hell in the morning.

By the time she had everything she needed half an hour had gone by. I had vaguely registered first Tommy and then Angel coming up the stairs on their way to bed. As I was about to close the door and retire myself, my mother came toward me. She stood so close, we could have been embracing.

"Sleep well, Mum," I said, resisting the urge to kiss her good night.

"Good night, Lee. I just wanted to tell you how much it means to me to be here."

"It's your house, Mum."

"No" — she actually touched my arm and held on to it — "I mean here . . ." And after a beat, "With you."

I shut the door and burst into silent sobbing on the landing. She had done something I had always wanted her to do and yet now I couldn't handle it. My face was wet with tears when I walked into my bedroom and Tommy sat up in bed.

"Hey, what's up with you?"

"Don't say a word. If I go into it now I'll be blubbing all night."

"It'd make a change from your snoring."

"*My* snoring? What do you mean, my snoring?" As usual Tommy succeeded in defusing my budding hysterics.

"But you're still pretty tense," he told me when, as I lay next to him, he leaned over and resumed the massage he had begun in the kitchen. I was naked for the simple reason that I could not find my nightdress. I could have sworn I had draped it over a chair that morning but it was impossible to find anything in a room inhabited by Tommy. He hadn't even spent a night there and my bedroom was already no longer my own. Despite the fact that I had allocated him shelf space in my closets, he had elected to dump his clothes all over the room. And in the bathroom, I had barely been able to find my toothpaste in amongst the newly arrived clutter of medicinal remedies. "Something's bothering you."

Trust Tommy to make the understatement of the year. I find out I have slept with the husband of my latest ghosting subject, my parents announce they are getting divorced, someone dies at the end of my garden, I discover there's a chance that my new lover may be beating up his wife. And Tommy boils it all down to *Some-*

thing's bothering you. Of course poor Tommy only knew about two of the above. Maybe he'd amend it to *Something's bothering me* if he knew about the other two. And maybe it was the guilt I felt about betraying him that was causing most of the tension.

"My mother's turned up," I offered by way of explanation. "That'll do it. Why is she here? Why doesn't she ever give me any warning? And she's going to give me hell about all the things I haven't taken care of in the house."

"What things?" he asked sleepily as he caressed the back of my neck.

I took him briefly through all the items on the list and he stopped massaging me and sat up.

"You know you're actually wailing."

"I am not."

"Yes, you are. Whenever you start talking about your mother your voice gets more and more anguished till you really are wailing. There's no other way to describe it. Now shut up and listen. I saw that list pinned to the fridge and I've been meaning to talk to you about it. I can do most of the stuff on it and, frankly, I'm surprised you haven't asked me before now. It's the perfect opportunity while I'm here. I'll come home from work, get into my overalls and turn into your friendly neighborhood handyman. Weekends too, no problem."

There was a very good reason I hadn't asked him. He always said he was going to do things for me and he never got around to it. But if I pointed this out to him, he got into a huff and said something like *Fine, if you don't want me to help you out, go get someone else, see if I care.* He never actually said *see if I care* but his expression did.

"You've had a rough time with this fire. I'd like to help you out. Let me do this for you," he persisted. "Go on, you know I'll do a terrific job and I'm cheap."

"Cheap?" I nudged him sharply with my elbow. "I thought you were free. Have you left much stuff in the upstairs bathroom, by the way? You can start by fixing the shower for my mother and Angel. We don't want them all crowding in with us. And while you're up there, the windowsills need looking at and the cornice is crumbling on the top landing and —"

He was snoring softly before I got to the end of my sentence. I leaned over and kissed the air above his nose, a kind of butterfly polar bear kiss. I was glad he was here. It was sweet of him to offer to help with the house and I knew it made sense to say yes. I needed to trust Tommy and allow him to do more for me. I knew it didn't help our relationship that I was always so quick to reject his efforts. It would make him feel good if I put him in charge of the house and it would suit me fine — that way I wouldn't have workmen traipsing through the house during the day.

I settled down in the kind of rosy glow of contentment I barely recognized anymore but I couldn't sleep. After a while I realized why. Something that had been niggling at the back of my mind for the past couple of hours finally rose to the surface.

But I don't know what she's doing married to someone as cool as Buzz. She's old enough to be his mother.

How did Angel know Buzz and Selma were married? And why had she lied to the police about him being in the garden?

Chapter 14

Once I found myself pondering the answers to those questions, I gave up trying to get to sleep. I went downstairs and retrieved Selma's package from the hall table. I opened the shutters to the garden to let in the moonlight and curled up on the sofa with the tape recorder on the floor beside me. It could have been a romantic setting but the sound of Selma's voice on her latest tape killed any semblance of fantasy.

"Nothing can describe how I felt when I first came to London," *she began and her tone forewarned that what I was about to hear would be real and unpleasant.* "The man I had loved and trusted had dumped me in favor of someone he'd known for just a few months. My self-esteem was at an all time low. I did not believe I would ever be able to count on a man again.

"The only thing that kept me going

was the role I had been offered as Sally McEwan in *Fraternity.* Sally was just about everything I was not. At least not at that particular moment in my life. She was tough, she was strong. She knew what she wanted and she went out and got it. And she had a man who loved her. He loved her so much, he was prepared to stand up to his family to defend her. Whereas I had banked everything on a man who kept our relationship hidden from his family and his friends. I had been a fool and now I was paying for it.

"It's safe to say that on arrival in London I submerged myself in Sally McEwan. I adopted her willful, attention-grabbing personality off screen as well as on. I hid behind her. Whenever I had doubts about something, I would ask myself *What would Sally do?* My instinct was to buy myself a little one-room apartment in some neglected area of London where no one would find me but, thanks to Sally, I plowed my money into a much wiser investment: a five-story mansion in fashionable Notting Hill. In fact, Sally guided me through all the decisions on how to behave that I had to make at that time, except one: the choice of a man.

"I noticed Buzz the minute he appeared on the set. He was the agent of one of the other actors. I noticed him because he had the strange romantic look of a gypsy. He wore exotic clothes in rich autumnal colors. Embroidered waistcoats. Boots with Cuban heels, that made him seem even taller than his six feet two inches. Long scarves in soft wool wound round his neck several times. He wore linens, tweeds, cottons, cashmere, never synthetic fabrics. My eyes followed him everywhere. He was loose-limbed and he loped around the set with a kind of easy grace.

"Sally McEwan would have waltzed right up to him and introduced herself as she did to her husband in *Fraternity* when she met him on one of his business trips to New York. Sally knew how to land her man all right. She was married to Jimmy McEwan by the second episode when he brought her back to England and she caused havoc by demanding a role in the running of the company he owned with his brothers.

"I wasn't Sally and I did not go near Buzz. I was too shy and vulnerable to approach him. I watched him from a distance.

"But he noticed me. Or rather he noticed Sally McEwan when they called me to do a scene with his client. He came right up to me when the director called 'Cut' and started a conversation. He took me out to dinner that night in Manchester and the next day we traveled to London together on the same train.

"At first I thought his interest in me was purely professional. From the get-go he talked about my representation — at the time I was still with my New York agent — and how I needed someone to look after my interests here in the UK. His concern was touching. I needed a protector. I had been raised by my father to believe I would always be taken care of. I had expected to marry a rich man who would look out for me as my father had provided for my mother and me. What I hadn't bargained for was the independent spirit that led me to become an actress and provide for myself. In satisfying that side of me I neglected to fulfill the need in me for a shield against the harsh reality of life. I saw my married lover as my shield but of course he was anything but.

"Buzz was considerably younger than I was but I swear I never noticed. He was so wise. He didn't come at me all gung-ho, telling me how he was going to turn my career around and take it to the next level. That would have been pretty dumb because in the soap opera world I was already pretty successful. He used a more subtle approach. He worked on my trust and he talked about how he sensed that I was sad in some way, he could see it in my eyes. He said he understood what it must be like starting a new life in a strange country and I should know that he was there to help in any way he could. I had already told him that I had no family left in the States — my parents were both dead, I was an only child, and my cousins were almost total strangers living miles away in Colorado. He told me this made him feel all the more protective of me. It was all pretty corny stuff and if I hadn't been in such a vulnerable state, I would no doubt have smelled an extremely large rat.

"I fell for his line but here's the kicker: Except for the occasional brushing of elbows, he didn't touch me. Never even gave me a peck on the cheek. And I began to yearn for him. Just before I fell asleep, his face would float before my eyes and I'd imagine what it would be like to make love to him. So when he finally kissed me at Kings Cross Station when he came to meet me off the train from Manchester, taking me in his arms and placing his lips on mine as I stepped down onto the platform, I was caught totally off guard.

"He knew exactly what he was doing. From that moment on I was his slave, and shortly after that — his client and then his wife.

"The first attack came about a week after our wedding. I came home from work and found him in the kitchen. From the minute I walked in he freaked me out by not saying anything. He didn't respond to my greeting, he just stood there staring right through me as if I wasn't there. I always rushed up to him and kissed him but now I found myself moving toward him tentatively, approaching him as if he were a potentially ferocious animal. And you know what they say about animals, they know when you're scared of them and it can make them jittery so they attack you.

"I told him I was going to fix him a drink and while I was pouring it, he reached out and stroked the side of my face. I relaxed. It was okay. He was being tender. I'd imagined the tension. Then suddenly *POW!* he slammed my head against the cabinets and accused me of cheating on him with one of the cast members of *Fraternity.*

"And that was pretty much what began to happen on a regular basis. I'd come home, he'd be quiet then he'd explode, throw me against the sink, the draining board and the dishes would go flying. I'd fall to the floor and crawl to the stove and he'd come after me and slam me against the oven. I'd grapple for something to use as a weapon, catch him by surprise, and then I'd run. That was the worst part, hearing him come after me, waiting for the hand on my shoulder that would pull me back just as I was halfway through the door. I tried never to let him chase me upstairs because then there was always a chance he would throw me down the stairwell.

"He seemed to have got it into his head that I was betraying him with cast members of *Fraternity*, that was the reason I had to be punished. No matter how much I swore it wasn't true, he refused to believe me. And after he beat me up he always begged for my forgiveness, told me he loved me. In fact he often told me he loved me *while* he was attacking me. The awful thing was that I didn't get the sense that he was angry during these attacks, just totally, desperately miserable — and I had no idea why."

The tape came to an end with an abrupt *click.* When I reached out to flip it over, I discovered she had barely used up one side of the tape and the other side was blank. I decided she must have been interrupted. Maybe she had heard Buzz coming home, slamming the front door behind him while she was in the midst of dictating, giving her just enough time to whip the tape out of the machine.

Two things struck me over and above the sickening details of violence. Selma's account of meeting and getting to know Buzz was the total opposite of what he had told me. Not only that but she'd said she had no family left. So whom had she been visiting when she'd gone to New York at Christmas?

More questions I didn't have the answer to and as a result I spent the night on the sofa going nuts. The smart thing to do would be to walk away from both Selma and Buzz. I should call Genevieve first thing in the morning — along with Cath and the elusive damp people — and beg her to get me a safe docile job writing the memoirs of an eighty-year-old landscape gardener in the depths of Gloucestershire.

But I was in too deep. I really wanted this gig. Having listened to Selma's tapes, there was no way I could turn my back on her now. I went back upstairs about 5:30 a.m. feeling very shaky and to my surprise I found Tommy wide awake and waiting for me.

"So where did you go?" He took me in his arms and nuzzled my ear. "Been clubbing, have you? Hip-hopping the night away somewhere?"

"I've been downstairs thinking," I replied.

"Sounds serious."

"It was. Is."

"Going to tell me what you were thinking about?"

"You don't want to know," I said.

"In that case I'm going to engage you in a little sex," said Tommy and before I could protest — which would have been my guilt-ridden knee-jerk reaction — he leaned over and began to suck my left nipple with unbelievable gentleness. My nipples are the most friendly creatures you could ever hope to meet. They perk up at the slightest provocation and now was no exception. I lay there, looking down at Tommy's head on my chest and stroking his hair. After a while his mouth moved off my left breast and over to my right.

I knew what to expect next. His sexual routine was second nature to me, like the sequence of events that prepared me for bed — removing my makeup, getting undressed, cleaning my teeth, patting my face with night cream, swallowing a zinc capsule, finishing a chapter. Just as all of this had to happen before I could begin to think about sleep, Tommy felt he had to arouse a certain area of my body before he could enter it.

I waited for him to progress to my navel and then on down to the insides of my thighs. Instead his head moved up and he began to kiss me long and deeply and then, before I knew what was happening, he had wriggled underneath me and I was sitting astride him, impaled. I hadn't even realized I was so ready for him. He reached up and began to knead my breasts. He was being quite rough and it hurt but I didn't stop him. He thrust himself up inside me and I began to ride with him, leaning forward and back, forward and back . . .

We came almost immediately. Together.

“Shh!” said Tommy, reaching up and pressing the flat of his hand against my mouth.

“What?”

“You yelled blue murder. Didn’t you hear yourself? We don’t want your mother running in.”

“I enjoyed that,” I said, leaning down to give him an Eskimo kiss. “Thanks.”

“Me too,” he mumbled. He was falling asleep. “Do it again in an hour.”

“You wish.” I laughed.

But he awoke at seven thirty and leapt on me. Literally. And this time there was no foreplay. It didn’t matter. I was so excited by his sudden urgency, I responded instantly. Afterward I lay there more or less stunned. He had succeeded in taking me right back to the early days of our relationship when we would awaken at odd times during the night and go into action in a frenzied ritual that would leave us exhausted. Only now I felt exhilarated.

I was wondering what kind of dialogue would accompany this renewed energy and whether Tommy already had a script prepared when the phone rang.

“Is that Lee?” It was a tremulous voice with an American accent. “It’s Selma Walker.”

Why was Selma Walker calling at eight o'clock in the morning?

"Selma, I've been meaning to call you. I swear I have. I feel dreadful. You must think I'm totally unprofessional but my mother arrived out of the blue from France along with a couple of unexpected guests and you know about the fire and it's just been hectic here. Did you have a good Christmas? How was your New Year? I got your tapes, I've listened to them and . . ."

Tommy was standing in front of me stark naked pressing the air down in front of him, signaling that I should stop yattering on like a maniac.

Slow down, he mouthed.

"Could we meet?"

I could barely hear her. Why was she speaking so softly? Then I nearly dropped the phone when there was a click and Buzz's voice suddenly said, "Selma, are you on the line? Let me know when you're off, okay?"

Buzz was there. That meant she was in London. It was midweek. Why wasn't she up in Manchester? I kept very still. He hung up.

"Are you there?" whispered Selma.

"I'm here. Of course we can meet. Where do you suggest?"

Please don't say come round to me, I pleaded silently down the line.

"There's a little café further along Blenheim Crescent. Shall we meet there in half an hour?"

I showered, dressed, and slipped out of the house before anyone could start demanding I make them breakfast. I turned the corner from Westbourne Park Road into Elgin Crescent and stopped dead outside the launderette. There was Max Austin with his laundry all laid out on the floor at his feet. He had requisitioned two machines and was peering at each yellow Post-it before removing it and throwing in the item of clothing. It looked as if some of the Post-its had got mixed up because as I watched he tossed a bunch of whites in with a pair of bright red boxers that might very well run. There was a pile of clothing with no Post-its at all and he was squinting at the labels in despair.

"Can I help?" I asked. I'd slipped in and crept up to stand right behind him.

He let out a short yell of surprise.

"Jesus Christ! Don't do that! You could have given me a heart attack."

"Sorry," I said. "Do you live round here?"

"I do now," he said without explaining

where he'd been before. "I have a flat in Wesley Square."

I knew Wesley Square. The houses were newly built and it had a nice little communal garden.

"Do the trains keep you awake at night?" The railway ran along the back of the square.

"Everything keeps me awake at night." He did look thoroughly exhausted. Crescent-shaped dark smudges fanned out under his eyes yet, I noticed with a jolt, just as I had when he'd first interrogated me, they were beautiful eyes, soft and expressive.

"Is your washing machine broken?" I asked him.

"I don't have one. There isn't room."

"Well, why don't you drop it off here and let them do it and pick it up later?"

He pointed to a sign saying BACK IN TWO HOURS. "Just as I told you. The bloody woman's never here. I can't come back in two hours."

I'd have liked to have stayed and help him but I didn't have time. "Look," I said, "give me the stuff you haven't sorted and I'll take it home and do it for you. You know where I live. You can pick it up from me later."

"Don't be daft," he said. "You're a writer,

not a washerwoman."

"Why can't I be both? Multitasker, that's me. I promise I won't make a habit out of it but it looks as if you could use some help. I've got to meet someone now but I'll pick up what's in these machines on my way back and do the rest at home."

He looked so grateful I felt an enormous sense of benevolence. It wasn't pure altruism on my part. I had an ulterior motive for doing him a favor. I needed to get back in his good books in case he had second thoughts about charging me with obstruction.

"My wife always did the washing. I don't know why I always find it such a nightmare, but I do."

His wife had been dead five years, according to Mary Mehta. Surely he could have mastered the art of laundry by now.

"That would be Sadie?" I said innocently.

"How did you know her name?"

"You were talking to her when I came into your office the other day."

He looked very embarrassed. "I suppose you think I'm going soft in the head."

"Not at all," I said. "I do it myself sometimes. It's comforting, especially when they're no longer around. I was sorry to hear about that," I added, hoping I wasn't overstepping the mark.

"Do you really? Have you lost someone too? Who do you talk to?"

Telling him how I swore out loud at my mother when she was safely in France and couldn't hear me wouldn't quite hit the right note so I mumbled something about a childhood dog and said I needed to be off.

"Are you sure about this?" he asked as we walked out of the launderette. "You've got enough on your plate what with all those people you've got staying with you."

"Oh, it's no problem. Call me on your way home," I said and left him at his car. About five minutes later, as I was wandering up the market, his words sank in. How did he know I had people staying with me? He was watching the house. He had to be. And if he was watching the house, he must have seen Buzz turn up on my doorstep the night before.

I stopped to say hello to Chris at his stall and thank him for the vegetables he had brought around. I didn't tell him I hadn't eaten any of them myself.

"You shouldn't have, Chris. It was an incredibly sweet thing to do."

A distinctly uncharacteristic flush appeared on his face and he scratched the back of his head, embarrassed.

"It was no biggie, honest. I could deliver veg to you whenever you wanted. Be a pleasure."

"No, no, I enjoy popping over to the market. I need the exercise."

"Nah, you don't. Best body in the market, yours is."

This was such a ludicrous stretch from the truth, I didn't really know what to say but it seemed Chris's cocky self had made a comeback.

"Seriously, I like coming here."

"Well, maybe I'll pop round anyhow, take a nice cuppa tea or coffee off you on my delivery rounds."

I smiled vaguely. The last thing I wanted was Chris knocking on the door when I was in the midst of trying to do some work. It was going to be hard enough as it was what with Tommy, my mother, and Angel taking up residence in the house.

"I hear you were one of the witnesses who saw someone in my alleyway on New Year's Eve."

"How'd you know that?"

"The detective who's investigating the case told me."

"You friendly with him?" He looked a little wary.

"Well, obviously I'm talking to him. I'm trying to find out what happened, Chris."

He nodded. "They say it's murder? That the fire was started deliberately?"

"They do. What made you notice the man you saw in the alley? Was he acting suspiciously?"

"Oh yes, he had a problem walking. You know, gammy leg." Chris came around his stall and began to walk jerkily down the road in the kind of dot-and-carry fashion people adopt when they favor one leg more than the other.

"That means he had a problem with his leg. It doesn't necessarily mean he was acting suspiciously. Did you tell Inspector Austin about it?" I wondered why Max hadn't mentioned it.

"I thought I had. But he was good-looking, this bloke. I confess I was on the lookout for geysers coming in and out of your house because of that man I saw leaving before Christmas."

"You spying on me, Chris?" I laughed, trying to make light of it.

"What if I am?" He grinned at me. "I've had my eye on you ever since we was nippers."

Had he always been this cheeky? Probably. I had an uncomfortable feeling that he thought seeing Buzz coming out of my house gave him the right to be more familiar with me, as if some kind of barrier had been crossed. Now he had an insight into my private life. I was wondering how to tactfully discourage this when someone touched my arm.

Selma was wearing dark glasses. I kissed her on the cheek in a nervous reflex action. I wasn't sure we were on kissing terms yet. The way she flinched was not a good sign.

"This is Chris," I introduced him. "Chris, this is Selma Walker."

"Oh, I know," he said. "*Fraternity*, right? My cousin's a big fan." He reached across his stall with a paper bag. "Maybe you could sign this for her."

Selma looked at him blankly as if she hadn't heard a word he'd said.

"Selma?" I took the bag and held it out to her. "Would you mind signing this for Chris's cousin?"

"Chris's cousin?" she repeated.

"Her name's Monica," said Chris.

Selma took out a pen. "What's her name?" she asked Chris.

She looked at me. "Monica," I said,

enunciating every syllable. It seemed rude but there was something wrong with Selma's hearing in her left ear. I was standing to her right and she could hear me but she couldn't hear Chris across the stall to her left. She scribbled her name on the bag and dropped it on the stall. She was incredibly jittery.

"Finish your shopping, I'll go on to the café. See you there."

As she walked away, Chris suddenly slapped his forehead. "That's it. That guy I saw coming out of your house before Christmas, it's him, innit? It was her fella. I make deliveries to her and that housekeeper always takes them in but when she's not around, he comes to the door. I hardly ever see her, Selma Walker. Who'd have thought?" He jerked his head in the direction Selma had departed. "She's in a bad way. You see too many of them."

"Too many of them what?"

"She's been beaten up."

"How can you tell?" I was astonished. I hadn't seen any bruises on her.

"Well, the dark glasses at this time of the morning is always a bit dodgy. The sun's not shining, is it? Could be a hangover but I'll bet you a bunch of parsley when she takes them glasses off, you'll see a great big shiner. It's the deafness that's the big give-away."

I was bewildered.

"Someone's given her a big walloping on the side of her head, bashed her ear up, poor girl. Most likely it's singing away inside her head and she can't hear nothing at all."

"You know," I said, more to see what his reaction would be than anything else, "that man you saw at her house, he's her husband, and they say Astrid McKenzie used to be his girlfriend."

"Blimey!" said Chris.

"But you didn't see him at my house on New Year's Eve?"

Chris stared at me for quite a long time. "Nah," he said finally, "can't say I did."

I paid him quickly and raced around the corner. Selma was sitting at the back of the café nursing a hot chocolate. She still had her dark glasses on.

"Thanks for coming," she said. "I caught the last flight down from Manchester last night. Now what will you have? Have a nice big breakfast, go on, eggs and bacon, lots of toast, how about a croissant? And here's another tape." She fished it out of her pocket and handed it to me. I was thrown. She was really churning them out and I hadn't even begun the book. When did she find the time?

"Coffee," I told the girl. "Thanks. I listened to the other tapes. I was shocked beyond belief."

"And you didn't know what to say to me, right?" She patted my hand. "It's okay. It hits everyone like that, not that I talk to many people about it. My makeup artist knows, obviously. She has to cover up the damage for the camera although he's pretty careful not to mark my face too much. I told you I was embarrassed by the story I would have to tell you, and now you know why. Domestic violence. It's no longer a taboo subject to the world at large, you read about it in the press but when it's on your own doorstep, it's a different story."

"It's just totally outside my experience," I stumbled.

"Of course it is, you and just about everyone else — at least up front."

As I babbled away she lifted her glasses away from her face for a fraction of a second. But it was enough; Chris was right. There was a livid gray and yellow circle around her left eye. I couldn't see the pupil, the swelling was so severe.

"You got the second tape?" she asked me anxiously.

I nodded. I couldn't tell her about Buzz's visit and the narrow escape I'd had picking up the package before he saw it.

"Now you understand why Buzz didn't want me to do a book. I had no idea he was eavesdropping when I talked to your agent that night in the Ivy and when she told me he'd called and had you over for an interview, I thought that would be it. He'd taken control as usual and would nurse the project along for a little while for appearances' sake and then find a way to kill it. That's why I had to meet with you personally, to see if you were someone I could trust, someone who would maybe help me make sure this book sees the light of day."

"Thank God Genevieve's got some interest in it," I said. "He really doesn't have a case for persuading you to drop it. Too many people know about the book now."

When I heard her next words I went totally cold. "He'll probably try to make a friend of you now," she said. "He'll want to know what I'm putting in the book."

Of course what she didn't know was that it had already happened. I had been nothing but foolish putty in his hands. He had seduced me. I had been in thrall to him and maybe if he had had more time to work on me, who knows what I would have told him. But surely, I told myself, surely the minute I heard what he had been doing to Selma I would have clammed up.

"If he asks you what's on the tapes," said Selma, gripping my wrist, "say I've started at the beginning with my childhood. That's what I've told him. He keeps asking to hear the tapes and when I won't let him, he hits me. He knows just when to catch me off guard so he can slam his palm into the side of my head before I run away. Once he fractured my cheekbone. All these" — she bared her teeth at me in a grisly smile — "replaced in the last two years. Lord knows what my dentist must think."

"I've only just met you," I said tentatively. "I don't have the right to tell you what to do. But surely your friends must try to get you to leave him?"

"I don't really have any friends over here." I was devastated by how pathetic she seemed all of a sudden. "I hooked up with him and then we only saw people he knew. I have friends back home but I'm too ashamed to tell them anything. I want them to think everything's going great over here. I mean, in a way it is. Over here I'm a star whereas over there I was just a daytime soap opera actress. I know it's all because of the character, because of Sally McEwan, it's her the fans care about but it still means I can go back to America and tell them I'm a hit."

"Ashamed?" What she was saying was incomprehensible to me. "Why would you be ashamed? He's the one who should be disgusted with himself. Hitting you over such a small thing."

"It's always a small thing that triggers him. Something you or I might see as small anyway but somehow it's a huge offense to him. Lee, I called you because I'm getting scared."

"You're *getting* scared," I said. "Your husband deafens you and virtually blinds you in one eye and you're *getting* scared." I tried not to sound too sarcastic but it was hard.

"I don't expect you to understand right away," she said, "but you're going to have to once you get into doing the book. What you have to accept is that I love Buzz. We go through cycles. Something takes hold of him and he takes it out on me but once he's hit me he's always full of remorse. And that's the best time. He's so sweet to me then, it's heavenly."

"Are you trying to tell me that in order

to receive love and affection from your husband you have to let him beat you up first? That's the sickest thing I've ever heard."

She looked at me with such sadness, I immediately felt awful. I couldn't think of anything else to do but reach out across the table and take her hand in mine.

"Thank you," she said. "I appreciate this. Of course it sounds totally insane to you. It *is* totally insane. I never know what it is that will trigger an attack of violence in him. When I came home after Christmas he knocked me down the minute I walked through the front door. *Why'd you have to go away and leave me?* That's what he yelled at me but we'd discussed it before I left and he'd said he was fine with my going back to the States for Christmas. He left me lying in the hall and went and made himself a cup of coffee. He called out to me, did I want one? And when I staggered into the kitchen to get it, he knocked me down again."

"Didn't you scream for help? Wasn't anybody there? What about the woman who was staying there? Had she gone? Wasn't Bianca there?"

"What woman?" She frowned.

"I ran into Bianca on the street and she

said there was a young lady staying there. She said she'd made a mess and she had to clean the house before you got back."

"Well, she must have cleaned it very well because there's no trace of her now."

"But don't you know who it was?"

"Lee, I don't want to know." She put her sunglasses back on and turned away from me. "Don't you see, that's why I have to write this book. I love him so much I let him get away with anything. I can't bring myself to leave him but when this book is published, everyone will know and he won't be able to get away with it anymore."

I wasn't listening to her. I was struggling to digest what she'd just implied. Buzz had had a woman there while she'd been away. He'd been cheating on her and it seemed she accepted it.

But I didn't.

How could I have been such an idiot? How could I have let myself be seduced by a sadistic, two-timing married man?

"It's just this time there hasn't been the sweetness afterwards. He's been beating me every day since I got back. He's really mad for some reason. Do you know what he does? He gets me down on the ground and he kicks me. He's the striker and I'm the football. When they had me go watch

Chelsea play for a publicity stunt, I almost screamed every time someone kicked the ball. It's his favorite thing, get me down on the kitchen floor and kick me — where it won't show."

"What about Bianca? Surely she must know. Doesn't she do anything?"

"Of course she knows but what can she do?"

"Call the police."

"What can they do? Nothing, unless I press charges, which I will never do. I don't want to involve Bianca any more than I have to."

"I saw how devoted she was to you," I said. No wonder Bianca always looked so grim.

"Oh, she is. She never says a word but from the moment she first saw me hobble into the kitchen black and blue, she began to make an extra fuss of me. It's embarrassing, sometimes, the way she worships me but it's a real comfort knowing she'll be there every day."

"Why don't you ask her to live in?"

"She won't. She has a relative — a sister, I think — who is very sick in some way. She lives with Bianca and Bianca takes care of her. Her need is greater than mine."

How do you know? I wondered. "How did you find her?"

"Buzz found her actually. He was in the newsagents one day and she'd just put up one of those postcards advertising her cleaning services. She asked him if he needed anyone and it coincided with our cleaner leaving. He hired her without even consulting me." She glanced at her watch. "Oh Lord, I have to catch my flight back to Manchester. I missed it last night. I'm sorry we had to do this so early but I wanted to give you this tape in person before I left. Could I ask you for a favor? Could I call my driver and reroute him to pick me up from your house? I just don't want to go back home with Buzz in the mood he's in."

"Of course," I told her.

But the minute we stepped through my front door I regretted it.

My mother was coming down the stairs as we came into the hall. She didn't see Selma behind me.

"Lee, the house is a disgrace!" I could tell instantly that she was in a state. Her squeaky voice always rose even higher in an attempt to command attention. It was comical and my father had always laughed at her when she was in full flow, which only succeeded in making her even more furious. When I was a child he would wink at me, encouraging me to join him in seeing the funny side of it, but as I grew older I began to understand how it infuriated her, that she couldn't help her silly voice, and I desisted. I wondered if he still tormented her like this and how enraged she must have become during their marital breakdown.

I nodded meekly, stopping in the doorway in an attempt to stall Selma.

"The place is absolutely filthy. What on earth have you been doing?" She was practically apoplectic by now and I couldn't delay Selma's entry into the hall for another second without seeming rude.

"Mum, this is —"

"I mean, I know you're not capable of cleaning a house, Lee, but whatever happened to Mrs. Jenkins?"

This was a tough one. I'd got rid of Mrs. Jenkins for two reasons. First I wanted to save money and second I couldn't stand having her around when I was trying to work. Pretty quickly I had realized that when I tried to do housework, I only succeeded in making the house even dirtier. An unusual talent but not one I could publicize. At that point I tried to retrieve Mrs.

Jenkins's services but the damage had been done. She was miffed beyond belief and refused to return. After that I took to executing lightning cleanups in the living room when I was expecting my friends and hiring a band of professional cleaners to blitz the whole house when my parents threatened a visit — something I had not been able to do this time because my mother had arrived without warning.

Selma saved me.

"Hello there," she said emerging from behind me to grasp my mother's hand. "I think I can help you."

"This is Selma Walker, you know, I was telling you about her last night . . ." Please God, let my mother remember.

"Of course." Suddenly my mother was all charm. "I'm Vanessa Bartholomew. Lee's mother." If she was surprised by the fact that Selma had not taken her sunglasses off after coming into the house, she didn't show it.

"Why don't I loan you my Bianca?" said Selma. "She's the perfect cleaner. I'm sure she'd welcome the extra work."

I had a fleeting vision of Bianca slaving away for days on end, informing my mother over coffee, "This house very dirty. Miss Selma have the clean house."

I started to say that I didn't think this would be such a great idea but my mother was already marching Selma into the kitchen.

I was about to follow when another figure appeared at the front door.

"Miss Bartholomew?" he said, consulting an order form. "Sorry I'm a bit late. Here about the damp?"

I put my finger to my lips in a desperate attempt to head him off at the pass. Too late.

"What damp? Did I hear the word 'damp'?" My mother emerged from the kitchen. "Tell me he's got the wrong house, Lee. Did I really hear him say he's come about the *damp?*"

Chapter 15

I used the arrival of Selma's driver as an excuse to make my escape. I felt bad about it. For one thing I still did not know the reason for my mother's surprise visit. I needed to have a talk with her, find out how things stood with Dad, but one look at her getting into her stride with the damp man was enough to send me scurrying into the street.

"The key to the basement's in the Vienna roast," I shouted to her. Let her work that one out for herself. I knew I just did not want to be there when she opened the door to the basement.

I was wandering aimlessly down Portobello Road, wondering what I could do to keep me away from the house for an hour, when I saw Buzz walking across the road toward me.

I didn't think twice. I just turned around and ran and as I did so I realized it was a stupid thing to do. I should have just allowed him to come up to me, chatted for a few minutes, pleaded an errand, and gone on my way. I would have been quite safe. What could he do to me with morning shoppers all around us? Now he knew I was deliberately avoiding him. He'd start to wonder why and pretty soon he'd put it together that it had something to do with Selma's tapes.

But I didn't stop. In a matter of days I'd gone from sexual obsession with Buzz to being downright terrified of him. It was hard to keep moving fast in the midst of the morning bustle of the market. The street was devoid of vehicles except for the odd truck delivering produce, but there were people everywhere. I crashed into someone, apologized, kept moving. After a while I was aware that a crowd was gathering to watch the chase. They were treating it as a bit of fun, cheering us on. Buzz was surprisingly nimble on his feet. I could sense him gaining on me and I began to panic. But then he tripped and fell against a stall, tipping an array of oranges, apples, pears, and lemons down the street.

Had I lost him? I didn't look back. I kept running, thankful I had gone to meet Selma in jeans and sneakers. By the time I leapt onto a passing number thirty-one bus, I had no idea where he was. I braved a glance out the window and I couldn't see him but that didn't mean he wasn't still after me.

As with train journeys, bus rides send me into a reflective state. Somehow I become immune to the chatter all around me, people getting on and off, the precarious swaying of straphangers, and start to gaze out the window, bringing whatever problems I had buried in my subconscious to the surface for inspection. Stuck in traffic for thirty, forty minutes, sometimes I even managed to resolve them by the time I arrived at my destination.

As we crawled along High Street Kensington, turning left into Earl's Court Road, I let my mind go blank and to my surprise my preoccupation with Buzz vanished. Instead I found myself thinking once again about Fred. The more I thought about it, the more I realized that Fred had made an impression on me that had nothing to do with his horrendous death. As the bus came to a standstill in the run up to the slow-moving Cromwell Road, the main exit to Heathrow, I returned again to the image of him gazing at Angel in adoration. No one had ever gazed at me like that. Tommy looked at me with affection sometimes but it was always tinged with amusement and backed up with a gentle poke at my ineptitude in some area.

But Angel had not even noticed. I felt sure she had at no time returned poor Fred's devotion and I wasn't talking about sex. She had strung his tender teenage heart along and then broken it. How *could* she? Those extraordinary blue eyes. In a year or two — maybe even in a matter of months — Fred's pimples would have disappeared and he'd have grown into his gangling frame. As we passed Earl's Court tube station I began to create for Fred the life he'd never have. I sent him to the Earl's Court gym, just coming up on the right, where he expanded his upper body until his protruding Adam's apple disappeared and he emerged a veritable Adonis. His stringy hair grew with miraculous new luster, he shed his anorak and faded jeans for tight-fitting black trousers and a billowing shirt open to the waist. Continuing on this seventies journey — I found it easier to place him in the *Saturday Night Fever* world of my own teenage fantasies because somehow I couldn't connect Fred with hip-hop — I sent him to a dance instructor, and from there to a series of clubs where he amazed everyone on the dance floor. Girls swooned at the sight of him and Angel had to wait her turn.

I was in the process of having Fred give Angel the runaround, taking her on a date and then not calling for weeks on end, making her suffer not knowing where she stood with him, when I saw we had reached the Fulham Road. The Royal Marsden Hospital was only a short walk away and Noreen's visiting hours were in progress.

But Noreen already had a visitor.

A delicate creature who looked almost as frail as she did was crouched on a chair at Noreen's bedside, immaculately dressed in a pair of tailored slacks and a soft wool sweater.

Noreen's face brightened when she saw me.

"Lee, how sweet of you to visit me again so soon. This is Marie-Chantal. Do you two know each other?"

Marie-Chantal said, "No, I don't zink so," very firmly in one of those infuriatingly exaggerated French accents and stood up. She came up to about my waist.

I smiled at her but for some reason she suddenly seemed in a hurry to be off. She clasped Noreen's hand very tightly for a second and beetled off down the ward lugging two enormous bags of supermarket shopping.

"So who is she?" I asked Noreen, intrigued.

"She works with Tommy at the BBC. Hasn't he mentioned her? I've met her several times and —"

Noreen seemed about to add something else and then changed her mind. All she said was "It's good that you two met."

A lightbulb went off inside my head. "Is she the one who's been giving Tommy French lessons?"

"Probably," said Noreen vaguely. "Ask Tommy to get the two of you together. She's enchanting."

I only stayed about twenty minutes with Noreen. I noticed — to my distress — that she tired more easily than on my last visit but she assured me she was on the mend.

"They're going to send me home in a couple of days. They say they've got it all — you know, the cancer — but I'm to come in for treatment regularly."

It was good news but I was secretly shocked. She seemed far too frail to be sent home to cope on her own. Tommy would have to sort something out for her. On my way home I realized I had forgotten to pick up Max Austin's laundry but before I did so, I popped into Tesco. The Caught on the Hop stir-fry had been fun but it had cleaned me out of food. I always felt a bit guilty going to Tesco when the market merchants were always on about how the supermarkets were taking away their business and how soon traditional street markets would be a thing of the past if we didn't support them properly. But they couldn't argue that a one-stop shop wasn't convenient, could they?

I ignored the filthy look Chris gave me — quite a change from his matey banter earlier in the day — as I bypassed his stall to go into Tesco and started running menus in my mind. How was I going to cope with catering for four, instead of one, every night? After the euphoria of the get-together we'd had in the kitchen the night before I'd found myself coming down to earth with a bump. On the bus back from the Fulham Road I realized I was actually dreading going home. I was used to walking into an empty house and going straight to my desk to work, secure in the knowledge that I would not be disturbed. This wouldn't happen anymore. How long was my mother planning on staying? How long before Angel found herself somewhere to live? How long before Max Austin nailed his man and I could release Tommy from his role as my protector?

In the meantime I had to think about feeding everybody. Deep down I was rather proud of myself that I was able to play house to so many people. This was something most women took care of as a matter of course, many with the additional responsibility of raising children. Quite frankly, I simply did not know how they did it and I admired them more than I could say. But I was a realist; I knew exactly what would happen. I would be thrilled and excited having people in the house for a few days, cooking and catering for them as I had already done for Angel, and then I'd want them gone.

Well, this time it wouldn't happen as fast as I'd like and I knew I'd better face up to the fact that I'd have to get used to it. I decided I'd cook for the next two nights and then I would draw up some kind of roster and pin it on the front of the fridge. Monday supper — Tommy; Tuesday — my mother; Wednesday — Angel. I paused. Was Angel capable of cooking a meal or would we all be given fish and chips? And could she afford it? Well, all I could do was ask.

I looked about but didn't see her on any of the tills. I approached the duty manager's desk but when I mentioned Angel's name, it caused quite a stir. Heads popped up all over the place.

"What's she done?" someone asked me.

"Is she coming back today?"

When it became clear that I didn't know what they were talking about, they told me what had happened. The police had arrived soon after Angel turned up for work and taken her away with them.

"They said they wanted to ask her some questions," said the girl on the next till.

I wandered up and down the aisles for a few minutes but I couldn't focus my mind on what to buy to feed everyone and I kept expecting Buzz to appear around every corner. The memory of our last encounter at Tesco and what had taken place in my hall shortly thereafter filled me with misery. Every way I looked I was trapped. I couldn't abandon the book because I couldn't let Selma down. But if I went on with it, I'd have to see Buzz. How was I going to get him out of my life?

As I was on my way out of Tesco, a woman waylaid me. I didn't think I knew her but she looked vaguely familiar, something about the color of her eyes.

"You were asking about Angel O'Leary," she said. She was older than I was, in her late forties probably. She looked haggard and worn out and her voice had a smoker's rasp.

"Yes, do you know why the police were looking for her?"

"She lives with you, doesn't she? You gave her that place to live in that burned down. Her mum told me she was back with you now. You've taken her in again. What you want to go and do that for, nasty piece of work like her?"

Suddenly I knew who this woman was. Her son had inherited her devastating ice-blue eyes that were fixed on me now. What had Angel said? *My mum knew Fred's down the bingo.*

"There's nothing I can say that will tell you how sorry I am," I said, aware that my words sounded trite.

"Well, why did you have to take her back in? If you hadn't given her a home in the first place, my Fred would never have gone there." Her voice was rising, bordering on hysterical. "Fred was my eldest. I've got four more back home and Fred's dad's not around anymore. I *needed* Fred. He was my oldest," she repeated.

"Have you buried him yet?" I asked.

Angel hadn't mentioned the funeral but she probably wouldn't have been welcome at it.

"We cremated him yesterday, what was left of him," said Mrs. Fox with no apparent irony. "And she never even bothered to show up. I hope he don't meet no Angels like her where he's going."

"Can I help you in any way?" A direct question, better than the ghastly *If there's anything I can do to help.*

"You can help me by trying to find out who started the fire."

"The police are —"

"IT WAS IN YOUR BACK GARDEN!" she screamed at me. "You've got to do *some*thing."

She was right up close to me, staring into my face, holding me directly responsible for what had happened to her son. Another woman came up and drew her gently away but it didn't make any difference. She'd got to me and I was glad that she had. I knew that the reason I kept thinking about Fred was because in some way I did feel responsible for what had happened. I wasn't a mother, I'd never had a child, and I didn't presume to think that the feelings I harbored for Fred's memory were maternal — yet in a way they were.

Standing in front of the checkouts with people wheeling their laden carts around me, I resolved there and then to do my utmost to find Fred's killer.

I barely recognized the house I had left two hours earlier. My mother had gone into action with a vengeance. Workmen swarmed everywhere — or so it seemed. In fact there were only two but the sound of whining drills made it feel as if the entire house was being taken apart. This was worse than I had ever anticipated and I sat down in a heap, wondering how on earth I was going to be able to write a word of Selma's book with all this noise going on.

The floorboards were up in the living room beside the kitchen and the damp man's head was poking through them. The smell was nauseating.

"Another month and your kitchen would have been in the basement," he told me cheerfully.

"Where's my mother?" I asked him nervously, expecting her to rise up out of the woodwork and strike me dead at any second.

"She's out back." He jerked his head in the direction of the garden.

I saw she was with Felicity Wood, her gardening club pal. They were walking about the blackened area around the summerhouse, striding through the ash, seemingly impervious to the stench that still lingered from the fire. In the spring and summer, Felicity came over once a week with a couple of hefty-looking men whom she proceeded to boss about, directing them to mow the lawn and dig and plant according to some grand scheme she had for her annual reinvention of my mother's garden. They were now scooping up ash with a shovel and tossing it into bin bags. I was feeling guilty enough about not having done anything about the house. Trust my mother to put me to shame about the garden as well.

I went outside. With Felicity there, my mother might just restrain from venting her wrath on me but to my surprise she didn't seem angry at all.

"There you are," she greeted me. "Isn't this marvelous? Everything's going to be cleared up in no time and then I've decided to ask Felicity to plant a memorial garden for that poor boy. Get a sundial or a birdbath or something. Nice idea, don't you think? Not sure what to do about rebuilding the summerhouse. Might be best to knock it down altogether. I don't think I'm going to want to barbecue out here anymore. There's been enough grilling of flesh, wouldn't you say?"

I winced and Felicity looked as if she might throw up. It was so like my mother to have the sweet idea of planting a memorial garden for Fred — something I should have thought of — and then spoil it all by talking about grilling flesh.

"And I've ordered a damp course for the whole of the basement. Just in time by the looks of things. Only problem is it'll stink the place out for quite a while. But thank God for your Tommy."

"Tommy?" How did he fit in?

"Oh, he really is a saint. We had a nice chatty breakfast together after you'd gone out — where on earth did you rush off to my first morning? Anyway, he told me about all the work he's doing in the house and I have to say I'm just thrilled. I'd no idea he was even living here and to find out he's really pulling his weight, well, we're going to make a great team."

She really was in her element taking charge like this. Where would we all be without her? Hadn't she arrived in the nick of time? Leave it to her to assemble her own personal task force to get the house and garden back in shape. As long as my mother thought she was invaluable, she was one happy bunny.

"Has that little blond creature who was living here found a new home?" Felicity asked me.

"Yes," I said. "At least I've taken her in for the time being."

"Thank God she left when she did."

"What do you mean?"

"Well, she must have gone out just before her summerhouse went up in smoke. She was here when I arrived on New Year's Eve. Then I went off to pick up some stuff from the market and when I returned, she'd gone. The summerhouse was empty."

"You were here, Felicity, on New Year's Eve?" I couldn't believe it. She must have been the woman the witness had seen.

"Only for a second. I was dropping off that little statue over there." She pointed to a tiny stone cherub standing on the ground beside one of the blackened shrubs. I'd never even noticed it. "I was doing some work in a garden in Dorset and I found it there. They said they didn't want it so I thought it would look wonderful beside the birdbath here in your mother's garden. I could have sworn I'd rung you to say I'd be dropping it off."

"No, you didn't, Felicity." *You never call before you come over,* I felt like adding but didn't. Felicity had a habit of turning up unannounced at the most inconvenient time to work on the garden. You'd be lying there, seminaked, stretched out on the lawn sunbathing and Felicity would appear with a team of men who would start digging all around you. "What time did you get here the first time, when you saw Angel? Did she see you?"

"You know, I don't think she did. She had the blinds down. She had a visitor, a man. They left together, that's when I saw her and I was out in the street by then. It was about four-thirty, quarter to five maybe."

Mrs. O'Malley hadn't mentioned a man with Angel, had she? I couldn't remember what Max Austin had said.

We went indoors and I left my mother standing in the rapidly disintegrating kitchen to go upstairs to my office and think about some work. I had to begin the book and all the activity in the house had delayed me. Sometimes I rolled out of bed and went straight to my desk to begin writing before the precious early morning fresh-from-a-good-night's-sleep inspiration evaporated. I would have to start locking the door to the little room off my bedroom that I had designated as my new office. As soon as Tommy ran out of places to dump things on the floor in my bedroom he wouldn't think twice about encroaching on the space where I worked. I had visions of trying to write with my feet sinking into a pile of T-shirts encrusted with dried sweat lying where he'd dumped them when he came in from his morning run.

I called Max Austin to tell him about Felicity but he was out and so was Mary Mehta. Well, they didn't make it easy for me to give them vital information either, did they? I transcribed the tapes Selma had given me so far and instead of feeling virtuous, I began to see myself as totally redundant. Selma didn't need a ghost. She was delivering her message in a clear, concise voice that I really didn't think I could improve on. If anything, my services might be required to assemble the material in a slightly more cohesive order once I had typed it up but apart from that I didn't see why she needed me.

It took me only a minute to realize I was lying to myself. I knew exactly why she wanted me. She had taken me into her confidence and she needed me as a buffer between herself and Buzz. There was no escape for me. I couldn't let her down. But what would she do if she knew that the person in whom she had chosen to place her trust, was someone who had already betrayed her?

I fretted all afternoon until I opened the door to Max Austin at around six o'clock. I was staggered. Since I'd seen him that morning he'd had what looked like a very expensive haircut. Not that I'm an expert on men's haircuts. It's not something Tommy goes in for very often. Then, when I took his overcoat in the hall, I noticed that he had changed his clothes. He was dressed casually but looking really quite spruced up in a pair of charcoal trousers and a black polo neck sweater. I had a fleeting moment of anger. Here I was doing his washing because I thought he didn't have enough time off from work to take care of it and all the time he'd been off getting himself fancy haircuts and decking himself out in some nice threads. But then it occurred to me that maybe he had a date. Maybe he was on his way to pick up someone whose appearance in his life might mark the end of his lonely days as a widower. My anger was instantly dissipated at the thought of the tentative relationship that would be unfolding over the next few weeks. But surely he wasn't going to turn up for a date with his washing in tow. That wouldn't be at all romantic.

He was staring at me and I don't blame him. God knows how long I'd been standing there fantasizing about his private life. I have to confess I'm a sucker for widowers, although the ones I usually feel sorry for are shrunken old men with white hair who shuffle down the road in a state of bewilderment that their beloved wife of fifty years has departed before them.

"It's still in the dryer," I said over my shoulder as I went up the stairs, "so I wonder if you wouldn't mind coming up to my office for a few minutes. It's rapidly becoming the only room in the house that's safe to enter. I've got something to tell you." I paused suddenly and turned around to confront him on the stairs behind me. It was rather odd looking down on him. He had a tiny bald patch on the very top of his head. "I forgot to offer you a drink. What would you like? Or are you on duty?"

He smiled at this. "No, I'm not — eh — on duty." He sounded as if it wouldn't make much difference if he was. "I'm picking up my washing and a Scotch and water — right up to the top — while I wait for your tumble dryer to run its course would be excellent. Thanks.

"You know," he said and his mournful face became quite animated, "we had a case last year where we found a woman's body parts in a tumble dryer. We were onto this bloke and we went round to nab him. We disturbed him in the middle of cutting her up. He flung everything into the dryer along with his washing and switched it on. Then he made a run for it. You'd think he'd have figured it out that the clothes would all turn red. It was a Miele. Sadie always said they were the best."

I couldn't move. Did he have any idea of the effect this grisly piece of information would have on me? I knew for a fact that this image of bloody body parts going around and around would pop into my head the minute I closed my eyes to go to sleep for the next six weeks. Was he going to go on like this? Was this the sort of thing you should expect from a detective off duty? Because if so he could leave right now.

He saw my face and was mortified.

"I'm sorry. You look quite ill. Are you all right? Sadie always liked hearing the gory bits but I know it can give some people a nasty turn."

"You have to deal with this sort of thing

every day," I said, pouring myself an even larger Scotch than the one I handed to him. And I never drank whiskey! "I don't know how you can stand it. What keeps you going?"

He looked at me in surprise. "It motivates me, quite frankly. The worse the condition of the body the more I want to go out and get the bastard who did the damage. My job is to catch the people who do these things so they can be punished and I *want* to see them punished. They're scum."

"All of them?" He sounded so vehement I was a little alarmed.

"Most. It's pretty grim out there but I've never regretted becoming a detective. *Never!*" he added, as if he thought I might contradict him. "I was the first one in my family to go to university and everyone thought I was mad but it helped when I entered the police force. I was on the fast track because of it, made detective ahead of my peers and they didn't like that one bit but it was worth it. Each time I put a villain away I'm a very happy man. *Very* happy." He jumped the last two steps on the stairs as if for emphasis. "So what is it you want to tell me?"

We'd reached the landing and I saw him

glance into my bedroom and take in all Tommy's clutter all over the floor. Once he was in my office he started to go around the room looking at all the photographs, peering at the books on my shelves. I removed a pile of manuscript pages from a chair and invited him to sit down. Now he was reading all my notes to myself pinned up on a slab of dark brown cork above my desk, anything from *Print out Chapter 9 with latest revisions* to *Buy Tampax* or *Tell Tommy Shagger called.*

"What's she doing up there? You know her?" He was looking at an old picture of Cath.

"She's an old friend. And Sergeant Cross's girlfriend. Have you met her?"

"Briefly. She's come to pick up Richie from work on the odd occasion."

I realized I was longing to know what he thought of her and I also realized he wasn't going to tell me.

"Is it serious?" I asked him.

He shrugged. "Put it this way. If she wants to be Mrs. Cross, she's going to have to be the one to do something about it. They moved in together but I have a feeling that was all her doing. Richie hasn't a clue about women."

And you do? I felt like saying. I was beginning to wonder if I was wrong about him. I had pegged him for a sad creature mourning his dead wife, desperately in need of someone to look after him but maybe it wasn't as simple as that. Maybe he wasn't as helpless as I thought. He was probably more than capable of taking care of himself, probably even preferred to do so. It had probably suited him to have me do his laundry for some reason because one thing I was sure of: Max Austin didn't do anything he didn't want to.

He leaned forward and tapped the photo of Cath. "Although maybe Richie's better off without her," he muttered.

"Why do you say that?"

"I thought you said she was an old friend," he said without elaborating further.

"Do I call you Inspector Austin or Max?" I asked him.

"Well, what do you want me to call you?" he countered.

"I'm Lee so I guess you can be Max."

"It's my name. So what have you got for me?"

"I've found the woman your witness saw."

"Oh yes?" To my intense irritation, he sounded skeptical.

"The woman who takes care of my mother's garden, Felicity. She was there around four-thirty on New Year's Eve. The summerhouse was okay. She saw Angel there and then she saw her leave." I paused for effect. "With a man."

"Yes, we know," he said and I nearly fell off my chair.

"You *know?* You've spoken to Felicity?"

"Of course. You told us about her, remember? Her number was in your address book. And we know Angel left with a man."

"Mrs. O'Malley told you?"

"She didn't actually. She omitted that little detail but once we went back and told *her,* she amended her statement pretty quickly. Amazing how you can jog people's memories just like that."

I was feeling rather deflated. I had so wanted to impress him with my discovery of Felicity.

"Well, at least you can eliminate one of the people your witnesses saw. Anyway Felicity couldn't possibly be a suspect. She wouldn't murder anyone in a million years."

"She wasn't the woman," he said quietly.

"What?" I wasn't sure I had heard him correctly. Of course Felicity was the woman.

"Our witness took one look at her and said they'd never seen her before."

Suddenly I realized what a nightmare his job must be. Half the time witnesses were unreliable and just when you thought you had found the person they saw, there was nothing to stop them saying *Oh no, you've got it wrong.*

"I suppose you also know that Buzz came round to see me last night?"

He nodded.

"Why is he free?" I asked, a note of desperation creeping into my voice.

"We've got no reason to hold him," said Max Austin.

"But you have, you have," I cried. "He beats his wife and he beat up Astrid McKenzie and you found his prints on the can of kerosene right here in my potting shed. Why haven't you arrested him?"

"We know why he lied about going to your house. Same reason you did. He wants to keep quiet about his adultery. And we know why he was in your back garden. But we've let him go."

"Why?" I could hardly believe it.

"Because he's not our man. He's got a cast-iron alibi. He took a can of kerosene round on New Year's Eve and that's why his prints are all over them, but he was seen leaving well before the fire started and someone was with him right through until the next morning."

I didn't like the sound of this. I remembered Bianca's complaint: *Young lady make mess.*

"So he didn't set the fire but he had something to do with it."

"Not necessarily. We didn't find any evidence of his having been at Astrid McKenzie's place."

"What about the other prints you found on the can of kerosene? And the footprints you think belonged to a child?"

He nodded.

"Well, whose do you think they are?"

"We don't know. We've talked to Kevin O'Malley and we've ruled him out. He wasn't in your garden when the fire was started. He was upstairs chatting to his friends on-line and we've got the times on the e-mails to prove it."

"You know those prints might have been Angel's."

Now he looked interested. "Why do you say that?"

"Well, you say they're small prints and Angel is tiny. Maybe she kept a can of kerosene in the potting shed for some reason."

"You're saying Angel O'Leary set fire to the summerhouse where she was living? Tell me, I'd really like to know, what do you think her motive was?" He was humoring me now, plainly amused by my attempt to play sleuth.

"Oh, no, of course I don't think that. I don't know what I'm saying. To think that Angel would start the fire would be crazy but then why would a child do something like that?"

"There are a lot of amateur detectives these days but I'll be honest with you, Lee, I didn't imagine you were going to turn out to be one of them."

"I just so hoped you had enough to put Buzz away. Do you understand the mess I've got myself into?" There was no stopping me now. I'd yearned to be able to talk to someone about Buzz, not that I'd imagined in a million years that that someone would be Max Austin. "I've been a complete fool. It was totally unlike me to let him seduce me, you have to believe me. It came out of the blue, I was going for a job interview, I didn't expect to meet someone and be violently attracted to them. I didn't know he was Selma's *husband.*"

He'd got up and was standing looking out the window. I couldn't see his face, couldn't tell if he was even remotely interested in what I was telling him.

"He beats Selma up too," I went on. "He knocks her about. That's what the book's going to be about. It's not her autobiography, she wants to do a book for victims of domestic violence like her. She wants to share her experience with them, use her celebrity to offer her support. But she told me that after all he's done to her, she still loves him and I believe her. There's something about him — I've been trying to work out what it is that made him so appealing. What do you suppose happened to him to make him the way he is?"

Suddenly Max Austin turned on me.

"Forgive me but you're talking complete crap," he exploded. "You're asking for my understanding about some torrid little affair you've been having. You're winding up to spout some bleeding heart liberal bullshit about how poor Buzz Kempinski was probably abused as a kid so that lets him off the hook for what he's doing now. Have you any idea how lucky you are?"

"Lucky?" I didn't get it.

"Yes, lucky. You've got away from this guy. You're not hooked into him like Selma Walker is, or Astrid McKenzie was, or countless others no doubt. When we were called round to Astrid McKenzie's place a few years ago we found her beaten almost to a pulp. The skin on her cheek was broken and the mess below her eye was like a blood orange, like overripe fruit. Pulp. And the word is she'd seen him again recently and lo and behold she's in the market the next day with a black eye. Seems like she wasn't one to learn her lesson the first time."

"My agent told me that she —"

"Yeah, yeah. We talked to her," he said and I was momentarily unnerved. I should have wised up by now to the fact that he must have talked to *everyone* surrounding the case. I began to wonder just how much he knew about my life. I kept to myself and led such a hermit's existence, I wasn't used to being under the microscope and I wasn't at all sure I liked it.

"You're trying to sell me on the notion that he's not all bad," Max continued. "Well I don't buy it even if it's free. Buzz Kempinski's a menace and nothing would make me happier than to pin this fire on him so I could nail him once and for all. But I can't. I *bloody can't.*"

He sat down again and leaned forward to tap my knee.

"I'm more frustrated about the fact that

I can't arrest Buzz Kempinski than I have been about anything in years. And as for suggesting that Angel O'Leary might be implicated in some way — that's the biggest irony of all."

"Why's that?" I was scared of him now. He was right to make me feel stupid but did he have to crush me so completely?

"You haven't asked me who his alibi was."

"Oh *no!*"

"Oh yes. They had a date for New Year's Eve. She said she was freezing cold in the summerhouse and she called him to ask him to bring her some kerosene for the heater. She'd run out. He turns up, they fill the heater, leave the can in the potting shed. Then they go off to celebrate New Year's Eve together — all night. It fits with the times we've got people saying they saw them plus we've got them on the closed-circuit TV coming into Ladbroke Grove from Blenheim Crescent a good half hour before Kevin O'Malley saw Fred arrive. Angel O'Leary was his alibi, all right. They'd been at it like rabbits all through Christmas."

As if to emphasize the horrible truth of what he was saying, I felt the dryer's final shudder vibrating through the house. Then came the sound of the high-pitched penetrating signal that meant the cycle had come to an end. It was broken and once it started, it wouldn't stop until I went downstairs and turned it off.

Just one more item to add to the list of things that were falling apart in the house.

Chapter 16

It was probably the understatement of the year to say I was shocked at Angel's duplicity. I never for one moment saw her as the deceitful little minx she clearly was. But maybe Angel didn't know about me and Buzz and how, for that matter, would Selma describe *me* if she found out what I had got up to with Buzz?

But I still didn't know how I was going to face Angel when she came home.

Home! I'd given her a home and look what she'd given me in return. I caught myself. I could see where this was going and I needed to snap out of it. At the very least didn't I need to warn her what she might be dealing with if she got involved with Buzz? How long before he started knocking her about? She was so tiny, just like Selma. And Astrid McKenzie. Didn't that make what he did to them twice as contemptible? Why couldn't he pick on someone his own size? Like me.

Max Austin was right. I'd had a lucky escape.

After he'd gone, stumbling down the front steps bearing his pile of washing before him in a giant Harvey Nichols bag, I returned to my office in search of distraction. He had promised to keep me informed as to his progress in tracking down the mystery arsonist and I supposed I had to be content with that. I pulled up my transcripts of Selma's tapes and began to read through them in the hope that they would take my mind away from the Angel problem. Okay, so I was procrastinating as usual, but in fact this was how I got things done. Displacement activity. Works every time. Do something else in place of the thing you don't want to do and in time this very activity will come to the top of the list to replace another dreaded chore.

I began to jot down notes as to how to proceed with the book and I was feeling quite pleased with myself until I came to the bit where Selma declared she had no family left in the United States.

So who had she been visiting over Christmas? Why had she told me she'd gone to see her family? Where had she been? Why had she lied? Had she even gone to America? Could it be that she'd stayed here and just made it seem like she'd gone abroad? I tried to continue with her transcript but I kept coming back to the same thing until finally I acknowledged what was lurking at the back of my mind.

Selma could have been right here in London on New Year's Eve. Selma was beaten up by Buzz. Selma was his wife. Selma had a few scores to settle. When it came to setting fire to the homes of Astrid McKenzie and Angel, Selma had a *motive!*

And Selma had tiny hands and feet — just like a child's.

But if Selma knew about Buzz's association with Astrid and Angel, did that mean she also knew about me? Somehow I didn't think so. I would have seen it. Surely I would have seen it.

Of course, once I started fretting about Selma, telling myself I had let my imagination come up with an utterly preposterous scenario, I had to find something to do to take my mind off *her.*

I checked my e-mail and was immediately confronted with yet another of my problems. In amongst the attempts to sell me Viagra and help me increase the size of my penis there was a message from Cath. Subject: *Ok. Let's meet.*

I had called her earlier in the day and

left an impassioned message on her voice mail, imploring her to get in touch. It had never occurred to me that she might send me an e-mail.

Okay. Calm down. Let's get together. See you in the Napoleon for a drink tonight at 7.

I looked at the little clock in the corner of my screen — it was 7:15. I shut down my computer, grabbed my bag and raced down the stairs and out the door. I could see Angel on the other side of the street coming home from Tesco. I ducked into the mews — Astrid McKenzie's mews — until she'd passed and then sprinted along Blenheim Crescent onto Talbot Road. The Napoleon was a pub on the corner of Chepstow Road whose actual name was the Prince Bonaparte but for some reason we'd never called it that. It had a noisy bar and a large room in the back where they served surprisingly good food. I found Cath sitting at one of the tables in the back, nursing a Diet Coke. That was a good sign given what Tommy had said about her drinking problem. I picked up a warming glass of Shiraz at the bar and carried it over to her. I leaned across the table to kiss her hello and she moved her head away so I was left feeling totally stupid. I was tempted to snap at her *What is your problem?* but I restrained myself and sat down opposite her.

"Sorry I'm late, I only just got your e-mail." I smiled. "It's great to see you."

She didn't smile back. I was reminded of Bianca and her perpetual scowl whenever she saw me. "I thought you'd be chained to your desk," she said. "I remember how you always used to check your e-mail all the time." She sounded almost accusing.

"Well, yes, I am working," I assured her. "I'm just beginning something, as a matter of fact. I'm ghosting a soap star's book, Selma Walker and —"

"Yes, I know," Cath interrupted me.

I was thrown. "How do you know? No one's supposed to know."

"I know a lot about what's happening with you, Lee. You've been a naughty girl, haven't you?"

"Well, don't sound so triumphant," I said, stalling, wondering what on earth she meant. "You were always the good girl and I always fucked up. Why should anything change?"

She smiled a little, not much but it was a start. "Selma Walker's manager," she said. "Are you ghosting his story too?"

Suddenly I got it. "Sergeant Cross?" She

nodded. "Is he supposed to blab to you about the cases he's working on?"

"No" — now she really smiled — "but he does. He told me about this fire in a summerhouse and that poor kid getting killed and then he told me about the woman who lived in the main house and how they'd found prints in her bedroom *and* the shed. He knows I like the gossipy stuff. He said they reckoned the woman was cheating on her boyfriend, which was a shame because he seemed like a really nice guy."

"But you didn't know it was me?"

"Not until much later. I asked him if he knew why you were there and I eventually got it out of him. So you've been giving Tommy the runaround?"

There was that familiar tone of disapproval in her voice. We'd only been sitting here five minutes and already I was beginning to feel defensive. Cath was always in the right. She always made me feel — I searched for the word — immoral and I resented it. *Calm down,* I told myself, *don't let her get to you.*

"He had no right telling you about Buzz." It sounded lame. "It's none of your business."

She looked a little sheepish. "I guess

not," she said. "And I'm sorry I didn't stop to talk to you. It was a bit of a shock running into you like that. And I really was in a hurry."

"But it doesn't explain why you wouldn't talk to me at the station."

"No, it doesn't," she said slowly. "All I can tell you is that I thought I might have some pretty shattering news that I was in a hurry to share with Richie. Poor guy, he said he felt he was caught in the middle between us. He did tell me to call you but he knew we had issues and he was nervous. He didn't know whether I'd want to talk to you. He didn't know what the boundaries were."

"*Issues?* You fall in love with my boyfriend and you can't handle it and you walk out of my life and you call it an *issue?* So what *are* the boundaries, as you call them?"

Suddenly she leaned forward, reached across the table, and shook me by the shoulders.

"I'll tell you if you really want to know," her voice had risen to an anguished squeak and I flinched at her touch. She was pretty upset. "I'll tell you what the boundaries are and then maybe you won't overstep them all the damn time. You were always hard work, Lee. Did you know that? You were always testing me and to be perfectly honest with you, I'd begun to wonder if it was worth getting back in touch with you. I'd had time to stand back and think about you objectively. You were always so confident, arrogant almost, and yet so vulnerable and needy. You always wanted to play it both ways. You were so self-contained, so much your own person, it was almost as if you didn't need anyone else in your life. I felt flattered to be chosen as your friend but I was never really sure how I fitted into your life."

Now she held my chin and turned my face to hers to check my reaction. I was stunned. Some kind of dam was bursting and I wondered if she'd been bottling this stuff up for years. No wonder she hadn't called me before, she was probably terrified of what she would say to me. Well, now I'd forced it all out into the open. I had only myself to blame and there was nothing I could do but sit and listen to it. Something told me she wasn't finished yet.

"You think I've stayed away from you because of how I felt about Tommy and you're partly right. I adored Tommy. For his kindness, mostly. I'm a sucker for a kind, decent man. And now I've found one of my own. You'll see, Richie is this great big benevolent bear and he's so good to me, I can't believe it. I don't think I was ever actually *in love* with Tommy, I just couldn't resist the combination of a good-looking man who was actually nice. And I couldn't stand the way you treated him. I couldn't understand why you didn't just snap him up and marry him. Or at least I did understand — you're attracted to the dark and dangerous type and Lord knows Tommy isn't that — but I was so angry with you for hanging on to him like a dog in the manger. I wanted a Tommy type and it bugged me that you didn't and yet you'd hooked one who was besotted with you."

"Back up a bit," I said. "I'm attracted to dark and dangerous types? Where'd you get that idea?"

"By being around you and watching you since we were twelve years old. Your eyes were always drawn to a black leather biker jacket whereas you could line me up a three-piece suit any day. You were always the adventurous one. I was always a little in awe of you. I was convinced one day you'd run away with a glamorous dark stranger so when you suddenly started seeing Tommy, I just didn't get it. It was so unfair. I think I always secretly thought you ought to leave the Tommys of this world for those of us who really needed them."

"I need Tommy," I said, surprised to hear myself admit it.

"So what were you doing fucking Selma Walker's manager?"

"Having fun."

"You are impossible," she said with what I thought was begrudging admiration. "I'm appalled at your behavior but I confess I want to hear all about it. You see, this is what I miss about you, Lee. You do things I never would and I get to live vicariously through you. You behave badly. You're moody. You sulk. You're arrogant. You say all the things I long to say and never have the guts to. You snare exactly the kind of man I want and then you cheat on him with the kind of man *you* want. You set out to have it all, you overstep all these boundaries I've been talking about, and you fucking get away with it. How do you do it?"

"Not this time," I said. "It's backfired on me."

"Really?"

"Really," I said.

You see, this is what I miss about you, Lee. Wasn't that what she'd just said?

Later, just when I was trying to go to sleep, just before the picture of the bloody body parts in the washing machine floated before my eyes, I knew I'd bring out Cath's pent-up assessment of my character. I'd examine it for the brutal grains of truth I knew were in there. But right now I was going to hang on to the fact that she'd said she missed me. Because I'd missed her too. I'd missed having someone to confide in. Cath and I were so different — as she'd just pointed out with rather unexpected candor — but we complemented each other. And there was no denying that a shared history went a long way toward cementing a bond. It was something of a relief to be with someone who knew me so well, who wasn't afraid to be honest with me, and I was intrigued by her sudden revelation that she had always been in awe of me.

"Look," I said, "let me tell you what happened with Buzz. Stop me if you know it all already but I think you ought to hear my side of it."

She shrugged. *Okay.*

"I met him when I went round to Selma Walker's house for my first interview. I thought I was going to meet her. Of course, it turned out to be his house too because he was married to her but I didn't know that at the time. No, really, I swear I didn't know." Cath's expression said *Pull the other one.* "All I knew was he was her manager. She wasn't there and it made perfect sense for him to interview me in her absence. It's just that he interviewed me as a sexual partner instead of as a ghostwriter and I was so instantly attracted to him, I responded in like fashion and — what can I tell you? — I got the job."

"What do you mean, you responded in like fashion? You fucked him?" Cath was incredulous.

"Not *then.* Cath, who do you think I am?" But the truth is I know I would have fucked him then if we'd got that far. "No, I ran into him later in Tesco and —"

Cath burst out laughing. "He ogled you over the biscuits, stalked you along the pet food, and finally threw you down in aisle four?"

"Shut up. I know it sounds hilarious but it's turned into a nightmare. I've got myself into a real mess and I want your advice."

"I'll bet you do. Where was Tommy while all this was going on?"

"We weren't speaking. It wasn't serious, just one of the usual ongoing tiffs. He forgot to record a TV program I really wanted to see and I was fed up with him. You remember how it was between us?"

"I remember you were always so bossy. It was always about him doing things for you, not much of the other way around."

My hackles went up and I started to lash back at her. Then I stopped. She was right. From where she stood it probably looked as if I never did anything for Tommy.

"We hadn't had sex in months — we have now," I added hastily when she leaned forward, "and frankly I suppose I was just ripe for exactly what you said earlier: an adventure with a dark handsome stranger. I fancied Buzz rotten."

"Then you found out he was married to your new subject when it was too late?"

"Exactly. Do you watch *Fraternity*, Cath?"

"When I have the time. She's an odd little creature, Selma Walker. Is she anything like her character?"

"The opposite."

"How's the book going?"

"I haven't even started it properly yet. She's dictating it on tapes and giving them to me and I'm listening to them and that's where it's all got nasty."

"She's found out about you and her old man?"

"Not that I know of. But she doesn't

want to do a regular autobiography, *My Life as a Soap Opera Actress.* She wants to do a book for battered women."

"How bizarre. Do her publishers know? Is this the mess you've got yourself into? They're expecting a juicy tell-all soap opera memoir and they're not going to get it? Why ever would she want to write a book for battered women?"

So Richie hadn't told her this part.

"Because she is one."

Cath was pretty slow. She just stared at me blankly. It was only when I said, "A book for battered *wives,* Cath," that the penny dropped.

"Good God! Has he — ? You? Are you — ?"

I shook my head. "I feel so stupid," I told her. "I never guessed, not for a minute and I saw them together. They seemed fine. You'd never have thought there was anything wrong although when I first met her, I caught a glimpse of a bruise on her back. She said she'd fallen over in the kitchen. Of course, that's probably exactly what happened but as a result of him knocking her down. I suppose I was so wrapped up in myself as usual, so busy fussing over whether she'd detect if there was anything between me and her husband, that I probably wouldn't have noticed if he'd whacked her over the head right in front of me. He conned me into doing the book." I told her how Buzz had witnessed Selma talking to Genevieve at the Ivy and then approached me without Selma knowing in order to seduce me so he could have access to the book's content. "How could I be so blind? Cath, I don't know what to do."

"This is a first for you, right?"

"A first?"

"Domestic abuse. You've never encountered it. I bet you thought it was a working-class thing. Man comes home from work, his dinner's not on the table so he knocks the wife about." Cath had a wry look on her face that I couldn't quite read. "You thought you were safe from that sort of thing in your middle-class ivory tower?"

"Oh, no, of course not, I —"

"It's a common misconception. And you are a bit of an innocent, Lee. You like the idea of a bit of edgy drama in your life but you want to be able to run back to your big fancy house when it suits you, where you feel all nice and safe."

It always made me uncomfortable when Cath drew attention to the difference in our backgrounds mostly because while I felt guilty about my privileged life, like most people in my position, I did nothing about it.

"It's not so safe, actually," I pointed out. "We've had a murder in the back garden."

"Lee, I'm not sneering at you. Honest. I'm just stating a fact. I'd probably be just like you if I'd lived in that house all my life. You *are* pretty blinkered but it's part of who you are. Like I said, there's an innocent quality. I used to be amazed at all the things in the world that passed you by. Women getting beaten up is something that happens all the time. *All the time!* We had a kid at school about a year ago who was getting knocked about and I got involved. His mother was the one taking the real beating and she brought charges against the boy's father. Doesn't often happen but she was pretty courageous."

The expression on Cath's face was very sad, as if the memory of what she'd witnessed had really shaken her.

"I had to give evidence," she went on, "and after it was all over I began to investigate. I started asking around about domestic violence and talking to people, reading about it and I learned a lot. I could throw statistics at you that would terrify the life out of you. In this country alone fifty thousand women and children flee their homes every year to get away from domestic violence. In the States there's a beating every nine seconds —"

"I hate the thought of Selma just being a statistic," I said. "I want to know what I can do to help her now."

"Well, you can start by not screwing her husband." Cath grabbed my hand when she saw my face. "Sorry. That was uncalled for. But why doesn't she get a restraining order slapped on him? Has she given you any indication that she's going to leave him?"

"Not until the book's published. She seems to think the only way she can expose him is by writing a book, then the whole world will know and he won't dare to come after her. But I haven't even started the book yet. By the time it's published, she could be dead. He came round the other night." Cath's eyes widened. "My mother had just arrived. Tommy was there. Angel. I got rid of him pretty quickly. But he could come back at any moment. What should I do?"

"Who's Angel?" asked Cath. I told her. "Right," she said, "the girl in the summer-house." And then I told her about the Buzz connection and she shook her head in disbelief. "I heard he had an alibi. What a bastard! You've got to stay away from him, girl. I'm going to talk to Richie."

"So how did you meet him?"

"Richie?" She looked at me oddly for a second. "He came to give a talk to my kids at the school about being careful with strangers. You know, after Soham — Holly and Jessica?"

I felt a little sick all of a sudden, remembering the grotesque murder of two beautiful little girls, by the caretaker at their school in the town of Soham near Cambridge, a man they had trusted. I recalled how he had actually hung around to help the police with their inquiries, when all the time he had disposed of the girls' bodies in a ditch not far away, even returning during the investigation to set fire to them.

"And he was so sweet with the children," Cath went on. "I think I sort of fell for him there and then. I'm surprised he hasn't mentioned Buzz's domestic violence history. It's one of his obsessions."

"Buzz seems to be one of Max Austin's obsessions, full stop. He's determined to get him one way or another."

She looked at me quizzically. "What do you make of Max Austin?"

I threw up my hands in a helpless gesture. What *did* I think of Max Austin?

"I'm not sure, to be honest. He seems so moody. One minute he's impatient with me, sarcastic almost, and then I get the feeling he could be quite gentle if he tried. He patronizes me, humors me when I try to suggest stuff about the case."

"You try to *suggest* stuff?" Cath looked incredulous. "What sort of stuff?"

I told her about what I'd surmised about Buzz.

"He must like you," she said. "If anybody else tried to suggest stuff like that to him, he'd bite their head off. But a word of warning: Don't try to play amateur detective. It's insulting. This is arson and murder we're dealing with. But you're right, there is a gentle side to him. Off duty, he used to be a really sweet man before the tragedy."

"What tragedy?"

She looked at me and shook her head. "I don't believe it. He hasn't told you? But then I don't suppose he would, would he?"

"I know about his wife dying."

"But did you know she was murdered?"

"You're joking!"

"I'm not. She went off on holiday on her own apparently, to some cottage in darkest Devon and when he couldn't raise her on her cell phone he got a funny feeling and went chasing after her. But he was too late. They found her body in a field. She'd been strangled and dumped under a hay bale, and her little dog — a poodle — had been butchered. They never found the killer. Can you imagine what a nightmare that must be for him?"

"What do you mean, they never found the killer?"

"Well, sometimes they don't. It's pretty ironic when you think about it. He's a murder detective and it's one case it seems he's never going to solve. He's an angry person but you can understand that. It's just that recently he's become so cynical. He's surrounded by the more despicable aspects of society day in day out and to be honest with you, Richie and I are quite worried about him. There doesn't seem to be anything else in his life. Richie thinks he's going a little crazy, quite frankly."

"He talks to his wife," I said. "I went into his office and he was talking to an invisible person called Sadie."

"His wife," Cath confirmed. "He's always done that. At first Richie and I thought it was quite healthy but we reckon he ought to be over it by now. It's been five years. He should be talking to someone else. Do you know" — she looked a little coy — "Richie and I were talking about it the other night and we wondered if he'd even had any sex since his wife died."

I giggled a little, Cath frowned.

"No, seriously. Richie's worried he might be heading for a breakdown."

"What was she like? Did you meet her?"

"No, I never did. Richie and I got together long after she died but he told me she was stunning. Colorful. Literally — she was black, or rather café au lait. But she was flamboyant. Richie showed me a picture of her. She was as tall as her husband and striking. I mean in-your-face striking — dangling earrings, bright red skirt, and purple blouse sort of thing. Very high heels, great legs although the calves had a bit too much muscle for my liking. Gigantic tits, long neck, high cheekbones, Sophia Loren eyes, lots of teeth —"

"Okay, stop" — I held up my hand — "I get the picture." But it wasn't a picture I was expecting. I found it hard to reconcile this image with the kind of woman I'd imagined as Max Austin's wife. I would have assumed he'd be married to what I call a background person. Someone with impeccable taste who stayed home and made herself invisible. He had struck me as someone who didn't like to draw attention to himself, which was more than could be said for his wife by the sound of things.

"But she was nice? Richie liked her?"

Cath made a face.

"Like? I don't know about that. He was seduced by her. Oh, don't look like that. I don't mean literally. Maybe 'charmed' is a better word. But she never stopped talking, never stopped laughing and Richie said whenever he went over to their house she always had loud music blaring. And she was smart. Richie had the feeling Max used to sound her out about his cases. He knows Max thought she had sensational instincts."

What a huge empty hole she must have left, I thought. What must it be like for him now when he went home? No noise, no more sharing his cases.

"Oh God!" I said. "I'm starting to feel really sorry for Max Austin."

"Well, let me tell you something that'll make it a whole lot worse. Listening to Richie I get the distinct impression she was a bit of a tramp. He went to a party with them one time and she danced the entire evening with different men, threw herself around the room. Max claimed he didn't dance and just sat there drinking. Richie said from watching her, he figured she was on intimate terms with at least two of those men. But Max seemed oblivious to what was going on. Either that or he was in denial. Richie said the way he spoke about Sadie, you'd have thought she was this meek little devoted creature who met him at the door every night with his slippers in her mouth."

Funny, I thought, that's exactly how I imagined her and he'd never even said anything about her to *me.* Shows how wrong you can be about a person.

"I need a refill," I said, getting up and turning to the bar. I'd done this deliberately to see what her reaction would be. I wanted to give her a chance to discuss her alcoholism with me if she felt so inclined.

"Nothing for me," she said.

"Oh, come on, Cath. This is a celebration, getting back together like this."

"Well, okay, I'll have another Diet Coke."

I made a face.

"I'm not drinking," she said.

"Party pooper," I said, in a teasing tone of voice, nothing heavy. She could pick it up or not, as she wished.

But her explanation, when it came, completely threw me. She shook her head again and then, to my astonishment, she burst into tears. I slipped around the table and put my arm around her. Cath might insist there was a lot wrong with me but she was a total mess herself and I couldn't figure it out.

She dried her eyes with a paper napkin.

"I'm pregnant," she whispered.

"No!" I said. "I mean, yes! That's great news, isn't it? Why are you crying? Why didn't you tell me the minute I arrived? Is Richie thrilled?"

When she didn't answer, I squeezed her shoulders a little.

"What's up, Cath?"

Eventually she rubbed her eyes and murmured something.

"What?"

She looked at me and I saw how distraught she was.

"He doesn't know."

I couldn't believe what she was saying. "You mean you haven't told him? Why? How far gone are you?"

"I was practically sure I was pregnant the day you saw me at the station. That's what I was rushing in to tell Richie. I'd decided he had to know."

"And?"

"It was hectic in there. He was busy. I don't know why I acted so impulsively, rushing to the station like that. It was neither the time nor the place. I don't know what I was thinking."

"Okay." I could imagine that it needed to feel special when you told someone you were expecting their child. "But why haven't you told him since then?"

"I was all set to tell him that night. We were due to go to his brother's for dinner and I thought I'd tell him on the way there and maybe we could announce it — like a family thing. But he got caught up and called to say he'd meet me there."

"Is Richie close to his brother? Do you like him?"

"We both like Alan a lot. He's sort of a joke, you know? He's big like Richie but in a roly-poly way. All warm and jovial all the time and of course the drink helps." She gave me a knowing look but I was a bit slow picking up on it. "He's a builder like their father but the truth is he's not very successful. When jobs go out to tender, Al never seems to be in the running. Richie's the responsible brother but to my mind he's a bit too responsible."

"What do you mean?"

"Al has five kids. Shirley, his wife, really

has her hands full because four of them are under six. Money is very tight and it seems every time we go there, Al has his hand out." Cath's face hardened. "Richie and I had a row about it on the way home. Al always hits on Richie, never says anything to their father because Richie insists the old man shouldn't be bothered. I asked Richie if Al had hit on him for money again and he suddenly became really defensive — *He's my brother, why shouldn't I help him if I want to?* sort of thing. It turned out he'd had a desperate call from Al the week before and he'd agreed to cover Al's mortgage for the rest of the year. On top of his own mortgage, it leaves him with virtually nothing. When I said how crazy it was he replied that he didn't need the money, it wasn't as if he had kids of his own, Al was family, he owed it to him, et cetera, et cetera. After that I couldn't bring myself to say anything about the baby."

"You know you have to," I told her.

"Or I could just have an abortion and he'll never know," she said and burst into tears again.

"Right," I said, "that's enough for tonight. You need taking in hand, Cath. You're coming home with me. I've got to feed the troops, we'll take this bottle of champagne for them, we'll pick up a Chinese takeaway, and you'll join us for supper. Forget about this for tonight. Besides I'm going to need backup when I confront Angel."

"Well I won't let you feed *her.*" Cath sat up. "What other troops do you have to feed?"

She laughed at me when I told her it was only Tommy and my mother and frowned when I explained about my parents' separation.

"But it's quite a big step in the right direction for you, Lee. Last time I saw you there was no way you would allow that many people in the house on a regular basis. How does it feel to be a normal member of the human race?"

I ignored the barb. I was rapidly coming to the conclusion that Cath's getting at me was a form of affection. I couldn't believe that I had never noticed how vulnerable she was beneath her take-charge exterior or that she could think of me as the confident one. I must have changed considerably in the years since we'd seen each other to be able to view her in such a different light.

"It's weird but I actually quite like it. But what you have to understand is that it's not exactly business as usual at the moment. Life is pretty crazy generally, what with someone getting killed in my garden and Buzz turning out to be a batterer and my parents splitting up. I haven't settled down to work and that's worrying me but I have to tell you, I'm rather proud of myself for being able to live like a normal member of the human race, as you call it. At the moment it's still such a novel experience that I haven't had time to take stock. Ask me again in a month or so."

"Good God!" Cath grinned. "Will everyone still be there by then?"

Not Angel after what she's done, I thought to myself. "Heaven help me — or her — if my mother's still there. But having Tommy there is comforting, believe it or not and . . ." I paused, not quite sure how far to go when discussing Tommy with Cath. "Our sex life seems to have taken on a new lease of life. Do you know, before Max Austin turned up today, I was just about to conduct an experiment. I wanted to see whether you could hear Tommy and me having sex from the top floor where my mother's sleeping. I was planning on simulating sex noises in my bedroom and recording it. Then I'd play it back and rush upstairs to see if I could hear it."

I expected Cath to laugh at such ridiculous behavior or ask me how I expected to reproduce the volume accurately on my tape recorder but all she said was:

"Why did Max Austin come round to your house?"

Something stopped me telling Cath I'd been doing his laundry. I had a feeling she'd have something disparaging to say about that along the lines of letting people walk all over me. I was trying to think of an answer when her cell phone rang. We were outside the Napoleon walking arm in arm along Talbot Road and she put her hand to her ear to block out the traffic.

"Talk of the devil," she said. "Hi, Max, what's up?"

I felt her go rigid and then slump against me and I quickly put an arm around her to hoist her up. After a few seconds she snapped her cell phone shut and dragged me to the curb.

"I need to get a cab," she said, holding out her arm. "Richie's been injured. Someone's hit him. He was okay but now he's blacked out and they've rushed him to St. Mary's. I need to get there, Lee. Max says it's pretty bad."

She kept repeating the words "pretty bad, pretty bad" over and over like a mantra as I hailed a cab and put her into it. And I tried to understand when she slammed the door in my face, shouted something to the driver, and left me standing there on the curb.

Chapter 17

My mother was standing in the bay window of the kitchen and when she saw me coming she darted away to open the front door. She met me at the top of the steps dangling a pair of briefs from her little finger.

"I found these in the dryer. Tommy says they're not his," she said accusingly.

I glanced up the street. Did she have any idea of the picture she presented, standing there waving men's underwear in public? Mrs. O'Malley would have a field day.

"Come inside, Mum." I pushed past her. My instant knee-jerk panic reaction was to assume they were Buzz's but after a second's reflection I realized they had to be Max Austin's.

"Well, I think you'd better have a good explanation as to why you're harboring a strange man's underpants — for Tommy if not for me."

"I've just seen Cath," I said knowing that

would get her attention.

"Cath Clark? Good Lord."

I gave her an edited version of the evening's events, leaving out what Cath knew about Buzz but blurting out in my overexcited state that she was pregnant before I remembered that she hadn't even told Richie yet.

"Where is she? You should have brought her home for a drink. I always liked Cath. I can still see her sitting here in this kitchen asking me to show her how to lay a table for a dinner party. And now she's going to have a baby." My mother shook her head and smiled.

Until I told her what had happened to Richie.

"Where's Tommy?" I asked, looking round. My mother seemed to be the only one there.

"Went straight out again after I showed him the briefs although I don't think there's any connection. Said he was going to see his mother in hospital. I was a bit disappointed, tell you the truth. I spoke to him earlier in the day and he said he'd be starting on the repairs to the house this evening but I couldn't very well stop him going to see poor Noreen."

I suppressed a smirk. She'd learn soon

enough. This was probably the first in a long line of excuses Tommy would produce to get out of doing the repairs.

"And you know Angel's gone," she went on.

"Gone out for the evening?" That was a relief. I wasn't looking forward to facing her.

"No, gone altogether." My mother looked quite affronted. "She was dragging her little bags down the stairs when I came in. Asked me to hold the door and walked straight past me into the street. Didn't even say good-bye or thank you. So which hospital have they taken Cath's boyfriend to?"

I shook my head. "St. Mary's. I hope she'll give me a call." I toyed with the idea of telling my mother Richie didn't know about his baby but thought better of it. It was all too complicated.

"Have you eaten?" I asked her. "You look exhausted, Mum."

"I *am* exhausted."

"Well, maybe you'd like to have an early night?"

"I won't sleep," she sniffed. Had she been crying? Were her eyes a bit puffy? "It's all getting a bit nerve-wracking. Someone was killed out there, Lee." She nodded in the direction of the garden. "I think about it just as I'm about to fall asleep and then I lie awake for hours. Your father called by the way."

So that was it. That was why she was upset.

"Was he calling you or me?"

"Who knows?" She shrugged. "But I behaved badly. I was shrewish with him. I snapped at him. I was sarcastic. All the things I swore I'd never be —"

"Mum," I said gently, "you're entitled to feel bitter. It's allowed. Dad's left you for another woman. Just admit to yourself how angry you are with him and you'll feel a whole lot better."

It made a change, me being the one doling out advice rather than the other way around. I felt quite superior.

She looked at me dubiously.

"I didn't realize quite how angry I was. I've been pretending to myself that our marriage just sort of came to a natural break, that I didn't care about Josiane, but" — she paused and there was a catch in her voice — "I think I do. It's odd. I don't want him back — at least not right now. I'm too angry with him for that. But I feel a bit dog-in-the-mangerish. I don't want him to have Josiane either. She's too young and — I don't know — she's too *French!*"

I laughed. I couldn't help myself. "Would it be any better if she were Greek or Norwegian?" But I knew what she meant. A French mistress was somehow a bit of a cliché.

"It's odd how your father is still so interested in sex," she continued. I wasn't entirely sure I was comfortable with the direction she was going but I had to let her get it all off her chest. "I have zero interest in that department these days, I have to tell you. I suppose that's why Ed drifted towards Josiane in the first place. I thought he was just like me, happy with just a cuddle every now and then. I thought we'd put all that stuff behind us and were ready to settle down to a nice calm old age."

"Well, you did say you were bored with Dad's conversation," I pointed out. "Maybe you were just bored with him full stop. You need someone new to get you going again."

She looked quite horrified at the thought. "I just don't have the energy. I'm too bored with myself to think anyone else might have any interest in me and as for sex, quite frankly, the thought of baring my arthritic old body to anyone fills me with disgust. You know something, Lee? I'm ashamed of myself. I've grown old while I wasn't looking and now there's nothing I can do about it. I'm sure if I'd been paying attention, I could have done something about it."

"Like what?" I asked, intrigued.

"Well, instead of bossing your father around all the time, instead of rushing round trying to run everyone else's lives, I could have sensed that maybe he needed me — you know, like he used to."

"Mum," I said softly, "you're beautiful and you'll find someone just like he has. If you want to, that is."

"Well, that's just it. I don't. I can't conceive of it. That's what's making me feel so weird. It's all over for me now and the strangest thing of all is that I'm *accepting* it so readily."

"I think you're just very, very tired. What you need is a good long sleep and you'll see things differently." I was aware that I was talking to her in exactly the same jolly, no-nonsense tone she used to adopt with me when I was a truculent teenager, convinced the world had nothing to offer me. "You go up and get into bed and I'll bring you up a hot drink to help you sleep."

To my surprise she obeyed me, quite

meekly. “I can’t tell you what it means to me being here with you,” she said as I helped her to her feet and she held on to my arm for support as we went up the stairs. “I have to confess I find I’m rather relieved that Angel child has gone. Now I can have you all to myself.”

I wished I’d had Tommy’s Aiwa stashed in my pocket to record those words. I hugged them to myself as I went downstairs to boil some hot milk but when I returned with the drink, she was already fast asleep. I bent over and kissed her on the forehead and remembered when she used to do the same thing to me when I was a little girl feigning sleep.

She had loved me then. But I loved her now.

Cath didn’t call but at two a.m. I was awakened by the sound of the doorbell ringing and there she was with Max Austin right behind her.

This was a Cath I had never seen, out of control, flailing her arms in front of her as if lost in a fog. In fact she was resisting the attempts of Max Austin to guide her into the kitchen. She was trying to tell me something but she couldn’t seem to get the words out in any kind of intelligible fashion. Her mouth worked silently, like a baby's searching for its mother's nipple, and her eyes pleaded with me to understand. I wrapped my arms around her and held her, letting her sob and heave against me. And then she was pried away from me, gently but firmly. I assumed Max Austin had taken over but it was my mother, woken by the doorbell and the commotion downstairs.

"Cath," she said in a voice that brooked no argument and that was all it took. Cath allowed herself to be led upstairs to be soothed by my mother. When they reached the landing on the first floor I distinctly heard my mother say, "And I hear you're going to have a baby. What a wonderful piece of news that is."

I moved to join them but Max Austin restrained me.

"Leave them to it," he said. "She needs mothering right now. She should have gone to her own wherever she is but she said she wanted to come to you. You were the first name out of her mouth. You may — I mean, if it's okay, she might need to stay with you for a few days. She shouldn't be on her own."

I nodded again. She could have Angel's room.

"Richie's dead?" I said it bluntly, wanting to know the worst.

Max looked quite taken aback. "No, no, no. Absolutely not." He paused. "Well, not quite."

"What happened?"

"You got any whiskey?" He nodded in the direction of the kitchen.

I poured him a glass, pulled out a chair for him.

"He's not dead but he's in a pretty bad way. Actually, he's in a coma."

I didn't say anything, just waited for him to go on.

"The irony is he got beat up right outside my house."

"Beat up?"

"He took a blow to the head. He was in pursuit of this bloke who turned round and belted him with a bit of lead piping, whacked poor Richie on the temple. I thought he was fine at first. He got up good as new and walked back to my place and then half an hour later he keels over and blacks out. I called an ambulance and they took him to the hospital and he hasn't come round since. Blood clot to the brain, so they say."

"What does that mean?"

"It'll either disperse and he'll be fine or

he'll —" He put his glass down slowly on the table. "It's a bloody stupid thing to happen to someone like Richie."

"Or he'll die?" I asked.

"Well either that or — you know — brain damage. Vegetable."

I wondered if he knew about the baby.

"Why would someone go after him with a bit of lead piping right outside your house?"

"It was in the mews round the back, underneath the railway line. There's this row of lockups in the arches. Most of them have been turned into garages, remodeling of old cars, that sort of thing. But there's one lockup, number nine, that I suspect is being used for something pretty nasty. I sometimes wonder if the whole area will have the curse of Christie hanging over it forever."

"What is the curse of Christie?"

"Don't you know the story behind Wesley Square?" he asked. He seemed to have gone off on a tangent.

I shook my head. It was just up the road but I'd only walked through it once or twice. To me it was just another modern housing estate, rather better designed than most. This was the sort of thing that exasperated Cath about me. I lived in a neighborhood rich in history but I hid myself away and didn't bother to learn any of it.

"You've heard of the serial killer John Christie? Ten Rillington Place?"

"Of course." Everyone had heard of 10 Rillington Place. "He murdered loads of women in Notting Hill Gate back in the forties, right? Cut them up and buried them in the garden. Strangled his wife too, didn't he? Then he gave evidence against someone else who was hanged for the crime. But they got Christie in the end, didn't they?"

"Yes they did. But do you know where his house is — or rather was? Ten Rillington Place? It's where I live. After the murders all the people living there in those Victorian terraces found they couldn't sell their houses. No one wanted to be anywhere near there. So the council tore it all down and rebuilt the whole area."

"Wesley Square?"

"I thought it was a rather appropriate place for me to live given my line of work. After Sadie was mur— After Sadie died I wanted to move somewhere else. I couldn't bear to stay in our old flat. I was looking to buy to be honest but I couldn't afford Wesley Square prices even back then. You can't own a house there on what a copper makes. The place is stiff with lawyers and TV producers, designers, architects, and the like. But then the real estate woman asked me if I'd considered renting and that's what I did. I've got a little studio at the top of one of the houses, belongs to some journalist who's living in New York. It's not a fancy place like this." He waved his arm round the room, shaking his head. I bristled a little. Was he taking a leaf out of Cath's book, having a go at me for being a snotty middle-class woman?

To my relief, he smiled. "It's just the one room and a kitchen and bathroom but I love it. The Metropolitan Line runs along the back of the houses and I lie in bed and listen to the trains rumbling by. I find it comforting, I don't know why. Everyone thinks I'm mad to live somewhere so small. They left me alone to begin with. I can imagine the sort of things they said about me. *He needs his space after the tragedy of what he's been through.*"

He smiled again, or at least his mouth did. His eyes seemed to have an expression of permanent sadness. He'd changed out of his smart clothes from what I could see beneath his scruffy raincoat. Maybe his date had canceled. Did that happen a lot? Poor lonely Max.

"But then they got it into their heads that I wasn't taking care of myself. Richie's taken to coming round to check up on me. He thinks I don't notice him taking a quick peek into my fridge every now and then. It's getting worse as a matter of fact. I think Cath puts him up to it. That's why he was there this evening. He came round with a takeaway about twenty minutes after I brought my washing home, wanted me to go for a pint afterwards but I'm afraid I sent him away with a flea in his ear. My bloody pride getting the better of me. Told him if he wanted to do something useful, he should take a look at what was going on in the arches. Next thing I knew he was back with a bloody great gash in his temple."

"What *is* going on in the arches?" Had he eaten Richie's takeaway? Should I offer to cook him scrambled eggs? I could understand Cath and Richie's concern. *I* was beginning to worry if he ate properly.

"I can't say for certain but I reckon there's a bit of child prostitution going on."

He said it in such a matter-of-fact tone — *This is what I have to deal with on a day-to-day basis* — that I felt sick. Surely I hadn't heard right.

"I'm not saying there's another Christie at large, no bodies buried under the park in Wesley Square or anything like that. But a few days back I noticed one of the locks had been broken and there were some strange comings and goings. The lady next door said she'd seen these young girls hanging around there during the day. She said they couldn't have been more than about twelve but when she asked them what they were doing, they told her to fuck off. Poor old dear, she was really shocked at their language. But she's got guts. When they'd gone, she sneaked up and took a look in the lockup through the window and saw a couple of mattresses on the floor."

"I don't believe it," I said. "How does something like that happen?"

"It's all crack related," said Max. "They give the girls drugs. I'm pretty sure that lockup was a crack house at one point. There was a shooting down the road last year. You think the Yardies are at a safe distance up in Harlesden in the next borough but they're all over nowadays. You see them with their bling-bling flashing."

"Their what?"

He looked at me and shook his head. "Where have you been? All that jewelry they wear, rocks and diamond stud earrings. They call it bling-bling. You know, like Puff Daddy."

"P. Diddy," I corrected him. "At least I think that's what he calls himself now, but he'll probably change that tomorrow." I might be up to speed on P. Diddy but I still felt like a total ignoramus. All this action going on so close to me and I was barely aware of it. I had no idea that such a thing as child prostitution existed in London. The only crime I knew about involving kids was the constant muggings and stealing of mobile phones.

"Who was it who hit Richie?"

"He gave me a description. He was walking towards the lockup as a bloke was coming out of it. He took off when he saw Richie. Richie gave chase, cornered him under the railway bridge, and that's when the man suddenly came at him with the lead. Richie hadn't even seen it in his hand. I've got a load of men going through the whole area right now. We'll get the bastard soon enough."

"What about — ?" I stopped. It seemed a little self-centered to ask about my fire when Richie was fighting for his life, but poor Fred's demise was always lurking at the back of my mind.

"What about your case?" Max gave me

another faint smile. "Don't worry. I hadn't forgotten about you although it's going to set it back a bit with Richie being in this state. I mean I can bring in someone else in his place but he was in the middle of a line of questioning I have a feeling might turn out to be quite productive and he hasn't brought me up to date on it."

I waited for him to tell me what it was but instead he said:

"So have you had any more bright ideas like the one about Buzz Kempinski?"

I glared at him.

"No, I'm serious," he assured me. "You got it wrong, he had an alibi, but you were thinking along the right lines. I'm curious to know in which direction you'll go next."

I looked at him, not quite sure if he was taking a piss. Then I decided to take the risk.

"Selma Walker said she went to visit her family in New York over Christmas but in the tapes I've been transcribing for her book she states that she has no family left in the world."

"Have you asked her about it?"

"Not yet. But if you think about it, she has — you know — she has a motive."

I waited for him to make some snide remark about my amateur detection, to produce some cast-iron reason why Selma couldn't be the murderer but to my surprise he said, "Tell me about it," and poured himself a bit more Scotch. "By the way if you want to get back to bed, just give me a shout. I only intended to stay a second, make sure Cath was okay with you."

I shook my head. I was tired, no question, but I was too wound up about Cath and Richie to contemplate going straight back to sleep.

"Two fires," I noted, counting them off on my fingers. "Astrid McKenzie and Angel — at least we assume Angel was the intended victim. Both women were — are sleeping with Buzz. Selma's his wife."

"It's a good point," he conceded. "I'll check the airlines for the day she left and returned — or said she did. See if she was listed going to New York. That's where she said she went, right? Does she strike you as a killer?"

I shook my head.

"Not even as a woman scorned? Maybe you're next on her list."

"She doesn't know about me and Buzz," I said.

"How do you know?" said Max and he was right. "Do you like her?" he asked, catching me off guard.

"I'm not sure," I said and it was the truth. "I have no reason to dislike her but I just don't feel entirely relaxed with her. It always happens when I meet someone whose book I'm going to ghost for the first time, I can feel them sizing me up, asking themselves if they can trust me. It's natural. But she seemed more suspicious than most. Of course, given what she had in store to reveal to me, I can understand why. She had to know I wasn't going to go running to Buzz." I felt a little guilty not being entirely pro-Selma. I'd actually begun to feel a distinct loyalty toward her and in fact she was the last person I wanted to see as a suspect — apart from the fact that if she was, I'd be out of a job.

"Ironic under the circumstances," said Max. "I hope for your sake she never finds out about you and Buzz, that he doesn't go and do a shitty thing like tell her."

I shuddered and he reached across the table and patted me on the shoulder.

"Don't worry. She decided to trust you and she was right. You're not going to talk to Buzz and even if she did find out what happened between you, my guess is she'd know you weren't entirely to blame, that it happened before you found out what a monster he was. But tell me, do you trust *her?*"

"I think she's fucked up. I think she's doing a very brave thing with this book, using her fame to reach out to other women in her situation but I'm not sure her story will come across as entirely rational. She still loves him, you know. She's still pretty much under his spell."

"But isn't that where you come in?" he said. "You'll make sure she gets her message across, you'll make her sound sane and wise and all the rest of it."

Listening to him, I had a sudden flash of ghastly inspiration. What if I were to ghost *his* story? The detective whose wife was murdered, how he coped.

"I'm going to make a cup of tea. Want one?" I stood up and reached for the kettle, as much to stifle my train of thought as anything, but I didn't hear his answer because my mother came crashing down the stairs and into the kitchen.

"She's asleep," she said. "Poor, poor Cath. Will he live, do you imagine?"

"Mum, you remember Inspector Austin. Cup of tea?"

"Oh no, I'm off back to bed." She wrapped her dressing gown more tightly around her in a faintly modest gesture as she shook Max Austin's hand.

"There's always a chance he might not live," said Max simply. "That's why I'm pleased Cath is here with you. But let's be optimistic."

I expected him to go once my mother had returned to bed but he lingered. How many whiskeys had he had? Maybe he was a little drunk by now. Maybe he needed to talk to someone.

"In spite of what you say," I said carefully, "it can't be easy carrying on after what happened. Did you and your wife have a lot of friends? Have they been supportive? Do you still hanker after the past or are you feeling your way towards making a fresh start, a different kind of life to the one you had with — Sadie?"

I was taking quite a risk being so nosy but I was genuinely interested. I was asking him exactly the sort of questions I would ask if I were preparing to ghost his story. The worst he could do was tell me to fuck off.

But he didn't even get the chance to do that because the front door banged and Tommy lurched into the kitchen.

"What's going on?" he demanded. He saw Max Austin and said rather defensively, "I'm drunk but I haven't been driving. I took a cab home."

"Tommy," I pointed out, "you haven't got a car."

Out of the corner of my eye I saw Max pick up his coat and slip out the door into the hall.

"What's he doing here at this time of night? Has there been another fire?"

I explained about Richie and that Cath was asleep upstairs.

"Cath?" Now he looked bewildered. "You never said she was back in your life."

"Well, she wasn't until tonight."

"How was she? Still crazy about me?"

I didn't laugh. Tommy could be so crass at times. There was Richie fighting for his life and he had to go and say a thing like that.

"Okay. Sorry, sorry, sorry. Sorry about her bloke. Sorry I'm drunk. Christ, where've you put her? Is she upstairs in bed with Angel?"

"Angel's gone."

"Sorry about that too."

"No, you're not," I told him firmly.

"Okay, I'm not. A man's not entitled to his own opinion when you're around, Lee."

Suddenly I was dog tired and I could feel my anger rising.

"So where the hell have you been?" I

challenged him. "It's nearly three o'clock in the morning."

"How do you do, Lee the Shrew." He reached for the whiskey and I moved it away from him. "I went to see Mum in hospital. Is that okay with you? I was there a lot longer than I expected so I had to go back to the BBC and work late to make up the time."

Until three in the morning? Well, okay, I wouldn't ask. Things were getting edgy enough as it was.

"So? How was she? Oh, and by the way, I've just remembered. There was someone with her when I went to see her. Who's Marie-Chantal?"

"Who?"

It had been a casual question but the way he said "Who?" in that oh-so-innocent tone made me pay attention. Tommy is a hopeless liar probably because it isn't something he practices very often. I know him so well that his delivery of one word can alert me to the fact that he's nervous.

"When I last went to see your mother she had another visitor, a French woman whom she introduced as Marie-Chantal. Noreen said she worked with you at the Beeb."

"Oh her."

He'd gone bright red. Now why would he go red at the mention of someone he worked with?

"Well? Why was she visiting your mother?"

"She likes her."

"How did she meet her?"

"I suppose I must have introduced them at some stage."

"You suppose. Tommy, who is this woman?"

"I think I may have mentioned her." He was looking very sheepish. "She's that teacher they brought in to broadcast that program. You know, I told you, when we were staying with your parents and you discovered I spoke French."

"She gave you French lessons. So you knew her pretty well?"

He was hopeless. It was written all over his face how well he knew her.

"Tell me all about it, Tommy," I said quietly.

"You just didn't seem to care anymore. You were writing all the time, you didn't want me round here. You made me feel like I was this awful person who kept interrupting your life, you didn't seem to want to take the relationship to —"

If he says *to the next level,* I thought, I'll kill him. But when he did I forced myself to curb my irritation. His mother was seriously ill. He must be far more worried than he let on. Whatever I was about to learn about Marie-Chantal I would have to deal with another time.

"So you worked with her on this broadcast and — ?" I prompted him.

"I liked her. She didn't make fun of the fact that I couldn't speak French. She corrected my pronunciation and after a while I began to get the hang of it and she told me I had a good ear. She offered to give me lessons. It began with the odd cup of coffee during a break" — *Exactly like he'd begun with me,* I thought wryly, *a cup of BBC tea and a Kit Kat* — "and then we had lunch and she took me shopping, showed me the sort of clothes she thought would suit me. She was very thoughtful in that respect."

Dear God! The number of times I'd tried to interest him in a new wardrobe. Just because she was French.

"Those sweaters you were wearing at Christmas?"

He nodded happily. He seemed relieved he didn't have to lie anymore. "Beautiful, weren't they? She has great taste."

I sat on my hands so I couldn't punch him. Now it seemed there'd be no stopping him. Did I really want to know the sordid details?

"Tommy," I said carefully, disguising my mounting indignation and hurt with a light conversational tone, "tell me, does Marie-Chantal suffer from cystitis at all?"

He looked at me in genuine bewilderment.

"It's an infection of the bladder," I explained pleasantly, "and it can be irritated by sex. I've had it from time to time. It's best to get up and pee as soon as you've finished having sex. Do you remember me doing that?" He nodded. "And another cure is some rather nasty medicine called mist pot cit."

"Oh, *that's* what that's for. There was a bottle in the medicine cabinet in my bathroom for ages and I hadn't a clue what it was doing there."

"Well, now you know."

"Poor Marie-Chantal. She must suffer from what's it called? She never said."

"It's a bit of a turnoff to mention it during sex."

"That's probably why —" He stopped. "Lee, I never — she —"

"Are you still seeing her? Have you just been with her? Is that why you were so late home?"

"Well, she was there seeing Mum and afterwards we went for a drink because I was upset, but we didn't — I mean, I haven't slept with her since before Christmas. Not since we went to France and you and I —"

And that made it okay? What had he done? Made it some kind of New Year's resolution to simplify his life and only have sex with me?

But the worst part about it was that I didn't really have the right to be angry with him because of what I'd done with Buzz. Of course he didn't know about that. But *I* did. The words "double standard" flitted through my mind.

"Are you angry with me?" He was giving me a wary look. I didn't say anything. "You are, aren't you?" he went on. "Listen, I've always loved you and I've always told you so, over and over again. It's you who doesn't love me, or if you do you have a pretty funny way of showing it. If you made me feel you loved me do you seriously think I would have played away? If you really want to know the truth, there have been times recently when I wondered if you might be seeing someone on the side."

So now he had to go and make me feel guilty on top of everything else. He was right, damn him. He was right about everything. I could feel the tears coming and if I spent another minute with him, I'd give myself away. All I wanted to do was take him in my arms and comfort him about Noreen but Marie-Chantal had come between us. When I moved toward him, he backed away.

"I know that look. You're mad as hell. I should never have told you. But you know what?" He took a step toward me and looked me right in the eye. "Maybe it's better this happened, that it's out in the open. You're mad at me but maybe you should just take some time out to think about why I got together with Marie-Chantal in the first place."

And then before I could make any further attempt to placate him, he walked right past me and out the door. I yelled after him.

"Tommy! Tommy, come back, for God's sake."

But he'd gone. Alone, I let the tears flow freely in my frustration and picked up the whiskey, by now nearly empty, and took a swig straight from the bottle. Then I heard the sound of someone coming down the stairs. Oh God, all I needed was my mother wanting a late-night chat. But then the front door slammed and I peeped through the curtains to see Max Austin hurrying into the night.

He must have gone upstairs to have a pee because the floor had been taken up in the downstairs cloakroom by the damp people. So at what point did he start coming downstairs again?

Just how much of my miserable exchange with Tommy had he overheard?

Chapter 18

I'd had rows with Tommy before — lots of them, generally when I was tired or fretful. For some reason I always took it out on him. What usually happened was that I would pick a fight with him over something small like what were his dirty socks doing under the bed when I had distinctly asked him to take them home or put them in the laundry basket.

Tommy always apologized but invariably with a smirk on his face and this only served to provoke me even more so I would start shouting at him. He would shout back for a while, just for good measure, so I could feel like I'd cleared the air. Then we wouldn't speak for a few hours so we would both know the point, whatever it was, had been well and truly made. Peace would be restored when my mood lifted and I'd forgotten whatever it was that had angered me in the first place. And here Tommy was smart. He knew exactly when it was safe to approach me again and once he did, we'd carry on as if nothing had happened.

But he had never walked out on me with such an air of finality before.

In spite of my exhaustion, I couldn't summon the energy to climb back up the stairs to bed. I suppose I harbored some hope that Tommy would return and beg my forgiveness. I found a load of washing-up in the sink and knew without a doubt that he had left it there. Maybe he had had a bite to eat before going to see his mother in hospital. A dirty saucepan, a bowl, a glass and some silver. Why was it beyond him to perform the simple task of reaching down and placing these items in the dishwasher?

And in spite of my craving for my bed, I continued to sit there waiting for him, dozing off every now and then and coming to with a start when I heard the sound of a key in the front door around 5:30.

I ran into the hall as the key stopped rattling and the door blew open from the cold early morning wind outside. Bianca stood there in her red duffel coat.

For a second I was totally baffled. When had I given Bianca a key? Then I remembered Selma's offer to my mother to send

Bianca to clean the house. My mother must have given her the key but what on earth was she doing here at such an ungodly hour?

"Good morning, Bianca."

She didn't answer, of course. Just let out a little shriek of surprise and then, when she'd recovered her composure, she gave me one of her impassive looks and stomped her feet hard on the floor to warm them, scattering bits of wet mud. Well, fine, she could clean it up.

There was something perverse about the way she refused to return any courtesies I extended to her, never answered my questions politely, and in spite of myself, I began to look upon it as a challenge. I would make her acknowledge me, whatever it took.

"Do you always start work so early?" I asked her, smiling warmly even though I felt like death.

"Why you no in bed?"

"Cup of tea, Bianca?"

"Where you keep Hoover?"

"Cup of *tea,* Bianca?" I persisted, the tone of my voice making it clear that I meant business.

"I drink the coffee."

I wasn't quite sure whether this constituted a point on her side or mine but I decided to let it go. At any rate, until I gave her instructions and showed her where everything was she couldn't very well start work. I wondered what she would have done if I hadn't been up. How could she possibly have known I would be downstairs to greet her at 5:30 in the morning?

"Sit down," I gestured to a chair at the kitchen table. "Black or white?" As it happened, knowing I wouldn't be going back to sleep, I had made myself a pot of coffee about an hour ago and it was still warm on the hot plate of the coffee machine.

When she didn't answer, I retrieved the key she was still clutching in her hand and laid it on the table in front of her beside a mug of black coffee. I pushed a jug of milk and a bowl of sugar lumps toward her, smiling at the giant fluorescent green label attached to the key ring with my name and address on it written in Selma's flowery scrawl, together with the words *DON'T FORGET!*

Bianca was nervous, I saw to my surprise. Her hands shook as she reached for the coffee. She was perched on the edge of her chair, in her coat, with her bag still hanging from her shoulder.

"Here, I'll hang that up for you."

I reached for the bag and she leapt away from me with the result that it fell on the floor between us. She was on her knees in a second, scrabbling around for her belongings. A photograph had fluttered over to the other side of the room and I went to retrieve it.

"Who's this?" I asked, highly intrigued. The photo was of an unusually beautiful woman. She was sitting on a bench, barefoot at the water's edge with her trousers rolled up to her calves. She was laughing at the camera, presenting the kind of carefree image I associated with advertisements for health clubs. She was a Latina, long black hair, dark flashing eyes, the whole bit. But she appeared so vibrant and engaging, I couldn't stop looking at the picture. There was something else about her, something that was bugging me. She was familiar in some way I couldn't quite put my finger on.

When Bianca said "Is my sister," it fell into place. There *was* a resemblance. Same set of the eyes except the sister's were larger. Same mouth except the sister's was wider. Same broad shoulders except the sister looked to be a good six inches taller than Bianca. It was a classic case of one sister getting all the good features and the other getting none. But it was more than that. The woman in the photograph had an open face. She looked like she would offer warmth, humor, understanding whereas Bianca's expression seemed to be permanently closed and disagreeable.

"Bianca, she's beautiful." Even as I said it I wondered how often she had heard this and resented the attention never focused on her. "What's her name?"

But Bianca's face softened slightly as she took the photograph from me. She didn't look resentful, only sad. "Maria," she said, "but she don't look like that now. Here" — she thrust another picture into my hand — "here is Maria today."

I gasped. If Bianca said it was the same woman then it was the same woman but I could barely see it. She was slumped in a wheelchair, about two stone lighter. The beautiful dark eyes were now sunken holes in her gaunt face with horrible shadows underneath and there was something wrong with her nose. I remembered a small straight nose in the other picture but here there was an ugly bump in the middle.

"What happened? Did she have an accident?"

I was trying to recall what Selma had told me. Something about Bianca having a sister who was sick and whom she took care of.

Bianca's eyes were very bright. She was blinking and I realized with a shock that she was trying to suppress tears. Should I go over and put my arm around her?

"What's the matter?" I asked as gently as I could.

But her opaque look was back and in answer to my question, she repeated, "Where you keep Hoover?"

"Bianca," I said, not bothering to hide my anger, "you can't Hoover at this time of the morning, you'll wake everyone up."

"Who here?" She looked surprised.

"My mother — remember, you met her. And my friend Cath is staying here. She is very tired. We have to let her sleep. She's at the very top of the house, you can work your way up there slowly."

"Where that girl sleep? She back with you?"

I had to think for a minute and then I realized who she meant.

"Angel's gone."

"Where she gone?"

"Bianca, I don't know. So why are you here so early?"

She shrugged as if it was obvious. "I clean you and then I clean Miss Selma."

I supposed that made sense. She was squeezing me in before Selma. She couldn't do me after because she had to go home and take care of her sister. I thought of something.

"Bianca, do you know? Does Selma have a sister — in New York?"

"Miss Selma no have sister or brother or mother or father. Miss Selma all alone."

"She has Buzz," I said and waited to see what Bianca had to say about that.

"Sometimes." Well, that was an interesting answer.

"Oh, you mean like he wasn't with her at Christmas? But that was because she went away. Do you know where she went?" I said it casually, deliberately not looking at her as if I wasn't really listening.

"She go to seaside."

"Seaside? The beach? She went to the coast near New York? I thought she went to Manhattan."

"No," said Bianca, "no New York."

"Are you sure?"

"Yes, I am sure. She send me postcard. Here, I show you."

Once again she produced it from her bag, clearly the repository of any number of interesting items. I looked at the picture of a strip of sand, at the bottom of an anonymous-looking cliff. It could be anywhere. I turned the postcard over and read that it was a place I'd never heard of in Devon. The postmark bore that out and the date showed that the card had been mailed on Christmas Eve. So Selma *had* lied about New York. She had been in England all along. She could have come up to London from Devon on New Year's Eve.

I read the message.

Dear Bianca,

I hope you and your sister have a wonderful Christmas.

I shall be returning January third. Please go by the house and see if Buzz is all right before I get back. Thank you. It's cold here by the sea but I am getting a lot done.

Happy New Year!

Selma

But I am getting a lot done. What did she mean by that?

Bianca suddenly snatched the card away from me and returned it to her bag. She took off her coat and stood there in a pinafore with a garish floral pattern over her skirt and jumper.

"I start the work," she announced.

I didn't have any option but to show her where the cleaning materials were kept and the cupboard under the stairs where the Hoover lived. To my horror, in spite of what I'd said — or maybe because of it — the minute I went upstairs she started up with the Hoover.

My mother was on the landing in a second.

"What in the world is going on?" She was joined almost immediately by Cath and they stood there in identical Viyella nightdresses with cabbage roses all over them. It took me a moment to get that my mother must have lent Cath one of hers for the night.

"Bianca's started work," I explained.

"Well, I'm going to go downstairs and stop her," said my mother. "This is ludicrous."

Cath was in tears and I wondered if she'd been crying all night. I helped her back upstairs to bed and offered her a cup of tea but she shook her head and turned away from me.

As would become clear as the day wore on, she had a migraine — a real one, not a hangover — and my mother insisted she remain in bed in a darkened room. She persuaded Cath to part with her house key and her address and a list of the things she might need over the next few days and then she disappeared to let herself into Richie and Cath's flat to pick them up. I said I would go but my mother would not hear of it and I knew what this was all about. Looking after Cath and doing things for her made my mother feel needed and kept her busy so she wouldn't have to face up to dealing with her feelings about the breakdown of her marriage. I had observed that she had been severely rattled by my father's call, just as I was rattled by her revelation that she seemed to think her life as a woman was over. I suspected she was angry with my father for forcing her to confront this in herself. But I believed that there was a side of her that would benefit from her new-found freedom if only she would allow herself to. I liked to think she was teetering on the edge of a diving board, excited about the leap into the fresh air that awaited her but still too nervous to take the plunge. Maybe I would just have to find a way to give her a big push from behind.

As for me, I was miserable when I still

had not heard from Tommy by lunchtime, especially when my mother revealed he had been intending to take the day off from work.

"He was going to start the repairs today. We agreed. I was woken up yesterday by a piece of plaster falling off the cornice above my head onto my nose. So where is he?"

I muttered something about him having to go away for an outside broadcast that the BBC had sprung on him at the last minute. She looked at me skeptically.

"A likely story." She was beginning to get his number.

I don't know why I didn't tell her the truth, that we'd had a row, he'd been having an affair, that I was devastated. I found it ironic that the only person I wanted to share my misery with was, in fact, Tommy. He was my best friend. Whenever I was unhappy he was always the first person I turned to. I could tell him anything, I knew he wouldn't lecture me like Cath did because he didn't have to. He knew who I was.

How things had changed. Normally I would be sitting at my desk trying to figure out how I could put off seeing Tommy until the weekend, desperate for a way to get some work done, dreaming of a nice quiet evening alone. Yet here I was, desperate instead for his return, desperate too to know where he was. He wasn't at the Beeb, his mobile was switched off, and I was terrified to go rushing down to the hospital to see if Noreen had heard from him because I might run into Marie-Chantal.

And on top of everything I was praying for Richie's recovery. There was no change, they told me when I called the hospital for Cath, who could barely lift her head off the pillow. I found an old bottle of sleeping pills in the medicine chest in the bathroom and made her take one. I knew you weren't supposed to do this but my mother hadn't returned with her migraine pills and I needed to know she was fast asleep so I could keel over myself. Having had no sleep the night before, I was wandering around the house like a zombie. The place was a pigsty and that made me feel even worse. My mother had scared Bianca away so forcefully that she would probably never come back.

I slept all afternoon and was woken by the sound of the doorbell ringing at six o'clock. I slipped upstairs, peeped in on Cath who was still dead to the world.

Where on earth was my mother?

"Coming!" I shouted, racing down the stairs again.

Max Austin was back in the fancy charcoal trousers and the polo neck sweater. Did he always get togged up in his best clothes at the end of the day to give himself a thrill? Or was he going on somewhere to resurrect the date I'd conjured up for him the night before? Tonight he'd added a black leather jacket to the mix and it didn't suit him at all. It was a bit desperate, a bit *trying* to be cool instead of actually getting away with it. He'd looked terrific in the voluminous dark overcoat he'd had on one time I'd seen him. He'd known how to wear that, allowing it to wrap itself loosely around him like a cloak. But this leather jacket was skin tight and a bit short at the waist with great big baggy shoulders. You could tell his own shoulders had got lost in there somewhere. I wondered if I could point out the discrepancy tactfully. After all, if he was trying to pull some woman, he might appreciate the feminine take on the situation.

When he said good evening and told me there was no change with Richie, I slapped myself mentally on the wrist. That should have been the first thing on my mind too, along with the nagging question of how much had he heard of my row with Tommy.

"I know, actually," I said, "I rang the hospital earlier."

I could sense him looking at me rather oddly and who could blame him? I was still in the nightdress I'd been wearing when he last saw me.

"Sorry about this." I held the door open. "Come in and I'll pop upstairs and get dressed. Won't take a second."

But he continued to stand on the doorstep.

"I only came round to tell you about Richie, see how Cath is. And I wanted to let you know there's no record of Selma Walker being on any flight to or from New York, on the dates she claims to have flown there and back."

"That's because she wasn't in New York over Christmas and New Year," I said, unable to hide the glee in my voice. "She was in Devon."

I told him about Bianca's early morning visit and her postcard.

"I'd better pay Selma Walker a visit tomorrow," he said, jotting something down in his notebook. "Why in the world would she lie about something like that? I don't think I like her as a genuine suspect but something doesn't add up. Are you due to see her at all?"

I shook my head. "I can't leave Cath at the moment. She's got a migraine and she's sleeping, which is probably the best thing for her at the moment. I couldn't believe the state she was in last night. I've never seen her like that. It looks to me like she'll need a fair bit of support until Richie pulls through."

Max smiled. "*Richie pulls through.* I'm glad to see we've got an optimist in our midst. She's lucky to have a friend like you."

I smiled back. "Richie's attacker, did you get him?"

"We got him. Tell her that from me, would you? With a bit of luck we'll have uncovered a nasty little operation he was running back in those arches thanks to Richie. He's . . ." Max paused and shifted uncomfortably in his leather jacket. "He's a good lad. Anyway, I'm off now. Go inside before you catch your death. And you're giving the neighbors an eyeful to boot."

"Thanks for coming round. Evening, Mrs. O'Malley," I shouted next door and waved. "How's Kevin?"

She ducked back behind the net curtain

in her bay window just as a cab drew up and my mother got out. I was about to go down the steps and help her with Cath's belongings when I realized she wasn't alone and I wasn't sure I ought to greet a total stranger in my nightdress.

And what a stranger! The man who followed my mother out of the cab was short and solidly built. He had the broad shoulders of a boxer and indeed his face was rather pugnacious until he smiled at me, flashing a set of even white teeth — save for a piratical gap right in the middle — that belied his age. My instant impression was *What a rascal!*

"Hold on to your hat," said Max Austin, still standing beside me on the doorstep. "It's Sonny Cross."

"Sonny Cross," I repeated. "Who's he?"

"Richie's dad. I left a message for him last night up in Liverpool. He lives up there now, it's where he's from originally. He must have taken the train down this morning. Don't be fooled by that thuggish appearance. He's a remarkable man. Richie's mother took off, abandoned him, when Richie and his brother were still toddlers and Sonny brought them up single-handed."

He didn't look thuggish to me. For a

start, unlike Max, he knew how to wear a leather jacket with a certain amount of cool. He had a white crew cut and, God help me, I saw a little flash of gold in one of his ears.

"Did he never remarry?" I was watching him extracting notes to pay the cab driver from a money clip. He was flash all right but he seemed to have the confidence to get away with it.

"No, he never did," said Max. "But it's not for want of half the women in the north of England trying. Richie grew up being spoiled rotten by a bunch of widows auditioning to be his stepmother. I don't know how Sonny does it, to be honest. He's got to be well into his sixties and the way Richie tells it, he's had a few problems with the bottle over the years."

"Hey, Maxie!" Sonny had come bounding up the steps to punch Max in the shoulder.

"Hey, Sonny," said Max, clearly not entirely sure about being called Maxie. "Glad you got my message. This is Nathalie Bartholomew. Looks like you've already met her mother."

"Vanessa? I have indeed. Your mother's a lovely Judy," he said to me. "There I was, just back from the hospital, sitting in my lad's flat wondering what to do with myself and in she walks. I hear you've got our Cath stashed away upstairs." It was odd hearing her described as *our Cath* by a complete stranger. I wondered how Cath's parents, an unassuming couple in Acton with none of Sonny Cross's vigor, would react to his proprietorial air. "I'm pretty chuffed to hear I'm going to be a granddad."

Max looked shellshocked.

"What's the matter, Maxie? Don't tell me he didn't tell you?"

"Richie doesn't know," I said.

"Well, he does now," said Sonny cheerfully. "I chattered on about it when I went to see him."

"Was he awake?"

"Well, no, not exactly but he will be soon."

And suddenly I knew Richie was going to be all right. Sonny Cross had the kind of confidence that left no room for doubt. If he said his son would wake up, then he would.

"I'm off," said Max. "Give me a bell, Sonny. We'll have a drink."

"Will do," said Sonny. "I'm bursting, love" — he turned to me — "where's your nearest loo?"

I remembered just in time that the floor-boards of the downstairs cloakroom had been taken up as part of the battle against the damp. I directed him upstairs to my bathroom, had a vision of my underwear lying all over the floor, and asked him if he wouldn't mind going up to the top floor instead.

"Don't mind a bit providing I can keep it in till then," he said, giving me a pat on the arm and saying "Nice frock!" as he glanced at my nightdress. "Leave that suitcase, Vanessa. I'll be back down in a minute."

But he wasn't and I assumed he must have found Cath in the little box room and stopped to say hello. I wound up helping my mother with Cath's suitcase and left it at the bottom of the stairs. In marked contrast to Sonny Cross's cheerful banter, my mother didn't say a word to me when she came in and that in itself was unusual. She normally never missed an opportunity to comment on something in the house no matter how short her absence from it. After a minute or two of silence I decided she was being downright shifty.

"So, you went round to Cath's, Mum. Everything okay? You took your time — or did you come back while I was asleep?"

"What could I do?" she said, sounding a

bit breathless. “He was sitting there waiting for Cath to come home. I couldn’t just leave him there. He wanted to go out, get a bite to eat, he was starving, poor man, he’d had nothing to eat on the train, the buffet was closed as usual, and I thought I’ve got to —”

“Mum, it’s all right. I’ve been asleep all day. It’s not like I’ve been sitting here waiting for you to come back. You don’t have to account for your whereabouts.”

“What’s he doing upstairs all this time? I thought he just went for a pee.” She seemed quite anxious.

“He’s with Cath, I imagine. Where did you go for your bite to eat?”

“Rather nice, actually,” she said. “A place called Snows on the Green, near Cath’s flat.”

I knew Snows on the Green. It was quite a smart restaurant frequented by media types. “He knew Snows? I thought he was from Liverpool.”

“Oh yes, and they knew him. He knows quite a few London restaurants, actually. In fact it took us a while to decide where to go. He wanted to take me to a place called Sonny’s in Barnes but we decided it was a bit far. Anyway, Snows was fine. I had a nice bit of smoked fish.”

"And a nice bottle of Bourgogne," said Sonny coming in. "She wanted to drink it with that cassis crap and that's the best for whatever it's called. Cath's pretty much out of it. I'll catch up with her tomorrow."

"It's called a kir, that cassis crap as you put it," said my mother, giggling a little. I wondered how many kirs she'd had.

"French nonsense," he said. "Why you have to spoil a decent glass of white wine is beyond me. And I hope your house in France is in better nick than this one." He wagged a finger in her face and pressed a piece of paper in her hand. "I've made a list for you while I've been upstairs. You've got rising damp, of course. I could smell that the minute I walked in the door. And your windowsills are practically nonexistent. There's plaster coming off the walls in every room I looked into and the ceiling's about to come down in that little room off the master bedroom on the first floor."

"Make yourself at home, why don't you?" I said, amused by his audacity. "And in fact I've got something that might interest you." I pulled my mother's list from the side of the fridge where Tommy had taped it safely out of sight.

"Right then," he said glancing at it, "you

know what needs to be done. Let's get to it. When can I start? Got to have something to occupy my mind while I wait for my lad to come back from the land of nod."

"When can *you* start?" I didn't get it.

"Sonny's a builder," my mother explained.

"Sonny," I said, moving toward him with my most brilliant smile, "let me get you something to drink."

"But what about Tommy?" said my mother.

"What about him?" I replied.

Sonny Cross was as good as his word and turned up at eight o'clock the next morning with a couple of helpers. We were all downstairs in the kitchen to greet him. Cath, having more or less slept around the clock, was up and about and intending to go back to work. I was touched to see the way her face lit up when she saw Sonny. They embraced and he patted her tummy.

"So when were you going to tell me?" he asked.

I froze.

"Who told you?" said Cath.

"Vanessa. Best news I've had all year."

"And you told her?" Cath looked at me

and I waited for the explosion. But it never came. Instead she gave me a rueful grin. "In a way I'm grateful to you for getting it out in the open. The only person I still have to tell is Richie." At this her face began to crumple and Sonny gave her a little shake.

"Now, now, now. That's not going to do anybody any good. We'll go to the hospital this afternoon, girl, just you and me. We'll stamp and we'll cheer and we'll wake him up if it's the last thing we do."

She went off to work, pale and wan and not before she'd called the hospital twice. I said that if she wanted me to, I'd go with her and sit by Richie's bed but she shook her head. "I can't do that," she said. "I can't go and sit there and do *nothing,* just wait. He'd be furious with me if he knew I was doing that. But thanks anyway." She squeezed my hand. "I'm lucky to have you, you know that, don't you? Tommy's not around? Your mum said he was away."

She knew me too well. My face gave me away. "I'm not going to ask," she said. "I don't want to know — not until you're ready to tell me anyway."

Sonny Cross had donned a pair of paint-spattered workman's overalls. They were unbuttoned to the waist and it didn't look like he had much on underneath. His chest hairs were white like the hair on his head and stood out sharply against his tan.

"You been abroad, Sonny? Winter holiday?" I asked as I made him a cup of tea.

"Tanning parlor," he said with a grin. "Works a treat. Got to keep looking my best, don't I?"

I had to laugh. The vanity of the man! "So you're happy about Cath and Richie?"

"Over the moon," he said. "Richie was always a bit shy with the ladies. I used to try and get him to look for a date on match.com like I do but he wouldn't hear of it. Said he'd meet the right girl when he was meant to and he was right."

"You find women on the Internet?" I was staggered.

"Of course, darling. You ought to try it. You too, Vanessa." He flung an arm round my mother's shoulders and to my amazement, she didn't push him away. Just stood there beside him, smiling and going a little pink.

"I couldn't possibly," I said. "It's too risky. I might get murdered."

Sonny looked at me and shook his head. "With that kind of attitude, you probably will," he said. "Bit of a nervous type, are you, love?" Now he drew me into his embrace on his other side and stood there between my mother and me. He gave us each a big fat kiss on the cheek and I noticed he gave my mother a little slap on the behind, which she didn't seem to mind at all.

"Now then," he said. "I'm going to need some music while I work. Some Motown would be nice, and some of that Atlantic Stax. Got any of that?"

Over the next couple of days he put our house to rights, turning us out of our bedrooms every morning but leaving them immaculate for us to return to in the evening. I was impressed by the way he put dust sheets down everywhere and ran up and down stairs with endless bin bags of fallen plaster. He rang the damp people, told them they'd done a rotten job and furthermore it wasn't finished and when they returned, he stood over them like a contractor until he was satisfied their work was done.

My mother made him and his coworkers endless cups of tea and ham sandwiches, and played him nonstop sixties soul music — "I Heard It Through the Grapevine," "River Deep Mountain High," Aretha, Smokey Robinson and the Miracles, Ben E. King. She put Stevie Wonder's "Uptight" on repeat and it resounded throughout the house over and over again till I thought I would scream. And all the time she danced about like a demented rock chick. I'd been here before. As long as I could remember, probably as far back as my playpen, her only real form of relaxation had been reliving her sixties moments and when she found she could compare reminiscences with Sonny Cross, there was no stopping her. To make matters worse, Sonny scored some grass one lunchtime from *A chap I met in the market* and they got stoned out of their minds at the kitchen table while I huddled in my office and thought *This could have been Tommy and me.* And of course once the grass appeared, the work stopped. It seemed the top floor of the house was doomed to remain a crumbling health hazard.

I'd been putting off going to Tesco, doing most of my food shopping in the market, buying a ton of vegetables at Chris's stall every day, which scored me an equal number of brownie points with him.

"If only more people were like you," he told me. "Seems like you've turned yerself into a vegetarian over the last few days. I'm proud of you, girl. 'Ere, 'ave a pound of French beans on me."

In the end, he sent me back to Tesco himself without realizing what he was doing.

"So that Angel you took in after the fire in her summerhouse, how's she doing? She become a vegetarian and all?"

"Actually she's not living with me anymore."

"Oh yes?" He seemed interested and I recalled Angel telling me how he'd hung about waiting for her outside Tesco. "Where'd she go then?"

"I've no idea," I said.

"Well, well, well. Looks like she's gone and left us."

"What do you mean?"

"She's done a runner on her job. They haven't seen her at Tesco for two or three days. Her mother's worried sick. Didn't your mum tell you? Mrs. O'Leary called your house to find her and your mother said she'd left."

I rushed to Tesco and stocked up on all the things I normally bought there like yogurt and cheese and the disgusting frozen meals Tommy seemed happy to live on — although who knew when I'd be catering for Tommy again.

In the evenings I found myself on my

own while Cath was at the hospital with Sonny and my mother was God knows where and instead of relishing the solitude I'd craved so recently, I *hated* it. I felt guilty about how little work I was doing. Genevieve was beginning to leave rather sharp messages asking if I was making any progress. I knew I should call Selma but I was terrified of encountering Buzz.

And as I finally retired to bed, kicking my way morosely through the various piles of Tommy's discarded clothing still lying on the bedroom floor, I added Selma and Angel to the list of people I was fretting about. Top of the list was Richie, and Cath by association, then poor Fred followed by my mother and lonely Max Austin as I always dubbed him. (Had he had his date? How had it gone?) And finally Tommy. By now I was seriously beginning to worry about not having heard from Tommy, that something terrible had happened to him and no one had told me. And after hearing about Angel's disappearance from Chris, I found I had a strange sense of unease about her. After what she'd done, it was weird that I should even care but I did.

But Selma was the person who was creeping to the top of the list. For some reason I really had the spooks about her and as it turned out I was right.

When the doorbell went in the middle of the night, my first thought was that Richie must have died and they'd sent someone to deliver the news to Cath. But when I peeped into Cath's room, she wasn't there and I assumed she must have finally decided to keep an overnight vigil at the hospital.

I shouted, "Who's there?" through the door and put the chain on. I heard a whimper from the other side and suddenly I knew who it was.

He'd really done a number on her this time. I was amazed she could even walk. Her right ear was bleeding and there were traces of blood around her nostrils. One eye was nearly closed and her right cheek was very swollen. And perhaps most horrible of all was that when she turned her head, I could see that her hair was matted with blood.

She fell into my arms as my mother came down the stairs behind me.

It's okay, Mum, I mouthed. "It's Selma Walker. I'll take care of her —" And then I stared in total shock. Coming down the stairs behind her, his tanned body naked except for the briefest of underpants, was Sonny Cross.

Chapter 19

With the image of Sonny Cross's amazingly compressed abs imprinted forever on my mind — I wasn't about to get into *that* now — I took Selma up to my bedroom and tried not to flinch every time I looked at the brutal evidence of Buzz's attack on her face. I attended to her cuts and swellings and ran her a bath in my bathroom. I left her to have a long soak and set about making up the sofa bed in my office.

My new little office, bang next door to my bedroom, was the most private room in the house and why I hadn't thought of working in it until the fire was a mystery to me. It could be reached either from the landing or by a small door in the far corner of my bedroom, not immediately visible as you entered the room. I was already making plans to offer Selma shelter and protection from Buzz. I would move the big cupboard on the landing in front of the door to my office. I deliberated whether to call Max Austin in the middle of the night and decided that I would wait till morning. If Buzz came looking for Selma tonight, I would dial 999.

"Are you sure you wouldn't like me to take you to hospital?" I asked when she emerged from the bathroom, her diminutive body somewhat dwarfed by my toweling robe.

"Not necessary." She managed a smile. "Nothing's broken, although I can't quite believe it. He was in a terrible rage. He went out last night, I don't know where. I'd gone to bed early, thought I was coming down with a cold. He stayed out all night, he wasn't there this morning when I got up. He got home around eleven and he came to find me immediately. He had on a pair of boxing gloves. He bought them the other day because he's taking lessons. And I was pleased about that. I thought it would be a way for him to find some kind of release for his anger so he wouldn't have to take it out on me. I was really happy for him." She paused, looked away from me and said something that left me speechless. "You know, I love him so much."

I love him so much. She said it with so much feeling, but I couldn't believe it. I'd slept with the man she was talking about,

I'd been infatuated with him for twenty seconds, but the minute I became aware of the violence he was capable of I had instantly begun to despise him. Yet only a short time after he had used her as a human punching bag, Selma was claiming she still loved him.

"It's okay," she went on, "I know I have to get out. Something set him off today and he was out of control. Once he was through hitting me he locked me in a closet and left me there all day. He's never done that before."

"How did you get out?"

"He thinks it's just a closet but it's actually a very small store room and there's a tiny window at the back that was hidden by cardboard boxes. When I moved the boxes, there it was. I'm so tiny I was able to squeeze through. It was quite a drop down the side of the house but I think I'm okay. I just ran for my life — to you."

"You can stay here as long as you want, Selma," I said, going over to her to put my arms around her but I stopped at the last minute. There was something about her that didn't encourage closeness. "You'll be safe in this little room. I'll be right next door. We'll call Inspector Austin in the morning."

"You call him," she said slowly. "I know I won't be able to bring myself to. That's partly why I've come to you, so you can help me to stay away from Buzz. He's going to be so sorry for what he's done. The more brutal he is the sorrier he is afterwards. He'll be desperate to find me and he'll get down on his knees and beg me to come back and I cannot afford to let that happen. Our reunions, Lee, they're the sweetest thing. I love him then more than at any other time. I start thinking maybe I'm responsible, maybe I provoked his anger in him in some way. When he tells me he can't believe what he did, that he loves me so much, we are *so close,* it's almost unbearable. That's why I've never left, you understand, Lee? Because the reunions are so sweet."

It was awful but I did believe her. I just don't think I could ever condone violence on that scale. I mean, I *know* I provoke Tommy no end but he would never *ever* lift a finger to me. Not that it looked like I'd have much chance to provoke him anymore.

"Of course," she went on, "everything's rosy for a couple of months and then I do something and he hits me again. It never lasts. I know that. I keep hoping the rosy times will last forever and I just have to accept that they never will."

I let her talk on and on. I hoped I'd retain everything she was saying. It would be invaluable for the book.

"It's the most dangerous time," she said, her voice gathering strength, "the contrition phase, because that's when you tell yourself that one day they'll change and that maybe that day has come. That's what I want the book to focus on. I've been there, I know what it's like, I can speak to them in such a way that they will identify with everything I'm saying. I'll tell them how I've always thought I could change Buzz and never more than during the periods following a beating when he was so ashamed and begging for forgiveness. But I was deluding myself and I want my readers to understand they are too. I want to give them a book that guides them through an abusive marriage and out of it while showing them they can still love him — but they *have* to get away.

"And speaking of the book, I'm here to give you these." She handed me a canvas tote bag I noticed she'd been clutching when she was standing on my doorstep. I looked inside and saw a stash of audiotapes, at least ten or fifteen. "Here's the book. You'll have everything you need on these tapes."

"But when — ?" I was speechless.

"Over Christmas. I have a little secret to tell you. I didn't go away to America. I stayed right here in England but I had to say I went to the States so Buzz wouldn't try to find me. I wanted to be alone to record these tapes out loud without interruption and without him accidentally hearing anything I said."

"Where were you?"

"In a house by the sea in Devon. It belongs to one of the cast members in *Fraternity.* He lets me have the key so I can use it when I want to. That's where I'm intending to go now. I called him and he said fine, no problem, didn't even ask why."

"What about *Fraternity*?"

"I'm on a two-week break. That's why I'm down in London. Ironically, my character, Sally McEwan's on a business trip to New York. I'll go to Devon till I have to restart work and then I'll ask for some kind of day-to-day protection in Manchester. That will be the time to tell the *Fraternity* production team the truth."

"We'll tell Max Austin first thing in the morning and have him contact the Devon constabulary. We don't want you feeling vulnerable down there."

But before I could call him, Max Austin was on my doorstep once again at nine o'clock the following morning. He was smiling and charming and back in the billowing overcoat that I found so romantic but when I told him about Selma, he switched to grumpy, moody Max in a second. He was furious with me for not calling him in the middle of the night.

"You've got my mobile number. I keep it switched on at night. What's the point of waiting till this morning to tell me? I should have gone round and picked him up straight away. That bastard's probably halfway to China by now. What were you thinking of?"

I took him upstairs to see Selma and he came down about twenty minutes later looking slightly mollified.

"Keep her up there. Don't let anyone in. She's insisting on going down to Devon — seems like she *was* there over New Year's, gave me the address and everything. I'll check it out."

"You don't believe her?"

"I'll check it out," he repeated. "Now I'm going to call a couple of the lads and go round the corner to pay a visit on your friend Buzz."

"He's not my friend —" I began but he'd gone before I could finish the sentence. I followed him out into the hall in time to get a glimpse of Sonny Cross's backside — now fully clothed, mercifully — disappearing out the door behind him. Well, well, well.

There was no sign of my mother who was usually up before anyone else and when Cath came down she went straight to the phone to call the hospital. The way she slumped at the kitchen table when she'd finished the call indicated there was no change in Richie's condition.

She looked totally exhausted.

"They let me sit by his bedside till four in the morning. I came home and tried to fall asleep but I don't think I got more than a couple of hours."

I set about making her breakfast. "You've got to eat," I said firmly when she made a face at the scrambled eggs and bacon.

"Don't say it. I know. *I've got to keep my strength up,*" she parroted in a weary tone. "I wish you'd all change the record. I'm grateful for everyone's support except when it starts coming at me in the form of clichés."

"Sorry," I murmured.

"No, I'm sorry," she said. "I really am. I don't know what's making me be so churlish. You don't look too hot yourself. What's up? Ah, I remember — where's Tommy?"

"This is going to take a minute," I told her. "Have you got time?"

"Of course," she said. "I'm going to the hospital in half an hour or so — it was a mistake going to work yesterday, I couldn't concentrate at all — but until then I'm all yours."

I told her the whole story, starting with the discovery of the mist pot cit in Tommy's medicine cabinet, which should have alerted me to what was going on. Cath shook her head in wonder. "I suppose it never occurred to you to ask him what it was doing there? No? Lee, this could only happen to you."

I went on to describe how Tommy started speaking miraculous French when we visited my parents. I gave her the sad news about Noreen and I described the sighting of Marie-Chantal at her bedside. I finished with Tommy's surprise revelations about his affair, going into malicious detail in my description of Marie-Chantal. "She's so neat, I expect she has a manicure every day and I doubt there's a single hair anywhere on her body."

"But she suffers from cystitis?" Cath reminded me.

"Yes," I laughed, "there is some justice in life."

I waited for her feedback on Tommy's behavior but before she could say anything, Max Austin was ringing my doorbell for the second time that morning.

"He's gone," he said flatly. "No answer when I rang the bell and a neighbor saw him leave this morning with a suitcase. Hi, Cath," he said, seeing her behind me. "How are you holding up?"

"Richie's just the same," she said. "I've got no option but to keep going. But what if he stays like this for months — ?"

I knew she was going to say years and couldn't bring herself to. Max shifted uncomfortably.

"Well, I guess we just have to face the fact that it might happen but on the other hand he may pop out of it this afternoon. Nobody could feel worse than I do, Cath. I was the one who told him to go and take a look round the arches behind my house. So I'm to blame, you want someone to shout at, shout at me if it'll make you feel better."

"It wouldn't," said Cath, "and you

mustn't feel responsible. Tell me, do you talk to him when you go and see him or do you think it's a waste of time?"

"I do," said Max. "I ask him questions. He was in the process of tracking down and interviewing as many of Buzz Kempinski's old girlfriends as he could find. I ask Richie about his progress because I want to know every damn detail about that bastard. He'd seen one of them the day he was attacked, the last woman Buzz was with before he met Selma. He was telling me about her when he came over with the takeaway. He was pretty shaken up by the state of her and this was years after Buzz had been with her. But I didn't get her name — I assumed I'd be seeing him at work the next day — and now I can't find it. There's nothing in his diary and I've searched his desk but I can't find anything. He got this call in the middle of the afternoon and shouted to me that he was going off to South London somewhere but I don't have the details."

Cath shook her head. "I was with Lee that evening. I hadn't seen him all day. We spoke on the phone and he said he'd been to somewhere like Peckham but he didn't say why. I knew he was going to check you out, Max, see if you were up for a beer or something. The next thing I heard was you calling me to say he was in hospital."

"Look," said Max, "we're going to get Buzz. I'll put a watch on the house so if he comes anywhere near Selma, we'll know. Tell her not to worry. I'm going to send someone round to take some pictures of her all beaten up. Cath, I'll see you at the hospital later."

"You haven't a clue, have you?" said Cath when he'd gone. She was grinning at me like a Cheshire cat and while it felt good to see her smile again, I was a little uncomfortable.

"About what?"

"He fancies you."

"Who does?"

"Max. He fancies you. It's clear as day."

"He does not."

"He never stopped looking at you even when he was speaking to me. He was all of a twitter. I've never seen him like that. Richie mentioned a while back that he'd been talking about you but I didn't catch on. I thought he meant talking about your case, not about *you.* Why did he have to come round to tell you Buzz'd scarpered? He could have just phoned you."

"I expect he wanted to see you, not me. Anyway he was here earlier this morning.

He was only going round the corner to Buzz's. It made sense for him just to pop back."

"What do you mean he was just here?"

"He was on the doorstep first thing and so I told him about Selma."

"What about Selma?"

When I told her she came over and hugged me. "What is it with you, girl? You seem to be running a refuge for women in trouble. Her, me, your mum. Weird occupation for someone who values her solitude as much as you do."

But I was still thinking about Max. "I suppose he has taken to turning up quite a bit lately. He was here to pick up his laundry" — at which Cath rolled her eyes — "then he turned up with you the night Richie was attacked, then he was back yesterday — asking how you were — and again this morning. But he's got a perfectly good reason. You heard him this morning, he's keeping me posted about his investigation into my fire. I asked him to."

"And you believe that? Any reason why he can't just pick up his mobile and give you a quick bell? You are talking about a seriously busy man and anyway it's the Family Liaison Officer's job — what's her name? Mary someone — to keep you in the loop. He doesn't have time to go making house calls every five minutes. Have you any idea of the hard time he'd give Richie, if Richie took to popping by to see some woman?"

"I'm not some woman," I protested.

"My point exactly," said Cath. "How long did he stay after your mother took me upstairs that night?"

"Quite a long time," I admitted. "He was still here when Tommy came home drunk and we had that row."

"And he heard it?" Cath leaned forward.

"You know, I'm not sure. I thought he left but maybe he was on the stairs listening."

"Well, there you are. He thinks you've broken up with Tommy and he's going to try his luck."

"But a couple of times he's been all dressed up in smart clothes, as if he's about to go out on a date."

"What sort of clothes?"

"Just — I don't know — better clothes than that sad suit and tie he normally wears. Like he'd made a real effort to impress someone. I assumed he was going on to meet a woman."

"Did it ever occur to you that maybe he was trying to impress you?"

"Oh, stop it, Cath." For some reason the idea bothered me. Had I made a fool of myself yet again? If what Cath said was true, no wonder Max was in such a state over Buzz. No, it was insane and I wouldn't give it another thought.

"I'll leave you to fret about it all day," said Cath knowingly. "Don't look like that, Lee. It's not the end of the world. You've probably brought a little sunshine into his life, think of it that way. He could use some, that's for sure."

"Call me from the hospital the minute there's any change," I told her and gave her a parting hug.

When I went upstairs to check on her, Selma suggested we use the time together to work on the book. She wanted to listen to the tapes together and take a break now and then to discuss how the material might be incorporated into the book. It wasn't how I usually worked but I appreciated the gesture of cooperation. I wanted to do as much for her as I possibly could. Sleeping with Buzz was probably the single most cheesy thing I had ever done. Although I prayed she would never learn about it, I planned to make it up to her by putting together the best book I had ever written.

I went into the bathroom, retrieved the

ghetto blaster where it was perched on a stool beside the bath and ejected the Waylon Jennings tape that accompanied Tommy's sing-along in the tub most mornings. I picked up a plaid wool shirt off the floor and a stray navy sock and tossed them into the laundry basket. And then the phone rang.

It was Max. I answered it by my bed and sat down rather suddenly, Cath's words still fresh in my mind. Selma came to the doorway of the office. I felt stupid and jittery as if I were answering the phone to my very first date and it made me more than a little abrupt with him. He was calling to tell me he'd made the necessary checks and Selma Walker was telling the truth about being down in Devon over the Christmas holidays.

"Well, of course she was," I shouted suddenly, aware of Selma standing right in front of me. "I never doubted it for a second. Why would she lie to me?"

"But you were the one who told me she was lying in the first place," he pointed out, clearly shaken by my tone, "about going to New York to see her family, don't you remember?"

"Oh, probably," I said.

"Well, I just thought you'd like to know."

He sounded totally dejected. "I still don't like the fact that she lied to you. I've only established she *went* to Devon over Christmas. Nobody has been able to confirm she was at the cottage on New Year's Eve. It's miles from anywhere apparently and no one had any reason to go near it. They were all too busy celebrating elsewhere. As I've said, I'm not happy with the idea of her as the prime suspect but as you yourself pointed out, she does have a motive. I mentioned Angel O'Leary and she said she didn't know who I was talking about. Earlier she had referred to your 'little blond lodger' and when I pointed out to her that Angel O'Leary was this person, she pretended she didn't know the lodger's name. Perfectly possible, I suppose, but I had the distinct feeling she was lying, that she knew much more about Angel than she was letting on. She could have driven up from Devon for the day. And there's another thing. When I spoke to her this morning, I noticed something. She has very small hands —"

I hung up on him. I didn't want to face what he was saying. Here I was, sheltering Selma from Buzz and instead of going after him, Max was trying to make it sound as if *she* were the criminal. Worse than that, he was holding me responsible for putting the idea into his head.

I stared at Selma's battered face and shuddered. Had Buzz told her about Angel? Had he taunted her, provoked her in some way that had driven her to extreme lengths?

And Max was right. She did have very small hands. She was reaching out with one of them now, pointing to the phone.

"Would it be okay if I called Bianca and told her where I was?" she said. "I always tell her where I am. She's the only person who has always known what he does to me. She'd be worried sick if I didn't let her know I was all right."

"Of course," I said, "make whatever calls you want. Will she be at your house? You're not going to call there, are you?"

"She has a mobile and only I have the number. I gave it to her for just this kind of emergency."

I left her alone to call Bianca and went downstairs to make us some coffee. When I returned, she'd inserted the first tape and was curled up on my bed.

As we listened, I realized this tape would be very useful for the proposal and I scribbled a note to remind myself to tell her that. Selma outlined in a lucid and rational way exactly how she felt her book would help other battered women. She spoke about what she had described earlier — the danger of the contrition phase.

Then, to back this up, in the second tape, she began to chronicle the beatings she had endured followed by the periods of calm when she had reversed her decisions to leave him. The saddest moments were when she talked about her abject surrender at the onset of each beating, how she knew that to fight back would only prolong the agony and might even prove fatal. The least resistance she put up, the sooner it would all be over and they could enter another sweet contrition phase. It was, she said, as if she were watching slow-motion action in a film. She would see the arm, or the weapon, raised above her and force herself to go numb while she waited for the contact, thinking that this was not really happening to her but to somebody else.

I sat there mesmerized. Selma's voice had filled the room and as she sat there listening to herself our eyes met from time to time and she smiled, or nodded to emphasize a point. And then, after what must have been close to two hours, when there was a slight pause on the tape — she was searching for a word or a phrase — in the silence that followed, through my open bedroom door, we heard Buzz's voice clearly and distinctly in the hall below.

"I'm so sorry to disturb you. Lee's expecting me."

Selma opened her mouth and I thought she was going to scream. I mouthed *No, no,no!* at her and signaled to her to stay in the office. I closed the door without making a sound and crept to the top of the stairs to listen.

"Is she really? I didn't know. Do come in." I heard my mother close the front door. She must have come downstairs while we were playing Selma's tape. I should have anticipated this and warned her not to open the door. She didn't know Selma was still here. More to the point, she probably had no idea who Buzz was. After all, she'd never seen him before.

"We're working together," I heard Buzz say smoothly and quite truthfully.

"I expect she's upstairs," said my mother. "Hold on, I'll just get her for you. Who shall I say it is?"

"Robert," he said, giving his real name. And that was clever. If my mother knew him by name, she would only remember us talking about Buzz.

"Lee," she shouted up the stairs with no

idea that I was crouching just out of sight. "Robert's here."

I didn't say a word, hoped she'd assume I'd gone out and send him away.

"Lee!" she shouted again. "Are you there? Can you come down please? I've got to leave, I'm having my hair done."

Oh Mum, please don't go. Stay where you are. Send him away.

"Don't let me keep you," I heard him say. "I can see myself up, I know where she works. I've been here before."

"Oh, have you?" My mother's voice indicated she was wavering. "Well, if you wouldn't mind. I really ought to be off. If she's not there, just come down and let yourself out. When were you last here? You know she's moved her office from the top floor to the door off the first landing?"

"I didn't actually," he said. "Thanks. I'll find her, don't worry."

And then everything happened at once. My mother went out the front door and he came bounding up the stairs yelling, "Lee, where are you? Lee?" and came upon me before I could even get to my feet.

"Eavesdropping? Bit beneath you, I would have thought. Here, let me give you a hand."

I shrank from him but he caught me by

the wrist and hauled me to my feet. And didn't let me go.

"What's with the spooky look? You've been really weird since you went away. Is it because of your fire?" he asked, taking my chin between his finger and thumb and giving it a tweak. "You didn't think I'd forgotten about you, did you?"

I imagined Selma listening to every word on the other side of the door. If he kept this up, my secret was out.

He let me go abruptly and moved toward my bedroom door. I leapt in front of him.

"Let's go downstairs. I'll make you a cup of coffee."

He stepped back and leaned against the wall, looking surprised.

"We've got a few things to catch up on, you and me," he said pleasantly and I shivered with fear. What was he playing at? "I've had a detective round to see me a few times, seems to think I had something to do with your fire. Now why would he have that idea?"

I said nothing. I wanted to shout at him about Angel being his alibi but I was inhibited by Selma being within earshot.

I couldn't help observing that he looked beautiful. It had already struck me that he was the same type as Max Austin but I had to concede that while Max was intermittently attractive, Buzz was the real thing. He had an edge to him that Max only exhibited when he was moody or angry but with Buzz it was there all the time, simmering under the surface. It reminded you that he was dangerous and unpredictable and there was no way you could have anything else on your mind when you were with him.

As I looked at him, I found myself thinking back to the conversation I had had with Max where I had raised the possibility that something in Buzz's past had turned him into the sadistic monster I now knew him to be. I recalled the way Max had exploded in rage at my *bleeding heart liberal bullshit* as he'd called it and to my surprise I suddenly realized that, ironically, at the precise moment he said it, Max had appeared as alive and passionate and sexually charged as Buzz himself. Still, I wondered about Buzz's past, his childhood — had he been abused himself?

With Buzz standing there before me I was in shock and, it seemed, when I was in shock my mind turned to inconsequential thoughts. When I had learned that Astrid McKenzie had been burned to death in her house all I could think was that it was a shame she had just had it painted and why did women in high heels do silly things like walk down cobblestone streets? Now all I could do was think back to my first meeting with Buzz — to a time of innocence before I had done something so stupid as to have sex with him. He had played me that jazz CD he had just bought with the tenor sax that wailed first urgently and desperately — and then softly and irresistibly and I wanted to ask him to remind me who it had been.

It was insane to be thinking something like that while Selma was in such danger and I was aware that it was some kind of defense mechanism kicking in to prevent me from showing how frightened I was.

"Selma's gone to Devon," he said suddenly, conversationally and I looked at him and forced myself to appear calm. "Chap phoned this morning, one of the cast members of *Fraternity.* He's got this house there and Selma's going there, apparently, to work on your book. Did you know? No? Now why is that, I wonder? He gave me the number and the address, just in case I wanted to join her. I just phoned her, as a matter of fact, but she wasn't there yet and her mobile's switched off."

So now Selma couldn't escape to Devon. Buzz came toward me again and I had a ghastly thought. Had he come around to see *me,* to resume our affair because he thought Selma was away? Maybe he had no idea she was even here.

I had to get him away from my bedroom.

"Come on, coffee," I repeated. I moved toward the top of the stairs but he caught me by the wrist and drew me to him. *Keep your head,* I told myself. *Don't scream, don't panic, don't let him know anything's wrong, just get him downstairs and out of the house.*

"Why have you been avoiding me? What's she been telling you? You know, I've missed you so much." He bent to kiss me and I turned my head so that his lips were buried in my hair. "You smell so wonderful, Lee. What's it called, your scent?"

"Jo Malone. Jasmine and honeysuckle," I said.

And suddenly he threw me against the banister and pinned me there.

"Selma uses Shalimar by Guerlain. She smothers herself in it every morning so the smell is always lingering wherever she is," he hissed in my ear. "That's how I know she's here. I could smell it the minute I came upstairs. I thought it might be your scent, but it isn't, is it, Lee? You've just set me straight there. This is like a children's game — it's stronger over here, am I getting warm?" Still holding on tightly to my wrist, he moved toward my bedroom door. "She's in here, isn't she?"

"No," I said as evenly as I could, "why would she be here? You said she was on her way to Devon."

"Well, maybe she's been here? You're lying, I can tell."

He gripped me and as my heart hammered away he held me to his chest, one hand pulling my head back by my hair so I had to look up into his face. And suddenly all trivial inconsequential thought evaded me and I found myself dwelling on something I'd heard on the radio recently: If you were murdered, it was highly likely to be by someone you knew.

Murdered! My old nightmare. Over and over again I'd imagined how it would be. Strangled till my eyes popped out of their sockets or smothered with a pillow. Would I be stabbed in the chest and die from a massive hemorrhaging of the aorta? Would I be hit over the head with a blunt object? What constituted a blunt object? I pictured someone picking up my laptop and bashing it into my temple, someone into whose autobiography I had managed to inject his or her true vile personality without realizing what I was doing.

And here was Buzz, someone I knew in the biblical sense even if I was a bit hazy about the rest of him. Was he going to kill me?

"Who is this man with the house in Devon? Are he and Selma an item? What's going on?"

"Nothing," I screamed because he was hurting me. "I don't know anything."

"Let her go!" Selma opened the door and came at him like a snarling little terrier and he released me abruptly. "Lee," she shouted. "Go and call the police."

But the sight of her did something to him and he began to lash out. I caught a glancing blow above my eye and felt blood trickling down my face where the skin was broken. Then he gripped Selma firmly by the elbow and began to propel her toward the stairs and when he put his hands on her and began to grip her hard it unleashed in me a rage I had never known before. I hurled myself at him and lashed out at him, pummeling him on the back, but it was no good.

What horrified me was the way Selma submitted to him. Her instinct was not to retaliate like I did but to go weak and allow herself to be half carried down the stairs. As I followed behind them, I stuck out my foot and tried to kick him in the back but I missed, lost my footing and was left clinging to the banister, screaming at him to stop.

He didn't make it out the house with Selma but it had nothing to do with me. As he opened the front door, one arm wrapped around Selma's waist, something knocked him sideways.

Chris might be short and stubby but his strength was singularly impressive. He sized up the situation in an instant and his fist shot out toward Buzz's jaw in a left hook that indicated he had boxing experience. He missed as Buzz dodged, but connected with Buzz's shoulder, sending him flying back against the coat stand and causing him to lose his balance and release Selma. Then he began to kick Buzz for all he was worth. Selma watched with a grim expression on her face, no doubt reliving moments when she'd been on the receiving end of Buzz's kicking. There was a ferocity to Chris's blows that I actually found pretty scary even though I wanted him to demolish Buzz as quickly as possible. He had Buzz down on the ground and he was going for his ribs. Buzz wasn't making any attempt to fight back and I could see he was in serious pain.

Suddenly Selma started screaming at Chris.

"LET HIM GO! You're going to kill him."

Chris glanced at her and Buzz seized his moment, rolling over and clambering awkwardly to his feet. Chris launched himself at Buzz to stop him going out the door but he was a second too slow. He made as if to go after him but Selma grabbed his arm and pulled him back into the hall.

"Let him go. Didn't you hear me? You were really hurting him."

Chris looked at her and shook his head in wonder. "Yeah," he said slowly, "I really hurt him. Duh? Like I was supposed to kiss him? He was on the point of really *hurting* you. I thought I was doing you a favor. Maybe I'd have done better to have let him kill the pair of you."

But if he was disappointed by Selma's reaction to his chivalry, he didn't need to worry about mine. I almost fell down the stairs again in my hurry to thank him. I flung my arms around him and clung to him like an hysterical orangutan. I thanked him profusely, stopping short of calling him my hero, but I was aware that I was going way over the top.

"Well, that's more like it," he said when I finally pulled away. "In fact that was very nice indeed." He looked me up and down. "Especially since all I came round for was that coffee."

Chapter 20

Selma fell apart almost immediately. She began to babble that she too was grateful to Chris but that she loved Buzz, that she knew he would be back and that while she dreaded it, she needed to know he wanted her. Didn't we understand? Didn't we know how much it hurt her to see Buzz and not be able to help him?

Help him? I could see Chris getting ready to remonstrate with her and I led her upstairs to calm her down. I managed to persuade her to lie down and take one of the tranquilizers that I had recently discovered were part of the arsenal of aids that helped her get through the day. She was brave, Selma, but she was not as tough as she made out and, as I was beginning to realize, this stand she was making against Buzz by doing the book was taking its toll.

When I had finally settled her and went back downstairs half an hour later, I assumed Chris would be long gone. But he was still there, sitting at the kitchen table, chatting to Cath who had returned from the hospital. She stood up and embraced me when I came into the kitchen.

"I can't believe what Chris has just told me, that Buzz was actually here."

"Thank God for Chris," I said, smiling at him. "You two know each other?"

"You remember the café Mum and Dad had when I was a kid? We lived above it in that tiny little flat?" She looked at me.

I nodded.

"Well Chris's family had their lockup in the mews right around the corner, where they kept all the produce for their stall in the market. I was always round there because his mum used to give me an apple or a few cherries if I caught her in a good mood. So where do you have your lockup now, Chris? Same place?"

He shrugged. Didn't look like he had the same kind of fond memories as Cath.

"How's Richie?" I asked her.

"No worse, no better," she said. "I just came back to get my toothbrush in case I want to stay with him through the night. Unless of course you'd like me to stay with you — in case Buzz — you know, in case he comes back."

"He won't be back," said Chris firmly.

"You heard the man," I told Cath. "You need to be with Richie."

She kissed me again on the cheek and called out, "See you tomorrow," as she went upstairs to get her stuff.

I expected Chris to get up and leave but he settled back in his chair and grinned at me.

"So what about that coffee then? Do I deserve it or what?"

Well, of course he deserved it. Absolutely. But with my mother out at the hairdresser's and Selma asleep, I would have welcomed the opportunity to get some work done in a house that was seldom this quiet these days.

But Chris had come to my rescue and Selma's. He had stood up to Buzz even though he was five or six inches shorter. He had been our savior, there was no other way to look at it and the least I could do was make him a cup of coffee.

"So what's with Selma Walker?" he asked me. "How can she say she loves that guy when he beats the crap out of her?"

"It's complicated," I said.

"It's sick, is what it is," he said. "What does she see in him? I mean, what is it with blokes like him? He looks like a bleedin' faggot with all that floppy hair. The only way he can show his strength is by beating up on his wife. You see it all the time, beautiful women falling for that type of man. I don't get it. I really don't."

I could hear the subtext in the whine in his voice. *What's he got that I haven't got?* I didn't answer. What was the point? I couldn't very well point out that Chris's bald head and uncanny resemblance to a bull terrier probably had something to do with it. He was chirpy enough, and I would have thought his natural confidence — albeit a little cocky — and his gift of the gab would have won him more than his fair share of dates but it looked like he had a bit of an attitude problem and that could be off-putting.

"What was he doing round here anyway?" he asked me suddenly.

"He'd come to get Selma. She's staying with me."

He looked up at me sharply and I realized I hadn't needed to tell him that.

"No, I meant that time I saw him coming out your house."

"I'm working with Selma on a book and he's her manager as well as her husband. We were having a meeting — about the book," I added hastily.

I could tell he didn't believe me.

"So if a guy got rough with you, you'd like it, would you?"

"No, of course not."

"So what kind of guy do you like then?"

"The coffee's ready," I said, ignoring his question. I was a little uncomfortable with how personal his questions were becoming. "You want milk or sugar?"

"Don't want to tell me?" He winked at me. "Bit shy, are we? Me, I like women with a bit of meat on them. And they've got to have nice friendly faces. I can't stand them stuck-up chicks who just point at the veg on my stall to show me what they want and never bother to speak to me. Not like you." He looked at me with a silly grin on his face. "You always have a nice chat with me. I look forward to it."

"I do too, Chris." It was a white lie. I enjoyed going shopping in the market and I always went to his stall because I was such a creature of habit. I hadn't been aware that we always had a *nice chat* but then I did make a point of exchanging a bit of conversation with everyone as I paid for shopping, more out of courtesy than anything else.

"Yeah, we've known each other a long time," he said happily. "Milk please, two sugars. I was only thinking the other day how we've sort of grown up together. My mum knows your mum —"

This was a bit of a stretch but I let it go. I heard Cath coming down the stairs and was disappointed when she left without coming back into the kitchen.

"Funny how you know Cath," I said. "I suppose everyone knows everyone growing up round the market."

"Like you and me," he said cheerfully, then his face darkened. "But listen, you want to watch that Cath."

"What do you mean?"

"She's a drunk. Have you ever seen her when she's shit-faced? She barely knows who you are."

"Not the Cath I know," I said truthfully. I didn't want to get into this with Chris.

"Well, speaking of drinking, I was wondering," he went on, "if you fancied going out Friday night? Maybe a spot of dinner somewhere? What do you say?"

What could I say? What could I possibly say that would let me off the hook and allow him to retain his dignity?

"Friday's tricky," I began.

"Well, Saturday's open. What about Saturday?" he nipped in quick.

"No, I might be going away for the

weekend," I lied. "That's why Friday wouldn't work."

"We'd better make it tonight then. Doing anything tonight?"

"I ought to be here, I ought to stay with Selma. Can't leave her on her own, not after —"

"I thought your mum was here? I saw her in the market yesterday. She told me she was over for a bit."

Okay, I'd have to spell it out for him.

"Chris, I'm not sure it would be such a good idea —"

"What d'you mean? It'd be a brilliant idea. I must admit I never thought of it before but what with you inviting me round for a coffee, it started me thinking."

I had never invited him around. He'd come up with that idea all by himself. I'd actually stressed I didn't want him to deliver stuff. I hadn't encouraged him. I had not!

I shook my head gently and whispered "Sorry" at him and smiled to say no hard feelings but he was surly now, stirring his coffee around and around with such a vigorous motion that it slopped all over the table.

"I didn't reckon on you being snotty as well," he said. "I thought you were different but you're like all the rest of them. *So nice to see you, Chris, your broccoli's the best in the market, Chris, it would save my life if you'd deliver to the house, Chris.* Oh, you're all over me when you want something, but if I suggest something as normal as a get-together that isn't fruit-and-veg related, you can't get away from me quick enough."

"Chris, it's not like that at all." I was genuinely horrified that I'd upset him. "Here let me top up your coffee. Tell me how your mother is. Will we ever see her back on the stall again one day? You should get her to help you out on Saturdays like you used to do."

But he continued to look at me with a belligerent expression on his face and I was wondering what on earth I was going to do with him when I heard the sound of the front door opening.

Tommy was the last person I expected to walk in at that precise moment but boy was I glad to see him. I leapt up and kissed him square on the mouth before he could indicate there was any tension between us. Chris looked on in amazement.

"Wow!" said Tommy. "Looks like you're pleased to see me." He grinned. "I stopped by to tell you that I just came from the hospital and they're releasing Mum on Friday. She really wants you to come with me to take her home. She doesn't know that we — you know — that we've had another —"

"Of course I'll come with you," I said quickly not wanting him to reveal we weren't speaking in front of Chris. "Thank God she's coming home. Tommy, this is Chris. You've heard me speak of his stall on the market and how it's my favorite place to shop. Chris, this is my boyfriend, Tommy Kennedy."

Chris's eyes widened at the word "boyfriend." He regarded Tommy dubiously. "I've not seen you in the market," he said.

"That's because I don't live round here," said Tommy, reaching over and finishing off my cup of coffee. I didn't say a word.

"So you two don't live together?" Chris perked up.

"Well, yes, we do as a matter of fact," I said quickly. "Tommy's just been away."

Tommy looked at me quizzically.

"Well, your stuff's still here," I said by way of explanation.

"Best be off," said Chris. "Can't be dilly-dallying. Got a stall to run."

"Nice meeting you," said Tommy.

"Ta for the coffee," said Chris and when

I saw him out to the door he muttered, "You never said nothing about no boy-friend. And he never stopped you seeing Selma Walker's husband, did he?"

He was gone before I had a chance to reply.

"Weird-looking bloke," said Tommy when I went back into the kitchen. "Listen, I'm sorry about the other night. I was drunk."

I was drunk and I also admitted that I'd been having an affair with a French woman. I could bring it up again or I could let it go. I opted for the latter. We weren't done with it yet, we'd have to deal with it sometime and I'd have to come clean about Buzz. To put a cynical slant on it, after Buzz's dramatic visit I needed Tommy back in the house. And to put a noncynical slant on it, I found I was desperately happy to see him.

I made him some lunch and filled him in on what had happened while he'd been gone. When he heard about Buzz he came over and took me in his arms, hugging me to him and stroking my hair.

"Sounds like all your worst nightmares came true," he whispered. "I wish I could come back and protect you."

I pulled away from him.

"No, it's okay. I want you to come back. We'll forget the other night. I didn't —"

"I've got to think of Mum," he said. "I've been wracking my brains trying to think who could look after her and then I realized the obvious person was me. I'm going to move into her house to look after her. I'm going home, so to speak."

But what about me? a voice inside me wailed.

"But what about when you're at work?"

"I'll hire someone to be there during the day. I can barely afford it but it's important Mum has someone with her. She's very weak and you know what she's like, she'll go lifting stuff all over the house and do herself an injury twenty minutes after I've left for work."

I need you, I kept thinking but my need couldn't compare with Noreen's. I was healthy, I was relatively young. It wasn't as if I would be alone in the house.

But it was agony. The more I listened to Tommy talking about his mother and how scared he'd been that he might lose her, the more I realized how much I loved him. He was a sweet person. Please, God, I hope I hadn't entirely blown my chances of living with him.

"I'm going to enjoy living with her

again." He was getting into his stride about Noreen. "We were always a good team. I'm her straight guy. She's the comedienne — as you know to your cost. She never stops talking, she has an opinion on everything under the sun, and more often than not she can make you laugh about it. I'm the opposite, I know. Yes I am," he insisted when I made as if to protest. "I'm just an ordinary bloke but she enables me to feel okay about it. She points out that someone has to be the straight guy, the one who listens and stays in the background otherwise how could people like her have any fun at all? And I find myself thinking that if I were like her, if I were an entertainer, a talker, a wit, and someone who always finds himself the center of attention then I'd never have the benefit of listening to people like her."

I went to the sink to rinse Chris's mug. Noreen had to be okay. I don't think I'd realized before just how much Tommy cared for his mother. Listening to him now I envied him his closeness with her.

"You know, people like me often get called boring," he went on, "but I reckon we're the lucky ones. We're always entertained. We don't get the praise and the attention but we have all the fun."

As I listened to him, I wondered if he was trying to tell me something. Did he want me to be more like Noreen, to be more of an extrovert?

"But where I'm really lucky," he went on, "is in the fact that she understands and accepts me for what I am. It's the saddest thing in the world when people aren't lucky enough to be understood by their parents."

Of course when he said that I burst into tears. He'd always known how much my mother upset me.

"But Tommy," I burbled through my tears, "if you're going to be with Noreen, when am I going to see you?"

"I don't know. I'm going to be pretty busy," he admitted, "but perhaps it's a good thing if we spend some time apart. We've been having plenty of rows recently."

I began to sob even louder.

"Oh, God, Lee, *please* switch off the blubbing. I'm not saying we're breaking up or anything like that. Mum would never allow it. No, seriously, I think we need to take stock, see where we want to go next."

To be translated: *He needed to take stock and see where he wanted to go next.*

"Anyway, as I said, Mum wants you to come and settle her in at home when she comes out of hospital. Doesn't trust me to attend to the finer details like shopping and making her bed. Can I count on you?"

"Of course," I mumbled, not looking at him. I had to stop crying and hold it together. I had to stop being needy, go along with his plan, and just hope that he'd come back to me when Noreen was fully recovered.

I didn't go with him to the door, knowing that if I did I might not be able to stop myself clinging to him on the doorstep and pleading with him to stay. But I peeked through the curtains and saw him encounter my mother returning from the hairdresser's.

Sonny Cross had a lot to answer for. There could be no other reason why my mother had taken it into her head to have a fuchsia streak incorporated into her otherwise snow-white hair.

They stood on the pavement for a long time, Tommy doing most of the talking, I noticed. When she finally came into the house her first words on entering the kitchen were: "Tommy's been telling what's just happened with that dreadful man. He says I'm to take care of you, Lee.

So there you are, with me here you don't need to worry about a thing."

Somehow this unlikely statement from my mother managed to make me feel even more frightened than I had been before.

Two days later Richie returned to the land of the living. Sonny Cross, who happened to be at his bedside at the time, reported that his first words were *What's for tea?* although we all had a hard time believing him.

That night Sonny and Cath went out and got rip-roaring drunk. I went along for the first half of the evening, until I realized with a shock that I just couldn't keep pace with them. At first I thought Cath was merely humoring Sonny, whose first words on leaving the hospital were "I've never felt so relieved in my life. This requires a celebration and you know what I mean by that, Cath."

To my surprise he took us to a rather seedy bar near the Earl's Court Road. I glanced at Cath, expecting her to turn up her nose but she seemed happy enough. Then it began to get nasty. Instead of ordering an apple juice, or something equally innocuous, when Sonny looked at her and said "The usual?" she nodded. "Yes, whiskey and ginger, thanks, Sonny." She'd downed two of them before I knew what had happened. When she asked for a third, I sat up sharply. What could I say? *Oh by the way, Tommy told me all about your drinking problem.*

"I expect you're looking forward to telling Richie about the baby?" I said finally.

"I expect I am," she said, not looking at me.

"I thought it wasn't wise to drink too much when you were pregnant."

"I've heard that too," she said and took a large gulp of whiskey.

Something about the way they replenished the rounds of drinks with barely any communication between them told me they'd done this before.

Cath was an angry drunk. Every time she raised her glass, her eyes challenged me to comment until finally I let her have it.

"Stop it, Cath! Stop it right now. Put down that glass and let me take you home."

"No way, José. Sonny and I are just getting started."

"You're a fool!" I was almost screaming

at her. "If you want to do this to yourself, fine. Well, not fine — but it's ultimately your call what you do to your own body. But you're carrying Richie's baby. Just stop and think for one moment about what you might be doing to harm the baby."

She said nothing and gave me a sullen look, which made me think maybe my reaction had got through to her.

"It's Richie's baby too. How can you do this to Richie while he's lying there in hospital? I'm flat out disgusted with you, if you really want to know."

"I don't, actually," she said infuriatingly. "You can keep that sort of information to yourself. And while we're at it, Richie doesn't know what I'm doing. He doesn't even know about the baby yet."

That did it. I reached out and grabbed her by the arm, pulling her to her feet. I picked up her bag and propelled her toward the entrance.

"Sonny!" she yelled but he was ensconced in a conversation with the barman and he didn't hear her.

I got her outside and hailed a cab but when I pushed her into the cab ahead of me, she clambered across the seat and let herself out the other side. I slumped down in the back of the cab and watched her stumbling down the street through the rear window.

"Want me to follow her?" asked the cabbie a little dubiously.

I shook my head at him in the mirror and asked him to take me back to Blenheim Crescent. At least I'd got her out of the bar.

The sound of Marvin Gaye singing "Ain't That Peculiar?" blasted me in the face as soon as I opened the front door. I came upon my mother executing some kind of Tamla Motown solo line dance around the kitchen table. I was relieved to find her in a better mood than when I'd left for the evening. She had fallen into a sulk because she had not been included in Sonny's invitation to celebrate Richie's recovery. In fact she had spent the last two days sitting by the phone like a neurotic twenty-something.

"What does it mean that he hasn't called?" she asked me repeatedly. "Is he waiting for *me* to pick up the phone, do you suppose? What do I do, Lee, tell me, *please.*"

I don't know why she thought I'd have the answer. After all, it had been eight years since I'd been on the dating scene myself although even if I had been single, I doubt if I would have felt able to comment on the mating habits of an aging rascal like Sonny Cross.

"It was the most exciting night of my life," my mother had confided on her return from the hairdresser's. She found me sitting in my office, still shaking from the effects of Buzz's visit and sobbing intermittently whenever I thought about Noreen. I had all but forgotten the sight of Sonny Cross's naked midriff hovering on the landing so I wasn't prepared when, before I could tell her what had happened, my mother launched into her lurid description of her night with him. "He completely woke me up, Lee. He did things to me I'd never even heard of. He —"

"Little too much information, Mum," I cut in quickly, heading her off at the pass before she could subject me to too many embarrassing details.

But Sonny didn't call her for an encore and she sat by the phone like a wet rag. I wasn't sure whether to be relieved or sad. Part of me suspected that it could only end in tears but I hated to see her so bewildered and desperate.

"Just try to accept it for what it was, Mum," I told her. "A fantastic night of passion, a once-in-a-lifetime experience.

Be glad you had it. Many people go through their whole life never knowing something like that."

She didn't even have the strength to take me to task for uttering such a veritable string of clichés. Less than a week ago I had been dreaming up ways to shield her from the sound of sex between me and Tommy, thinking she would be shocked and embarrassed. Indeed, she was the one who insisted she had *zero interest in that department.* Well she had been proved wrong. Now she had to accept that it was my father she had zero interest in, not sex.

"One night is not enough." Her voice had a slightly crazed edge to it. "Can't you understand? Now I've come alive again I want *more.*"

I did understand. Lord knows, I'd wanted enough of Tommy when I'd first met him and although I didn't want to go there, Buzz had had a similar effect on me in the not too distant past. In a way I was reassured to learn that nothing seemed to change as you got older. I just found it a little disconcerting hearing about it from my mother.

Nor did I relish the thought of guiding her through the dating process.

"Where's Selma?" I asked. I'd only felt

comfortable leaving Selma knowing my mother would be home. And of course I'd left strict instructions that she was not to open the door to *anyone.*

"Upstairs. I took a tray up to her. She hasn't been down all evening. So put me out of my agony. How was Sonny? Did he say anything?"

"Nothing, Mum. Sorry. He never mentioned you." I was being cruel to be kind and I hated the way she flinched. "It was a pretty strange evening, if you really want to know. He and Cath started getting pretty loaded."

"Well, that's that then," said my mother.

"What's what?"

"He's drinking."

"Who, Sonny? Well, yes. We went out for a drink."

"But he's not supposed to. He's — you know, he has a problem. That's how he met Cath."

"What do you mean? He met Cath because she's his son's girlfriend."

"No" — my mother shook her head — "it's the other way around. Cath met Richie through Richie's father." *Ah,* I thought. That was why she had given me an odd look when I asked her how she met him and then come up with the Soham explanation. "I always had a feeling years ago that there was something about Cath, something she wasn't telling us. I never liked to ask but I thought that was probably why she stopped seeing you. I thought maybe she was in rehabilitation somewhere."

"You know about Cath's problem?"

"Sonny told me. He and Cath met in AA. They went to the same meetings before he moved back to Liverpool where he's from originally. By the way," she added guiltily, "he's not supposed to have told me that and I shouldn't have told you."

"But he asked her if she wanted *the usual,*" I said, knowing even as I said it that that confirmed everything she'd said. "What should we do? How could he lead her astray like this?"

"How do you know it wasn't the other way round?" asked my mother fiercely. "He didn't touch a drop when we had lunch. When he told me I asked him if he minded me drinking. I'd already had all those kirs on my own. You can imagine how I felt."

"Looks like you've been putting it away tonight too," I said, pointing to the empty bottle of wine in the middle of the kitchen table. “Was that why you were doing your Tina Turner impersonation?”

She didn’t reply and I sensed she was embarrassed that I had caught her reliving her sixties moment with Sonny.

“What are you doing?” She eyed me moving round the table, picking up dirty plates and glasses. There were so many, it dawned on me they’d probably been there for days, accumulating after each meal. Strange that my mother had not whipped the place into shape. Normally she was the one trying to restore order and I was the slob telling her to leave it to the morning.

“I’m clearing up, Mum. I’ve never seen the place in such a mess and it doesn’t look as though Bianca’s going to come near us again.”

“Oh, she came this morning.”

“Who did?”

“Bianca. You know it was most odd. I was up early and she let herself in while I was making myself a cup of tea. But when she saw me she turned and fled. I ran after her, saying it was fine, we needed her, please come back but she disappeared round the corner.”

“She was coming to see Selma, Mum. Selma called her and told her where she was.”

"But why would she come early in the morning?"

"She's scared of running into Buzz, I imagine."

"Haven't they found him yet?"

"No," I said slowly, "they haven't."

When I said *they* I meant Max Austin and I was furious with him. Selma was going out of her mind with worry about Buzz and she had also been perplexed as to why she had not heard from Bianca. So when Max rang my doorbell the next morning, I stood in the doorway making no move to invite him in. He hadn't anticipated this and as a result he was halfway through the door before he realized I was blocking his path. His face was about six inches from mine and I found myself thinking he had very long eyelashes, much longer than mine and it was really rather unfair.

There was a definite *moment.* He could have stepped back instantly and he didn't. *Damn it, Cath's right,* I thought, *he's going to make a move on me.*

But I was wrong. In fact he did the opposite. He turned his back on me and jumped down the front steps like an excited child — a tall, gangling, excited child, his long arms waving in the air and his raincoat billowing out behind him.

I was so taken aback by this display of energy, I didn't know what to do.

"Come for a coffee," he said. "I've just been to see Richie, managed to have a bit of a chat with him. I wanted to tell you about it. Tell Cath to keep an eye on Selma or has she gone to work?"

"She's not around," I said.

"Where is she?"

"You may well ask."

"Sounds like you've got a few things to tell me too. What about your mother?"

I ran upstairs to get a jacket, yelling "Going out for a coffee, be back soon." I was annoyed with myself for accepting Max's invitation so readily but he seemed to have that effect on me. I wanted to talk to him about Cath, bring him up to speed about everything else that was going on, tell him about Noreen. I was angry with him but in a rather odd way, he had become part of my life.

We settled at a table in Books for Cooks farther down Blenheim Crescent. It was a bookshop that sold cookery books and they had a little café in the back where they served food cooked from the recipes in the books they sold. We were rather early for lunch but they didn't seem to mind serving us a coffee and a slice of some delicious-looking angel cake.

"You seem angry with me for some reason," he said as soon as we sat down. He appeared to have put his childlike enthusiasm on hold and he surprised me with his perception. "Have I done something to offend you?"

"You haven't found Buzz," I said. "I'm worried about Selma. You've got to find him."

"You think it's a piece of cake finding someone who doesn't want to be found? You think we'll holler and they'll come running? What you don't seem to realize is I haven't got the manpower," he said defensively. "If Selma Walker wants to come down the station and press charges, fine. But in the meantime she's safe enough with you and I'm a homicide detective with a case to solve. Buzz Kempinski is a rotten piece of flesh but he's already proved he's not the person I'm after. Angel O'Leary's still missing, by the way. Maybe they've gone somewhere together. The word's out on Buzz but quite frankly my best bet is to keep a watch on your house. He'll be back for Selma and we'll get him then. Until that happens, you've just got to be patient and get control of all your guilt."

"I'm sorry, *what* did you say? Guilt?" I was mystified.

"Selma Walker. You want to make it up to her. You want Buzz out of the way so she never learns what happened between you two."

Was he right? Surely I wanted Buzz apprehended because I didn't want him to harm Selma anymore. But a new dart of alarm hit me. If Buzz appeared, what would happen to him? Max said they were keeping a watch on the house. Were there firearm officers lurking in the vicinity, poised to bring him down in two shots?

"Will you give him any warning, you know, if he turns up?"

"Before we shoot?" Max shook his head in exasperation. "He's not a drug dealer as far as I know. You're not running some kind of crack cocaine house, are you? If he comes back and he gives you a bit of aggro trying to get in to see Selma, we'll do something about him. Meanwhile, I'm concentrating on who's been setting fires and trying to kill his girlfriends. I wish there were someone I liked for it apart from Selma Walker but she's beginning to look like a pretty good fit. Her hands are small. It's logical the other set of prints on that can of kerosene in your potting shed are hers because Buzz brought it over from her house. But why would her handprints be all over the letterbox at Astrid McKenzie's mews house?"

"Are they?" I nearly spilled my coffee in surprise. "Are they *Selma's* prints?"

"I don't know whose they are. Whoever it is they haven't got a record. But someone with small hands managed to get them all mucky with wet pink paint over there and leave plenty of evidence. I'm going to have to come and question Selma again, take a set of her prints."

I was shocked. "You *can't* put her through something like that when she's recovering from an attack by Buzz. She's put her trust in me to give her shelter. I can't allow you to waltz in there and accuse her of being a killer. It's totally insane."

He shifted in his chair and shook his head at me.

"I mean it," I said. "I won't let you get near her."

"Well, then give me something she's touched," he said. "Something I can lift her prints off. If they're not a match — and if she can produce someone in Devon who was with her New Year's Eve — then I won't need to upset her, will I? Meantime, you can keep her warm for me."

I didn't say anything. He made it sound so easy but what if they *were* Selma's prints? It would mean I was harboring a murderer and then what would I do?

"So besides the child —"

"Who may not be a child," he reminded me. "Don't forget I've got another witness who says the person wearing a coat with a hood up — an anorak or whatever it was — they say this person was bigger than a child, more like a small adult. That's why we're wondering about Selma —"

"But what about the witness who says they saw a *woman?* The one who wasn't Felicity. Maybe that could have been Selma? Did they say she was a small woman?"

"Ah," said Max, "forgot to tell you, I've sorted that one. It was your neighbor Mrs. O'Malley. She's the worst kind of person to interview in an investigation. Forgets to tell us Angel left with Buzz. Also neglects to tell us she went out into your alley to shout at Kevin to come in for his dinner. He was in your garden kicking a ball around on his own. He told us his mum called him in otherwise we'd never have known."

"You said you'd been to see Richie," I suddenly remembered. "Did he tell you anything?"

"I'm on my way to see the woman he interviewed the day he was attacked. His head's not too clear and he can't remember the details but he told me where to find her name and address. But he was clearly disturbed by his visit and I want to see what it was that freaked him out."

"This is the woman Buzz was involved with before he met Selma?"

Max nodded.

"And if it wasn't Selma you think maybe it was one of his old girlfriends seeking revenge?"

"No!" The way Max looked at me made me feel I was totally stupid. "How do you come up with that motive? Why would his old girlfriends who'd been beaten up go after the new ones? They'd want to warn them to stay away from him more like. And we want to find them to warn them that someone's going after people Kempinski's been involved with for some reason."

"Has Cath been to see Richie? I mean today, this morning?"

"Not as far as I could see. You didn't seem to know where she was. What's happened?"

I told him and asked if he knew about Cath's drinking.

"I did actually," he said, not looking at

me. “Richie told me when he first met her. Asked me if I thought it’d be a problem.”

“What did you say?”

“What could I say? Of course it could be a problem. It always is unless they do something about it. But the bloke was falling in love with her. He didn’t need to hear that. He was too far gone. I must say, she could have picked a better time to fall off the wagon.”

I didn’t regale him with the details about my mother and Sonny Cross, although I did want to discuss it with someone. Instead I told him, “It’s very sad. Noreen’s pretty sick.”

“Who’s Noreen?”

“Tommy’s mother. She has pancreatic cancer. Weren’t you there when he came back from seeing her that night? Didn’t you hear — ?”

Didn’t you hear our flaming row? Didn’t you witness me throwing him out of the house?

Max looked at me now and I waited for him to say *What do you mean? I left when he arrived.* But he didn’t say anything like that. He just asked, “So what’s the deal with Tommy?”

“The deal?”

“You and him?”

"What about me and him?" I could feel myself bristling.

"Well, you know — if you had that number with Buzz Kempinski?"

That *number?* Why did he keep going back to me and Buzz?

"I don't see that it's any of your business," I began.

"Well, yes, it *is,*" he cut in.

"As part of your investigation?"

"As part of my investigation — into you."

He left it dangling. I could pick it up and run with it or I could ignore it.

"Oh not you as well," I said before I could stop myself.

"What's that supposed to mean?" He looked a bit offended. I'd have to be careful. I explained what had happened with Chris, how he'd left in a huff when Tommy had shown up, tried to make light of it.

"Yes," said Max, "I got the impression he was a bit chippy."

"Chippy?"

"Chip on his shoulder. I was talking to another guy like Chris the other day, someone who's grown up in this area, seen a lot of changes. It's a very affluent neighborhood but there's a lot of riffraff mixed in and that's part of the problem. Chris sees these fancy stores and businesses springing up all around him, he witnesses extremely rich people moving in and turning his old neighborhood into an area of multimillion-pound houses. On top of that, he has daily access to women way out of his league when he sells them a pound of carrots and then he has to go home to whatever poxy accommodation he's always lived in. He starts to think it's not fair and who can blame him? And speaking of Chris" — he looked at me intently — "the person I really want to find is the man he says he saw in your alley. He's the one who was there the closest to the time the fire was started."

"How would you go about finding him if he doesn't come forward?"

"All we can do is run the CCTV over and over. It shows everyone who entered and left Blenheim Crescent from both Ladbroke Grove and Westbourne Park Road but can you imagine how many people there were coming and going on the afternoon of New Year's Eve?"

"But it'll help that he limps?"

"What do you mean?"

"Chris told me the man had a bad leg. Walked funny."

"I don't believe it!" Max was thoroughly exasperated. "What is it with these people? Can't they remember to tell me anything? I'll have to talk to him again. He never mentioned anything about a bad leg. He and Mrs. O'Malley are a right pair. So," he said, sipping his coffee, "what about my other investigation — ?"

Uh-oh, we were back to that.

It wasn't another Chris situation by any means. I had to admit that I liked Max Austin and I enjoyed talking to him. But I felt sorry for him. I thought of him as a sad suit, not as exciting romantic potential. He had a vulnerable air to him, which wasn't surprising given what he'd been through with his wife's murder. Plus, I could imagine how I would feel if I'd had the courage to make a tentative approach to someone and they turned me down flat. If I was going to deflect his "investigation" into me, the least I could do was let him down easy.

So what did I do? I sent him such a mixed message that he probably didn't know if he was coming or going.

I leaned over and kissed him very gently near his left ear and whispered, "I love my Tommy very much."

And then I picked up the bill and said,

"This is on me. Walk me back to the house and I'll give you something Selma's fingered."

It was agony walking back along Blenheim Crescent. He didn't say a word, gave me full on moody Max all the way home, and when I rushed inside and returned to press one of the tapes Selma had given me into his hand, he took it and just kept on going. I went back into the house, wishing I'd put him in his place instead of kissing him, especially when I saw Selma standing at the bay window. She must have seen me hand him the tape cover because the look she gave me made me feel quite uneasy.

But I'd meant what I'd said to Max. The truth was I'd fallen in love with Tommy all over again when he'd come around earlier in the week, and when he rang the doorbell and said, "I've got Mum outside in the car. Sorry I didn't give you much notice but it'd be great if you could come up to Islington with us now," I grabbed my coat and rushed outside with him, suddenly knowing without a doubt that helping Tommy was what I wanted to do more than anything else.

Chapter 21

Poor Noreen was desperately frail and could barely manage more than a weak smile at me when I climbed into the car. She fell asleep as we became stuck in traffic on the way up to Islington and when we arrived at her little house in Bewdly Street, Tommy lifted her out of the car and carried her inside as if she were a baby.

What he would have done if I hadn't been there, I have no idea. He had not prepared the house for her homecoming in any way. He hadn't gone shopping for provisions or even made up a bed. All he had succeeded in doing was to dump his belongings in a heap on the floor in the spare room. We settled Noreen on the sofa tucked under a rug and I wandered about the house making a list of things that needed to be done. Finally, I turned to Tommy.

"You know, it would make a lot more sense if she stayed down here on the ground floor," I said. The house was tiny — in a row of what I think were once artisans' cottages — and the only bathroom was on the ground floor with two bedrooms upstairs. "Otherwise she's going to have to contend with the stairs every time she needs the loo."

So we moved her narrow single bed downstairs to the L-shaped living room and placed it by the window so she could keep an eye on what was happening. Tommy went back to work and I went shopping. I spent the afternoon cooking, making meals that could be stored in the freezer and easily defrosted by Tommy — and indeed by Noreen when she felt up to it later on.

For supper that night I made moussaka, one of Tommy's favorites. Noreen picked at it for a minute or two and fell asleep almost immediately. Tommy and I retreated to the kitchen. I watched him pouring dishwashing liquid into the dishwasher and decided maybe the time had come to start thinking about moving in with him, if only to stop him ruining Noreen's appliances. I was contemplating how to bring up the subject out of the blue when he suddenly said, "Damn!" very loudly and started dabbing himself in the chest area.

He turned to face me, looking very Tommy with his hair all rumpled, and I saw that his sweater displayed a moussaka stain that would no doubt prove impossible to remove.

"How did that happen?" he said. "This is my favorite sweater."

It looked familiar and suddenly I knew where I'd seen it.

"Take it off, Tommy," I said sharply. "It's ruined. Throw it away."

"Oh, no, they'll be able to deal with it at the cleaners. Probably cost me a fortune but they've sorted out worse stains than this for me."

"I'm surprised you haven't chucked it out before now." My voice was really on edge now.

"Oh, you've recognized it." He had the nerve to grin at me. "This is a very fine cashmere sweater. Just because Marie-Chantal gave it to me, I don't see why —"

"Well I do," I snapped. "Get rid of it." And then, although I should have let it go at that, I asked what I had been dying to know. "Is she going to stay at the BBC?"

I held my breath. I had dealt with the existence of Marie-Chantal in my usual way by behaving like an ostrich. If I never mentioned her then she would go away and I could pretend Tommy had never had anything to do with her.

"Actually, she isn't." Tommy pulled the sweater over his head and scrunched it into a plastic bag he fished out from under the sink. "She's going back to Lyons in a couple of weeks." He was facing me, barechested, and I resisted the urge to stroke the fine hair between his nipples. He'd lost a little weight, I noticed with surprise. He looked extremely edible. "Satisfied?"

"Are you still — do you still see her? Have you slept with her again?"

What was the matter with me? She was going. Why couldn't I leave it alone?

I knew why. I knew exactly what I was doing.

"I haven't had sex with her since before Christmas." He was frowning at me now. "We've had lunch a few times, there's no harm in that, we've become friends — but no sex."

"How do I know you're telling the truth?"

I believed him implicitly, but I had to twist the knife in a little deeper. I wasn't done yet.

"Because I expect you to trust me, Lee, like I trust you." He was looking very serious now and his arms were crossed protectively across his bare chest.

"You shouldn't trust me, Tommy." Now it was my turn to get serious. "Haven't you ever wondered why I haven't made more of a fuss about Marie-Chantal?"

"You made plenty of fuss about it the night you found out."

"But I haven't gone on about it. I didn't mention it the other day when you came round."

He shrugged. He was looking very nervous now.

"I didn't drag it out because you weren't the only one having an affair."

He started shaking his head and waving his hand as if to push me away along with whatever I had to tell him. *No, don't tell me. I don't want to hear.*

"No, Tommy, listen. I have to tell you. I've been trying to work up the courage to tell you. I slept with someone, more than once. It was at the end of last year, probably right around the time you and Marie-Chantal were —"

"Don't tell me." Tommy had found his voice at last. "Don't tell me who it was, don't tell me all the details. I couldn't stand it. Just promise me you're not seeing him anymore."

I chickened out of telling him it was

Buzz because how could I explain that I had slept with the man who had come around and almost beaten me up? All I said was, "So now you see you can't trust me."

I don't know how I had expected him to react. Anger, maybe. Tommy rarely lost his temper and then it was usually because he felt patronized or that I was being particularly snotty. It was a form of self-defense. He sometimes lashed out when he didn't quite understand what I was talking about but didn't want to reveal his ignorance. I had thought he might distance himself and wallow in an extended hurt sulk. What I never imagined in my wildest fantasies was that he would come over and hug me.

"We're quite a pair, aren't we?" he whispered.

I couldn't believe this. "You're not angry? You're not hurt? You don't care that I had sex with someone else?"

"I care desperately," he said and when I looked up I could see it in his eyes. "But I'm not that surprised. Right before Christmas our relationship was about as bad as it could ever be. If you want to know the honest truth, I sometimes wondered if we'd make it through the New Year. If you're telling me that's when you had your affair, then all I can say is that, inasmuch as it ever could, it makes sense for it to have happened then. If you'd said you'd had sex with someone *since* Christmas, I'd feel a whole lot worse. I felt we grew close again, that time at your parents, didn't you? I felt we had a chance" — he looked down at me — "I feel we still do."

He made it all so simple. Somehow he had managed to shoulder everything I had thrown at him, acknowledge that it hurt him and exonerate me at the same time. As I clung to him, I marveled that I could be so stupid as to come so close to letting this guy go. He was a wonderful, generous man and I really didn't deserve him. And he was absolutely right. There was nothing to be gained in sharing the details of our respective infidelities. Now was the time to move on.

Of course I stayed the night, having first called my mother to establish that Selma wouldn't be on her own.

"Oh no, Bianca's with her," explained my mother. "It seems Selma called her and asked her to come over and in fact it's worked out perfectly because Bianca's cleaning the house as we speak. She's going to stay here with Selma. That's okay, isn't it?"

"Well, if *you* don't mind," I said.

"Oh, I won't be here. I'm going to spend the night with Sonny and then, guess what, your father's in town — *without* the wretched Josiane, imagine that! — and he wants to meet me for lunch tomorrow so Bianca being here is perfect timing."

I left a message for Max Austin to call me. I wanted him to be aware of the situation and to be sure to have someone watching my house in case Buzz turned up.

But he didn't call back until the next day and then he seemed more interested in telling me about how he'd had another chat with Chris who had confirmed that the man he saw had had a limp.

"But I can't find anyone under eighty-four on the CCTV with a limp and certainly no one coming in or out of Blenheim Crescent round about the time of the fire," said Max, sounding rather desperate.

"So maybe he's still there," I pointed out. "Maybe he lives in Blenheim Crescent."

As I said it, I closed my eyes. The killer could be living right beside me.

"That's a good point," said Max, a little too gleefully for my liking. "Or maybe he just had a limp the day of the fire and now he's recovered and is walking normally. But if the lab comes back and says Selma's prints aren't a match for the ones on the kerosene cans then right now he seems to be my most likely suspect. Now, I want to update you on this woman I've just seen. Buzz's old girlfriend."

I suppressed a sigh. I didn't want to have to think about Buzz now. I wanted to devote the day to Noreen.

"What was she like?"

"Beautiful," he said without hesitation and I was intrigued by the vehemence in his voice, "and ruined."

"What do you mean?"

"Well, she can barely walk. She's in a wheelchair most of the time. Her face is smashed to bits but the weird thing is she's not at all bitter. That bastard Buzz beat her up all the time she was with him and yet she's determined to put it behind her, even said the reason she's in a wheelchair was an accident and partly her fault. They were having an argument in the car and she claims she provoked him, made him hit her so he took his hand off the wheel and that's why the car crashed leaving her a semicripple. There were photos all over the place of her before it happened. He certainly has a type, that Buzz. He likes the

Latin look. Your looks have always seemed more Italian than English to me."

"And Selma's got all that jet-black hair," I said. "But how do you explain Astrid McKenzie? She was a real Scandinavian type."

"Yeah, well," Max sounded put out, "she didn't last long. Anyway, I see how this woman got to Richie. It was weird, the person she was really worried about was her sister."

"Her *sister?*"

"Yes, she says she wants to move on but her sister won't let it go, even after all this time. She said it had turned into some kind of obsession with her sister. She was worried she was on the verge of a major breakdown. I was driven mad. There I was trying to warn her that there was some lunatic who seemed to be going after Buzz's old girlfriends and all she would talk about was her sister. I gave up in the end. Told her to call us if Buzz came anywhere near her."

"What was the sister's name?" A bizarre scenario was beginning to unfold in my mind and its sheer plausibility was sending shivers of dread through me.

"I can't remember. It's here somewhere in my notes. Why do you want to know?"

"Well, what was *her* name, the beauty in the wheelchair?"

I didn't really need to ask. I knew what he would say.

"Maria," he said, "Maria Morales."

"Max," I shouted down the phone. "I've got it! I know who the sister is. It's Bianca."

"Bianca?" He sounded confused.

"She's Selma Walker's housekeeper. And she's very short and she has very small hands and feet."

"You're trying to suggest she might have started the fire?" He sounded very skeptical.

"That's exactly what I'm saying. It all fits. They could be her prints on the cans of gasoline, the ones you thought were a child's. And she has a coat with a hood. A duffel coat. I've seen her in it. I'm telling you, if you saw her running down the garden in the dark, you could easily mistake her for a child."

There was a silence, as if he was considering it.

"No," he said finally, "it doesn't work. There's no motive. I could see her going after Buzz in revenge for what he's done to her sister and to Selma Walker — in fact I think that's what Maria seems to be afraid of, that she's going to wreak some kind of awful vengeance."

"But if it turns out they *are* her prints on the cans?"

"There's a perfectly good reason why they should be there. Buzz brought those cans over to Angel on New Year's Eve from Selma Walker's house. If Bianca was the housekeeper she might well have handled them too before they left the house. But if it makes you feel better, okay, I'll swing by sometime and check out this Bianca."

He wasn't taking me seriously. I couldn't believe it. I almost hung up on him in my hurry to get back to Blenheim Crescent. Selma was alone with Bianca. Noreen would have to manage on her own for the rest of the day. I'd interviewed a woman who was going to come and take care of her for an hour or two every day but she wouldn't be starting until tomorrow.

I took a cab and picked anxiously at my cuticles as we came off the Westway and ran straight into a bottleneck around Paddington Station.

When we finally arrived at Blenheim Crescent, I let myself into a house that was so clean I barely recognized it. Bianca was calmly chopping vegetables for a stew when I walked into the kitchen. I didn't have the nerve to confront her with something like *So, Bianca, have you been setting fire to people's houses in between scrubbing and polishing?*

"Floor wet. You be careful." She glared at my feet as she greeted me.

"Is Selma here?"

"She upstairs and she work hard." Why was it that Bianca always sounded so accusatory? The way she looked at me, I immediately felt as if I'd been shirking my duty in some way, leaving Selma to do all the work.

I scanned a note from my mother: *Gone to lunch with your father and if I'm not back tonight, it's because he wants me to go with him to the West Country to see Aunt Hilda.* Hilda was my father's stepmother, the only remaining member of the grandparent generation of our family. I wondered if they were going to tell her of their separation.

Before going up to the top floor to see Selma, I nipped into my office to call Tommy and explain why I had abandoned Noreen. He said he'd make a point of being home early but he was as dismissive as Max Austin about my Bianca theory.

"I think you've gone barking mad," he said cheerfully. "It sounds like a lunatic take on *the butler did it.*"

The fact that he showed no concern that I intended to stay in the house with Bianca confirmed that he wasn't taking me seriously.

Maybe I was overreacting. The more I thought about it, the more ludicrous it seemed and I couldn't bring myself to share it with Selma. All I said when I finally joined her was: "Selma, I'm back now so Bianca can go home."

But Bianca was still there at ten o'clock that night having cooked us a meal and cleaned the kitchen afterward. She had pulled up a chair to sit beside the dishwasher and I realized that she intended to stay until it had finished and unload it. She didn't seem to trust me not to make a mess of the kitchen she now had under her control. Selma pleaded tiredness and asked if I would mind if she had an early night. I didn't want to be left alone with Bianca, so I followed her up to bed.

I barely had time to register that I too was exhausted. I fell asleep within seconds of my head hitting the pillow.

And then I awoke with a start and glanced at my clock to see it was 2:30 in the morning.

I lay for a second or two wondering why

the air was so close that I could hardly breathe and then I shot out of bed as I registered the strong smell of burning. Creature of habit that I am, I automatically reached for my dressing gown and put it on. Then I did what was possibly the worst possible thing to do when a house was on fire. I staggered across the room and opened the door, letting in the air, and a wall of smoke hit me full in the face as I peered out to the landing.

Someone materialized out of the thick black fog that was enveloping me and I felt myself being hoisted up and over his shoulder.

"Breathe into this," he said, handing me a wet rag and pressing it to my face.

I couldn't see his face but there was no mistaking Buzz's voice.

Buzz was carrying me down the stairs in a fireman's lift. It felt as if we were going down into Hades because there were flames licking the bottom of the stairs and the kitchen already appeared to be a blazing inferno. It was the same scenario as before. There was an overpowering smell of kerosene and once again it seemed as if someone had pushed a torch through the letterbox. Any minute now the fire would reach the staircase and take hold. I took the wet rag away from my face long enough to yell:

"What about Selma?"

"Where is she?" he yelled back.

"Top floor. And Bianca? She was here too."

"Left a while ago," he yelled over the crackling of the flames. "I caught her letting herself in to Elgin Crescent and forced her to give me her key to your house. I came over to see Selma again. I let myself in and this is what I found. We don't want to open the front door and let the air in. Is there another way out of the house?"

"If we can make it to the downstairs cloakroom, we can get out the window onto the terrace and from there go down to the garden."

"Here's my cell phone," he said, thrusting it into the pocket of my dressing gown, "I'm going to let you down over the banisters into the corridor before the fire gets there. You can make it to the cloakroom. Call 999 as soon as you're outside. Ready?"

And then before I could say another word he had lowered me to the ground and turned around to dash back upstairs to find Selma.

I made it to the cloakroom but I couldn't

get the window open. I had a moment of sheer panic and then I wrapped my thick woolen dressing gown firmly around me and heaved myself at the glass, shattering it in all directions. Then I realized I would not be able to climb out through a single pane so I picked up the umbrella stand and whacked it as hard as I could against the window frame until it smashed. As I climbed out onto the terrace, I could hear the wail of approaching sirens. Someone had beat me to alerting the fire department.

A crowd had already gathered in the road outside the house and their heads were craned toward the upper floors. Selma was at one of the windows and I thought I could hear her screaming above the roar of the flames. The windows of the ground floor had now blown and smoke was billowing out into the street where the heat was palpable.

Suddenly I saw Bianca standing with a policeman and I rushed over to him.

"She started the fire! She caused all this. Don't let her go."

He looked at me as if I were the one who was dangerous.

"This lady called the fire department, miss. You've got her to thank that they're on their way."

I looked at Bianca in amazement. Was this true?

"Who alerted you?" I asked him, still not prepared to let Bianca off the hook.

He looked sheepish. "Actually I was supposed to be here anyway, keeping an eye out for the man who's in there. I was away from the scene for a few minutes. You know, call of nature."

"Mr. Buzz make me give him key." Bianca suddenly came to life. "He hit me the face." She was crying now, a pathetic tiny figure. "But I follow him and I see fire."

"*Buzz* set the fire?" Was this possible? If he was the one then why had he risked his life to save me — and Selma?

"I don't know," said Bianca. "I here, fire already burns. I call fire engine. Miss Selma give me phone." She held up her cell phone proudly. "But Miss Selma in there." She started wailing and held up her arms as if in prayer to Selma at the window above us.

And then the fire engines began to pour into Blenheim Crescent from Ladbroke Grove. Watching Selma, I felt about as helpless as the time when I had watched on television while a Formula One car exploded in flames on a racetrack with the driver still trapped inside. Selma did not appear to be on fire but she was plainly hysterical, clawing at the windowpane, screaming at us although we couldn't hear a word. I could see flames through the landing window and knew it was only a matter of time before they reached her.

And then she suddenly disappeared from view and my heart went dead. She must have slumped to the floor, overcome by smoke. All around me people were screaming. The police had arrived and were doing their best to keep everyone on the far side of a hastily erected barrier. Now the road was a mass of hoses being hefted by the firemen and once they went into action, I was staggered by the speed with which they rescued Selma. The ladders went up to the window, the glass was broken and within seconds a fireman reemerged with her inert body draped over his shoulder like a pashmina shawl. He gave a thumbs-up, she was still alive, and the crowd around me breathed a collective sigh of relief. Five minutes later and it would have been a different story.

The police were having a hard time keeping the crowd that had gathered at bay. A woman standing close to the waiting ambulance suddenly shouted out:

"It's Selma Walker from *Fraternity*!" and there was a huge surge forward. I was jostled and buffeted and I began to panic.

I could no longer see what was happening at the entrance to my house and I tried to duck under the arm of one of the policemen.

"Oh, no, you don't," he said, wrapping a restraining arm around my waist from behind and pulling me backward.

"It's MY house," I said, struggling. "There's a man trapped inside there. He hasn't come out."

God knows how but the crowd heard me above the roar of the fire and suddenly everyone stopped shouting and turned to watch as what seemed like an entire posse of firemen swarmed through the front door dragging a long hose.

We waited, spellbound, hands clasped in front of our mouths and eyes pinned to the upper floors of the house. The jets that were propelled up from the engines outside the house had succeeded in dousing the flames that had now reached the roof but through the windows I could still see fire licking its way up the stairwell and enveloping the landing.

After rescuing me, Buzz had gone back up the stairs. A sense of dread began to travel through my body until I was shivering with apprehension.

Responding to some invisible signal, the ambulance men suddenly ran to the top of the steps with a stretcher just as two firemen emerged with Buzz's body. They laid him on the stretcher and I don't know how I caught it — my eyes were straining to catch a glimpse of Buzz over the shoulders of the people in front of me — but I saw one of the firemen give an infinitesimal shake of his head. Then he threw a blanket over Buzz's body. Not just his body, but over his head as well.

It was insane but just as they reached the ambulance, one of the back doors blew shut and they laid Buzz down on the ground for a second. The policeman restraining me did not anticipate my reaction and he let go of me as I shook him off and darted across the road to pull the blanket off Buzz.

I stared down at him for a second and then I started chattering to him like an imbecile. "You're all right, Buzz. You're fine. We've got you now. You're going to be okay." As I spouted this inane gibberish, I registered that his flesh was seared and coated in soot. His hands were red and raw and still slightly clenched. His mouth was a white circle of pain in his blackened face. And as I finally understood that he was dead, it felt as if the flow of blood to my heart had slammed into a high seawall and I slumped to the ground.

I didn't pass out. I just sat there on the ground, sobbing, and when I could catch my breath, I screamed at the crowd, at the police, at the departing ambulance.

I felt someone put their arm around me and coax me gently to my feet.

Chris had a blanket and he wrapped it around my shoulders and began to slowly lead me away from the mayhem outside my smoldering house.

"It's okay, love. I've got you. Calm down, calm down," he said over and over again. "You're in shock. What you need is a nice cuppa tea. My lockup's close by. I'm going to take you there, okay? Nice cuppa tea, just what you need."

He talked to me continuously, soothing me, as I allowed myself to be led all the way along Blenheim Crescent to Powis Mews. He had his lockup there in a row of garages where mechanics worked all day long on car maintenance.

"Buzz is dead," I told Chris. "They rescued Selma but they couldn't save Buzz."

"Well, that's justice, innit?" said Chris,

the comforting tone suddenly gone from his voice and replaced with a savage rasp. "He started the fire, didn't he?"

"Did he — did he really?" Buzz was a monster but I don't think I had ever really believed he was capable of arson and murder as well.

"Of course," said Chris, squeezing my arm. "I saw him go into the house, didn't I?"

"Did you?" What was Chris doing outside my house at two in the morning?

" 'Ere we are." We had arrived at Powis Mews and he had upped his pace. Now he was almost dragging me along the cobblestones. He stopped halfway along the mews, reached down, and pressed a button that released the garage door to his lockup. It rumbled up and back and he propelled me inside into the gloom.

Even though I was in a state of shock I registered that Chris was acting strangely. No longer the comforting presence who had led me away from the scene of the fire, his grip on my arm was now nothing short of brutal and I pulled away from him. This seemed to enrage him and he leapt on me. I kicked him as hard as I could and struggled to break free but he was much too strong for me. I remembered the force with which he had attacked Buzz in my hallway and realized I had no hope of overpowering him.

"Why are you doing thi— ?" I screamed at him before he stuffed a foul smelling rag in my mouth, gagging me. He secured it around my head and then pulled the cord free of my dressing gown and tied my hands behind my back with it. Then he ducked outside again, pressed the button, and the door began to descend.

Before I was left in the pitch black of the lockup, in what was left of the light as the door rolled downward, I saw them, standing in a line beside boxes of vegetables: can after can of kerosene.

My wrists were tied but my fingers were free. I didn't waste a second and began to work my way around the wall in the darkness, searching for the light switch.

If there was one.

I'd been down Powis Mews before. I'd seen these lockups. Once the door was up, the owners didn't need any more light to find the box of carrots or lettuces they'd come to get. Had I ever seen a lightbulb dangling? I couldn't remember.

I felt the splintered wood of crates containing apples and then there was a gap. No shelves. Moving along with my back to the wall, my hands reached down and found what seemed to be the fabric of an old armchair. I almost tumbled into it and my fingers touched something that, when I understood what it was, caused me to silently scream and moan in panic behind my gag.

My fingers were resting on hair. Human hair, dry and unhealthy as if it had been over-bleached. Moving downward I felt skin — a nose, a mouth gagged with something, like mine was.

I fought to hold back the vomit that rose in my throat before it seeped into the gag.

I was trapped in a lockup in total darkness with a body — a body that no longer responded when touched.

I recoiled, stumbling backward into a crate on the floor and losing my balance. I hit the ground with a sharp bump to my right hip and lay there for a second, shaking. I inched my fettered body across the floor like a slow-moving snake until I was on the other side of the lockup to the body in the armchair. Then I flinched as it occurred to me that there might be other bodies lurking in the darkness. There was a stench in the place and while I was not familiar with the smell of dead human flesh past its cremation date, I was pretty sure that what caused my nose to twitch was the stink of rotting vegetables. So how long had the body been dead? If indeed it was dead. I knew I should slither back across the floor and touch it again, try to wake it up but nothing on earth would persuade me to do so.

As I lay there in the darkness I heard a little *beep* somewhere in the region of my left thigh and I remembered that Buzz had given me his cell phone to dial 999. What I had heard was the little *beep* that tells you to check your messages.

I rolled over, frantic, wriggled about until the phone fell out of my pocket onto the floor. Then I rolled back and over until my fingers found the phone. But it was useless. I am pretty hopeless at dialing a tiny cell phone with my stubby fingers at the best of times but trying to find the talk button to turn it on and then the 999 digits, fumbling in the dark with my hands tied behind my back, was impossible. And in any case, even if I had been able to roll over quick enough to get my mouth to the phone, I was gagged so all the emergency services would have heard would have been muffled grunts.

I had to keep calm. I had to stop myself from imagining what Chris had done to the figure in the armchair, what he would do to me. I had never been in a place that was so totally unilluminated. It had to be near dawn. Light seeped into bedrooms whatever kind of blackout you installed. You could always see *some*thing. Now, lying in this dank, foul-smelling lockup, I was as good as blind. And of course my imagination began to run riot, producing rats waiting in the blackness to come forward and nibble me. I moved a little to ease the stiffness that was beginning to invade my joints and my fingers touched something slimy.

I screamed behind the gag and then relaxed. It was a leek. I reached farther, searching for something that would in some way enable me to escape, maybe a crack in the wall I could poke through, and encountered more fallen fruit and vegetables. An onion, a big round football of a cabbage, oranges with firm skin and similar smaller objects, lemons or maybe limes. Pointy carrots, stubbier parsnips, and hard little garlics.

Having fallen to the ground, I couldn't get to my feet again and I lay there, exhausted and semiconscious until the sound of the mechanics arriving for work told me that the long night was over. I heard the sound of garage doors rumbling up and open, and the wheels of the milkman's van trundling over the cobbles delivering to the back entrances of the houses on the other side of the mews. I couldn't shout out.

Then Buzz's cell phone rang.

I thought fast. I rolled over, raised my upper body as if I were doing push-ups and crashed my face down onto the phone, hoping I'd hit the right button. I heard a voice say hello. I groaned and moaned and coughed, knowing it was futile but convinced it was better than doing nothing.

"Are you okay?" I heard a woman's voice say and I shouted "Help!" aware that it sounded like "He—."

Suddenly the lockup was flooded with light as the door rolled up and Chris came in and kicked the phone across the floor away from me.

I could see now. I could raise my head and look over at the armchair and the body slumped in it, bound and gagged as I was.

It was Angel.

Shockingly weak, barely able to open her eyes, but she was still alive. I could see that now.

Chris ignored us. He went straight to the row of kerosene cans, picked one up and began to pour the contents over everything in the lockup. Soon the smell of rotting vegetables was replaced with the stomach-turning reek of paraffin oil and bile rose in my throat.

"Shame," he said, pulling a matchbook from his pocket, "probably won't find another lockup this close to the market. Still, the insurance money'll come in handy." He struck the match, tossed it inside, and ducked quickly into the street before the door rumbled down again.

I wasn't in darkness anymore. The fire enabled me to see. As the flames rippled along the floor on their kerosene trail toward Angel and me, devouring crates of fruit and vegetables as they went, I flashed on Astrid McKenzie waking up to a wall of fire around her bed, and poor Fred trapped in my summerhouse. And the more recent image of Buzz's seared flesh.

And I realized that in all my nightly fantasizing on the kinds of violent deaths I might encounter, I had never come up with something as horrendous as this.

Chapter 22

I awoke to find Tommy leaning over and peering at me as if I were a caged animal at the zoo.

I was in a hospital bed and Max Austin was sitting in a chair in the corner.

"She's opened her eyes. She's looking right at me. She's going to be fine. What did I tell you? I said she'd be fine."

"Tommy," I said in a feeble whisper, and then I remembered the final moments in the lockup.

"Now, now, now, take it easy," said Tommy when he saw my expression change, "you're okay and I'm here. I'm not going anywhere. Give me your paw, that's it, hold on tight then you'll feel safe. I've brought your stuff in. Didn't know which nightie to bring so I've got the blue one with the ribbon as well as the shortie pajamas you look so cute in."

"In the middle of winter?"

Tommy laughed. "Hear that, Max? She's

about to give me a bollocking for bringing in the wrong stuff. Nothing wrong with her."

He was right. It seemed I'd had an extremely lucky escape and there was nothing fundamentally wrong with me other than a little smoke inhalation. Poor Angel, it turned out, was not in such a good state. The flames had reached her as she sat trapped in the armchair. Her feet had sustained second-degree burns and she wouldn't be walking very far for the next few weeks.

"We got you out just in time," said Max. "You were lying right at the front of the lockup but she was farther back and the rope binding her feet had already caught fire. Sorry," he said as he saw me grimace, "I'll spare you the details."

"But how did you find me? How on earth did you know to come to Chris's lockup?"

"Okay, one thing at a time. First of all, how did I figure out it was Chris who'd been starting the fires?" Max pulled his chair up to my bed. After Tommy had done his fair share of fussing about over me, Max had persuaded him to go to work, assuring him that I'd be fine.

"Have you got him?" I sat up suddenly.

What if he came into the hospital in the middle of the night and sloshed kerosene all over the ward?

"We've got him," Max assured me. "He's not going anywhere, don't worry."

"So how — ?"

"You remember I was going to go back and search for the man with the limp on the CCTV, the one Chris said he saw going into your alleyway?"

I nodded.

"I kept going over and over it and I couldn't find anybody with a limp. So then I thought I'd look for Chris and see if I could see him looking at anybody in particular near your house. I went back and found the moment he came into Blenheim Crescent from Portobello Road. That was about an hour earlier. He was coming and going on a pretty regular basis, going back to the stall to pick up more stuff, reappearing with a fresh crate. Don't forget we can only see him at the end of the street, there's no CCTV actually in Blenheim Crescent. The last time the camera picked him up before the fire started was at the corner of Portobello and Blenheim and I saw him put his crate down on the pavement and reach into it for something. I could see his face clearly, then he turned around and headed off toward your house and all I could see was his back view — a small figure in a hooded anorak. It was just a fleeting glimpse before the camera switched to something else."

"The anorak, the hood —" I stared at Max.

"Exactly!" he said. "But wait — I had them blow up the footage as big as it would go and guess what he got out of his crate?"

I shook my head in exasperation. *Haven't a clue. Get on with it.*

"A pair of gloves. So my next stop was Mrs. O'Malley. For someone who seemed to spend her days peeking through her net curtains, I'd come to realize she had a surprising capacity to forget the essential details. She forgot to tell us she went into the alleyway herself to call Kevin in for his dinner and —"

"She saw Chris and never told you?"

"She saw Chris and never told me. *Oh, he was just going round the back to make a delivery. I didn't think nothing of it.* I remembered you said he didn't deliver to you. She called Kevin in from your garden and left Chris there —"

"So it was Chris your witness saw running down the garden in a coat with the hood up. He described him as a small adult, not a child."

"But the other witness who said he saw a child was right too because Kevin had been running about there a few minutes earlier — in his anorak with the hood up."

"And the gloves?"

"Chris put the gloves on to hide his fingerprints. He was carrying what looked like a crate of veg but in fact he had a can of kerosene hidden under some cabbages. He had time to drench a rag in it and throw it in the summerhouse and run."

"He wanted to set fire to Angel?"

"She spurned him. He chatted her up outside Tesco but she didn't want anything to do with him. He really resented her. You have no idea how chatty he's been with us. He's given us the whole story. All you have to do is show him a bit of attention, make him feel he's got an audience, and you can't shut him up."

I shuddered. It all seemed to fit. The more I thought about it, the more I realized that Chris had needed very little encouragement to latch on to someone.

"When he learned it was Fred who had been in the summerhouse," Max continued, "he picked his moment to go after Angel again and take her to his lockup."

"But he asked me if I knew what had happened to her after she left my house. He was the one who told me she hadn't been turning up to work at Tesco, told me her mother was worried sick."

"And all the time he had her locked up. That was how he got his kicks," said Max, "brazenly talking about the crimes he'd committed to deflect the attention away from him."

"But what about Astrid McKenzie?"

"Same thing. He delivered to her. He told me that when I first interviewed him. His prints were all over her kitchen and front door and when he explained about the deliveries, it gave him a legitimate reason for being there. Several people confirmed she'd started having him deliver and her cleaning lady testified that he was always hanging around in her kitchen and she'd heard him asking Astrid out. Said he didn't take it too well when she turned him down and she had to spend a little time reassuring him it wasn't personal, that it was because she already had a boyfriend."

"Just like I did."

"Part of the problem was Buzz Kempinski. Chris knew about Astrid and Buzz, you and Buzz, and then Angel and Buzz. When we interviewed him it was quite clear that was what drove him over the edge. He just couldn't stand it that you'd all give Buzz what you wouldn't give him."

"But where did you pick him up?"

"At his stall. After he left you and Angel locked up he went to work, business as normal. Like I just said, that bravado is part of his makeup. Right after he set fire to Astrid's mews house he told us he was hanging about in the street the next morning and he didn't exactly make himself scarce after he set the summerhouse alight. He helped us with our inquiries, didn't he? Told us about the man with the bad leg —"

I turned to him. "So who was that?"

"A figment of his imagination, someone he made up to put us on the wrong track — and he almost succeeded. And you know, you did have a point with Bianca. We've talked to her too. She went round to Astrid's and left her fingerprints in the pink paint on the letterbox — *and* she went round to confront Angel in the summerhouse on New Year's Eve. But Angel wasn't there."

"Why did she want to see Astrid and Angel?"

"We're not entirely sure but she was out to destroy Buzz in some way. She set him up. She had to find some way to get to him. She put the ad for a cleaner in the newsagent's and then waited around until he came and saw it. Bit of a long shot but it worked. He hired her having no idea she was Maria Morales's sister. She might have wanted to warn Astrid and Angel about him, she might have hoped to enlist their help in bringing him down in some way. She did talk to Astrid but we'll never know what about. She's a sick woman. Selma's going to see she gets some help."

"But how did you know to come to the lockup? You still haven't told me that."

"You have Cath to thank for that. She bumped into Chris at your place recently and when she saw him with you it triggered something she hadn't thought about in a long while. A long time ago, fifteen years maybe, when Chris was still a teenager, she saw him set fire to a warehouse."

"She *saw* him! What did she do? Did she report him?"

"She did — but his mother covered up for him. Swore blind he was with her all night. And there was another problem."

"What was that?"

"Cath was drunk that night. When she went round to the police station and reported what she'd seen she was legless.

They didn't believe her and when Mrs. Petaki gave him an alibi, the whole thing was dropped. But when she saw Chris in your kitchen something started stirring in the back of her mind. She finally put it all together in the middle of the night and she called you but of course you weren't picking up — so she called me."

"Oh my God!" I lay back on the pillows and shut my eyes.

"I was on to him by then in any case. The minute Mrs. O'Malley told us she'd seen him I went round to pick him up at his mother's, which is where he still lives. He wasn't there, of course, because he was hanging around Blenheim Crescent, waiting for the right moment to stuff another of his kerosene-soaked torches through your letterbox. So his mother directed us to go all the way out to Hounslow near the airport. She told us Chris got up at about two every morning to go out there to his wholesaler's to buy the produce to sell at the stall. One of the joys of a produce merchant's life. She said if we didn't pick him up before then that's where we'd find him. But of course we didn't and then, as we're racing back to London, I get the call from Cath and she —"

"Directs you to the lockup."

"So we got back to Mrs. Petaki and demanded that she gives us the key. Just — in — time. We drove her over to the mews and she identified the lockup immediately. We opened up the door —"

"As I was about to become a roast with two veg."

"Twenty-two veg," he said with a faint smile, "at least."

"If Cath hadn't called you I'd be dead by now?"

"We'll never know," he said.

I knew it was going to be a long time before I stopped thinking about that.

"How's Richie?" I asked to get my mind off the subject of how I was almost barbecued.

"Richie's absolutely fine. He's coming out of hospital tomorrow."

"You don't look too happy about it," I remarked.

"I'm delighted about it but there's a slight problem. Since she called me that night Cath's gone AWOL."

"She's missing. Have you called the police?"

It just came out. Did he have to look at me as if I were a complete idiot? It's what anyone would have said.

"She's not exactly missing. She's going

to work during the day. It's the evenings she's not around. She's not at home, she doesn't answer her mobile, and the truth is I just don't have the time to go to every bar in Notting Hill looking for her."

"Oh," I said, "you think that's what's happened?"

"I should imagine."

"And Sonny?"

"Blazing the trail, I shouldn't be at all surprised. According to Richie it wouldn't be the first time."

"But she's *pregnant!*"

"Exactly. You'd think she'd be more responsible."

"But she's the responsible one. I'm the one who always ran wild."

"No, you're not," he said simply. "Look at you. You've had to put up with your house being destroyed, someone getting killed in your back garden, Selma Walker and your mother turning to you for shelter, Buzz Kempinski rampaging through your house, not to mention a visit from a certain rather unpleasant market merchant. Most people would have fallen at the first fence. I've been keeping a watch on you and I have to tell you, I'm impressed. You were even beginning to come up with a few mildly helpful comments on the detection front. Just as well Richie's on his way back to join the world. Few more weeks and he might have found he'd been replaced in his job."

I thought *mildly helpful* was a bit patronizing but I let it go.

"*And* I had to help you with your laundry."

He actually blushed.

"So you did. And thank you. Anyway, now you know the whole story. You're going to be out of here in no time. I'll look out for your book when it comes out. Maybe you'll even decide I deserve an early copy — a what do you call them? A proof?"

He was saying good-bye. He was signing off. As he stood up, I realized with a jolt that this would probably be the last time I would see him. He had no reason to keep in contact with me now.

"You know," he said as he went to the door, "about the washing. I've got a handy tip for you. When I do the ironing, I find one of those plant mister things are perfect for spraying the clothes for when you want to steam them."

"Why don't you just get a steam iron?" I asked him.

"I have. I've got one."

"Well then, you don't need a spray. Just fill the iron up with water, press the button with a little picture of steam on it, and Bob's your uncle."

"Really?" He sounded amazed. "Well thanks," he said perfectly seriously, "thank you for that." And he was gone before I could say anything else.

A piece of paper had fallen out of one of his pockets and I leaned out of bed to pick it up.

1 lb. mince for shepherd's pie. Lamb best.
Half pound carrots
Small frozen peas
Half pint milk
Harpic

It was a sad little list, the pathetic sign of someone shopping for one. Not so long ago, I reflected, that had been me but was I going to go back to that? That was what I had to decide.

I didn't have to make any immediate decisions for myself, it seemed, because my mother had all the answers. She came rushing in to see me about half an hour after Max had left and within ten minutes of arriving she was pulling the curtain around my bed and breaking down into loud howling sobs.

"You have *got* to be okay," she said, grasping my hand lying on the bed. "I need you, Lee."

This didn't make any sense. I was the one recovering in hospital but *she* needed *me?*

"Is it something to do with Dad?" I asked nervously. "Has he upset you again?"

"Oh, God, no," she said dismissively. "The minute I saw him I knew I was — what do you say these days? *Over* him? The irony was that he wanted me to go back to him. That was what the lunch was supposed to be all about. Seems like Josiane is proving to be rather too demanding already and he doesn't think he's going to be able to cope. Well, tough!" She squeezed my hand for emphasis and I yelped in pain. "No, darling," she carried on, "I need you to come home soon because I've come to depend on you. I find the thought of you not being around completely terrifying. I need you to hold my hand."

She gave one of her inane giggles that was meant to signify *Oh, look at me, what a silly billy I'm being.*

"Oh, Mum," I said, suddenly feeling more weary than ever, "what about Dad? Where's he going to go?" I felt bad for my father. I'd been so preoccupied with having my mother living with me that I'd barely given him a thought. Nor did I want to dwell on what my mother's reaction would be when I eventually made contact with him.

"Where's he going to *go?*" She seemed bewildered by my question. "Where he's already gone," she said very matter-of-factly, "back to France. And while I remember, he wants you to call him. He's hoping you'll go over there and stay with him soon."

I expected her to scoff at the idea but she surprised me.

"You know, you should go, Lee. Take Tommy. Ed may not be part of my life anymore but he is your father. Go and see him, will you? Promise me that."

I nodded. I was touched by her apparent lack of animosity toward my father.

"But what about you? Where will you live?" Even as I asked her the question, I had a sinking feeling I knew what the answer would be.

"Well, I'll stay here with you, of course. I've seen Selma and she says we can stay with her in Elgin Crescent until we can get back into the house. I'm not going to move in there until you're out of hospital, I wouldn't feel comfortable, but you have to admit, it's the perfect solution. She needs someone with her and we'll be right around the corner from Blenheim Crescent. I'll be able to oversee the building work but believe me, it's going to take some time to make the place habitable again. It's great, isn't it?"

"What is?"

"Well, who'd have thought we'd find the perfect way to get all the repairs done in one fell swoop. Have the place burned down and get the insurance to take care of it all."

That was one way of looking at it.

"I'm going to hire Sonny to do the job." She was looking at me out of the corner of her eye. "Brilliant idea, what do you think?"

"Have you heard from him?" I asked, ignoring her question. I thought it was a dreadful idea given her apparent emotional neediness as far as he was concerned.

She shook her head. "No, I haven't but that's not really the point. He's the best person for the job." Now she was nodding furiously as if trying to convince me what she was saying was the truth. "Oh, I know what you're thinking, that we don't want an unreliable drunk taking care of the house." I wasn't thinking anything of the sort but I let it pass. "What you probably don't understand is that those men he had working with him on our repairs — they were all in AA. They're a bunch of independent contractors in recovery, each with their own operation. I think the electrician's called something like Higher Power. But, of course, if you don't think it's a good idea —"

"Mum," I said, "it's your house."

It was sweet of Selma to invite my mother and me to move into her house while ours was being restored. It was so handy being right around the corner. We could run back and forth to check on the builders' progress and pick up stuff we needed — what was left of it. When I saw the damage for myself, I nearly collapsed again. The roof had a gaping black hole in the side of it and the upper part of the house was covered with soot and there were charred holes where the windows had been. My computer had apparently been overcome with heat exhaustion and it was doubtful it would ever work again. Selma was sweet about this too. She treated me to a spiffy new laptop the day I came home from hospital.

As luck would have it, my bedroom escaped serious damage other than everything being covered in soot, so Selma's tapes were intact. Once I was installed in Elgin Crescent we would set to work on them on the days she wasn't up in Manchester.

I had never been farther than the ground floor of Selma's house and the upstairs was quite an eye-opener. Selma's bedroom and bathroom took up the whole of the first floor of the house. She had recently had them upgraded in a stark modernist decor, just a vast wrought-iron four-poster bed with two austere glass bedside tables and everything else hidden away inside built-in storage. I think I would have felt as if I were sleeping in a cage but if that's what appealed to her, fine. But one floor up my mother was in heaven with the same space decorated in lush chintzes and a terrifying amount of scatter cushions that would take a person half an hour to remove before going to bed. And when she saw the marble bathroom, she flipped. I did too but it was at the sight of the Jacuzzi rather than the marble. There was nothing better to soothe an aching ghostwriter's shoulders and if Sonny Cross could see his way to installing one at Blenheim Crescent then as far as I was concerned he was in like Flynn.

I was given the run of the top floor. "You'll be able to work up there in peace and quiet," said Selma and I ran up the final short flight of stairs, clutching my laptop in expectation. On one side of the landing I found a little bedroom under the eaves, sparsely furnished but perfect for my needs with its own bathroom. On the other side of the landing was a closed door. Presumably this was where I was meant to work.

When I opened the door, I found a monastic cell. It was a square room at the back of the house with only one window but the view from that window was spectacular. The house was so tall that from the top floor you could see clear across the bare trees of the communal gardens to the railway that ran high above Max Austin's flat in Wesley Square. There was a glass-and-chrome table and a chair and a telephone, and over in the corner, abandoned on the floor, an old stereo system still hooked up to giant speakers standing in opposite corners of the room. I kneeled down and hit the POWER button, looking for a tape deck that would be useful for working on Selma's book. Once I'd found it and discovered it to be empty, I did the same with the CD OPEN/CLOSE and saw there was something in there.

I pressed PLAY out of idle curiosity and the room was filled with the desperate animal wailing sound of a tenor sax. I recognized it instantly. It had marked the beginning of the nightmare journey on which I had unwittingly embarked when I first stepped into this house before Christmas. I had last heard it downstairs in Selma's kitchen. I had danced to it, and as I stood here letting it infuse me once again with romance like a needle shooting pure heroin, I realized with a start that this barren room I had been assigned at the top of Selma's house was where he had listened to it.

I was standing in Buzz's office.

Finding myself in the one place that had been uniquely Buzz's, I snapped. Grief erupted from me in great heaving sobs. I think I howled for more than an hour, hugging myself and wallowing in my grief, hiding under the roof where no one could hear me. Buzz had been a monster who had performed dreadful acts of violence but knowing that did not rid me of a certainty that I would remember for the rest of my life that moment when I had known I would have sex with him. Buzz had *got* to me in that split second when I was standing downstairs listening to this music, and later he had aroused immense passion within me of a kind that I had never known with any other man. I could blame it on Houston Person and his saxophone. I could throw away this CD and see if all disturbing memories of Buzz were discarded with it. I could do that but I knew perfectly well that I wouldn't. Buzz had died an agonizing, searing death but I would keep him alive by hanging on to this CD and playing it in secret.

Because for a brief period of time I was convinced that I loved him. Apart from the sex he had been a virtual stranger to me but it didn't matter. I was mourning the loss of a loved one and I felt all the more wretched because I could not share my sadness with anyone. Repression bred confusion. I mourned him but I felt guilty doing so and thus I felt even worse.

As the days went by and nothing changed, I knew I had to talk to someone and there was only one person besides Max Austin who knew about me and Buzz.

The person I had to thank for saving my life.

My last news of Cath had been Max Austin telling me she'd gone AWOL. I thought for a minute and then rang her parents. Her father answered the phone and after a few minutes of catching up, he gave me Cath's address and told me I'd find her mother there too. Sure enough, when I rang the bell — I didn't call first for fear Cath would refuse to see me — her mother answered the door.

Wendy Clark had been a nurse and she always treated people as if they were her elderly patients on a geriatric ward, shouting at them as if they were deaf. *So how are we this morning? Going to eat your breakfast for me like a good girl?*

"My goodness, Lee! You're *JUST* what we need," she boomed. "Come in, come in. Don't hang about out there. We don't want you catching a chill."

She enveloped me in a bone-crushing hug and I was reminded of how different she was from my own mother.

"Hello, Wendy. Visiting Cath, are you?" I inquired. "Is she here?"

"I'm staying here for a while," said Wendy. "Someone's got to keep an eye on her. You heard what happened?"

I shook my head. "She hasn't been in touch in quite a while."

Wendy looked at me in surprise. "You mean not even after your house — that fire — ? She told *me* all about it. How come she didn't call you?"

I shrugged. "So what happened to Cath?"

"She was so drunk the other night, she had a nasty fall, and she nearly lost the baby. She needs total rest for a while and she's off work for a couple of weeks. Of course the best thing would be if she went into rehab again but she's never listened to what I had to say about that. Maybe you could talk some sense into her. Go on through, she's in the living room. If you could stay with her for an hour or so, it'd give me a chance to pop out to the shops."

"You can't leave her on her own?" I was shocked. And intrigued. From the sound of it, Cath's pregnancy was now common knowledge and suddenly here was Wendy bringing Cath's alcohol problem into the conversation as if we had both been discussing it for years. Which we most certainly had not.

"I could leave her. Of course I could but I don't," said Wendy, putting on her coat. "See what you can do, there's a love."

I half expected to find Cath in a belligerent mood but she smiled at me, patted the sofa for me to sit beside her. I took in my surroundings. This was the first time I had been to the flat she now shared with Richie and I have to say I was not impressed. It lacked the coziness I found essential in a home but then Cath had never been a nester. The room I was standing in was pretty bare and exuded the kind of soulless atmosphere that said its inhabitants probably spent more time out than in — and not just at work.

I sat down beside Cath and to my surprise she put her arms around me and drew me to her.

"I should have been in touch. I'm sorry, Lee. I'm really, really sorry. I can't forgive myself for the fact that I could have identified Chris as the person who was setting those fires so much earlier than I did. I know I saw him set fire to that warehouse but then I would think, maybe I *was* too drunk to know what I was seeing. But I should have remembered him when —"

"Shh!" I said. "You did remember and you saved my life and I'm here to thank you. That's all that matters."

Her remorse and her unexpected gentleness caught me off guard and I found myself dissolving into tears.

"Do you need a place to stay?" she asked. "You can always come here. We've got room and God knows, you'd be a welcome change from Mum. The house was insured, wasn't it? The repairs will take a while but once they're done, you'll have a brand-new house for free. Think about that, try to forget about what you've lost."

"It's not the *house!*" I said. "I don't care about the *house.*"

"But now Chris is caught you should be able to relax a bit by now — it's all over." She patted me on the back. "You've nothing to worry about anymore. Why are you still so upset?"

"It's Buzz!" I shrieked. "I can't seem to lay him to rest."

"You're not still seeing him?" She looked appalled.

"He's dead, Cath. Didn't you hear? He died in the fire, in my house. He was trying to rescue Selma."

Her hands dropped from my sides and she stared at me. "Richie told me a bloke died in the fire but I didn't realize it was *him.*"

"He died trying to save Selma," I repeated. "I wouldn't speak to him again after I found out he was beating her up. He must have felt so betrayed when he found out I was giving shelter to her. He came round, Cath, and I was terrified of him but in the end he turned out to be a hero. How could he beat a woman almost to a pulp and then risk his life going into a burning building to save her? He loved her, Cath. She always said they loved each other and I never believed her but she was right. But what I've finally realized is that I think I loved him and it was pointless. It was dumb and stupid and I feel like a total fool. If I hadn't got involved with Buzz, he wouldn't have met Angel and —"

My voice was bordering on hysterical.

"Now stop this," said Cath firmly. "Listen to me, Lee. You were not in love with him, you were in *lust*. You were obsessed about him and you didn't get a chance to let this obsession play itself out."

"But why do I feel so awful? Why am I so screwed up about his death?"

"Guilt," said Cath simply. "He turned out to be a bad person, someone you ought to be ashamed of having been involved with. Yet you can't deny that you were attracted to him — even after you knew what type of man he was. Oh, don't deny it. You'll never move on if you're in denial."

And then, as I sat there thinking about

what she had said, she got up and reached behind the sofa for a bottle of vodka.

"Don't say a word," she warned me as she raised the bottle to her lips. "Join me? There's a glass in the kitchen."

I was on my feet, pulling the bottle away from her before she could take a swig.

"Stay out of this," she yelled at me but I noticed she did not try to go after the bottle. Maybe she'd just been testing me. "Don't start telling me what to do about my drinking if you want us to stay friends. I thought you'd be the one person I could count on not to judge me."

"Well you thought wrong," I told her, "and anyway where is it written that I can't say boo to you."

"You're the one who's screwed up her life —" she began.

"Yes," I shouted at her, "yes, I have screwed up my life recently but not totally, not irretrievably. I made a bad mistake getting involved with Buzz but at least I am acknowledging it, I'm asking what I should do about it. You're the one who's in denial, Cath. You're the one who's fucking up her life. Get real! Do something about it before —"

I stopped. She was walking toward the sink with the vodka. As I watched she upended the bottle and poured the contents down the drain. As she turned to me, the look she gave me was heartrending.

"I'm trying," she said with an incredibly sad look on her face. "Please understand that. I'm going to go back into rehab and I swear I'll make it work this time but I need help. I don't know why I'm so mean to you sometimes. I need your support, Lee, truly I do. You've every right to get angry with me but please — please don't."

And suddenly I realized that was exactly what she needed. I should be showing her gentleness and acting in an encouraging way instead of shouting at her. I opened my arms and she came to me.

"I'm the worst kind of friend you could possibly have," I whispered as I held her. "I *am* judgmental and I know it's wrong but it's because I'm so worried about you. You've never talked to me about your problem. I just don't know how to behave about it. You're going to have to help me."

"It's a deal," she said. "I never told you because I knew you'd come down hard on me. I was scared I'd lose you."

"You won't," I assured her. "God knows, if we've come this far it looks as if we're stuck with each other. I'm going to be a lamb from now on, I'll do anything you ask except give you alcohol."

"*Any*thing?" she said.

I nodded.

"So would you be the baby's godmother? Richie and I would be thrilled."

"There's nothing I'd like more," I told her.

"And there's something else." She looked at me.

"Yes?"

"We've already asked Tommy to be godfather and he's said yes."

What? She'd gone behind my back and contacted Tommy — before she'd asked me — and he hadn't said a word — and —

But even as I found myself getting worked up, I began to smile. I had to let go of the old resentment. I had to start thinking about how both Tommy *and* Cath were going to be in my life again.

"What I want to know is how on earth I can wait another six months until the baby's born," I said. "It's going to be so exciting for all of us."

"Well, how do you think *I* feel?" she said. "I'm going to need you to give me as much time as you can spare."

But as it turned out I didn't have that much time on my hands — which was just as well since I was distracted from thinking about the fire and Buzz and Fred and all the drama of the past six weeks. Selma and I set to work in short bursts of time snatched when she wasn't in Manchester and I found myself wondering what kind of story she would have delivered if Buzz had not died. One thing was certain: It would not have packed nearly as strong an emotional punch. But while Selma's message was tragic it was also emphatic. While my pain resurfaced during those sessions when she hammered home how much she and Buzz had loved each other, I managed to keep a check on my emotions in her presence.

Selma was a strange one. We would never become close beyond a professional relationship and she told her story to me in a detached, almost clinical way. She described how when he began to beat her up, she made every excuse under the sun to stay with him. She had told herself that if she stood by him he would change. She whispered how unbearably tender their lovemaking was in the aftermath of violence, so much so that she was always given false hope — and reading these passages, the reader could not fail to support her decision to stay. She confessed that in the beginning she often thought she might be the one who was to blame. She told of the extraordinary lengths to which she went to keep her suffering a secret because she felt so ashamed. And bit by bit she allowed her despair to filter through in the book as the cyclical pattern of violence emerged, until finally she knew she had to leave him.

I think I was more proud of the work I did on Selma's book than of anything I had done in the past. The thing that impressed me most was that Selma never lost sight of the fact that she was writing a book for those less fortunate than herself. She acknowledged she had money and that she was lucky in a way that many others were not. But right from the very beginning of the book she advocated flight. Do not give him a second chance, was her advice despite the fact that she had stayed for so long. No matter how much you love him, you *have* to leave him the instant he shows any violence. Exhort him to seek help but do not stay with him. The message was reiterated throughout the book right up to the moment where Selma herself ran away to seek shelter at my house.

Of course Buzz's attempt to save her life in the final chapter was the ultimate contrition phase, a gesture more dramatic than their sweetest reunion, and his subsequent death made her story all the more heartbreaking. But even in the midst of her grief, Selma still maintained that she would not have gone back to him.

We did our homework. We dazzled the reader with horrifying statistics of domestic violence throughout the world; we gave advice on what to do once you'd left; we provided checklists on how to spot a potential abuser early on. But ultimately what we delivered was a killer story with a message from a household name whose face appeared in thirteen million living rooms three times a week. Genevieve declared she would have no trouble in "selling the shit out it," which I found to be an unexpected expression from the person Buzz had described as a "vision of loveliness in pale pink and lilac" at that unforgettable first meeting with him.

And then just as we were wrapping up the first draft and I was rolling up my sleeves to hammer out the revisions before handing it over to Genevieve, Tommy announced that Noreen's helper was moving to Australia with her husband. But, he added, this had prompted him to come up with a wonderful idea.

Why didn't I move in with him and be the one to take care of Noreen while he was at work?

Chapter 23

What with one thing or another, I hadn't seen much of Tommy since I'd moved into Selma's house. On the odd occasion when he'd come down to visit me, I could see he felt uncomfortable there. Tommy didn't do grand and that was one of the things I had always liked about him. There were times when I could have done with him having a bit more aspiration in life but his blatant dislike of the ostentatious trappings of wealth made sense to me.

Somehow I had got immersed in writing the book with Selma and although I made the odd visit to Bewdly Street, it was more to see Noreen and sit with her a while than anything else. There was nothing acrimonious going on between Tommy and me, we talked on the phone regularly but the weird thing was that I had begun to really miss him.

In a way, I enjoyed it. I *savored* missing him because it was a new experience. In the past I'd thought about Tommy when he wasn't with me and I'd needed him intermittently and summoned him to satisfy that need, either in my bed or as a stalwart against the marauding world on the other side of my front door. But while it was awful to have to confess such a thing after eight years of being someone's significant other, apart from the four months when we split up, this was the first time I really did miss *him.* It was a combination of the way I'd felt when we were first going out, that kind of visceral craving you get for someone that doesn't really even require them to speak. In that way I missed the reassuring sight of his sheer bulk slumped at the kitchen table or spread-eagled flat on his back across the mattress. I missed the smell of him. His pheromones. He might be a slob around the house but Tommy was meticulous about having clean shirts and linen.

It was an unexpected turn-on but then the other thing I missed was his constant ability to surprise me. On a visit to Noreen while he'd been at work I'd found evidence — books and language tapes — that he was learning Russian. At first I worried that he might be contemplating ordering a mail-order bride on the Internet as the *on dit* was that the Russians were the best value in the looks department. But it turned out that the new owner of Chelsea FC was a Russian who couldn't speak much English and Tommy was entertaining aspirations to become his translator. It wasn't as crazy as it sounded because within a matter of weeks, Tommy appeared to be fluent. When he gabbled away to me in Russian he was probably talking utter gibberish for all I knew but he sounded authentic. He had a natural gift for languages, with or without Marie-Chantal. Who would have thought?

I called him back and said I'd come up to Bewdly Street that night and we'd talk about it.

But Tommy had a crisis at work and didn't get back until ten o'clock by which time I'd fed Noreen and settled her down for the night and was more or less ready for bed myself.

We went upstairs to his bedroom — where I almost changed my mind and went home. He claimed to have tidied up for me but of course Tommy's version of tidying up a room was nothing like anyone else's. All he had done was to pick up his dirty clothes that were usually strewn all over the floor like an extra carpet. Now they were arranged in neat little piles — but they were still on the floor. I closed my eyes and said nothing.

We got into bed and lay there side by side in silence for a while.

"Tommy," I said tentatively when I noticed his eyes were closed and I wondered if he had fallen asleep. "I've thought about your idea."

"Give me your paw," he said, opening his eyes and snuggling up against me, taking my hand in his. "Okay. Fire ahead. I'm listening."

"I was thinking maybe I could give you a hand with Noreen."

"Stoked if you would." He began inching my nightie up my leg with his toe. "Stoked" was his new word. It had replaced "cool" and "crazy" but seemed to mean the same thing.

"And I might as well move in with you."

The toe stopped halfway up my calf.

"Did I hear you correctly?" The sheet was pulled up to his nose and his eyes peered over the rim at me, very wide.

"But, now, listen, I want to set some ground rules," I said, "literally. I want us to have separate rooms. You'll be here and I want you to let me have your mother's room all to myself — for work — and to sleep. At least until your mother moves back upstairs."

We both knew this wouldn't be for quite a while, if ever.

"You mean we wouldn't share a bedroom?"

"Well, of course we would. We'd share two. You'd invite me to yours and I'd invite you to mine."

"If I was a good boy?"

"Something like that."

"But I'm not a good boy," he said, moving my nightdress up my body with his hands now.

It was the perfect plan, I reflected in the afterglow of what Tommy insisted on calling Soviet sex. This involved a lot of nibbling and mumbling of sweet nothings in my ear in Russian, spoken softly and with great tenderness. It would be cramped with the three of us living at Bewdly Street as I'd requested but I knew I had to have my space. It would be good for me to move on. Blenheim Crescent had always been my mother's house and now that the insurance was going to cough up for the extensive repairs she planned, she could reclaim it.

But there was something missing. If I was going to take this huge step and move in with him didn't we need to make it official? Marie-Chantal might be safely back in France but Tommy's dalliance with her had shaken me out of my complacency. Living with him would be bearable, providing I had my own room to retreat to and being on-site I could control the chaos throughout the rest of the house. I didn't really want control of Tommy. I would prefer to encourage him to control himself. But now that I had finally realized how much I loved him, I wanted to hang on to him.

"Tommy," I whispered to the outline of his head in the glow of the television, "will you marry me?"

I was rewarded with a resounding snore. Given that it was Tommy I took that for a yes.

Later that night I sat up in bed beside him in the darkness and tried on Mrs. Kennedy of Bewdley Street, Islington, for size. Nathalie Kennedy. Lee Kennedy. I'd keep Lee Bartholomew as my writing name, of course. Oddly enough the Mrs. Kennedy part didn't bother me at all. Now I'd made up my mind that was what I wanted, I liked the idea of being a wife. I looked down at Tommy lying flat on his back with his arms resting by his sides on the covers as if he were trying out his coffin. I studied his huge paws and wondered if I ought to buy him a ring. I was the one who had proposed after all.

But as the night wore on and I couldn't get to sleep, I started to dwell on the notion of living full time in Islington instead of just visiting. And that's when I began to get very nervous indeed. What had I been thinking? There was no way I could live anywhere other than Notting Hill Gate. Now that I had finally come to terms with the knowledge that there were shootings and stabbings and crack-cocaine dealing on a mass scale just the other side of my front door — not to mention possible juvenile prostitution; now that I had survived two fires; now that I had finally found a way to get the repairs carried out throughout the house without actually having to be there to oversee it; now that I had finally grown up enough to entertain the thought of no longer living alone; now that I had finally come to terms with survival in the heart of twenty-first-century Notting Hill, why was I even thinking of going to live elsewhere? Tommy would have to be the one to move.

I passed out for a few hours through sheer exhaustion and then I got up and dressed, leaving Tommy a note. The Victoria Line was deserted on the journey down to Oxford Circus and even the Central Line, normally jam-packed, was relatively empty. I walked up Portobello Road from Notting Hill tube station and once I reached the top end, I had to start dodging the market merchants on their way to set up their stalls as they trundled their loads of vegetables and fruit along the street.

This was something I could never leave, the dawn stillness followed by the early-morning madness as the market came to life. On one of the stalls a boombox was blasting "By the Rivers of Babylon" for all it was worth and a woman shrieked out of a second-floor window for it to be turned off.

At Mr. Christian's in Elgin Crescent I nipped in for one of their chocolate brownies. It tasted so good, I bought another and hurried across the road, stuffing it into my mouth as I went. I didn't want Selma, whose doll-like frame was testament to the strict organic diet to which she adhered, to witness my early-morning sugar freak-out.

And then, as I turned into Westbourne Park Road, I realized I couldn't just expect Tommy to pack up and move to Notting

Hill just like that. What about Noreen? I fished my cell phone out of my pocket and woke him up.

"Where are you?" he said. "I'm looking all around and you're not here. Are you under the bed in a sulk or something?"

"I've left you a note," I told him. "Go downstairs and read it and then call me back on my cell."

"You've left me already," he said wearily. "I thought it was too good to be true."

He called back almost immediately.

"Well?" I said.

"Well what?"

"Moving to Notting Hill, what do you think?"

"Fine, no problem, but hadn't we better wait until your house has had a few repairs done to it?"

"You mean you don't mind? I mean I know I said I'd move in with you in Islington but —"

"You seriously think I believed you for half a second?" He sounded incredulous. "You could never survive long term in Islington. I knew you'd be going back to Notting Hill sooner or later."

"You did?" Now it was my turn to sound incredulous.

"There's just one problem about me

moving in with you," he said and my heart sank.

"Your mother?"

"No," he said, "*your* mother. She's planning on living there, isn't she? In fact it's two problems. I'm not living in a house with you and your mother. And you're right — I think I do need to bring Noreen with me."

"Tommy," I said, "I've thought of something. Now that the damp in the basement has been fixed —"

He interrupted me. "Do we have to do this now? We're going to take care of our mothers one way or another and we're going to do it together. That's just about all that needs to be said right this minute, isn't it? I've got to get to work."

"One more thing —" I heard a sigh on the other end of the phone but my anxiety was nearing fever pitch. "Just before you fell asleep I asked you a question."

"Maybe I fell asleep and never heard it," he said.

"Maybe you did," I replied.

"So if you manage to make it back to my bed one night and you stay there for long enough, I'll give you my answer."

"I'm not quite sure how to take that." By now I was extremely nervous.

“I should take it with a glass of champagne,” he said and I smiled with relief.

“I love you, Tommy,” I said and then screamed as a pair of jeans came flying out of the doorway to the launderette on the corner and knocked the cell phone out of my hand. If Tommy replied I didn’t hear it. I retrieved my phone, picked up the jeans, and took them inside, depositing them on the pile for which they were intended. There were more piles of dirty clothes in front of each of the machines and without even thinking about what I was doing, I set to work, sorting the whites from the coloreds and weeding out the delicates altogether.

When I reached one of the giant dryers banked along the far wall, I was just in time to rescue various items of clothing whose care labels I knew would bear the explicit instruction “Do not tumble dry.” I waited patiently until their owner’s head emerged from the drum of the adjacent dryer.

“Well, good morning,” said Max Austin as he straightened up and his face betrayed his delight in seeing me. “I think we’ve met before.”

The employees of Thorndike Press hope you have enjoyed this Large Print book. All our Thorndike and Wheeler Large Print titles are designed for easy reading, and all our books are made to last. Other Thorndike Press Large Print books are available at your library, through selected bookstores, or directly from us.

For information about titles, please call:

(800) 223-1244

or visit our Web site at:

www.gale.com/thorndike
www.gale.com/wheeler

To share your comments, please write:

Publisher
Thorndike Press
295 Kennedy Memorial Drive
Waterville, ME 04901